MOON
OVER
THE SUN

First Edition: May 2025

ISBN 978-0-9743937-2-8

Library of Congress Control Number 2025908380

Printed in the United States of America

Published by:

Hallelujah Publishing
www.hallelujahpublishing.com

For more information visit:

www.moonoverthesun.com
Instagram poetry madness: @rdcoyote007

Scan to access the soundtrack on Apple Music™:

MOON
OVER
THE SUN

R.D. Coyote

three o'clock
she walks in sight
seen from above
as love takes flight

her beauty stands
without compare
as midnight curls
dance on air

her quiet allure
bold yet fair
a silent strength
beyond all care

she floats along
with silent ease
barefoot and light
like an evening breeze

love grows strong
as time slips by
bringing his heart
to a soulful cry

a battle fought
deep from within
fear of rejection
and courage thin

the world calls out
but she holds still
a silent ache
he cannot spill

her memory clear
now a distant tear
a love once close
now nowhere near

for decades long
the years are passed
upon her bench
he sat steadfast

She rose with dawn
then slipped from view
but left behind
a light that grew

he waits with faith
beneath wide skies
for just a glimpse
of olive green eyes

Where baggage rolled
and arrivals came
he searched the crowd
and spoke her name

world's vast canvas
its beauty wide
yet she lingers
by his side

love is patient
beneath each year
gathering silence
until she's near

he waits alone
with steady grace
for the one
he can't replace

trusting fate
to show the way
before their lives
converge one day

bound for love
on a midnight run
chasing break
of morning sun

moon meets sun's
tender flame
together at last
in heaven's name

M.P.

I never saw you again, but I never gave up hope.

PROLOGUE
00:00:00:01:30:17

My old Porsche 914 hummed beneath me, steady as breath. The wheel felt worn and familiar beneath my hands—scarred leather shaped by time and memory. Fir Island Road was strangely quiet this time of day. No other cars. No movement on the farmland. Just me, the open road, and the weight of something long unfinished riding in the passenger seat.

Then—the whistle. Sharp. Piercing. Cutting through the stillness like a blade. I eased off the gas. The red warning lights at the train crossing flashed to life. The gate groaned down, metal joints stiff with rust. I rolled the Porsche to a stop just shy of the tracks, and I let out a slow breath.

The train came fast. A blur of steel and shadow, cars clattering past in a rhythm that felt both relentless and inevitable. I stared straight ahead, but I wasn't really seeing it.

My grip on the wheel tightened. Not new tension. Just the old kind. The kind that never left. In the rearview—nothing. Just the road behind me. Empty. Quiet.

The train rushed on, unstoppable, bound for somewhere it had always been going. No hesitation. No regret. Just motion. I watched the steel cars—graffiti-scrawled sides, rusted metal, box after box of something bound for somewhere else. No passengers. No faces. Just cargo and noise and the long, low groan of distance.

The train didn't care about the track behind it. Only what lay ahead.

I wondered what that felt like. To move forward without doubt. Without constantly looking back. I hadn't done that in a long time. Maybe not ever.

I'm fifty-five years old, and for reasons I still don't fully understand, this road didn't exist until now. Not in any real way. Maybe it was always waiting. Or maybe it only appeared once the past stopped holding it shut.

The scent of aged leather drifted up from the passenger seat. I reached for my old bag beside me—weathered, softened, familiar. I'd carried it for years. Long past its usefulness. Maybe that was the point.

Inside, beneath old travel receipts and a half-filled notebook, was the one thing I never let go of. A brittle newspaper clipping. I hesitated. Then unfolded it, slow and careful, the way you handle something sacred. The creases were deep from too many years of folding, unfolding, remembering.

The ink was smudged in places. But she was still there. Captured mid-air beneath fluorescent lights of a gym. Curls flying, eyes locked on the ball. Her body arched in motion, arm outstretched, fingertips just grazing the edge of a perfect set. A moment of pure, suspended grace.

My thumb brushed the edge of the photo—not her face this time. I wasn't sure what I was looking for anymore. Warmth? Proof? Or just a reason. I'd looked at this image more times than I could count. Each time trying to understand what had stayed with me. Why she had stayed with me. Not a lover. Not even a friend.

Just a girl on a bench.

And yet—everything changed the moment I saw her.

The bag has always sat next to me, holding more than just what I carried. Maybe it held the reason. Or maybe just the reminder. But I wasn't chasing anything. Not this time. Not running. Not searching. Not trying to rewrite the past into something cleaner than it was. I was just moving forward—toward something quiet. Unfinished. Waiting.

Something that had never really let go. And maybe now... I was finally ready to answer.

The final car rattled past. The warning lights dimmed. The gate lifted with a mechanical sigh. I folded the clipping carefully. Slid it back into the bag. Sealed it away like a secret. The road was open again.

I eased the clutch, shifted into gear, and felt the engine answer— low and sure, like it remembered exactly how this was supposed to go. The tires hummed against the pavement. The wind found the open window and slipped in like an old friend, as if it knew exactly where I was headed. ♪

♪ *"Simple Twist of Fate"* by Bob Dylan

◐

17

34:01:29:05:45:23

The sun hung low, gilding the sky in soft gold. Morning warmth spilled across the valley, touching everything with light. The McPolin Barn stood unchanged—its whitewashed walls glowing against the backdrop of rugged peaks, a quiet sentinel to a town that never quite stayed the same.

I coasted my Porsche to a stop along the roadside. The engine gave one final, reluctant hum before falling into silence. I leaned over the passenger seat and popped open the glove compartment. My fingers brushed loose papers and crumpled gas station receipts before landing on what I needed—a fresh roll of Kodachrome. The label was slightly worn, the spool cold against my skin.

I threaded the film into my Nikon, hands moving by muscle memory. I'd done it a hundred times before. Maybe more. At twen-

◎

ty-two, I already knew that repetition could be its own kind of comfort. Ten years earlier, I probably would've rolled my eyes at that.

The camera rose to my eye. I framed the barn in the viewfinder. The world always looked better through glass—cleaner, quieter, contained. Freezing it on film felt like holding time still, even if just for a breath. I took aim at the barn.

Click. The shutter broke the silence.

Click. Another frame. Another second sealed away.

I let the camera rest in my lap and exhaled. My breath clouded the windshield. Stillness never sat easily with me—not then. Not now.

Route 224 - Park City

The engine rumbled back to life, and I pulled onto the road flanked by snowbanks and low-slung fences. Park City, Utah had a rhythm all its own—half mining town nostalgia, half ski-town bravado. Old ghosts and new money stitched together by chairlifts and restaurants. But my mind was already higher. Already climbing.

The crunch of snow under my boots was the first thing I noticed when I stepped out of the car. It was sharp and clean, like a page turning in winter. The air bit at my cheeks—dry, pine-laced, familiar. That kind of cold that makes you feel alive again, like maybe your heart knows how to beat in rhythm with the mountains.

I crouched beside the car, fastening the buckles on my ski boots. That sharp snap of metal locking into place—it always felt good. I don't know why. Just a small, certain thing in a life that hadn't offered much certainty lately.

I stood slowly, letting my gaze drift toward the wide stone staircase that led up to the base lodge at Park City Resort. Skiers crisscrossed in slow, choreographed chaos—skis slung over shoulders, laughter carried on clouds of breath, poles tapping against ice-slick steps. It was early still, but the slopes were waking up.

And then—I saw her.

A red flash against the pale wash of snow. Fire walking through frost. She moved down the steps like she'd always known the rhythm of this place, like the cold bowed away from her. Red snowsuit, dark hair pulled back in a braid, goggles pushed up onto her forehead. Her face was flushed from the altitude or the cold or just being alive, and her smile—her smile was like sunlight on glass. It hit something in me I hadn't realized was exposed.

I wasn't ready. I froze. Halfway through adjusting my gloves, suddenly unsure of what to do with my hands. I wanted to stand straighter, brush the frost off my jacket, say something, anything—but my body locked up in that old, stupid way it always did.

I don't know what it is about me. Once I'm in it—once I'm talking, I'm fine. I can be present. Engaged. Even funny, sometimes. But that first moment? That first spark of possibility? I choke. I overthink. I get caught in the machinery of my own hesitation.

She passed me, her boots clicking against the stone. And for a second—just a second—she glanced back. It wasn't a long look. Barely more than a flicker. But it felt like an open door. A question. An invitation. Or maybe she was looking for the bathroom. Hard to say. I've been known to mistake eye contact for fate.

And still, I said nothing. The words were there, perched just behind my teeth. "Hey. Nice day for it, huh?" Something stupid. Something human. But my mouth stayed shut. I just stood there, fists clenched in my gloves, like a boy watching a train leave the station.

And then she was gone.

Swallowed into the shifting tide of color, movement, and ski jackets. I let out a breath I didn't realize I'd been holding. My chest felt tight in that familiar, aching way. One second. That's all it takes. One second too long, and the moment's already moved on without you.

I shook my head and turned toward the lift. I told myself I came up here to escape. That I didn't come looking for connection. But sometimes, when you're not looking—someone walks by in red, and you remember how lonely your hands are when they're not holding anything.

The chairlift scooped me up, pulling me into the sky. A hush settled over the world as I rose above the slopes. The world up here always made more sense—clean lines, wide sky, momentum carrying you forward whether you were ready or not.

I let my gaze wander—over the ridges, the sharp shadow of the summit stretching across the bowl, the clustered roofs of the base lodge growing smaller behind me. Farther out, the valley opened like a quiet promise, soft with light and untouched powder. Up here, it was just me, the hum of the wind, and the slow, steady drift of the lift. For a few minutes, everything made sense.

The chairlift swayed gently as it climbed, the cables humming overhead. Each time my chair passed over a tower, the rollers clattered above me—sharp, rhythmic, familiar. A sound so familiar it might as well have been stitched into the fabric of my memory.

Below, skiers carved across soft powder, their lines clean and looping, etched like calligraphy across the slope. Temporary, but not forgotten. Not yet. The kind of tracks the wind would soften eventually, but for now, they held.

I lean back into the padded seat, letting the cold air kiss my cheeks. The sun had just begun to burn through the morning clouds, casting long shadows across the trees.

This—this is where it all started. I must've been five the first time my father clicked me into skis. I remember how big his hands looked, tugging my mittens tighter, cinching my jacket, adjusting my goggles with a kind of quiet reverence, like skiing wasn't just sport—it was a gift. His patience back then felt endless, his voice low and steady as he skied backwards in front of me, arms outstretched, ready to catch me if I wobbled. Which I did. A lot.

But that was also the year I saw *The Spy Who Loved Me*. That opening sequence—Bond soaring down the mountain in his yellow suit, chased by gunmen, leaping off a cliff, the Union Jack parachute flaring open like a dare to gravity—I must've watched it fifty times. Maybe even twice a day that summer. I didn't care about the tuxedos or the gadgets. It was the snow. The freedom. The sheer audacity of it. ♪

Okay, that's a lie. I definitely wanted the Lotus Esprit that turned into a submarine. It didn't have an ejector seat, but it was still too cool to care.

That's what lit the match. After that, I didn't want to just ski—I

♪ *"Nobody Does it Better"* by Carly Simon

wanted to fly. My dad used to joke that I was trying to outrun something, even back then. Maybe I was. Or maybe I just believed, in my little-kid heart, that if I got good enough, fast enough, I could be that bold. That untouchable. That free. Just like *007*.

Skiing took hold of me. The speed, the edges, the way the world narrowed into a single clean line—I was hooked. Same way he was. Decades later, he still skis. Still sharp. Still graceful. And when we're on the mountain together, it's like nothing's ever changed. We don't talk much out there. We don't need to. The rhythm of it, the shared motion—it says more than words ever could.

The divorce was hard. On all of us. I was too young to understand the details, but old enough to recognize that some houses weren't meant to hold two people forever. My mom and dad never made me choose, and maybe that's what shaped me most of all. They let me love them both. No guilt. No games. Just... space. Still, skiing became our thing. My dad and me.

Every turn I make now—every perfect carve into untouched snow— it still feels like he's there, just ahead of me on the run. Not yelling back instructions anymore, but leading in silence. The way he always has.

Ahead of me, I hear the rhythmic thump of the lift operator's broom striking each chair, knocking off the fresh snow in practiced sweeps. It's a sound I've always loved—steady, part of the mountain's morning ritual. Like the mountain is waking up, one chair at a time.

The chair crests the ridge. I pull down my goggles and tap the snow from my gloves. Below, the slope unfurls—gleaming, endless, untouched. First tracks. There's nothing like it. Except maybe a perfectly struck 7-iron… or sex, I guess. Hard to say. So far, my short game's more consistent.

Thaynes

The run opened before me, untouched moguls stretching out like a song waiting to be played—each bump a note, each line its own rhythm. I took a breath, tracing the slope with my eyes, letting the right line reveal itself.

The zipperline.

That perfect thread through the chaos—tight, clean, direct. Not for the timid. It demands precision, timing, flow. One mistake and you're off it. But when you find it, when you hit it just right, it's like dancing with the mountain. Like flying in slow motion.

This was Thaynes. Where the real skiers played. Not the wide, forgiving groomers with their easy turns and California crowds. Here, you earned it—turn by turn, leg by leg. Moguls didn't lie. You either flowed—or you paid the price.

I pushed off. ♪

The first turn came like breath—light, effortless, a soft carve into the powder. Then another. My skis floated over the moguls, finding their rhythm, each movement a quiet conversation with gravity. The cold stung my cheeks, but I barely felt it. I wasn't thinking. I wasn't anything, really—just motion. Just flow.

Up here, I could forget. Up here, I was allowed to vanish. No past. No future. Just the zipperline. Then—A flash of movement. Too fast.

♪ *"Lonely Boy"* by The Black Keys

☾☽

Too close. A snowboarder cuts across my path, sudden as a snap of wind. I swerved. Tried to adjust.

Caught an edge.

The world tilted—sky, snow, sky again—and then: the slam. Breath gone. Vision blown wide with white. I hit hard. The impact echoed through my ribs, spine, all the way up into my teeth. Snow sprayed upward, then fell like ash. For a moment, I couldn't move. Just lay there. Staring up at the sky.

My chest rose and fell—ragged, but steady. My heart thudded loud in my ears. Everything else had gone still. The snow settled around me, soft as dust on a forgotten photograph.

Above me, the sun burned bright. Silent. Unmoved. And all I could think was—Even here, even now...You can't hold the line forever.

Snowboarders. *Whatever.*

☾

The headlights slice through the darkness as I turn into the familiar driveway of the Snowflower Apartment complex. I misjudge the curve—again—and the crash of trash cans sends a clatter echoing down the alley.

Perfect.

The Porsche groans to a stop. I cut the engine, step out, and take a breath. The March air still carries winter in it—dry, sharp, and clean. Cold clings to my jacket like memory, the kind that hasn't quite let go.

Inside, the warmth hits like a wall—along with my roommate's music. The kaleidoscope of Def Leppard pulses from the TV, all electric color and chaos. Our apartment smells faintly of popcorn, old pizza, and ambition. ♪

Robert's on the couch, buried in cushions, wearing a Pink Floyd tee two sizes too big. He looks like he hasn't moved since I left this morning.

"Any revelations on MTV today?" I ask, toeing off my Sorels.
"I've decided to marry Downtown Julie Brown," he says, eyes still locked on the screen. "She understands me."

I smirk. "How does Julie feel about this?"

"She doesn't know I exist yet."

"Well, Rome wasn't built in a day."

He finally glances over. "Oh—your mom called."

The answering machine blinks. I hit play. *BEEP.*

"It's your mom – the retail realm is in dire need of your help. Grandpa's convinced your eye for detail is the missing ingredient. Apparently, my attempts at rearranging have been labeled as 'creative chaos,' and I can't argue with that. Give me a shout when you can. Love you. Mom."

The fridge groans open as I hunt for sustenance.

"Ready for a culinary masterpiece?" I hold up a slice of cold pizza like a prize.

"Always! Cold pizza—the best kind. How were the slopes?"

♪ "Pour Some Sugar on Me" by Def Leppard

∞

"A Greatest Hits kind of day—first tracks, no lines... and one spectacular face plant."

He grins. "Let me guess—snowboarder?"

"Obviously. Will they ever embrace the true symphony of skis?"

"Never," Robert says solemnly. "Once you cross over to the dark side, all is lost."

I smirk, grabbing a slice from the box. "You know... Vader came back at the end."

Robert raises an eyebrow. "So you're saying there's hope?"

I shrug, taking a bite. "Some part of me still believes."

"Any snow bunnies?"

"One. But... another face plant."

Robert raises his slice like a toast. "And that, my friend, is why we're solo on a Friday night."

"Maybe we should watch The Pick-Up Artist?" I suggest, flopping beside him.

"Good idea. Maybe we'll learn a thing or two."

We dissolve into the kind of dumb laughter only twenty-some-things in a dead-end apartment can really master. The kind that masks the fact that we're both floating, directionless. Waiting for something to break loose.

"You know, this pizza's the real star tonight," Robert says.

"We should open a joint selling nothing but day-old cold pizza."

"Instead of skiing moguls, we'll be pizza moguls."

"Maybe you could seduce Julie Brown with your secret tomato sauce?"

"Brilliant! We'll show Jack Jericho how it's really done!"

For a moment, I forget I'm searching for anything else. But it always comes back—the quiet, the hum beneath everything.

I'm not made to stay still.

☾

The next morning, I sit at the kitchen table, sunlight striping across the tile, coffee warm in my hands. The latest issue of *Wander* Magazine is cracked open beside me. I dial my mom.

"Hey Mom. How's the empire holding up?"

"Oh, you know, your grandfather's at war with the mannequins again. When are you planning on coming down?"

"Next month, after ski season wraps up."

"No hurry. I wouldn't want to interrupt an intimate affair with the slopes."

"I don't know if I should be discussing intimate affairs with my

$$\textcircled{O}$$

mother," I say with a laugh, but my eyes drift back to the magazine. A want ad catches my attention.

Wander the World. Seek the Extraordinary.
Now Hiring: Travel Photographer.

The words burn into me. I reread it twice. Something inside stirs. Something I didn't even realize had been sleeping.

$$\newcommand{\moon}{}\text{☾}$$

The mountains are shedding their white—patches of green clawing their way up from beneath the snow. Like they're trying to remember how to be alive again.

I load my gear into the car: skis, boots, camera bag, duffel. It all fits too easily. Like I've been waiting to pack up and go since the moment I arrived. Robert stands in the driveway, holding the last bag like he's handing over a torch.

"Taking Pow Life on the road, huh?" says Robert.

I toss the bag in. "Just chasing the next chapter, my friend."

He grins, already slipping into air guitar mode—shoulders rocking, one foot planted for dramatic flair. I laugh, shaking my head. He salutes with his imaginary guitar, still riffing as I climb into the driver's seat.

Interstate 15 - Mt. Pleasant

The sun was to the east casting the Porsche's long shadow across the freeway as I headed south. The mountains were behind me now, their

◎

snow-covered peaks shrinking in the rearview mirror, while the desert stretched wide ahead—empty, open, waiting.

I rolled down the window, letting in the cool air. It carried the scent of dry earth and sage, a stark contrast to the crisp alpine bite of Park City. This was the feeling I chased—the in-between places, the quiet roads where the only sound was the hum of the engine and the occasional whisper of wind against the car.

I flipped on the radio. A thread of static gave way to a song—slow, spare, like dusk stretched into melody. A voice low and rough around the edges drifted in, backed by acoustic guitar and something else I couldn't quite name—maybe longing, maybe memory. ♪

It wasn't a love song, not exactly. More like a story told from the in-between—the place where the light hasn't quite broken and everything still feels raw. The lyrics spoke of motion before meaning, of kicking up the dust before the sun comes up. That restless space where you move forward because standing still hurts worse.

It suited the road. I let it play. Let it fill the car like the fading light. It didn't tell me where I was going, just reminded me why I'd left.

The road stretched before me, a ribbon of asphalt winding through southern Utah. I barely needed the map—I'd driven parts of this route before, but never with a destination that mattered.

Highway 9 - Hurricane

Highway 9 took me through the outskirts of Zion, the canyon walls rising like ancient sentinels on either side. Red cliffs burned in the afternoon light, streaked with shadows that shifted as the sun sank lower. I pulled over at a scenic overlook, stepping out and stretching my legs.

♪ *"Before the Sun"* by Gregory Alan Isakov

⦾

I grabbed my Nikon, adjusting the settings by muscle memory. The weight of the camera felt solid in my hands—something real, something permanent. I lifted it to my eye. *Click.*

My uncle Eddie gave me my first camera when I was twelve—a beat-up Canon with a cracked lens and a strap that smelled like the inside of an old suitcase. He was a war photographer in Vietnam and used to say photography wasn't about the image—it was about what you felt when you took it. Light. Shadow. Waiting for the moment most people missed. I didn't get it then, not really. But I loved the quiet of it. The patience it required. The way it made the world slow down.

A photograph was never just an image. It was a moment stolen from time, a fragment of something that would never happen the same way again. I framed another shot—the way the road curved into the distance, disappearing between the cliffs. *Click.*

Maybe that was why I liked photography. It let me hold onto things I'd otherwise lose.

Highway 163 - Monument Valley

The land opened up into something vast, Monument Valley rising from the desert like a dream. The towering sandstone buttes stood untouched by time, their deep red hues shifting as the sky changed above them.

I pulled over again. The silence here was different. Not empty. Not lifeless. Just still. I stood by the car, watching as a hawk drifted high above the mesas. This place felt sacred in a way I couldn't explain—like it had existed long before me and would go on long after. I raised the Nikon. *Click.*

The road ahead stretched endlessly forward, a perfect, iconic view

⦾

of the highway slicing through the desert toward the horizon. The kind of place that made you feel small in the best possible way. I let the moment linger before turning the key.

Highway 90 - Paradox

The road unwound before me in long, quiet stretch—miles of open country, empty fences, and sun-touched mesas. This was Paradox Valley, and despite the name, nothing about it felt contradictory. If anything, it made perfect sense. There was something sacred about this kind of stillness, the kind that only exists far from cities and airports, far from the urgency of schedules and traffic lights. Rural America had always held that pull for me. The pace. The space. The way it didn't apologize for being what it was.

The *Paradox General Store* came into view as the road bent. I pulled over slowly, dust kicking up behind the tires. The building stood like it had been waiting for me—weathered wood glowing under the sun, paint faded to near watercolor, a rusted Coke sign clinging to the front wall with stubborn pride. I stepped out, camera in hand.

Framing the shot, I felt that familiar shift in my chest—that quiet thrill of finding something real. Not curated. Not polished. Just real. *Click.*

And for a moment, standing there alone on a two-lane highway in the middle of nowhere, I felt more connected to the world than I ever did in a crowd. I tucked the camera back into my bag but didn't move right away. I hadn't been shooting long enough to call it anything serious, but something about it felt right in my hands—like a language I didn't have to translate to understand. Like it knew something, even if I didn't. Most of my friends were already polishing college essays and planning internships, charting lives that looked suspiciously like their parents'.

⟐

Not that there's anything wrong with that. It just didn't feel like mine. I wasn't lost exactly. Just… not ready to pick a direction. But the camera? It felt like a direction. And for now, that was enough.

But here, with nothing but open country and that infinite sky, those prescribed futures felt impossibly small. I wasn't sure what I was looking for yet, but I knew it was out here somewhere – in places forgotten by time, in moments that passed unnoticed. Not in the rush of city life or the safety of the expected. That much, at least, I knew for certain.

Highway 145 - Telluride

The desert faded behind me as I climbed higher into the San Juan Mountains, the air growing thinner, colder. The last traces of winter clung stubbornly to the peaks—patches of white against the deep green of the pines. The final stretch wound through a narrow canyon, the road twisting alongside the rushing river.

I turned off the radio. Some places demanded silence. ♪

I rolled the window down, listening to the water crash against the rocks. It was a different kind of wild than the desert—louder, more alive. And then the sign appeared at Society Turn:

TELLURIDE 3

A slow breath. I wasn't sure what I was expecting. Maybe nothing. Maybe everything. All I knew was that I'd made it.

The familiar landmarks appeared like old friends—places that had shaped me, watched me grow, held my memories when I wasn't there to tend them. I could still see myself—nine years old, pedaling my battered Nishiki ten-speed up Lawson Hill, glove hanging from my back

♪ *"Moonlight Mile"* by The Rolling Stones

pocket, on my way home from Little League practice. The sun always too high, the air always thin. I used to think the town was too small. Now it felt enormous with memory.

I didn't fit in right away. I was the California kid with sun-bleached hair and Ocean Pacific shorts, showing up on the first cold morning without a clue what mountain weather really meant. The local boys eyed me like I didn't belong. Maybe I didn't—at least not until they found out I ruled at dodgeball and kickball. After that, I always got picked first.

After school, we'd pile into the *Underground*, blowing our allowance on the Asteroids and Galaga machines, the air thick with nacho cheese, until our hands cramped. We thought we were kings then—piloting that little triangle through space, blasting rocks to dust, shouting over each other about who had next. It was nothing. And it was everything.

And the skiing—That first terrifying run down Spiral Stairs. Knees knocking, goggles fogged, chasing the older kids through the bumps Telluride was famous for. I didn't know it then, but I was learning how to fall and get back up. Again and again. I was always the last one down. Until I wasn't. I learned how to pay the bills one rut at a time.

The road curved one last time, and the town came into view—tucked away like a secret between the mountains. The Victorian buildings stood in their neat rows, painted in faded blues and reds against the towering backdrop of Ajax Mountain.

Something in me settled—a weight I hadn't noticed until it lifted. The tension in my shoulders eased. My breathing deepened. There was a certainty here I hadn't found anywhere else. A sense of belonging that went beyond reason or explanation. I moved around a lot as a kid. But Telluride always felt like home.

16

34:01:12:22:23:35

The town felt like it was half-asleep, caught somewhere between winter's departure and spring's reluctant arrival. The last patches of snow clung stubbornly to shaded rooftops, while the sidewalks had already surrendered to the sun, damp from the slow thaw. I pulled my coat tighter across my chest, boots tucked beneath the bench, knees close together.

This was my place. Not something I owned—but something I returned to. A quiet kind of belonging, the way certain corners of the world quietly claim you when no one else does. My fingers traced idle patterns into the worn wood beside me. The surface was rough, weathered by years of mountain air and passing strangers.

A Porsche turned the corner in front of me, gliding smooth and clean into view. The sun caught its white paint, too polished for this dusty stretch of Colorado Avenue. The Ski Utah license plate caught my eye.

POWLIFE.

A skier's car. Someone who knew the mountains. Someone passing through. The driver—just a flash. A man, maybe twenties. Older than me, but not by much. His face was gone in an instant. The sound of the engine lingered longer than he did.

I watched the space where the car had been, unsure what had drawn me to it. A feeling, maybe. A flicker. The kind that doesn't explain itself. A sharp clatter pulled me back.

Down the sidewalk, Mrs. Jenkins shuffled with her grocery bags— slow, deliberate, like each step had to be negotiated. Falstaff padded beside her, patient and enormous, his thick fur catching the light. The bags swung low against her thin frame, and her coat hung loose at the shoulders, like it remembered the shape of someone younger..

People passed. Some looked. Most didn't. I waited. Waited for someone else to help. No one did. I stood. My hands moved before my thoughts did—boots scuffing the pavement, arms reaching. One bag, then another.

"Thank you, dear," she said, smiling.

I nodded. That was enough. The words were there, the way they always were. But I didn't speak them. We walked side by side. Falstaff huffed, his giant paws making soft sounds on the sidewalk. At the bench, she paused to rest.

I set the bags down gently and watched her ease onto the bench. The town kept moving. No one noticed. I glanced at my hands—empty now, but still holding more than I could say. Then, quietly, I sat again.

The house looked exactly the same. And somehow—not at all. I eased the Porsche next to my Grandfather's Jeep CJ7, cutting the engine as the last of the daylight stretched long across the lawn. The Victorian still stood with its gingerbread trim, painted in the soft pastels Mom loved—sky-blue siding, butter-yellow shutters. A house that belonged more in a fairytale than a mountain town.

The scent in the air hit me before I stepped out: pine, woodsmoke, melting snow. Familiar. Distant. Like a song I used to know by heart. I sat there for a moment, fingers still wrapped around the steering wheel. Coming back wasn't bad. Wasn't good. Just… strange.

The front door swung open before I could reach for it.

"Well, well," Mom called, leaning against the doorframe, arms crossed. A smile tugged at her mouth—wry, warm, unmistakably hers.

"Look what the wind blew in. What's the snow story this time?"

Her hair was piled in a messy bun, streaked with gray, a smear of paint across one wrist like a signature. Her sweater was an explosion of color—turquoise, fuchsia, something that might've been orange. Mom always dressed like she'd walked through a canvas and kept going.

I grinned and stepped inside, letting the familiar creak of the hardwood settle under my boots.

"Oh, let's see…" I pretended to think. "I taught a yeti how to do a daffy."

From the kitchen table, Grandfather chuckled. "Now that's something I'd pay to see."

◯

He sat exactly where he always had, an old deck of cards spread in front of him. The lines on his face had deepened, but his eyes still had that glint—sharp, knowing, like he saw more than he let on.

"Well, you're in luck. He's joining the circus next week."

Across from him, Mom smirked. "Telluride's been quiet without your ski magic."

"Yeah, I'm sure the whole town's been in mourning."

Gilmore, the orange Persian shop cat, lifted his head from the windowsill just long enough to confirm I was not, in fact, food. Then went back to ignoring me.

I stepped toward the table, peeking over Mom's shoulder at her cards. Grandfather groaned, rubbing his temple. "She's winning again, isn't she?"

I shrugged. "You had to ask?"

Mom fanned her hand out with theatrical flair. "Luck of the draw, boys." A full house. Grandfather mucks his cards.

"Speaking of magic—did I ever tell you about my days as a part-time magician? Pulled rabbits out of hats. Confounded the locals."

Mom rolled her eyes. "Here we go…"

I leaned against the counter, arms crossed.

"Confounding the locals, huh? Seems you're still up to your old tricks."

❀

He tried to keep a straight face, but his eyes twinkled. The room filled with laughter—the easy kind. The kind that makes time bend a little, like maybe it never moved at all. And just for a moment, I didn't feel like I was passing through.

Charm & Whimsy

The brick facade of the store had been standing longer than anyone could remember, its weathered exterior radiating the kind of warmth that only came from years of stories passing through its doors. Inside, the air carried the scent of old books, beeswax candles, and aged cedar, a mix of timeless nostalgia and quiet magic. This place had been in my family for years. And yet, I still wasn't sure I belonged here.

I stood behind the counter, arranging a delicate row of hand-painted ceramic mugs, shifting them slightly to the left, then back to the right, like some invisible equation would suddenly make them sell.

Across from me, Mom and Grandfather observed in quiet amusement. Behind them, Gilmore was draped dramatically across the windowsill, his orange fur soaking in the sunlight. He blinked at me lazily, the picture of royal indifference.

Grandfather finally spoke, his voice low and certain. "Your grandmother always said beauty is in the details."

I sighed, leaning against the counter. "Yeah, I get the details. I just struggle with the big picture."

Grandfather shuffled his deck of cards absentmindedly. "Well, even Picasso started with a blank canvas."

◎

The soft chime of the doorbell echoed through the shop. I looked up, and—She stepped inside.

She wasn't like anyone I'd ever seen before. Dark curls framed her face in wild, untamed spirals, and her olive-green eyes held a kind of quiet intensity, like she was always deep in thought.

She moved gracefully, but there was something hesitant about the way she stood just past the doorway, as if she were adjusting to the atmosphere before letting herself belong to it.

I didn't even realize I was staring. Then—my elbow clipped one of the coffee mugs, sending it wobbling dangerously. I lunged for it, barely catching the handle before the whole display went crashing down.

Across the counter, Mom and Grandfather both turned, amused. The girl hadn't noticed. Or at least, she didn't let on if she had.

She wandered further inside, her fingers grazing the spines of old books, drifting over the delicate porcelain figurines, taking in the world of *Charm & Whimsy* like someone flipping through the pages of a story. I swallowed, forcing myself to focus, but my gaze kept betraying me, drawn back to her without permission.

Mom stepped forward, her voice warm. "Can I help you find any-thing?"

The girl smiled politely, shook her head. She kept moving, eventu-ally stopping near the window. Gilmore lifted his head, blinking at her as if appraising her worth.

I waited for him to do what he always did—ignore, dismiss, or, if he was feeling particularly generous, tolerate. Instead, he let her stroke his fur, even shifting slightly into her touch. Something in her expression softened, just for a moment. A quiet kind of peace, something real. Then—her gaze flicked toward the door.

Mom was the first to speak. "Come back anytime, dear."

The girl smiled.

No.

I didn't know why the thought hit me so suddenly, but it did. I could have said something. I should have. Instead, I watched her go, the door chime ringing softly as she slipped out onto the sidewalk, disappearing into the sunlight.

Grandfather turned toward me, his sharp blue eyes catching something in my expression I hadn't meant to reveal. He leaned forward, resting his forearms on the counter. Grandfather exhaled through his nose, shaking his head.

"Next time, say something—unless you're ready to watch her walk out that door for good."

I've been perfecting the art of saying nothing for years. And I'm getting too good at it. Especially with girls. Most of all, the *beautiful* ones.

Mom tilted her head. "Did that intriguing girl catch your eye?"

I opened my mouth. Closed it. Finally— "She… had really beautiful hair."

Grandfather leaned back in his chair. "The biggest regrets in life come from the chances we don't take, Michael."

Mom stifled a laugh. "You might need more than noticing her hair to win her heart."

I exhaled, "Like a transformation into Fabio?"

Mom rolled her eyes. "Fabio would be quite the leap."

Grandfather frowned. "Who's Fabio?"

That finally broke me. I laughed—an exhale, a release. But as the laughter faded, as the door chime settled into silence, my gaze drifted back toward the entrance.

I'd passed this shop a hundred times. Maybe more. Always meaning to step inside, always telling myself next time. It sat like a quiet story tucked into the street—easy to overlook, easier to postpone. But today, something tugged. Not hard. Just enough.

The door gave with a soft creak, and I stepped over the threshold.

The shop smelled like history—not of dust or decay, but something gentler. Aged pages. Melted wax. Polished wood worn smooth by years of handling. It was the kind of scent that slowed time, stretched it thin between the past and whatever came next.

I paused just inside, letting the space settle around me. Shops like this had their own hush, their own rhythm. You didn't rush a place like this. You listened. You breathed. The chime above the door faded behind me, swallowed by the warm quiet.

Charm & Whimsy.

⦾

Even the name felt like something half-remembered from a child-hood dream. Light filtered through lace-curtained windows in soft, slanted gold. Dust motes floated like suspended thoughts. The walls were lined with narrow shelves, their spines crowded with forgotten books, odd trinkets, and porcelain figurines so delicate they looked like they might shatter if you breathed too hard.

A place full of things left behind.

A place full of things waiting to be found.

I moved carefully, letting my fingers graze the edge of a hand-made leather journal, the worn cover soft beneath my touch. Beside it, a stack of old novels leaned against a silver picture frame, the glass slightly cracked, the image inside blurred with time.

Everything here had a story.

Then—chaos. A ceramic mug teetered on the edge of the counter, bumping into another like a warning shot. He lunged, catching it just in time. Across the store, the older woman and man—family, maybe—turned toward him with matching expressions: calm, affectionate, faintly amused. The kind of look people give when they've seen some-one grow up clumsy and stay that way.

I looked away, focusing on the shelves. If he was embarrassed, he didn't say anything. If I was amused, I didn't show it.

The cat watched me from his throne by the window, his fur an explosion of deep orange against the lace curtains. He had the expres-sion of someone deeply unimpressed with the world. I knelt beside him, careful not to startle him. He didn't move.

A test.

I reached out slowly, my fingers skimming his fur. Soft. Warmer than I expected. He let out a long, slow breath, shifting just enough to lean into the touch. I exhaled, too.

Time pressed forward, reminding me I wasn't meant to linger here. I pulled my hand away from the cat. His tail flicked in protest, but he didn't move to stop me. I stepped toward the exit. The chime rang softly above me as I pushed the door open.

The woman at the counter called out goodbye. I smiled, just enough to show I'd heard her. Then—the door closed behind me.

Outside, the air met me like a gentle exhale—warm and fragrant with new blossoms. I slipped my hands into my jacket pockets and followed the curve of the sidewalk, past shopfronts spilling window boxes and wind chimes. The sun filtered through the budding trees, dappling the pavement in soft, shifting patterns. A breeze stirred the scent of cut grass and something else—popcorn, maybe, or hot dogs warming in foil—carried from the park ahead.

At the edge of the park, I climbed the bleachers and settled onto the top row. The wooden planks, worn smooth by seasons of use, were warm beneath me. Below, the little leaguers moved across the field in a scattered rhythm, their laughter bright as birdsong. I let myself sink into the moment—quiet, unhurried. Just the sound of spring unfolding around me, one pitch at a time.

There's something about baseball. I never followed the rules, never played the game, but watching it… there's comfort in the rhythm. The familiar sounds. The cheer of the crowd. The crack of a bat, the thud

of a missed ball against the chain-link backstop. Even the soda pop—
syrupy and fizzy—tastes colder at a ballgame. Sweeter. Maybe it's the
ice in the paper cup, or maybe it's the way sunlight softens everything
it touches. I don't know. But I know the feeling.

I let my bag drop beside me, the worn leather slumping against the
seat. The weight inside was familiar—books, journals, and a choice I
wasn't ready to make. With careful fingers, I reached in, pulling out the
UC Berkeley letter.

*We are pleased to inform you that you have been awarded a full scholarship to
our English Literature Program.*

The words were already etched into my mind. Every sentence read,
reread, turned over like a stone in my palm. A full scholarship. A place
waiting for me in a world of libraries and poetry, of classrooms and
words. And yet— Beneath the letter, another piece of paper peeked
out. Thin, glossy, printed in bold hopeful letters.

Make a Difference. Change the World.

I pulled out the Peace Corps brochure, unfolding it slowly. The
image of smiling children in a faraway country stared back at me, their
eyes full of something Berkeley could never give me.

Something else slipped from my bag. A greeting card from my
Grandparents—light blue, decorated with embossed gold lettering.
It landed between the slats of the bleachers, face-up. I picked it up,
smoothing the edges.

*We always knew you were destined for greatness. Congratulations on the
Berkeley scholarship! We are so proud of you!*

⦾

I swallowed. Destined for greatness.

I traced the Berkeley seal with my fingertips, but my eyes kept drifting back to the Peace Corps brochure. One was a road already paved for me. A future others had imagined on my behalf. The other—a blank space. A leap into the unknown.

The breeze stirred my curls, cool against my skin. Across the valley, the snow-dusted peaks stood silent, watching.

Then—*CRACK.*

The sound of a bat connecting with the ball rang sharp through the air. I looked up. Below, a young player had swung hard, sending the ball soaring into the sky. The outfielders turned their heads, tracking its arc, waiting to see where it would land.

For a moment, it hung in the air, weightless, suspended between where it had been and where it was going. Just like me. I exhaled, my grip tightening around the papers in my lap.

Highway 145 - Ophir

There's something about driving with the top down that makes driving feel less like transit and more like experience. The air doesn't just slip past—you wear it. You smell the pine, the asphalt warming in the sun, the sharp trace of snow still clinging to the peaks.

Sound doesn't hide behind glass. You hear the hum of the tires on the pavement, the engine's low growl as you lean into a curve, the wind pressing against your chest like it's testing you. With the top up, you're watching the world. With it down, you're in it. ♪

♪ *"Running to Stand Still"* by U2

The highway curved south through the Ophir Loop, winding through the shadow of the mountains like a ribbon pulled loose. Farther down, I eased the Porsche onto a gravel shoulder, letting the engine settle into silence. Pines rose on either side of the road, towering and dark, their needles dusted with the last breath of winter.

Trout Lake opened before me in perfect stillness, a pane of glass reflecting the sky back at itself. The blue was impossibly deep, the kind of color that only shows up at high altitudes and in memories you're not sure are real.

I stepped out into the quiet, camera in hand. The air still smelled like pine and snowmelt, sharp and clean. A hawk cried out above the ridgeline, its voice trailing into silence. No traffic. No voices. Just the wind shifting through the trees and the faint lapping of water against the shore.

Along the far edge of the lake, a row of canoes rested in the shallows. Red, yellow, turquoise, faded green—sun-worn but still bright. They were half-tucked into the reeds, tilted slightly, as if waiting for someone to come back for them. They looked like memories, stranded. I adjusted my lens. Framed the shot. *Click.*

I moved a little closer, shifting the angle—trying to catch the exact place where the reflections blurred. The mountains mirrored in the lake. The pop of color from the canoes. The way the water carried everything and held nothing. *Click.*

I wasn't just photographing the scene. I was looking for something quieter. Something underneath. A pause in time. A reason to still believe in stillness. Sometimes the light hit just right—just for a second—and the world held its breath. And sometimes, that was enough. *Click.*

15

34:03:00:00:38:41

The pen hovered over the waybill, the ink smudged just slightly where I'd hesitated. A FedEx box sat open beside me on the counter, my portfolio carefully tucked inside—a year's worth of work, frozen moments in time, all leading up to this.

The weight of it wasn't much, just a handful of prints, a letter, a hope. But in a way, it felt like everything. I pressed the pen down, signed my name, then sealed the package. Leaning back, I let out a breath.

"I am in need of life support. Anyone want in?"

Mom didn't look up from where she was reorganizing a display of handmade candles. "A mochaccino, please."

Grandfather set his cards down, tapping the table thoughtfully.

◑

"You know, maybe it's time I switch things up. No black coffee today."

I raised an eyebrow. "History in the making?"

Grandfather leaned back in his chair, considering. "Sometimes you gotta keep 'em guessing."

"What's next? Socks with sandals?"

He gave me a flat look. "That'll be the day."

Mom finally turned toward me, crossing her arms. "What's in the box?"

I paused in the doorway, sunglasses dangling from my hand. The morning sunlight spilled across the wooden floorboards. A small smile pulled at the corner of my mouth.

"Just trying to prove there's still magic in the world."

And then the door chime jingled as I stepped outside. Telluride had a way of holding time in place—brick storefronts, old signs, people who seemed to belong to every era at once.

Like the Civil War Guy.

The first time I saw him, I wasn't entirely sure if it was a costume or some kind of tear in the fabric of time. He wore a long, navy-blue coat with gold buttons, creased leather boots worn at the toes, the whole look so precise it felt like he'd marched straight out of 1863 and hadn't quite caught up to the present. He walked with slow, deliberate

◍

steps, chin high, as if he were carrying something invisible but heavy. It should have looked absurd. It didn't.

I turned back for a second look, but—a figure ahead.

At first, just a silhouette. Backlit. Still.

Then the light shifted, and time didn't exactly stop—but it forgot how to move forward. Or maybe that was just me. Some part of me stopped keeping track of anything else.

Her.

She moved through the sunlight like it was parting just for her, a golden halo spilling across her shoulders. Barefoot. A long sundress catching the wind, swaying around her ankles. Midnight curls wild and unbound, twisting like they had a mind of their own.

The whole world should've stopped.

She wasn't real. Couldn't be. And yet—she was.

She looked like a dream I forgot to write down. Like every song lyric I never understood until that moment. I kept walking, pulled forward by something unseen—some thread stretched tight between us long before this. Like the whole rotation of the earth had tilted just enough to make this moment inevitable.

She blew a bubble. Pink. Iridescent. Perfect. It floated in the space between us, weightless and waiting.

Then—*POP.*

I blinked.

She kept walking, slipping past me like a warm breeze. I caught a trace of something sweet—coconut, maybe, or sugar. I turned, desperate for one last glimpse—

Gone.

Just the corner. Just the quiet.

I've never believed in ghosts. But maybe—just maybe—I'd just seen one. Not the haunting kind. The kind that leaves something behind. A ripple. A question. A reason to keep looking.

"That girl is so beaut—"

Before I could finish the thought—

CRASH.

I collided full force with something solid, sending an explosion of napkins, mustard packets, and diced onions flying into the air.

"Hey! Hey! Watch where you're going!"

The Hot Dog Man was legendary. Thick mustache. Perpetual scowl. The undisputed king of condiments and grudges. He ran his tiny hot dog stand like it was a kingdom under siege—strict rules, no substitutions, no nonsense. And now, his world was covered in spilled sauerkraut.

"Sorry, sorry!" I held up my hands, trying to help, but he swatted me away like an unruly pigeon. "Let me—"

"I got it! I got it! Just move along!"

I took the hint, backing away as he muttered about "damn dreamers walking around in a daze." Maybe he wasn't wrong.

The town felt different when you walked without shoes. I liked the feeling of it—the warmth of the sunbaked sidewalk, the cool patches of shadow between buildings, the slight give of earth when I wandered onto the grass. It made the world feel more real. Or maybe it made me feel more real.

The sundress swayed around my ankles as I moved, the air stirring through the fabric, light against my skin. The whole town hummed around me—the quiet chatter of café conversations, the distant jingle of a bicycle bell, the occasional thud of boots on pavement. It was one of those days where nothing felt urgent.

I turned onto Colorado Avenue, the brick storefronts casting long shadows over the sidewalk. Telluride was a town where time didn't seem to move quite as fast—it held things in place, stretched moments longer than they should be.

Then, a presence. Someone up ahead. I didn't look at first, but I felt it—the way the air shifted slightly, like something had settled into place without a sound. That subtle pull. That sense of being seen.

The boy from the store. Still a stranger. But not invisible. Tall, dark hair catching the sun, posture caught somewhere between confident and uncertain. For half a second, it felt like he wanted to say something. I walked past, the space between us so small, but impossibly vast.

And as I passed, I blew a bubble. Soft pink, expanding, stretching—then *POP.*

The spell broke. I kept moving. I didn't look back.

I rounded the corner onto Pine Street, fingers wrapping instinctively around the strap of my bag. The ground here was rougher—small cracks in the pavement, the jagged texture of stone. I paused, reaching down, slipping on my flats. The leather was soft from wear, molded to the shape of my feet.

Across the street, the Post Office stood quiet and expectant. The blue mailbox waited just outside, dignified in its usual place. I stepped forward. My bag felt heavier now. I reached inside—fingertips brushing the worn edges of my journal, the soft tangle of my scarf, the unmistakable shape of the envelope. I pulled it out slowly.

US Peace Corps.

The address neatly printed in my own careful handwriting. The ink caught the sunlight, and I stared at it, my thumb tracing over the letters.

If I let go of it now, it was real. No more wondering. No more balancing between two roads. I took a slow, steady breath. Then, with quiet certainty, I opened the metal slot of the mailbox and let the envelope slip from my fingers. A soft, final thunk as it landed inside.

It was done.

I closed my eyes for just a second, letting the weight settle. Then, without another glance, I turned and walked away.

$$\textbf{\textcircled{0}}$$

$$\text{☾}$$

The metal door creaked slightly as I pulled it open. The FedEx Drop Box stood just outside the courthouse, its chipped purple paint warmed by the sun. Inside, the slot gaped open, waiting.

I held the package in my hands, the weight of my portfolio light, but heavier than it should be. I should have felt nervous. Or relieved. Or something. Instead, I hesitated.

The voice in the back of my head whispered the usual doubts— What if it's not good enough? What if they don't even look at it?

Then, another thought—one that hadn't been there before. What if you don't take the shot? I exhaled. I looked at the address one last time.

Wander Magazine.

Then, without another second of hesitation, I dropped it in. A soft thunk. No taking it back now.

I let my fingers linger on the edge of the slot for half a second, then stepped away. A small step. But maybe the first one toward something bigger. The moment hovered. Just long enough for the chill to settle on my skin, for the weight in my chest to shift—lighter, not gone.

I turned, letting the smell of bread and espresso draw me across the street, warm and familiar. A few minutes later, I stepped out of the bakery, balancing a cardboard tray filled with coffee. The steam curled into the crisp mountain air, catching sunlight like breath.

Three cups. One for Mom. One for Grandfather. One for me. And yet, I barely noticed the warmth seeping through the cups into my palms. I scanned the street. Looking for something. Looking for someone.

⟨O⟩

The sidewalk stretched ahead—familiar faces, the steady rhythm of Telluride life. But she wasn't there. No sundress caught in the wind. No midnight curls shifting in the light. Nothing. She was gone. Like she'd only been passing through.

The door chime jingled as I stepped back inside. The familiar scent of old books and candle wax wrapped around me, grounding me back into the world I knew. Mom turned from behind the counter, her expectant gaze landing on the coffee tray in my hands.

"Did you bring life support?"

I blinked, processing the question for half a second before realizing she meant the coffee.

"Yep… Yes. Crisis averted."

I set the tray down, pushing a cup toward her, another toward Grandfather, who was already watching me with that quiet, knowing expression. He lifted his coffee, inspecting it like he was not sure what to make of it yet.

"You seem a bit off. Anything catch your eye out there?"

I hesitated. Then shrugged. "Oh, just the usual town happenings."

Grandfather took a slow sip, his weathered hands wrapped around the cup, eyes never leaving mine. Then, with the smallest smile, he said, "Well, sometimes, the usual in this town is more captivating than you think."

Before I could respond, the door swung open again, bringing in a rush of cool air and feathers.

Ms. Eloise had arrived.

Her mismatched socks peeked out from under her layered skirts, and a dramatic, wide-brimmed hat adorned with an explosion of feathers sat slightly askew atop her head. She swept into the store, arms open, as if embracing the air itself.

"Well, hello, Charm and Whimsy! Any new trinkets to tickle my fancy today?"

Mom smiled. "Always, Ms. Eloise. Anything particular you're looking for?"

Ms. Eloise glided toward a shelf, her fingers trailing over a crystal ball, as if expecting it to answer before she did.

"Ah, just searching for a hint of the extraordinary. Maybe a potion for good luck or a charm to ward off socks that disappear in the laundry?"

I bit back a chuckle. Leaning toward Mom, I murmured, "I've got a feeling her sock collection is legendary."

Mom, without missing a beat, whispered back, "And she thinks that crystal ball can predict her next great adventure."

We exchanged a knowing glance.

Ms. Eloise turned, holding up a mug decorated with swirling gold script. "This, my dear, will be my cup of fortune. What tales will it tell during my tea time?"

I gave a small bow. "May your tea be filled with adventures, Ms. Eloise."

She winked, then turned back to the crystal ball, pressing both hands lightly against the glass. For a second, she was completely still. Then, she looked toward the window. Her voice softened.

"Ah, the circles of destiny are closing in. Time has a funny way of bringing people together. And sometimes... it leaves a trail."

She twirled away, her hat shifting slightly as she swept out the door, her feathers dancing in the breeze. I watched her go. I wasn't sure why. Maybe it was nothing. Just Ms. Eloise being Ms. Eloise. Or maybe—I glanced back toward the window, toward the street where I had last seen the girl who didn't belong to this world. Maybe she was right.

The Sheridan

The *Sheridan* was one of those places that held stories in its bones. Low-lit sconces cast a warm amber glow over the polished wood, reflecting off the antique mirror that stretched the length of the bar. The air carried the scent of aged bourbon, cedar, and the distant trace of pine drifting in from the mountains beyond the heavy oak doors.

Laughter and quiet conversations hummed around me, but I wasn't really listening. The ice in my Old Fashioned was melting, slow and inevitable, much like the unraveling thoughts in my head.

Lauren moved behind the bar with the kind of effortless confidence that came from years of watching people drink their worries into something manageable.

Her wavy hair caught the low light, framing her face as she worked, her practiced hands sliding bottles across the mahogany counter like an artist arranging a palette.

She paused in front of me, one eyebrow raised. "Another Old Fashioned? Or should I just bring the whole bottle?"

I exhaled, rubbing a hand across my jaw. "Maybe the whole shelf. I'm toasting the slow death of my love life."

Lauren smirked, tilting her head. "Oh, so we're upgrading from Old Fashioned to existential crisis?"

I lifted my glass. "I'm multi-tasking."

She gave me a look, one that carried just enough amusement and just enough knowing—the kind of look that made you wonder how much she'd already figured out.

Then, before she could respond—A stool scraped across the floor.

"I'll have what he's having. Clearly, it's working wonders."

I didn't have to look up. The voice was smooth, edged with dry humor—the kind that belonged to someone who'd never truly struggled, but understood the concept well enough to sympathize.

Brandon, the architect.

I'd met him a few times before, and I liked him. He slid onto the seat beside me, a sharp contrast to the bar's rustic charm—his tailored jacket just slightly undone, his hair styled just enough to look like he hadn't tried.

◎

"Rough day?" he asked, signaling to Lauren without needing to look at her.

I swirled the remaining ice in my glass. "Aren't they all?"

Brandon leaned in slightly, studying me. "You're looking at that drink like it owes you money."

"More like it holds the answers."

He nodded toward it. "Does it?"

I exhaled. "Well… there's… this girl."

Lauren was polishing a glass, but her movements slowed.

Brandon smirked. "It's always a girl."

I took a sip, then set the glass down. "She's… breathtaking."

Lauren's hands paused imperceptibly on a bottle.

"But she's too young," I continued, as if saying it out loud would make the whole thing easier to dismiss.

"It feels like there's this giant wall of bad timing."

Brandon leaned back slightly, studying me the way a gambler sizes up the table before placing a bet.

"Then climb it. Or tear it down. Walls don't move on their own."

I let out a wry chuckle. "Easy for you to say."

⦿

Brandon shrugged, lifting his freshly poured drink.

"True. I've got plenty of walls I'm hiding behind."

Lauren returned with my refreshed drink, setting it down closer than necessary. Her fingers brushed mine—just barely, but enough. I glanced up. For the first time, I really saw her. She held my gaze for a moment—a flicker of something unreadable, something patient, something waiting. Then, just as easily, she was gone.

But not before she said, just under her breath—barely more than a murmur:

"Some walls are there to keep people out. Others? Just to see who'll try."

I watched her walk away, the words landing harder than I expected. She hadn't said them to me directly. Or maybe she had.

Brandon tilted his head toward her retreating figure, eyes gleaming. "Case in point."

I rolled my eyes, dismissing it with a shake of my head. "That's just friendly bartender banter."

Brandon laughed. "Sure, keep telling yourself that."

I took a slow sip, the bourbon warming its way down. Maybe he was right. Maybe he wasn't. Either way, it didn't change the fact that my mind was still somewhere else.

I set my drink down. "What about you? Any walls in your life?"

⟆

Brandon sighed, running a hand through his hair. "Monica."

He didn't have to elaborate. I already knew.

"We've been doing this… on-again, off-again thing," he admitted. "Great when it's light, a trainwreck when it's not."

"And?"

He exhaled, looking down at his drink. "And I run. Every time. I tell myself it's timing too, but really… it's just fear."

I turned my glass slowly in my hands.

"Maybe stop running," I said finally. "Might surprise you."

Brandon smirked. "Easy for you to say."

I let out a quiet chuckle. "Yep. I don't take my own advice either."

The laughter between us was lighter this time, the kind that comes from two people calling out each other's bullshit but not being mad about it.

In the mirror behind the bar, Lauren adjusted her pendant, her eyes meeting mine for a second before flicking away.

Brandon caught the glance, but said nothing.

Instead, he picked up his glass and swirled the liquid inside.

"So," he said finally, "what's your next move?"

I stared at the ice melting in my drink.

"Not sure I have one."

Brandon smirked. "Then make one. Before someone else does."

I lifted my glass in a small toast. "To bad timing."

Brandon clinked his against mine. "And the walls we pretend we can't climb."

The whiskey burned smooth down my throat, but the thought remained. Maybe timing wasn't the real problem. Maybe I was.

The classroom smelled like pencil shavings and old paper—familiar, faintly comforting. Late sunlight slanted through the tall windows, warming the tops of desks and catching dust motes mid-air, like the whole room had slowed just enough to breathe.

I sat near the back, my journal open, the lines already half-filled with the beginnings of something. A scene? A thought? Maybe a poem. I wasn't sure yet. Sometimes the writing led me before I even knew where we were going.

Mrs. Munson paced at the front of the room, her heels soft against the linoleum as she talked about tone and emotional resonance—how the unsaid was often more powerful than the obvious. She had this way of looking at you, like she could already see the story forming just behind your eyes. I liked her. She didn't treat us like kids. She treated us like writers.

My pen moved without much effort, the words spilling onto the page. I was writing something about leaving. About the way it feels to pack without knowing if you'll ever come back. It wasn't about me, not exactly. And yet, it was. It always was, somehow. Around me, classmates slouched in their seats, half-listening, half-doodling. Someone near the front was chewing on the end of a highlighter. Another stared blankly out the window, lost in some better daydream. But I liked this room—its quiet corners, the weight of its silence. It felt like one of the only places I could think clearly. Like my thoughts didn't have to explain themselves.

My gaze drifted toward the corkboard at the front of the class. The flyer still hung there—the one about the national writing competition. Mrs. Munson had slipped it into my hands over a year ago.

"I think you should go for it," she'd said. "Even if you don't think you're ready." So I entered. Secretly. Quietly. The scholarship offer arrived three months later. Berkeley. Full ride.

And now everything had changed—except it hadn't. Not yet. I tapped my pen against the edge of my journal, glancing around the room. These kids were my classmates, my hallway hellos, my lunch-table acquaintances. In a year, we'd scatter. Different cities. Different futures. Some of them would stay. Others would try to leave and never quite manage it. And still, part of me wondered—what would I leave behind?

I looked down at the page. The words were still coming.

Later, the school parking lot pulsed with the familiar rhythm of after-school life—engines revving, car doors slamming, the distant echo of laughter rising like static over the low thrum of teenage conversations. The air smelled like warm pavement and gasoline. I leaned against my dusty silver Honda Civic, arms crossed, the sun-soaked metal pressing into my back.

Beside me, Allison perched with the ease of someone born for golden hour. Her long, sun-bleached hair caught the light like spun sugar, her sunglasses pushed up into the soft waves. She wore a skirt that fluttered in the breeze and a worn Bowie tee, her wrists stacked with jangling bracelets that sparkled when she moved.

Allison didn't traffic in pretense. She said what she meant and expected you to do the same. There was nothing soft or filtered about her—just presence, full and unflinching. She had a way of cutting straight through the noise, not to wound, but to clear the air. Being around her felt like opening a window after too long. Sharp. Bracing. Necessary.

She was the kind of friend who would steal fries off your tray and threaten anyone who looked at you sideways. Who'd skip class with you not to go anywhere, but just to sit under the bleachers and breathe. She knew when I needed silence, and when I needed someone to be loud on my behalf.

She didn't speak for me. But she never let anyone ignore me either.

In tenth grade, some chick made a crack about the fact that I didn't talk much. Allison didn't blink. She stood up, looked her dead in the eye, and said, "Oh yeah, bitch? Keep it up, and your next period's gonna be from someone else's boyfriend."

I wasn't exactly sure what she meant by that—but that girl never said another word to me. Like, *ever.* She never made me feel broken. Just… different. And somehow, better for it.

Allison didn't hover. She flanked. She stood beside you like a wall, daring the world to try its luck. And if you fell, she didn't ask what happened. She would just brush the dirt off your knees, toss you a piece of gum, and say, "Let's burn something small and symbolic."

She was my translator. My compass. My riot when I needed one.

Everyone needs a friend like Allison—not a mirror, but a shield. We weren't opposites, exactly. More like different instruments in the same piece. She was the brass section—bold, bright, loud when she needed to be, impossible to ignore. I was strings—quieter, layered, but still part of the same music.

Then I felt it—that almost-electric shift in the air. I didn't have to look. I already knew.

Zach.

He moved across the lot with that same relaxed confidence that always made me feel like I was watching a movie where I didn't belong. His tall frame, backpack slung over one shoulder, dark hair tousled by the wind, heading toward his red VW Bug like he had all the time in the world.

Allison nudged me with her elbow, sharp and knowing. I turned just enough to glare, but she was already grinning like the ending had been written and she was just waiting for the scene to catch up.

I brushed a curl from my cheek, trying to shake off the heat blooming in my face. And then—he slowed. Not toward his car.

Toward me.

"I got you," she murmured. "I'll handle this."

Allison practically vibrated beside me, but I barely noticed anymore Zach adjusted his bag and stepped closer, close enough that I could see the small crease between his brows, the slight dimple in his cheek when he half-smiled. His eyes met mine, and for a second—just a second—something passed between us.

I smiled. Small, shy, but real. And without hesitation, he smiled back. Something in my chest loosened. Warmed. For the first time, I let myself believe he'd seen me too. Not just now. But before. We had a bit of history.

And then, of course—

"So, Zach," Allison said, flipping her hair and grinning, "How do you feel about threesomes?"

Zach choked. Visibly.

I could feel my soul trying to exit my body through my eyebrows. And just like that—the moment passed. But I would remember it anyway.

The soft glow of candlelight flickered across the counter as I shifted the display, arranging the handmade beeswax candles into something that looked both deliberate and effortless.

Outside, the slow rhythm of Telluride life unfolded—shop doors swinging open, voices carrying in the crisp air, footsteps against the sidewalk. Then, movement.

A dog trotted down the sidewalk, his thick coat a swirl of black, white, and rust. His gait was unhurried, confident, like he wasn't just passing through but surveying his domain.

I watched him, tilting my head slightly. Something about him

◍

felt… different. Like he knew something the rest of us didn't. I turned to Mom, who was adjusting a rack of postcards.

"Mom, what do you know about that dog that wanders around town?"

She barely glanced up. "Oh, that's Falstaff. He's a bit of a neighborhood explorer."

"Falstaff, huh? What's his story?"

"He belongs to Mrs. Jenkins, but he's got a knack for wandering off."

The phone rang. Without missing a beat, Mom snatched it up, her voice sliding into full theatrical mode.

"Whimsy, are you in need of magic?"

Mom listened, already handing me the receiver. "Please hold for your ticket to his world."

I rolled my eyes but took the phone. Brandon's voice beamed through the line.

"Yo, thought we could unravel some mysteries. Can you swing by around three tomorrow? Apartment 3B, above the post office."

"Do these mysteries have anything to do with Ms. Eloise's missing socks?"

"Why yes, that is exactly it," he deadpanned.

I smirked. "Roger that. I will bring my protégé, Dom Perignon, for assistance with this delicate matter."

I hung up, shaking my head. A soft bark interrupted my thoughts. I turned. Falstaff sat at the shop's open door, his head tilted just slightly, his intelligent brown eyes fixed on me like he was waiting for something.

I crouched down, resting my forearms on my knees. "You lost, buddy?"

His tail wagged once. Slow. Deliberate. Not lost. Just… watching. I reached out, scratched behind his ear, and he leaned into it like we'd known each other for years. Then, from the corner of my eye—*Her.*

She crossed the street with a wicker basket on her hip, curls catching the light like spilled ink. There was something about the way she moved—unhurried, unaware, like the world made space for her without her asking.

For a second, everything tilted. My breath caught—just a hitch in my chest, but enough. The kind of pause your body makes before your mind can explain why.

She slipped into the crowd at the farmer's market, swallowed by the rhythm of the town.

I exhaled, only then realizing I'd been holding it.

When I looked down, Falstaff was still watching me. His tail gave another deliberate wag—just once, like he'd seen something I wasn't ready to name.

The sidewalk hummed with life as I made my way toward the farmer's market, the sun warm against my shoulders, my basket swinging lightly at my side. The scent of earth and citrus, fresh basil and lavender drifted through the air, weaving together in a way that always made me feel… anchored. I'd always been drawn to things that grew.

Maybe it was the patience of it—the quiet way a seed became a sprout, the way roots stretched unseen beneath the soil long before anyone noticed the change. Growth wasn't loud. It wasn't sudden. It happened in small, invisible ways until one day, something beautiful unfolded. That kind of quiet transformation made sense to me.

I drifted through the rows of stalls, my fingers grazing the edges of wooden crates, burlap sacks, and sun-warmed produce.

The asparagus was crisp, the radishes bright like polished rubies. I traced my fingertips over the delicate leaves of butter lettuce, feeling the life in them, the way they held onto the morning's coolness.

At the next stall, a basket of strawberries caught my eye—plump, red, bursting with sweetness. I leaned in, inhaling the sun-ripened scent, my mind flickering back to summers spent barefoot in the backyard, fingers stained red from picking berries too ripe to make it to the kitchen. I smiled softly and added a handful to my basket.

Then—the herbs. Potted basil, cilantro, thyme. Tiny leaves, fragile but persistent, already reaching toward the light. I picked up a basil plant, cradling the small ceramic pot in my hands.

There was something about tending to living things—watering them, watching them thrive—that made the world feel… kinder. Like no matter what else was happening, no matter how uncertain life felt, this was something I could nurture. Something I could keep alive. I slipped the basil into my basket, tucking it between the strawberries and radishes.

The flower stall was an explosion of color—tulips, daffodils, sunflowers reaching for the sky. Flowers had their own kind of silent language. Tulips meant new beginnings. Daffodils meant hope.

I ran my fingers along a bucket of purple irises, their petals velvet-soft against my skin. Wisdom and courage, according to my grandmother's old book of flower meanings. Beside them, peonies unfurled in lush pink abundance—prosperity and honor, but also bashfulness. I smiled at that contradiction.

The air was sweet with the scent of freesias, their fragile stems holding clusters of blooms that seemed impossibly delicate. Friendship and trust, according to that same dog-eared book I'd pored over as a child, pressing flowers between its pages like secrets I wanted to keep.

Wildflowers stood in casual bunches—black-eyed Susans, cornflowers, and Queen Anne's lace gathered together like old friends having a conversation. They weren't cultivated or perfect like the roses that dominated the center display, but there was something honest about them. Something that didn't need to announce itself.

I leaned closer, inhaling deeply. Lavender meant devotion—or so I'd read. I'd always loved how flowers carried meanings, how people throughout history had used them to say things they couldn't put into words.

My hand hovered over a small bunch of forget-me-nots, their tiny blue faces turned upward like miniature skies. True love. Remembrance. Faithfulness.

I wondered what flowers I might choose to tell my own story someday.

14

34:00:13:24:04:35

I knocked on Brandon's door—a three-beat rhythm, casual but expectant. He opened it almost instantly. There he was—effortlessly put together, like someone who just naturally existed in a permanent state of looking like he had better places to be.

"Fashionably on time," I said.

Brandon leaned against the doorframe, arms crossed. "Dom is required for entry, sir."

"Robin Leach took the last bottle," I said, smirking. "So I brought this."

I held up my offering—a box of Strawberry Hill wine, the kind of stuff that probably violated several international treaties on good taste.

Brandon's eyes narrowed. "Two Buck Chuck?"

I lifted the box a little higher. "Why, yes. The finest."

Brandon stepped aside, waving me in. "Well, it does pair well with my poor life choices."

Inside, the place felt warm, lived-in, and full of half-finished ideas. Sketches and architectural drawings were spread out across every available surface. Some were meticulously detailed, others half-sketched bursts of inspiration that probably wouldn't go beyond the coffee table. Hanging over it all, like some kind of holy relic, was a framed poster of mogul skiing legend, Donna Weinbrecht.

I pressed my hands together and bowed deeply. "Donna... Hail to the Queen." I said, reverent. Brandon mimicked the gesture, grinning.

I wandered toward the bay window, which overlooked Colorado and Pine, the heart of town. Below, the street pulsed with movement— locals, tourists, laughter, music drifting from somewhere down the block.

I exhaled. "This place is incredible. It's like Telluride's beating heart."

Brandon flopped into a chair, stretching out like a king surveying his domain.

"Mi casa, su casa, my friend."

I took the seat next to him, letting the quiet hum of the town settle around us. Then, the courthouse clock began its three o'clock recital.

The chimes rolled through town, but I barely noticed. Because something else had just pulled my attention. A dusty silver Honda

Civic eased into a spot across the street. I sat up slightly, my pulse ticking up a notch. At that moment, a girl stepped out of the car.

Her.

Still no name. Just the girl—the one who hasn't left my thoughts since the moment I first saw her. She moved without hurry, a book tucked under her arm. Then—she sat. On a bench. A bench I'd walked past a thousand times without noticing. My breath caught, just slightly.

"Brandon, it's her."

Brandon followed my gaze, scanning the street. "Who?"

I gestured. "The girl I was telling you about."

Brandon took one look and exhaled. "Ah. The mystery beauty, driving a car that's seen better days."

I barely heard him. I was still watching her. The way she sat there, completely unaware of the weight of my stare. The way the sunlight caught in her hair. The way her gaze drifted over the street, almost like she was waiting for something. Or maybe someone.

I shook my head slightly. "Think of her as a rose among the thorns. It's not about her car; it's her… ethereal aura."

Brandon snorted. "Ethereal aura? Is that a new fragrance?"

I smirked. "It should be—but her essence would be impossible to duplicate."

⦿

Brandon leaned back in his chair, studying me. "What makes this Mona Lisa so special?"

I snapped my gaze away from the window just long enough to glare at him.

"Mona? She's hideous, man."

Brandon laughed. "Hey, don't disrespect the classics."

I shook my head, leaning forward. My voice was quieter now, more certain.

"No contest. She's the most beautiful girl in the world."

Brandon exhaled, shaking his head. "Oh, the most beautiful girl in the world. Our lives are forever changed."

I barely heard him. I'd never talked like this before. Not about anyone. I turned to him,. "You've been staring at those drawings of yours for way, way too long, dude. They've warped your ability to recognize perfection."

Brandon finally let out a real laugh, shaking his head. "Touché."

We clinked glasses, but even as I forced myself to lean back in my chair, I knew. That girl—whoever she was—She wasn't going to fade away.

I took a slow sip of the wine. It tasted like regret, optimism, and crushed strawberries. Perfect. Two Buck Chuck had never seen a moment this sacred.

The bench was cool beneath me, its surface smoothed by time, by hands that had gripped it, by the weight of people who had stopped here before moving on. I should have been moving too. But instead, I stayed. I let my book fall open in my lap. *The Essential Rumi,* translated by Coleman Barks. The wind caught the pages, flipping them gently before settling on one.

Let yourself be silently drawn by the strange pull of what you really love.
It will not lead you astray.

I traced my fingers over the words, lightly, as if they might change beneath my touch. Something about them made me feel unsteady.

Did people always know what they loved? Or did they sometimes walk right past it—blind, uncertain—only to recognize it too late?

A gust of wind brushed my curls across my cheek. I tucked them back, letting my gaze lift from the book. Across the street, the Hot Dog Man was already mid-monologue, gesturing wildly at a group of tourists clustered around his silver cart.

"Ketchup?" he barked, scandalized. "Nobody puts ketchup on a hot dog!"

Then, with theatrical disgust, he snatched the tray right out of one tourist's hands.

"No hot dog for you!"

The tourists looked baffled—part unsure if they were being scolded, part convinced they were being inducted into some sacred

☾

rite of summer lunch. He wasn't actually angry; that was just part of the act. Half street vendor, half performance art.

I smiled to myself, watching it unfold like a one-man play. He took it seriously—his rules, his cart, his kingdom.

I liked ketchup on mine. Always had. I wasn't sure what that said about me—but I knew better than to admit it on that sidewalk.

Telluride had a way of pulling you into its rhythm. I had lived here most of my life, and still, sometimes, it felt like something was waiting here—just out of reach.

☾

The phone rang, cutting through the quiet hum of *Charm & Whimsy*. Dust particles danced in the afternoon light streaming through the antique shop's bay windows as I barely looked up from the photography magazine I was flipping through.

"Charm and Whimsy, this is Michael."

"Michael, hey—it's Jane from Wander magazine."

My finger, which had been lazily tracing a camera review, froze. *Wander* magazine. I sat up straighter, my grip tightening on the receiver.

"Jane, hi—" I tried to sound casual. "Thank you for calling."

"We got your portfolio," she said, her voice warm but professorial. "And, wow. We love your work."

My heart skipped. "Seriously?"

A small laugh, then confirmation. "Seriously. You have a way of capturing a place—makes us feel like we've been there. That shot of the red rock arches with the storm rolling in? The way you caught that moment where sunlight broke through the clouds? Breathtaking."

My heart hammered, the weight of her words sinking in. *Wander* magazine. The kind of place where careers weren't just made, they were carved into something permanent.

I cleared my throat. "I always try to tell a story with each shot."

"It shows. That's exactly what we're looking for. We want to see more—something fresh, something that pushes your versatility. What are you working on now?"

The question caught me off guard. The truth was I hadn't shot anything new in weeks. But this wasn't just a courtesy call. This was a door creaking open.

"I've got a few new shots I'm really excited about," I heard myself say. "A series on the hidden corners of Telluride that most tourists never see. Some perspectives that I think would be perfect for *Wander.*"

"Good. Can you get them to me by Friday? The editorial team meets Monday."

My stomach tightened. Three days. "I will Fedex them over to you right away."

"Looking forward to it, Michael. This could be the beginning of something great."

I hung up, my hand still wrapped around the receiver, my brain catching up with what had just happened. Then, it hit me. Holy shit. A slow grin stretched across my face, followed quickly by a wave of panic. I needed new material. *Fast.*

"Did you just win the lottery?"

I turned to see Grandfather standing there, wiping his hands on a rag, his expression already knowing. The scent of furniture polish clung to him, as familiar as his skeptical smile.

"Better than that," I said, still grinning despite the knot in my stomach. "Wander magazine is interested in my work."

His eyebrows lifted, his voice laced with something I hadn't heard from him in a long time—pride.

"Well, well. The world's finally catching on."

Mom entered from the back, a vintage brooch in her hand, her eyes lighting up. "They'll see what we all see—someone who pours his heart into everything he does." She paused, studying my face. "So why do you look terrified?"

I ran my hand through my hair. "Because I just promised them new work by Friday, and I've got nothing."

Grandfather's eyes crinkled at the corners. "The best shots are always the ones you haven't taken yet."

I nodded, my pulse still racing, something shifting inside me. This was happening. This was real. This wasn't a maybe. This was a door opening. And I wasn't ready—but I had to be.

The Honda's door creaked as I pulled it shut, the sound oddly comforting. Familiar. I sat for a moment in the stillness of the driveway, hands resting on the steering wheel, watching the way the afternoon light filtered through the windshield and dappled the dashboard in gold. It was just before three. Like always.

I reached for a cassette case tucked into the glove compartment—its cracked hinge barely holding on, corners softened from years of use. Flipping past old mix tapes and hand-labeled memories, I found the one I always came back to. The tape inside had warped from sun and time, but it still worked.

I slid it into the deck. The familiar hum of the tape catching. Then those opening chords from the old cassette filled the car—warm and raw, like a voice from the past reaching back through the static. ♪

The song had always felt like a message meant for someone else. But lately, I'd started to hear something in it that felt like mine. Not the exact words, but the feeling underneath. That the world was out there—beautiful, unpredictable, full of sharp corners. And no one was going to warn you when it started to shift.

I backed out of the driveway, gravel crunching under the tires, and turned onto the road. The wind rushed through the open window, warm and restless. My hair whipped across my face, wild and untamed, but I didn't care. Not today. Two miles to town. It wasn't far, but it was enough space to breathe. To think. To not think.

The song wrapped around me—not soft, not loud. Just steady. Honest. Like it knew what it meant to feel like you're standing at the edge of something, not quite a kid anymore, but not sure what comes next either.

♪ *"Wild World"* by Cat Stevens

☾

I didn't know where I was going—not really. But the world felt like it was about to tilt, and part of me wondered if I was ready for it.

The tape hissed faintly as it turned, and the wind rushed in, carrying the smell of pine and dust. The sky was wide and empty above me. The road ahead curved gently towards town.

And I kept driving. Not to escape anything. Just to hold the feeling a little longer. Of motion. Of music. Of maybe becoming.

☾

The air outside felt different—thinner, quieter, like I'd stepped into a world slightly out of sync with the one I'd just left behind. I turned up Colorado Avenue, the phone call still echoing in my mind. Possibilities humming just under the surface. A flicker of something bigger, just out of reach.

Half a block ahead, an old Chevy pickup sat crooked along the curb, its bumper rusted and sagging, like it had given up long before the engine did. Next to it, a figure hunched on the sidewalk—

Scary Gary.

He was talking to a fire hydrant. Not near it. *To it.*

Hands gesturing like a magician mid-spell, wild gray hair exploding from his head, a cigarette dangling dangerously close to his lip. I nodded as I passed. Gary didn't acknowledge me, too deep in his performance. Something about a broken promise and "the peanut conspirators." Same routine, different audience.

I kept walking. Then—a shimmer of dusty silver. My eyes snapped forward.

☾

The Honda. And behind the wheel—*Her.*

The girl with the quiet gravity. The one I kept telling myself to forget, even as she took up more and more space in the corners of my mind.

I slowed, pulse hitching, watching as she passed. The window was down, her curls lifted by the wind—dark, wild, catching the light like strands of ribbon spun from night. There was something hypnotic about the way they moved, untamed and perfect, like they belonged to another rhythm entirely.

She didn't see me. Or if she did, she didn't show it. There was something precise in the way she drove—steady, focused, like she was tracing the same route she always did. Like this wasn't coincidence. Like it was something else entirely.

And then the courthouse clock began its slow, mechanical count-down. I looked up. Three o'clock. The hands aligned with a soft click I felt more than heard. I stood there for a moment, still watching the street even though she was already gone.

Behind me, Gary broke into a round of applause—directed at the hydrant. I almost smiled.

She drives past here at three. I didn't know what it meant yet. But I was starting to wonder if she lived her life in patterns—and if, maybe, I was beginning to learn the shape of them.

☾

The air was thin at 10,000 feet, the kind that burned your lungs but cleared your head. I'd left Telluride before dawn, driving the winding mountain roads with my headlights cutting through darkness and low-hanging mist.

The turnoff to Woods Lake was easy to miss—a dirt road that most tourists sped past on their way to the more famous overlooks.

I pulled Gramps' Jeep into the small clearing that served as a makeshift parking area, empty except for a single pickup with local plates. Perfect. The lake was still a half-mile hike through dense forest, but that's what made it special—you had to want it.

The weight of my camera pack pressed against my shoulders as I navigated the narrow trail. Grandfather's words from yesterday echoed in my mind:

The mountain reveals itself to those who climb it with purpose.

Purpose I had—Friday's deadline loomed large. Jane was waiting, and these shots needed to be more than good.

They needed to be honest.

I emerged from the tree line just as the first direct light hit the western shore of the lake. The scene before me pulled the air from my lungs more effectively than the altitude. The lake sat like a perfect mirror in a natural bowl formed by the surrounding peaks, their snow-dusted summits reflected with perfect symmetry in the still water. A thin layer of morning mist hovered just above the surface, catching the golden light and diffusing it like nature's own softbox.

This wasn't the postcard Telluride. This was the Telluride that locals guarded, that required effort, that rewarded patience.

I set up my tripod at the water's edge, careful not to disturb the perfect stillness. My fingers moved with practiced precision despite the cold—switching lenses, adjusting settings, screwing on filters. The first shots were wide, capturing the entire basin with the lake as the centerpiece. But it was when I switched to my 70-200mm that the real magic happened.

I focused on where the mist curled around a half-submerged log on the far shore, creating patterns that resembled ghostly figures dancing above the water. *Click.*

The way the aspens at the edge trembled slightly in a breeze too gentle to feel, their golden reflection rippling. *Click.*

Time disappeared. The world narrowed to what I could see through my viewfinder—light, texture, movement, moment. I worked methodically, checking my light meter between shots, making notes in a small pad about exposures and compositions. I'd shoot three rolls here if I had to. This place deserved the film.

As the sun rose higher, I noticed what I'd been too focused to see—a patch of wildflowers on a small rise caught the light in a way that perfectly framed the lake. I repositioned my tripod, incorporating this new foreground. The composition was immediately stronger— more layered, more intimate. Not just showing a beautiful place, but inviting the viewer to step into it, to smell the pine-scented air and feel the mountain chill.

That was what Jane had responded to in my portfolio—not just pretty pictures, but doorways into experience. Places that felt real because they were real, captured by someone who knew them, loved them, understood their moods and secrets.

I worked until the light changed, shooting variations, experimenting with exposures and perspectives. By the time I finally lowered my camera, my film canisters were safely tucked away and my fingers were numb. But I knew I had it—the shots that would make Jane and her editorial team lean forward in their chairs.

These weren't tourist snapshots of Telluride's famous views. These were windows into the heart of a place most visitors never saw, the hidden Telluride that required you to venture beyond the obvious.

As I packed up my gear, I felt the tension in my shoulders ease. *Wander* wanted something fresh, something that pushed my versatility. Woods Lake at dawn wasn't just photogenic—it was authentic. And I hoped it was enough.

The bench had warmed in the sun. Across the street, the last patches of snow clung to shaded corners, but the trees had begun to whisper green again—small, bright leaves pressing through like the world had decided to try one more time.

A breeze lifted the scent of lilac and melting earth. The kind of air that makes you think anything is possible. The kind that used to make me want to run.

But today I stayed.

People passed—couples with coffees, dogs tugging at leashes, a man pushing a stroller with one hand and shielding the sun from his eyes with the other. All of them moving, choosing, heading somewhere.

Something inside me had shifted. Quietly. Like when the thaw begins—not all at once, but slow, silent, sure. I didn't know what came next. But I felt the pressure of it rising, like the creek near Bear Creek Falls in spring—gentle, then sudden.

I'd spent so long surviving. Drifting between routines. Smiling when I was supposed to. Helping where I could. Letting time pass like pages I wasn't reading. But lately, I could feel the edge of something. The faint outline of a life that wasn't built on waiting.

Maybe it was the season. Maybe it was the sound of water running again. I tilted my face toward the sun, eyes closed. Some decisions don't come all at once. Sometimes they arrive like spring—impossible to ignore once they've taken hold, even if you're not quite ready to bloom.

The door chime jingled as I looked up from a crossword puzzle. And then—a hurricane of color and movement entered.

"Hello, lovers of Charm and Whimsy!"

Penny. A swirl of paint-streaked overalls, wild hair, and boundless energy, a canvas tucked under her arm like she had just emerged from battle. She spread her arms wide, like a magician revealing a great illusion.

"Behold! My masterpiece—'Deer in the Headlights.' A symphony of colors and emotions, don't you think?"

Grandfather squinted at it. "More like an acid trip through the forest."

Mom, always the diplomat, smiled. "While we appreciate avant-garde, our customers usually prefer charm without deer-induced panic."

Penny pressed a hand to her heart, dramatically wounded. "But this piece tells a story—a Bambi thriller, if you will."

Then—a bark. Everyone turned. Falstaff stood in the doorway, his brown eyes steady, his tail flicking once. Something in me jolted. I glanced at my watch.

2:57.

Without thinking, I bolted for the door. I hit the sidewalk at a sprint. Falstaff trotted after me, tail wagging, as if this were some game he had been waiting for me to play.

I barely dodged the grumpy Hot Dog Man, who frantically waved me away from his stand. Falstaff, however, was not one to ignore potential opportunities. He slowed, sniffing at the air—clearly enticed by the scent of sizzling hot dogs.

The Hot Dog Man scowled at Falstaff, arms crossed.

I barely registered the interaction. I was already halfway up the stairs to Brandon's place, reaching above the door for the spare key.

The courthouse clock began to chime. I flung the door open, rushing toward the window. And then—there she was. The Honda pulled into a spot near the bench.

She stepped out, her movements fluid, natural, the kind of effortless grace you don't realize is beautiful until you see it up close.

Beside her—another girl. Golden hair, bubbly, radiating a different kind of energy. They sat, their heads close together, talking, laughing.

Then—a flash of pink. A bubble. It hovered for a second before— POP. I grinned.

There was something mesmerizing about it—the way she sat there, the way she existed in this little moment of time, unaware of the fact that someone, somewhere, was watching her and thinking—I need to know her name.

Dinner at the house always had a certain rhythm. The scent of something rich and slow-cooked lingered in the air, a warmth woven into the very fabric of the house. The same Victorian home with gingerbread trim I'd grown up in, the same dining table where birthdays, holidays, and everyday nothings had unfolded over the years.

Some things never changed. Mom in her colorful, artsy outfits. The faint sound of Gilmore, our spoiled Persian cat, stretching lazily on the windowsill. The soft clink of silverware on ceramic as we ate.

Across from me, Grandfather sat with his usual quiet presence. He never hurried through a meal. He treated dinner like a slow unraveling—a time for thought, for conversation, for the kind of wisdom that never felt like preaching.

And, right on cue, his voice came steady, even.

"Heard anything from Wander yet?"

I stabbed a roasted potato, shaking my head. "Nothing at all."

A pause. Then—his slow, knowing nod. "They're probably just taking their time to make sure they recognize your genius."

I smirked, reaching for my drink. "More like they're deciding if they remember who I am."

We both took a sip—his, black coffee; mine, something colder, something that didn't settle quite as easily. The thing was, I wasn't just waiting on *Wander*. I was waiting on something else, too. I just wasn't sure what.

"This waiting…" I exhaled, rolling my glass between my fingers. "It's brutal."

Grandfather leaned back slightly, his chair creaking like an old house stretching its bones.

"Well, you know the old saying."

I glanced up at him, smirking. "The one about patience being a virtue, or the one about good things coming to those who wait?"

He shook his head, sipping his coffee. "No, the one about the early bird getting stuck in traffic."

A laugh escaped me before I could stop it. Mom chuckled, shaking her head, and even Gilmore flicked his tail like he was mildly entertained.

Grandfather always had a way of grounding me.

He let the laughter settle before leaning forward slightly, hands resting on the table.

"The hardest part is always the first step. But once you take it, you'll see—it's not the fall that matters, it's the flight."

Something in his tone made me pause.

I looked at him then, really looked at him. The lines on his face, the steady certainty in his voice. He wasn't just talking about *Wander* magazine. Or photography. Or even career choices. It was bigger than that. It was about risk. About movement. About knowing when it was time to stop standing at the edge and finally jump.

I swallowed, letting the words settle into the empty spaces inside me. Dinner continued, but my thoughts lingered.

After we ate, Mom wandered into the kitchen, humming as she rinsed the dishes, and Grandfather started shuffling a deck of cards, his way of saying the night wasn't over just yet.

"Up for a game?" he asked, eyes twinkling behind his glasses.

I exhaled, rolling my shoulders back, shaking off the weight of waiting.

"Yeah," I said, leaning forward. "Deal me in."

Outside, the wind stirred through the old tree in the yard. The house was the same. The people were the same. But somehow, tonight, everything felt just a little different. Like something was about to begin.

Dinner at our house always felt like a stage play. Soft lighting. Polished silverware. Conversations that followed a script. I sat at the dining table, my plate barely touched, listening as my future was shaped around me like I wasn't even there.

"So, dear, have you made any plans yet? Berkeley must be thrilled to have you."

⓪

Grandmother's voice was warm, expectant. Encouraging in the way that wasn't really asking—it was confirming.

I nodded faintly, keeping my eyes down, feeling the weight of the words before I even heard them.

"It's such a great opportunity," Mom said, her smile soft, proud. "We're so proud of you."

Dad nodded, his voice steady, certain. "Berkeley will open doors you wouldn't believe. Don't worry about anything—we'll handle the costs." That was never the issue. Money. Security. Opportunity.

They had built this path for me before I even knew how to walk it. And now, they were holding out their hands, waiting for me to take the first step.

"It's the best path." Grandmother added, her tone soothing. "You'll have security, a career. We just want what's best for you."

Best for me. Or best for them? I swallowed, folding my napkin in my lap, pressing the fabric between my fingers like a lifeline.

"This is your chance," Mom said. "You've always loved writing. Imagine the professors, the internships."

My eyes flicked to the family photo on the wall. The four of us, smiling, taken years ago in the backyard, the sun setting behind us. Frozen in time, frozen in expectation. Would I always be this? A version of myself that belonged to them, to their dreams, to their carefully laid-out map?

⟲

"This is everything you've worked for," Dad continued. "We just want to see you succeed."

Success. What did that even mean? A degree on the wall? A safe, respectable career? Or was success waking up in a place I had chosen, with a life that felt like mine?

I picked up my fork, forcing a weak smile as I pushed food around my plate. No one noticed. They kept talking like my future was already decided. Like I wasn't even in the room. Like I wasn't screaming inside.

July

The courthouse clock looms above town, its hands inching toward three like some silent, all-knowing god.

Tick. Tick. Tick.

Each second pulled me closer—or pushed me further away. I couldn't tell which. I just knew I was out of time.

So I ran. ♪

The heat pressed down on everything, thick with the scent of sun-warmed pavement and melted sugar. My shirt clung to my back. The air shimmered.

I burst out of *Charm & Whimsy*, nearly knocking over a display of floral mugs, and tore down the sidewalk. Falstaff was already ahead of me, tail a blur, weaving between tourists in wide-brimmed hats and locals sipping iced tea like the world wasn't quietly unraveling.

The condo rose into view. I raced up the stairs. I fumbled with the

♪ "Flower Power" by Greta Van Fleet

key—dropped it—damn it—scooped it up with shaking fingers and flung the door open. Window. Now. And then—There she was.

Lounging on the bench like she'd always been there. Sundress fluttering in the breeze. A paperback open in her lap. One hand flipping pages, the other holding a strand of pink bubblegum between her lips.

She blew a bubble—delicate, slow, round. POP. She didn't look up. Didn't know she was being watched. Didn't know that somewhere, someone was completely undone by the sight of her turning a page.

I leaned against the windowsill, chest heaving. But it wasn't the running. Not entirely. It was her. It was always her.

I never meant to sit here. It wasn't planned. There was no intention behind it, no poetry. Just a moment—one I didn't know I needed—between where I'd been and where I was going.

So I sat.

And then, I came back. The next day. And the one after that. Now, three o'clock calls me here like the tide—gentle, certain, impossible to resist. My path never changes. Past the Pharmacy window with its dusty plant that never quite blooms. Past the Hot Dog Man, forever glowering behind his cart like the world personally betrayed him. Past the bookstore mural, the edges of the paint curling like old leaves.

And then I sit. The bench is warm in the sun. The world hums around me—dogs barking, strollers squeaking, wind rustling through the free box—but here, everything slows. It doesn't stop. Just… softens.

I pull out a piece of bubblegum from my pocket. Bubble Yum.

⦾

Watermelon. My favorite. It's a small ritual, almost childish, but there's something comforting about it. The stretch. The snap. The soft burst of sweetness. People don't expect me to be the kind of person who still chews gum, who blows bubbles just to see how round they can get before they break. But I do. I always have.

There's something about it—this tiny, fleeting joy—that reminds me I'm still allowed to take up space. To play. To be a little foolish in the quiet. I unwrap the gum, tuck it between my teeth, and let it bloom.

I open my copy of *Plainwater* by Anne Carson, not always to read, but because it gives my hands something to do. The pages are soft at the corners, the spine curved from being carried too many places. Carson understands longing in a way that makes me feel less alone with mine—her words about distance and desire, about the spaces between people. How she writes about water as something that both connects and separates. Sometimes I just need to hold something that makes sense of the things I can't articulate.

I don't look for meaning in it. I don't ask why this bench, why this time. Some things aren't questions. They're patterns. They just begin. And they continue.

August

The air felt different now—thicker, softer, like even the sunlight had started to exhale. The last stretch of August clung to town with a golden kind of warmth, like a season reluctant to say goodbye.

I walked this time. Slowly. Past the surly Hot Dog Man, arms crossed as usual, his permanent scowl tracking me like a camera panning out of spite. I nodded like we had some unspoken truce: I won't ask what you're angry about if you don't ask what I'm doing here again.

Then—I ran. Up the stairs. Through the door. Straight to the window. And just in time. Her car pulled up, familiar now, like a recurring dream I couldn't shake. Dusty, silver, deliberate. She moved like she meant to go unnoticed, and yet somehow... never could.

But today—she wasn't alone. The golden girl stepped out with her, laughing, balancing two cones of melting ice cream. They sat on the bench, legs tucked beneath them like they were ten years old again— or like they'd never stopped being ten. It was beautiful—the kind of beautiful that sneaks up on you, soft and unannounced.

She smiled—really smiled—at something the golden girl said. Tilted her head. Took a slow lick of ice cream. Her eyes crinkled. Her shoulders relaxed. I leaned forward, breath catching, pressing a hand over my face like that might somehow protect me from how much I felt all at once.

I had no idea what they were talking about. But I wanted to. I wanted to be the reason she smiled like that. I wanted to sit beside her and forget time existed. I wanted to know what flavor she picked, whether she licked the drip or let it fall.

I wanted to belong in that small, sunlit moment. But I didn't. I watched her through glass instead.

The heat lingered, golden and thick, wrapping around town like a second skin. Even the shadows felt warm, stretched thin across the sidewalk like they'd given up trying to stay cool.

Allison handed me the cone—strawberry. She always remembers. We sat on the bench, our legs folded beneath us like we were still made of playgrounds and pinky promises.

The ice cream melted fast, sticky rivers tracing down the cone. I licked it slowly, letting the cold shock my tongue, then settle. I liked the way it made the world pause for a second.

Allison talked—about a weird dream she had, her neighbor's dog that kept getting into her tomatoes. Her voice was light and fast and full of movement, like wind chimes in August.

"Next time that rat gets off his leash and into my tomatoes, I'm lacing a meatball with antifreeze and letting God sort it out."

I nodded, smiled, and laughed. But mostly, I just listened. I liked the way her words filled the space without needing to be answered. I let the day melt with the ice cream, slow and soft. I let myself be still.

This—this was the kind of moment I didn't trust. Because it felt too good. Too quiet. Like if I reached for it, it would vanish. But for now, I just sat in the sun with my best friend, licking strawberry ice cream and pretending I could believe in moments like this.

September

The air had changed— thinner, as if summer had been wrung out of it. Somewhere in the distance, I caught the faint trace of woodsmoke. It clung to the edges of things. A quiet promise that something was ending.

I wove through the sidewalk crowd, heart pounding with every step. I didn't know why I was running. Only that I needed to get there. That I didn't want to miss it—miss her.

I made it.

And there she was. Sitting on the same bench, as if it had always

belonged to her. A light cardigan pulled around her shoulders. Her sun-dresses replaced now with softer layers—earth tones, longer sleeves, clothes that understood the quiet of fall.

She was writing. A journal balanced delicately on her lap, one hand curled around a pen, the other anchoring the pages against the breeze. I watched her pause—pen resting gently against her bottom lip, eyes distant, lost in some thought I would never be part of.

She didn't look up. Didn't know I was there. Or maybe she did. I leaned against the window, barely breathing. Just watching her. Like a man looking through glass at something he believes in but doesn't dare touch.

The air is cooler now—crisper, more honest. The kind that brushes your skin and makes you breathe a little deeper without meaning to. Fall is settling into Telluride like an old friend, unhurried but certain. I pull my cardigan tighter and tuck my legs beneath me on the bench, the wood cool against my jeans.

Above me, the aspens have begun their transformation—leaves shifting from summer green to molten gold, trembling like coins in the breeze. The mountainside is streaked with fire and sunlight, as if someone took a brush to the landscape and didn't hold back. It's stun-ning. Almost too much. The kind of beauty that makes your chest ache for reasons you can't quite explain.

I rest the journal in my lap. I like its weight—like it grounds me, like it agrees to hold whatever I can't yet say aloud. I tap the pen gently against my lip, watching the long shadows stretch across the sidewalk. The light is different this time of year—lower, richer, the kind that turns everything to honey just before dusk.

⦿

I want to write about that golden light and the way it folds over the world like a soft blanket. I want to write about the strangers who pass by without knowing they're part of something—like they're walking through a story that hasn't finished yet. I want to write about the way some places don't let go, even when they should.

I want to write about the feeling I get sometimes—like I'm not alone, even when I am. Like someone is watching, but not in a way that frightens me. In a way that makes me feel... known.

But I don't. Instead, I write about the wind—the way it slips beneath collars and carries the scent of something fading, like woodsmoke and memory. I write about the smell of old pages drifting from the bookshop, the sound of leaves crunching beneath passing footsteps. I write about the taste of strawberry ice cream eaten slowly, long after summer has gone.

I write about this bench. And how I keep coming back to it. Like it's waiting. Like it still matters. Even if I don't know why.

October

Falstaff barked. Not a warning. More like a signal—like he knew something I didn't, and couldn't wait for me to catch up. I followed. I ran down the street, keeping to the shadows, avoiding the sidewalk out of habit or instinct. Ducking between parked cars like I might scare the moment off if I came in too directly.

The heat was gone now, replaced by that brittle kind of cold that crept through the seams of your coat, settling deep. The town had shifted, too. Scarves wrapped tight. Steaming cups held between gloved hands. Store windows glowing softly in the early twilight, halos of light pooling onto the sidewalk.

By the time I reached the window, she was already there. Wrapped in a scarf, hands curled around a paper cup, a quiet kind of stillness in her body. The golden girl beside her was laughing—something open and free—and Falstaff trotted up to them like he'd always belonged there.

He stopped at her feet. She smiled and bent down to stroke his head. Slow, gentle, present. Something inside me tilted. Just slightly. Like the world had shifted one degree to the left and was suddenly, inexplicably better for it.

I let out a breath I hadn't realized I was holding. And for the first time—I smiled, too. Not a grin. Not a smirk. Nothing performative. Just something quiet. Something real.

The cold has a different kind of bite now. Not sharp exactly, just... settled. It gets into things. Into the cracks of town, into your sleeves, into your thoughts if you let it.

I wrap both hands around the warmth of my cocoa, grateful for the way it anchors me. I watch the steam curl upward, soft and slow, dissolving before it can become anything else.

Allison was beside me laughing—something open and unfiltered, her breath turning to mist in the cold. "I told him, if you're gonna quote Nietzsche, at least put on pants first." She shook her head, still laughing.

I hear the soft thud of paws before I feel him beside me. Falstaff. He settles at my side like he's always belonged there—solid, calm, unapologetically present.

His eyes meet mine, steady and knowing, like he sees things in

⦿

people we haven't admitted to ourselves yet. I press my fingers into his thick fur, feel the living weight of him beneath my hands.

Something stirs. Not fear. Not sadness. Just that quiet flicker of recognition. Like remembering a name you haven't said in years. Like hearing the echo of something you don't quite understand, but already trust. A moment before the moment. A heartbeat before something shifts. The whisper of something that hasn't happened—

—but already feels inevitable.

The Red Banjo

I stepped into the *Banjo*, the warm scent of dough, melted cheese, and oregano wrapping around me like an old memory. I made my way to the counter, nodding to the guy behind the register, my hands finding the worn surface as I leaned into it. I'd been in here so many times he didn't have to ask who I was.

"Hey, your pie will be ready in a sec."

I nodded, fingers tapping lightly against the counter, my eyes drifting across the room—casual, not looking for anything in particular. And then I stopped. A booth near the window.

Her.

She sat across from two other girls. The golden girl from the bench, and another I didn't recognize. Loud, animated, barely pausing for breath. But her—she was quiet. The sun caught in her curls, turning them to fire, painting gold into black. She wasn't laughing. Wasn't even really listening. Her fingers twisted the edge of a napkin, delicate, restless. Her pizza sat in front of her, untouched, growing cold. She was somewhere else.

A small smile. A slight shrug. But in that tiny movement, I saw something. I recognized it. The hesitation. The way someone smiles when they don't know how to say they aren't sure anymore. The other girl didn't notice. My fingers froze mid-tap. Because I knew that feeling. That weight of expectation. That quiet pull toward something else. Somewhere else. Someone else.

The pizza guy slid the box across the counter. "Hot outta the oven!"

The spell shattered. I blinked. Exhaled. Took the box and turned to leave. The words sat heavy on my tongue—something unformed. Something stupid and reckless and real. But I didn't say them.

I pushed the door open. Stepped outside. And then—it happened.

Through the glass. A flicker of movement. Her eyes lifted. Not by choice. Like something unseen had tugged them upward. Toward me.

Our eyes met.

The world slipped out of focus. Edges blurred. Time bent. It wasn't just a glance. It was a knowing. Recognition. Curiosity. A pause in the rhythm of the universe.

Her fingers stilled on the napkin. And then—she looked away. My pulse thundered in the quiet. I stood there, the heat of the pizza box pressing into my palms. Just for a moment.

Then I walked. Because I didn't know what I would do if I stayed.

The smell of oregano filled the air, mingling with the hum of conversation and the faint clang of silverware on plates. I wasn't hungry. But I came anyway. Because it was easier. Because Allison and Sarah could fill the silence—could say the things I didn't have the energy, or the courage, to find words for.

Sarah was already deep in college plans, talking about professors and dorms and the endless doors about to open. Allison bounced beside her, soda in hand, practically glowing with anticipation.

"Can you believe it? Soon, we'll be at college!"

"I know! I can't wait to get out of here. Dorm life, classes, freedom!"

And me? I smiled. Small. Automatic. The kind you give when there's nothing to say, but people expect something anyway. I twisted the edge of my napkin, slow and steady, until the fibers began to fray beneath my fingertips.

"You all set for Berkeley?" Allison's voice was bright and expectant. That kind of question that already assumes the answer.

I gave a shrug. A half-smile. Something light enough to float away. Sarah didn't notice.

"I heard Berkeley is amazing. You're gonna love it! That campus, those hot professors…"

Her voice blurred, like it had been turned down a notch. My gaze drifted—out the window, to the soft blue sky stretched quiet and wide above the buildings. To the movement of people on the street. To the places I wasn't going.

And then—without choosing to—I looked up. It felt like something shifted in the air. A thread pulling tight.

My eyes lifted. And met his.

The boy from the store. Time caught. The sounds of the restaurant fell away. His gaze was steady. Unflinching. Like he was seeing something he hadn't expected—but had been waiting for anyway.

Something moved between us. Not words. Not even thought. Just the echo of something that hadn't happened yet—but already mattered. I inhaled. And looked away.

My fingers stilled on the napkin. The air felt different now. Something had changed. I just didn't know what it meant. And I wasn't sure if I wanted to.

The pizza was hot, greasy, and perfect. I sat back on Brandon's couch, box between us, the faint hum of Telluride's streets filtering in from the window. The condo still smelled like ski wax and takeout, a weird but familiar combination.

Brandon grabbed another slice, chewing thoughtfully before giving me the look.

"So, any enchantress news?"

I wiped my hands on a napkin, the image of he still burned into my brain.

"I just saw her at the Banjo."

◐

I shook my head, exhaling. "That girl is so incredibly beautiful."

Brandon snorted. "She's just a girl."

I gave him a deadpan stare. Right.

And the Mona Lisa is just some chick with a weird smile.

Truth is, I've never understood the obsession. People pack into the Louvre like sardines just to stare at that tiny painting behind bullet-proof glass. They act like it's sacred. Like she's whispering secrets only they can hear. But if you actually look at her—really look—she's... not much. Kind of hideous, honestly. No offense to Da Vinci. And yet people wait in line for hours. Some cry. Some say she changed their life. I've never gotten it.

But maybe that's the point. She's beautiful to someone—because they've decided she is. Everyone's just a face in the crowd until you really look. Then, sometimes—suddenly—they're not. The girl on the bench isn't just a girl. Not to me. She stops me. Tilts my whole world, just slightly.

"Not exactly Jennifer Connelly, either, " he said.

I scoffed. "Jennifer is a distant second."

He raised an eyebrow. "Grace Slick?"

And for a second, I see her—Grace at Woodstock, in that white fringe dress, electric and otherworldly, like she'd swallowed the stage whole. I hesitated. ♪

Then shook my head. "Nope," I said. "Not even her."

♪ "White Rabbit" by Jefferson Airplane

Because there's something about the way she exists—without trying, without needing to be seen—that undoes me more than any spotlight ever could.

Brandon, not ready to give up, gestures toward the poster of Donna Weinbrecht still hanging in its place of honor. Ski goddess. Mogul queen. Our shared crush.

I barely glanced at it. "Not even close, dude."

Brandon leaned forward, eyeing me like I had finally lost my grip on reality.

"You have seriously lost your mind."

I shrugged, reaching for another slice.

"I read somewhere that delusion is more fun than reality?"

Brandon shook his head. "If you keep up the delusion instead of acting, you'll just end up with more regrets."

I smirked, leaning back. "Anything else, Yoda?"

Brandon didn't even hesitate.

"Yeah. You can't move mountains by whispering at them."

I let that one sit for a second. Then sighed.

"I don't even know her name."

Brandon grabbed another slice, shaking his head like this was the greatest tragedy in the world.

"I guess you're just gonna have to use *The Force* to get her to tell you, then."

I raised a brow. "Does that work? I don't recall Luke Skywalker having a girlfriend."

Brandon chewed, thinking. "It wasn't Princess Leia?"

I nearly choked on my drink. "She was his sister, dope."

Brandon froze mid-bite. "His girlfriend was his sister?"

I looked at him. Shook my head. And ate my damn pizza.

The gym smelled like sweat, popcorn and the faint tang of floor polish. It always did on game days. My sneakers squeaked across the varnished court as I jogged to my spot, the volleyball dry in my hands, the polished wood gleaming under the lights.

We were playing Norwood. They were good—always were. Sharp serves, clean passes, the kind of team that made it look easy. And every single one of them looked like they'd stepped off the stage at a small-town Miss America pageant. Perfect braided hair, perfect teeth, long limbs like they were grown in some secret lab behind a cattle barn. What did they feed those girls over there? Beef and moonlight?

Norwood was a ranching town—grit and cattle and Friday night rodeos. Their girls grew up on hay bales and hard work, all strength and symmetry, like volleyball was just another chore they were naturally good at. Telluride was different. A mountain town—ski racks, money, and tourists. Our parents ran the ski shops, the bakeries, the chairlifts. We didn't have cattle, but we had grit. We chopped wood and shoveled the driveway before school. Worked weekend jobs. Came to practice with windburned cheeks and chipped nail polish.

Our maroon and gold uniforms looked sharp, but we were a ragtag bunch. Guts over polish. The culture clash always showed on the court—cowgirls versus mountain girls.

Coach Carly clapped twice from the bench. "Let's go girls!"

I nodded, moving to the front row. My job wasn't flashy—I wasn't the one slamming the ball across the net or diving for impossible saves. I was the setter. The quiet in-between. The one who kept her hands ready, eyes up, listening for rhythm in the chaos. I liked it, even if no one noticed what I did unless I messed it up. Allison elbowed me at the net, just loud enough for our bench to hear.

"Pretty sure they serve hay at halftime over there."

Classic Allison. All fire and one-liners. She had no filter and even less fear, which made her the best kind of teammate—and the worst kind of opponent. She made the game feel bigger than it was. I leaned on that more than I let on.

Across the gym, just behind the bleachers, a man stood with a camera pressed to his face. I recognized him as the reporter from the *Telluride Times*. Probably covering all the fall sports at once. He zoomed in, adjusted, stepped to the side. Not watching the scoreboard. Watching us.

I wondered what he saw. A quick set to the right. A spike clean over the net. Girls shouting, jumping, chasing the moment. But not what it felt like to be inside it—the thrum of sneakers on the floor, the way a perfect pass moved through your arms like music. I wondered if he'd catch that part. The part that mattered to us.

The whistle blew. Sarah stepped up, bounced the ball once. I crouched into position, fingers spread, ready. My job was to make the play happen. To get the ball to the girl who could finish it. I didn't need to shine. I just had to connect. And maybe that was enough.

I shoved another heavy mound of snow off the storefront steps, the rhythmic scrape of metal against ice the only sound besides my own breath. The cold settled deep, quiet and sharp, like it had teeth. My exhales fogged in front of me, curling upward before vanishing into the stillness.

Charm & Whimsy stood behind me, still dark inside but already warm—its windows fogged from the inside out, soft golden light beginning to stir against the glass. A single candle flickered in the display window, its flame trembling in the draft like a heartbeat.

All along the street, the town held its breath. The sky above was pale blue and infinite, stretching wide over rooftops dusted clean. Somewhere in the distance, another shovel scraped against concrete. A dog barked once and then fell silent again. The air smelled faintly of pine and woodsmoke, like every chimney in town had whispered itself to life just before dawn.

I leaned on my shovel, stretching my back. And then—I looked up. My grin came slow. I already knew what kind of morning this was. The ski runs into town gleamed under the first kiss of sunlight, pristine and untouched, etched in shadow and light. It dumped last

⦿

night—ten inches at least. Maybe more. The kind of powder that only shows up when the stars align.

A perfect morning. A *Pow Life* morning.

The Plunge

The chairlift groaned softly as it carried us up the mountain, swaying slightly in the wind. Brandon sat beside me, hands tucked into his gloves, goggles pushed up onto his head. Below us, the town shrank, the rooftops of Telluride coated in white, the streets still half-asleep.

"Gonna be a good one," Brandon murmured.

I nodded, watching our line unfold beneath us, the steep pitch of The Plunge waiting. A deep breath. A tightening of my boots. This was why we lived here. ♪

For this.

The first few seconds of dropping in were always weightless. A fraction of a second where the world tilted, and everything else fell away.

Then—the first turn. The snap of edges biting into powder. The sensation of floating, cutting, shifting with the terrain. The Plunge was steep. A long, unforgiving mogul field that could make or break a skier in an instant. The bumps were the size of Volkswagens, a never-ending maze of snow-covered giants.

I bent my knees, absorbing each hit, my body moving in rhythm with the mountain.

Turn. Recenter. Turn. Recenter.

♪ *"Daymarks"* by Catching Flies

⑩

The world became motion. Snow sprayed into the air, sparkling like shattered glass as Brandon powered down beside me, his movements fluid, effortless. For a moment, we weren't just skiing. We were flying.

The burn in my legs was real by the time we skied to a stop at Coonskin base after a full day of turn and burn. I pulled off my goggles, grinning like an idiot.

"Pow Life, baby!" I shouted, breath coming in sharp, uneven gasps.

Brandon, still catching his own breath, slapped a hand against his helmet. "You said it. Epic conditions. Now—let's conquer the bar."

I laughed, unclicked my bindings, and slung my skis over my shoulder. The walk back into town always felt different after a day like that. Like something in me had been reset. Rewired. The world felt sharper. Cleaner. Like I'd used up everything unnecessary just getting down the hill.

The sun cast long, syrupy shadows across the sidewalk as we made our way up town, boots crunching over salt-streaked pavement. The winter light had a way of softening everything—gold at the edges, a little worn down in the best possible way.

As we passed the *Ladle,* I saw three girls at an outside table, sharing something I couldn't hear, laughter spilling between them like steam off cocoa.

And then... I saw her.

The way her curls caught the sunlight, wild and gold-tipped, like the world had briefly turned its lens to focus only on her. I kept walking, but my eyes stayed with her. Brandon's voice beside me faded into background noise.

◐

My body moved forward, but my attention didn't follow. Which is how I missed the hot dog line. My skis clipped someone's shoulder—then another—and suddenly, the neat row of hungry skiers waiting for lunch collapsed in slow-motion chaos. Two people went down hard. Arms flailed. Someone's ski pole clattered against a trash can. A hat went flying into a snowbank.

I froze mid-step, heartbeat thudding in my ears, ski tips crooked, adrenaline spiking. Brandon and I dropped our gear and lunged forward, helping the fallen back to their feet. Apologies flew out of me, fast and useless.

"Sorry—I wasn't looking—I didn't mean—"

One guy scowled at me like I'd stepped on his dreams. A woman brushed off her coat like I'd ruined her dry-cleaning and her entire week. Then came the voice. Low. Gravelly. Familiar.

"You," it said, thick with judgment. "You again?! Mr. Magoo!"

I turned to see the Hot Dog Man glaring at me from behind his cart like I was the worst thing that ever happened to ski season.

I held up a dropped glove like it might redeem me. It didn't.

"I swear," Brandon muttered, grinning as he leaned close, "I can't take you anywhere."

The Iron Ladle

The warmth of my hot cocoa seeped through my gloves, the steam rising in soft spirals. I curled my fingers tighter around the cup, letting the heat find its way into my hands.

Allison and Sarah sat across from me, their voices twining around dorm assignments, course catalogs, what to pack, who they might become. I nodded when it felt right, sipped my drink, let their excitement roll past like a breeze through an open window. It wasn't that I didn't care. I was just tired of pretending I still belonged in the conversation.

But my focus kept drifting—slipping out past the edges of our table, toward the street and its ordinary motion. The scrape of boots on pavement. The crunch of snow being shoveled nearby. Wind tugging at the corners of store signs. The world just… continuing.

And then—A crash. Laughter. The shuffle of sudden movement. And a voice—sharp, theatrical, full of long-standing grievance.

All three of us turned automatically. Because everyone in this town knew that voice. The Hot Dog Man. Unmistakable. He didn't just sell hot dogs—he announced his opinions. With volume. With judgment. With a strange kind of permanence, like he was part of the town's plumbing.

A small crowd had gathered near his cart. Someone had clearly knocked something—or someone—over. There was a lot of gesturing. A glove being held up like a peace offering. The usual ski season chaos.

Allison squinted toward the commotion. "What now?"

Sarah shrugged, sipping her drink. "Tourist drama."

Allison grinned. "Some rich bitch probably broke a nail. Better call 911."

I laughed under my breath. The town changed with the seasons, but some things—like Allison's commentary—stayed exactly the same.

Their conversation picked up again, smooth as snowmelt. But I kept listening. Not to the voices—but to the silence underneath them. To the moment after something unexpected happens, when the air shifts, just slightly, and everything feels different even if you don't know why. I held my cocoa a little tighter. And let the wondering stay.

The shop smelled like Christmas remembered—cinnamon and pine boughs drifting through the air, weaving into the familiar scents of old paper, melted candle wax, and something warm and quietly sweet, like cloves tucked into an orange. It was the kind of scent that didn't just fill the room—it settled in your chest. A feeling more than a fragrance.

A soft crackle drifted from the old speaker near the register—vinyl. The quiet hush of static gave way to the gentle hum of a classic Christmas melody, something old and unhurried. Old Blue Eyes. That voice wrapped around the room like a knit blanket—worn, familiar, full of warmth and memory. ♪

Charm & Whimsy was transforming—garlands wrapped around shelves, twinkle lights flickering in the window, delicate ornaments hanging from the rafters like stars suspended in midair.

Grandfather adjusted his Santa hat, the red fabric slightly askew, giving him the look of a holiday rebel. I hung another string of lights along the counter, stepping back, arms crossed.

"Alright, folks, let's sprinkle some holiday magic… and a touch of New York sophistication."

♪ *"Santa Claus is Comin' to Town"* by Frank Sinatra

◎

Mom gave me a look over her glasses, her lips quirking. "We're not competing with Fifth Avenue, darling. We want customers to feel like they've stumbled into a holiday rom-com."

I smirked. "So, more mistletoe or more misty-eyed moments?"

"Both," she declared. "Christmas is all about balance."

I adjusted a strand of garland, then turned. "So, Mom. What do you want for Christmas?"

She barely hesitated. "I want to learn how to paint. Maybe I'll take a few lessons from Penny."

I coughed. "The maestro of mayhem?"

Grandfather chuckled, straightening a stack of books.

"All Penny-inspired art should come with a warning label… about haunting your dreams."

We all laughed. Mom shook her head, but I caught the way her fingers toyed with the ribbon she was tying—like she was already picturing herself at an easel, brush in hand.

Maybe she was serious. Maybe this year, we should all ask for something we actually wanted.

The phone rang, the old rotary bell cutting through the moment like a call from another century. I grabbed the receiver. "Whimsy and Mayhem!"

◯◯

"Hey," Brandon's voice came through, casual, familiar. "You up for some ice skating?"

I leaned against the counter. "Will Katarina Witt be there?"

"I'll make a few calls and see what I can do."

I grinned. "Count me in then."

I hung up and turned toward Grandfather. "Hey, Gramps. You up for some ice skating adventure?"

He rubbed his chin, eyes twinkling. "You know, it's been a while since I showed off my Eddie Shore skills."

I pointed at him. "Eddie Shore is coming too."

Brandon, still on the line, clearly baffled. "Who's Eddie Shore?"

☾

The air smelled like frost—and *impending doom*. Twinkling fairy lights stretched above the rink, glowing softly against the deep blue of the winter night. Skaters glided effortlessly across the ice, laughter spilling into the cold air, their scarves trailing behind them like banners of victory.

I sat on the ice-cold bench, staring at the pair of rental skates in my hands like they were medieval torture devices.

"Skates. Ice. What was I thinking?"

Brandon smirked, already lacing up with the confidence of someone who'd clearly done this before. Grandfather, beside him, tied his boots with slow, practiced hands—his fingers moving with the ease of old muscle memory.

Brandon shot me a sideways glance. "You look like you're prepping for a space mission, Michael."

I gritted my teeth, yanking at the laces. "More like a mission impossible. How did I get roped into this?"

Grandfather chuckled. "Because I told you I could skate better than you."

"And because," Brandon added, grinning, "I told you Katarina Witt would be here."

I glanced around the rink, feigning disappointment. "Still not seeing her, Brandon. I thought you had connections?"

He just laughed, finishing his laces and stepping onto the ice like he'd been born on it.

Grandfather followed—not just staying upright, but actually gliding. Gliding. Like some kind of silver-haired hockey legend. Eddie Shore, I guess. Whoever that was.

I sighed. This was a mistake. I took a deep breath and pushed off the bench. Or tried to. What actually happened was a kind of unholy flailing motion, followed by my legs completely refusing to cooperate. For a few blessed seconds, I stayed upright. Then I started to move. Then I started to panic.

Brandon weaved through the skaters, turning effortlessly, clearly enjoying himself. "Come on, Michael! This is gonna be epic!"

I muttered, "Yeah. Epic. Right."

I shuffled forward—tentative, hesitant—and immediately regretted all of my life choices. Brandon spun to a stop in front of me, looking way too comfortable.

I narrowed my eyes. "Is your last name Gretzky?"

He smirked. "Just a hidden talent, my friend."

I shook my head. "Architectural genius, mogul master, and now mad skating skills. Are you sure you're not on a Wheaties box?"

Brandon laughed and skated backward with zero effort. I, on the other hand, was channeling every ounce of energy into not eating ice.

And then—I saw her.

Just beyond the rink, walking past the storefronts. Her dark curls caught the golden glow of the holiday lights. Hands tucked into her coat, she paused in front of a window display.

She stood there for a moment. Still. The kind of stillness that felt intentional. Like her body was here, but the rest of her had gone somewhere else entirely. Somewhere I wanted to be.

My skates made the slightest wrong move—and then gravity did the rest.

Straight into a pair of unsuspecting skaters. One yelped. The other cursed. I sprawled in a heap, a tangle of limbs, regret, and freezing cold humiliation. The Hot Dog Man wasn't here, but I was pretty sure I'd just ruined someone else's night.

Brandon skated over, grinning down at me. "Did you forget how to stop?"

I groaned, rubbing my shoulder. "Yeah. I might've missed that part of the lesson."

I looked back toward the storefronts, searching. She was gone. Then I looked at the skaters I'd taken out.

They were *pissed.*

The shops along the skating rink felt different at night. By day, they were bustling—skiers, travelers, locals running errands. But now, in the quiet of a winter evening, they felt like tiny glowing storybooks, each window a page waiting to be turned.

I moved slowly, letting my eyes drift from one storefront to the next, taking in the small, intricate worlds tucked behind glass.

Sunshine Books

The first display belonged to the bookshop. Stacks of hardcovers and paperbacks rested in a carefully arranged pyramid, dusted with artificial snow. An open book sat at the center, its pages frozen mid-turn, as if someone had just been interrupted.＊

＊ *"The Snow Child"* by Eowyn Ivey

◯◯

A small sign read: *For those who wander through words.*

I tilted my head. That's what books had always been for me—places to escape. To disappear. A home when I wasn't sure where else I belonged. I traced a finger lightly over the glass. My breath bloomed into a soft cloud against it. Then I moved on.

Frost & Found

The next window was from the artisan shop—tiny, quiet, and always half-lit, like it didn't need to announce itself to be known.

A small Christmas tree stood inside, draped in white lights, its branches adorned with handmade ornaments. Each one different. I leaned closer. Some were painted glass globes, tiny mountain landscapes floating inside them—little San Juans, frozen in time. Others were carved wood, smooth to the eye, painted in soft hues. One was a miniature cabin. Another, a silver snowflake so delicate it looked like it would melt if you touched it.

And then I saw it: a small ceramic moon, with a golden sun tucked beside it. Opposites. But together. I exhaled, pressing my fingertips to the glass. The kind of ornament that belonged to a tree with history. Not one designed for appearances, but for meaning. Collected slowly. Chosen with care. I had never owned a tree like that. But maybe, someday, I would.

I thought of Allison. Her tree wouldn't be coordinated or themed—it would be loud, chaotic, full of clashing colors and ridiculous glitter-drenched disasters we'd made in sixth grade. But right in the center, she'd hang this. A sun and moon. It was her, really. Always pulling in opposite directions. Always keeping both sides lit.

◯◯

Maybe I'd come back for it. Maybe it would be the right kind of Christmas for something like that. Something that said, I see you. Even the parts you don't always show.

I stepped back from the window, my breath having left a small cloud on the glass. In its center, the sun and moon ornament seemed to float, suspended between worlds. Between what was and what could be. As I turned to leave, my reflection briefly superimposed over the display—a ghost perusing treasures behind glass.

Zia Sun

Farther down, the jewelry shop window shimmered under golden light. Diamonds and sapphires blinked under the spotlight like distant stars—gorgeous, sure, but loud in their way. They demanded attention, catching the eye and holding it, all sparkle and perfection. But it wasn't the expensive pieces that caught my attention.

It was the quiet corner of the display—simple silver charms, tucked away like they weren't trying to be noticed. A feather. A tiny leaf. A sliver of moon. A cluster of stars no bigger than a thumbnail. They didn't shimmer like the rest. They glowed—soft, unassuming, patient.

My grandmother says charms carry meaning. "You don't pick them," she told me once, holding my wrist as she fastened a seashell onto a bracelet I'd worn until the clasp gave out. "They pick you."

I leaned in, my breath fogging the glass, and studied each one like it might blink or speak or move. I wondered which one would choose me. And what it might be trying to say.

⦾

Weekends

A few doors down, the next window glowed with warmth and color. Scarves in soft wool and bold knits draped elegantly over wooden displays. Stacks of folded sweaters—deep cranberry, pine green, soft winter cream—promised warmth and comfort. A line of boots stood like sentinels along the bottom ledge, dusted with a sprinkle of fake snow.

I lingered longer here. Imagining what I might pick out for my Mom. A chunky knit in her favorite color. Maybe something for Daniel, too. Gloves. A flannel shirt he wouldn't think to buy for himself.

I wasn't sure when the shift had happened, but somewhere along the way, Christmas became more about others. About small gestures. Warmth passed from one hand to another. Maybe I'd come back tomorrow.

The Toy Box

The last window belonged to a small toy shop. Soft lamplight spilled across the snowy sidewalk. A wooden rocking horse stood among stuffed animals and tin soldiers. A music box sat open, its ballerina caught mid-spin.

For a moment, I was seven again. Face pressed to cold glass in December, heart full of wonder. Now, I only lingered for a second. Then I turned away.

I was just about to keep walking when I heard it. A sudden clatter. Shouts—one surprised, one annoyed. And then, unmistakably: someone cursing.

I glanced toward the ice rink. A few skaters had turned to look. A small crowd forming. People helping someone up from the ice. I couldn't see much—just a flurry of motion. A tangle of limbs. The glint of skates under the lights. I smiled faintly. Shook my head. Then kept walking.

The Jeep crunched to a stop on the overlook, tires grinding over packed snow and gravel. I cut the engine and sat for a moment, my breath ghosting the windshield, watching it fade.

Bridal Veil Falls stood ahead—frozen mid-descent. What was once thunderous now hung in silence, turned to ice. A suspended river of white and pale blue, jagged and glistening in the afternoon sun. The canyon air bit at my cheeks the moment I stepped out, sharp and dry, carrying the faint scent of pine and cold stone.

I opened the back of the Jeep, unlatched the tripod, and cradled the camera like something fragile. The snow here was undisturbed except for a few boot tracks and crampon prints that veered off toward the base of the falls.

I spotted them halfway up. Two climbers. Tiny against the massive face of ice—one in red, one in black—slowly making their ascent. Every movement deliberate. Every swing of the axe echoing faintly against the canyon walls. They moved with the kind of focus I envied. Purposeful. No hesitation. I framed the shot. *Click.*

I adjusted, zoomed in, caught the tension in the rope between them—the thread that connected one human life to another on a wall of ancient, frozen water. *Click.*

Mist still hovered at the base where meltwater fought to breathe beneath the ice. The light caught it just right—sun filtering through

thin cloud, turning the surface into glass and shadow. I crouched lower to capture the contrast. The stillness above, the shift below. *Click.*

I breathed into my hands, camera tucked under my coat while I waited for the light to change. Somewhere behind the cliffs, the sun was already considering its descent.

It was beautiful. But not soft. This wasn't the beauty that invited you in. It was the kind that warned you to keep your distance. Quiet, dangerous, and worth respecting.

The climbers were nearly at the midpoint now. A figure against a frozen fall. Suspended. Somehow still moving. Somehow still alive. *Click.*

The highway was quieter than usual. I could still hear it from my room—cars threading through the valley below, distant and softened by snow. Out here, at the edge of town, everything always felt one step removed. Quieter. Slower. Like the world had exhaled and forgotten to breathe back in. But the house was warm.

The smell of bacon reached me first, curling under the door. Then the soft clink of plates being stacked, the familiar sputter of the coffee maker, the scrape of a chair against the kitchen floor. I could hear the fire crackling, too—faint, steady, not something I usually heard. But today, I knew why. My dad must've gotten up early to light it, the way he always did on Christmas morning. Just the rhythm of a morning I knew by heart.

I pulled on socks, wrapped myself in the cardigan from the back of the chair, and stepped into the hall. The tree glowed quietly in the corner of the living room, its lights blinking in slow, uneven patterns. A few gifts sat beneath it—some wrapped, some tucked into reused

☉

bags, one with a bow held on by a piece of tape. My name written in my mother's handwriting.

I stood for a moment, watching them. Remembering the years when the tree had seemed ten feet tall, when I'd wake up before dawn and sprint down the hall, convinced I'd hear sleigh bells. The paper had been shinier then, the magic louder. Now it was quieter. Smaller. But not gone.

On the mantle, our stockings hung in the same order they always had—Dad's, Mom's, Daniel's, mine. My brother's stocking still had its place, even though he hadn't been home in awhile. Eighteen Christmases for me, and they'd never once switched places. The thought of next year settled strangely in my chest—not quite sadness, not quite excitement. Just awareness. Eighteen years of the same traditions, and nothing lasts forever. Maybe I would be here. Maybe I wouldn't.

I touched the small ceramic ornament hanging near eye level—a lopsided star I'd made in third grade, painted blue and silver, my initials scratched into the bottom. Every year, I'd search for it first when the ornaments came out of storage. Every year, Mom would say, "This old thing again?" with that smile that meant she'd never dream of putting it away.

My eyes drifted to Dad's collection of snow globes arranged on the bookshelf—one from each Christmas since I was born. Eighteen now, the newest still unwrapped, waiting for this morning's ritual. He'd pretend he hadn't bought one, act surprised when we'd "discover" it among the gifts. I'd shake it first, then pass it around our circle, each of us making a silent wish as the snow settled. Some traditions were too important to outgrow.

I crossed to the window. The valley was still, silvered in frost. Smoke curled from a distant chimney. A single car moved down the highway, its taillights fading into the blur of snow and light.

☾

Behind me, toast popped. A drawer opened. The soft pour of coffee into a mug. From the hallway came the sound of Dad's shuffling steps—he'd be wearing those ridiculous reindeer slippers I'd given him three Christmases ago, the ones with bells that had long since fallen silent.

I turned and walked to the kitchen, the floor cool under my feet. My mother stood at the stove in her robe and slippers, spatula in hand, back slightly hunched in that familiar way that meant she was focused. Dad would be out in the garage by now, digging through the bins marked XMAS in his impossible handwriting, looking for the special Christmas mugs—the chipped one with Santa always reserved for him, the snowman one for Mom, mine with the tiny handprints from kindergarten.

I didn't say anything. I just walked over and wrapped my arms around her from behind. She let out a soft breath—half surprise, half knowing—and reached for my hand, giving it a squeeze. No words. Just warmth. This was Christmas. And for now, it was enough.

☾

Grandfather always played Bing Crosby on Christmas morning. Not the record—the CD now, though he still complained about the sound quality. "Flatter," he'd say, gesturing vaguely at the speakers with his coffee mug. "No warmth." But still, Bing's voice filled the kitchen while my mother made pancakes in the shape of Christmas trees, a tradition she refused to outgrow. ♪

I stifled a yawn. Same songs, every year. I sometimes wondered if anyone had written a new Christmas song in the last thirty years, or if we were all just sentenced to an eternal loop of Bing, Nat King Cole and Brenda Lee. But I knew better than to suggest anything else. Grandfather would sooner cancel Christmas than play anything else.

♪ *"White Christmas"* by Bing Crosby

I stood at the window, watching the mountains catch first light. Snow had fallen overnight, dusting the pines, softening the world. My camera sat on the table, untouched for once. Some mornings weren't for capturing.

"Michael, set the table," Mom called, not looking up from her careful pouring of batter.

Grandfather chuckled from his chair by the fire. "Remember when you used to wake us up at five? Banging those pots and pans?"

"That was one year," I protested, gathering plates from the cabinet.

"Three," they said in unison, a well-worn correction.

I arranged the plates—the chipped holiday set that only appeared in December—and the silverware my grandmother had collected piece by piece from garage sales before I was born.

"Think it'll stick?" Mom asked, nodding toward the snow outside. Always practical, already calculating whether to salt the driveway.

"Not enough," Grandfather said. "But beautiful while it lasts."

That was Christmas with them—Mom focused on details, making things work; Grandfather seeing the beauty in what didn't. And me somewhere in between, quiet witness to their balanced orbit.

We didn't do mountains of presents or elaborate decorations. Just these small rituals: pancakes precisely flipped, Bing Crosby slightly too loud, the three stockings hanging from the mantle—one now empty for eleven years.

Mom slid a misshapen tree pancake onto my plate. "Yours," she said, the way she always did, as if I might mistake it. I nodded my thanks and reached for the syrup.

The mountains burned gold now, the light spreading across the valley. Another Christmas, cataloged not in photographs but in the muscle memory of traditions that needed no explanation.

Stubbie's house buzzed with life. Voices collided in waves of warm, drunken laughter. The air smelled like champagne, pine, and the last hours of a fading year. Music pulsed—something smooth and familiar. Another Sinatra classic drifts through the noise. ♪

There's just something about Sinatra—he always shows up when people are celebrating. Weddings, toasts, New Year's Eve countdowns. Like he's the soundtrack to every moment where someone tries to believe the best is still ahead. I don't even know when it started for me, but now, whenever life tilts toward joy—even the messy kind—I half-expect him to be playing somewhere in the background. Like the guy's always leaning against the bar, tie loose, drink in hand, reminding you to feel it while it lasts.

I let out a low whistle, surveying the scene.

"Wow. Stubbie's been moonlighting as a party planner. Either that, or he's got Sinatra on retainer."

Brandon smirked, cracking his knuckles. "And here we thought only the mountains knew how to throw snowballs. Let's get drinks and blend in."

♪ *"Fly Me to the Moon"* by Frank Sinatra

Blend in. Right. That had been the plan. Until the punch happened. Brandon watched as I took another sip of my third drink.

"Easy on the punch. We're here to celebrate, not audition for SNL."

I waved him off. "This is celebration. You know—joy, life, the turning of time. Stop killing the vibe."

The room tilted slightly. Okay. Maybe that last glass wasn't strictly necessary. I turned back to the crowd. And then I saw her. The enchantress. The most beautiful girl in the world. Here. Now.

She walked in with the golden girl, and suddenly, the whole party narrowed to a single frame. The noise faded. The crowd blurred. The only thing I saw was her. Hair wild, catching bits of gold from the chandelier light. She moved like time didn't apply to her. Like the world could spin and she'd remain steady at its center. A gravitational pull. My pulse kicked up.

Brandon pats me on the back and grins. "It's time to move mountains. Go." And against my better judgment—I did.

The moment I stepped forward, the crowd doubled. Tripled. People shifted, hands clapped my back, laughter swelled around me. Someone twirled past, nearly spilling their drink on my shoes.

The music changed. Someone spun me straight into a couple mid-spin, arms flailing in what might have been swing dancing—or a very committed attempt at it. ♪

I barely stayed upright. Move. Pivot. Weave.

♪ *"Dancing in the Moonlight"* by King Harvest

She was only a few feet away now. She turned, laughing at something the golden girl said. Almost there. Almost—

The door swung open. A new figure entered. Some dude. Familiar to her, clearly. Instantly magnetic. Her entire posture changed. Eyes lit. Shoulders softened. She smiled, already turning toward him. Like gravity pulled her towards him—no hesitation. No glance in my direction.

I stopped. Just short. Then came the final obstacle. A very, very large one. Standing directly in my path, arms crossed like a border guard, was none other than Telluride's own Civil War Guy. In full 1860s regalia. Because of course.

I stared up at him. He stared back. I blinked. And then, with the confidence only New Year's punch can provide—I saluted.

"So. How's the war coming along?"

The party was alive. Laughter bubbled from every corner. Glasses clinked. Voices blurred into a bright, breathless symphony. But I felt... elsewhere. Like watching a scene from a movie where the soundtrack keeps playing, but the character has drifted out of frame. I should be here. I should be excited. New Year's Eve. The turning of the year. The promise of forward motion.

Allison looped her arm through mine, tugging me deeper inside. I let her pull me. Then—just as we stepped through the door—it opened again behind us. A small shift. Not enough to be noticed. But enough to change something in the air.

I turned—just for a second. But before I could focus, before I

◑

could understand why—Zach walked in. And whatever had pulled my attention... vanished.

Allison squeezed my arm, beaming. Zach was familiar. Solid. A face I'd known since childhood. His presence felt like certainty. Like a book I'd read a hundred times and could quote without turning a page. He was the safe answer. The sensible choice.

I let myself be pulled toward it—toward him.

But even as I moved, something inside me hovered. Detached. Watching. There had never been anything wrong with Zach. That was the problem. He was kind, handsome, polite in a way that made parents love him and teachers remember him. I knew the shape of a future with him. And for a long time, I thought that was what I wanted—something knowable. Something I could count on.

Still, something flickered at the edge of awareness. A thread, a tug—like I'd almost remembered something important. Like trying to catch smoke with my bare hands—there, then gone. But Allison nudged me. Zach smiled. I smiled back.

☾

The first thing I registered was pain. A dull, merciless pounding in my skull, like someone had taken a jackhammer to my temples.

The second thing I registered was light. Blinding, offensive, unholy light. I groaned, shifting on Brandon's couch, trying to escape the merciless sunbeam currently cooking my face. No luck. I was a vampire caught in daylight, too weak to fight back.

The third thing I registered was Brandon's voice.

◍

"Morning, Sleeping Beauty."

A sharp pain shot through my brain as I winced. Talking? This early? Did he have no respect for the dead?

I cracked one eye open, barely lifting my head. "Who hit me last night? Iron Mike?"

Brandon leaned against the doorframe, mug of freshly brewed coffee in hand. He took an obnoxiously slow sip, enjoying my misery.

"You really embraced the spirit of the season."

I groaned again, flopping back against the cushions. Slowly—painfully—memories of the night before started piecing themselves together. New Year's Eve. Stubbie's party. Brandon handing me a drink. Me enthusiastically accepting.

Then—The girl. I shot up—too fast. The room tilted wildly. I swayed, gripping my forehead.

"Did I talk to the enchantress?"

Brandon snorted. "You did make an attempt."

That didn't sound good.

I stared at him. "An attempt? What happened?"

Brandon grinned, sipping his coffee like he was savoring the absolute disaster he was about to describe.

"You ended up in a lively chat with the Civil War Guy."

⊙⊙

I blinked. "The… Civil War Guy?"

"Yep. Right in your path. A human barricade to destiny."

I closed my eyes, exhaling slowly.

"And before that?"

Brandon smirked. "You were trying to impersonate Tony Manero before he interrupted."

I peeked at him. "…Saturday Night Fever?"

"Yep."

"This can't be good."

Brandon patted my shoulder. "Fear not, my friend. The secrets of last night are lost to history."

Right. That meant I'd made a complete fool of myself.

Brandon strolls over, setting a steaming mug of coffee on the table in front of me. I reached for it like a dying man grasping for water in the desert.

"Is a cup all you got? I need an IV of coffee before I die, please."

Brandon grinned. "Drink up, Tony."

I groaned, taking my first sip. This was going to be a rough one.

The morning light is merciless. It slants through the blinds in sharp angles, casting lines across Allison's face where she's buried half under a throw blanket and half under what I think is last night's denim jacket. Her eyes are closed. One sock is missing. Glitter trails down her arm like she tried to fight off the disco ball and lost.

I sit curled up in her desk chair, one leg tucked beneath me, cradling a chipped mug of lukewarm tea. The mug says *I Came. I Saw. I Made It Awkward.* Fitting. The tea is weak—barely more than warm water with ambition—but I drink it anyway.

The room is a battlefield: mascara-streaked tissues, a half-eaten granola bar fused to its wrapper, one sad balloon sagging against the ceiling like it gave up around midnight. My dress from last night hangs limply over the back of the chair, sequins catching the light in quiet flashes. There's a faint smell of hairspray and something suspiciously citrusy.

She stirs again, squinting at me like I've done something offensive by existing. "You're doing the thing."

She means the silence. The stillness. The way I tend to disappear even when I'm in the room. I raise an eyebrow. That's all.

Outside, the frost clings to the edge of the windowpane—the kind that melts slowly, like it's reluctant to let go. Just like that moment last night at the door. That breath of something… other. The thing that made me turn.

I still don't know what it was. Only that it vanished the moment Tom stepped into the frame.

Familiar. Safe. Predictable. But not what pulled at me.

Allison flops onto her back with a groan. I glance over. Her hair is doing something unspeakable, and there's an eyelash stuck to her cheek. Somehow, she still manages to look like the cover of a very expensive hangover.

She lets out a sigh that sounds like it came from the depths of her soul. "Can I throw up in your shoes?"

I press the mug to my lips, hiding a smile as I grab my shoes before it's too late.

The phone rang. It was just a sound. A familiar, everyday noise. Nothing special. Except—I knew. I felt it in my chest, a shift in the air, a pause in the universe. This was the call.

I wiped my hands on my jeans, suddenly aware that my palms were sweaty. The shop buzzed around me—soft voices, the murmur of a customer asking about a music box, the faint sound of a wind chime shifting near the door. But none of it mattered. The phone was ringing.

I grabbed it, pressing it to my ear. "Charm and Whimsy."

A pause. Then—

"Michael! Jane from Wander. We've made our decision."

I went completely still. Every muscle locked. My grip tightened on the counter, knuckles pressing white. The weight of every photograph

I had ever taken, every shutter click, every hour spent chasing the perfect light—all of it hung in the space of a single breath.

A second stretched into a year. And then—

"The job's yours—if you still want it."

My heart slammed so hard against my ribs I was surprised she didn't hear it through the phone.

I felt myself exhale, too fast, too loud.

Then—a grin broke across my face.

"Absolutely!"

Jane laughed, the kind of warm, knowing laugh that told me she expected nothing less. "Knew you would."

A pause. A shift. The first step into something bigger than I had ever let myself imagine.

"Can you be in Boulder in two weeks to discuss your first assignment?"

Two weeks. The timeline felt unreal. Like I had spent years standing on the edge of a cliff, staring at the drop—and suddenly, I was already mid-air.

"I'll be there."

Jane's voice was light, teasing. "Good. We'd hate to give it to some-one else."

I shook my head, even though she couldn't see me. "Not a chance."

A door had opened. One I had been pressing against for years, waiting for the lock to click. Now, it had.

Jane gave a quick goodbye. I hung up. The world rushed back in. The wind chime near the door. The soft rustling of a paper bag. The faint hum of music from the radio. All the same. But—not. Because I wasn't the same. A slow, unstoppable grin spread across my face. This was the beginning. And I had just said yes. ♪

The wind moved softly through the aspens, their pale leaves flickering like coins in the afternoon light. I curled deeper into the chair on the porch, my fingers resting lightly on the open pages of *Tess of the d'Ur-bervilles* by Thomas Hardy. I had read the book before. But something about it felt different today. My eyes traced the passage in front of me:

Did they sacrifice you? he asked.
I was ready to be sacrificed, she said.
I could not help it.

I exhaled slowly, letting the words settle. Wasn't that how life worked? You weren't always the one making choices. Sometimes, you were just… carried along. By expectations. By fate. By the quiet, invis-ible weight of what other people wanted for you. I closed the book, running my hand over the cover, feeling its softly worn edges.

Then—a sound. Distant, familiar. The low rumble of the mail truck. The engine hummed as it rolled up, the brakes screeching as it pulled to

♪ "Jamming" by Bob Marley

⦿

a stop at the bottom of the driveway. I barely looked up as the mailbox clanked open. Routine. Ordinary. A part of the rhythm of the day. The truck rumbled forward, turning the bend, disappearing down the road.

I stood, stretching, tucking *Tess* beneath my arm before making my way down the porch steps. The stack of mail was unremarkable. A bank statement. A flyer for a furniture sale. A crisp white envelope addressed to my mother. Then—A letter addressed to me.

I stopped. The air shifted, tightening around my ribs. I turned the envelope over. I ran my thumb along the edge, hesitating. Then, I looked out toward the road, toward the place where the mail truck had disappeared. The wind rustled through the trees. And I stood there, holding something I wasn't ready to open.

☾

Brandon poured another glass, the deep red swirling against the candlelight. I turned it in my hand, watching the way the light bent through the liquid. I should have felt nothing but excitement. This was it.

The moment I had been chasing since I was a kid with a camera and a dream. The opportunity to see the world. But instead—there was this weight in my chest. Something I couldn't shake.

I exhaled, swirling my wine again. "I'm thrilled about the job. It's a dream come true. But…"

Brandon looked at me over the rim of his glass. "But what?"

I stared out the bay window, where the lights of Telluride twinkled against the dark.

"It's the town, the mountains, my family, and… well, you know."

Brandon set his glass down, smirking. "The elusive enchantress?"

I let out a soft laugh, shaking my head. "What else could it be? Your insane ice skating skills?"

"I was hoping it was my mountain charm."

"You mean the flannel shirts and commitment issues?"
We clinked glasses. And yet—the ache stayed.

I leaned back against the couch, rubbing my thumb over the stem of my glass. "She's the most beautiful girl in the world, Brandon. An angel of the first degree."

Brandon shrugged, taking a slow sip. "If you say so. Lotta fish in the sea, my friend."

I shook my head. "From my eyes, that is impossible to imagine."

Brandon sighed, setting his glass down with a soft clink.

"Look, I get it. She's got a hold on you. But maybe this job will give you some perspective."

I stared at the wine, my reflection warped in the deep red.

I keep telling myself she'll be there tomorrow. That three o'clock won't vanish while I'm gone. But something about it feels... delicate. Like a thread that could snap if I stop showing up.

"Maybe. I just can't shake the feeling that if I leave, I might miss my chance."

☾☽

Brandon exhaled, running a hand through his hair.

"Life's all about chances. Sometimes you have to take a leap and trust that everything will work out."

I sighed, leaning my head back against the couch. Brandon stretched out beside me, watching the flames flicker in the fireplace.

☾

The courthouse clock struck three. Its chime rolled through town in slow, deliberate waves—deep, resonant, final. I turned the corner onto Colorado Avenue, my pace quick. I was late. Not by much, but enough to feel it. Enough to feel like maybe it mattered.

And then—I saw her.

Across the street. Already there. She sat on the bench, her posture relaxed, legs folded beneath her, like the day belonged to her. My breath caught.

I stopped just before the curb, heart tightening. I wasn't ready, but I was done waiting. I took one step forward, my mouth suddenly dry, palms damp with nervous anticipation.

"Breathe," I whispered to myself. "You can do this."

I was just about to cross the street when a voice called out behind me.

"Hey, Michael! I've missed you at the bar. Where have you been hiding?"

I turned to see Lauren, her familiar smile bright and expectant. I hesitated, caught off guard by the interruption.

⟦O⟧

"Oh, hey... Lauren. Just busy, I guess." The words came out flat, distracted. She stepped closer, enthusiasm undimmed by my lukewarm response.

"Some friends and I are heading over to the *Dollar* for some live music later. You should join us."

I glanced back across the street, just in time to see a guy sitting down beside her, handing her a drink. The same guy from Stubbie's party. My stomach sank. Whatever courage I'd mustered evaporated like morning dew.

"Uh, yeah, that sounds great, but maybe another time?" I heard the uncertainty in my own voice.

Lauren's smile faltered slightly, though she quickly masked her disappointment. "Sure, but next time I won't take no for an answer."

I managed a weak smile in return. "Well, I avoid confrontation, so I'll just say yes now."

Which, of course, I do.

She laughed, the tension broken. "Okay, deal. Talk soon!"

As she walked away, I was left standing there, frozen between two directions - the path I just committed to and the one I was too afraid to take. And just like that, I was no longer part of the frame.

I backed away from the curb, slow and quiet, like I hadn't been there at all. My steps were different now. Not rushed. Not driven. Just... leaving. Behind me, their laughter carried faintly across the street. Light. Distant. Already fading.

The wind had a soft bite today—not sharp, but whispering of change. The kind of breeze that snuck under your sleeves and reminded you that the season was shifting, even if you weren't ready to. The warming air carried hints of new growth and possibility, but April's temperament remained unpredictable, winter not quite ready to release its grip entirely

I sat on the bench just before three. Not because I was waiting. But because… I was there. Maybe out of habit. Maybe out of hope. The town moved gently around me—strollers squeaked, dogs barked in the distance, someone's radio played a song I used to know. Then I heard footsteps.

Zach.

He came from the bookstore side, his usual rhythm—steady, confident, just a little too pleased with himself. He handed me a drink. He always remembered. Like Allison did.

I smiled. Laughed at something he said. It was easy with him. Safe. Familiar in a way that didn't ask for much. We'd known each other for years. We'd kissed once, after a late movie, when the town was quiet and the stars felt close. It hadn't meant much. But it hadn't meant nothing either. Sometimes, I thought: Maybe that's enough. Maybe comfort was a kind of love.

But even as I laughed, something flickered in the corner of my vision—like a shadow brushing past. A weight. A thread tugging at the edge of my attention. I glanced around the street, but no one was there. Just the breeze, tugging at the leaves. Just the sound of the clock's echo, fading behind us. I took a sip of the chai.

Zach said something else. I smiled again. But a part of me stayed quiet. A part of me still wondered who hadn't shown up—and why I hoped they had. We sat in silence, the kind that didn't need words.

I stood by the window, hands in my pockets, staring at her bench. It looked the same as it always did—worn wood, familiar shadows, a place she always returned to. Every day at three, she was right there. I told myself it was just coincidence, just routine. But something about it felt… fragile. Like a window that might close the second I stopped showing up.

I wished I had that kind of certainty. Instead, all I had was a one-way ticket out of here and a feeling I couldn't shake. Brandon stepped beside me, holding out a small, wrapped gift. I looked at him, brows raised.

"Open this on your way."

I took it, turning the weight of it in my hand. Light. The edges of the paper were slightly creased—Brandon wasn't much for perfect folds. Something tightened in my chest. I managed a small smile.

"Thanks, man. Friends like you are hard to find."

Brandon exhaled, shaking his head slightly, like he wasn't great with sentimental moments but was letting me have this one. His gaze flicked to the window, to the world outside, to everything I was about to leave.

"You're not just leaving Telluride," he said. "You're taking a piece of it with you."

The courthouse clock chimed in the distance. Slow. Deliberate. Marking time. Counting down. I turned toward the sound, listening. I'd heard that clock ring a thousand times before. But never like this. Never like it was saying goodbye.

⦾

"And leaving behind a big piece of my heart, too, I'm afraid."

Neither of us spoke after that. Just the clock. Just the sound of time moving forward—whether I was ready for it or not.

☾

Mom held onto me longer than usual. Her arms tight. Like she could hold me here if she just didn't let go.

"I will really miss having you around, darling."

I swallowed the lump in my throat. "I'll miss you too, Mom."

Grandfather gripped my shoulder, his hand warm and steady.

"Remember, your roots remain, no matter where you go."

I nodded, words stuck somewhere between gratitude and longing. I bent down, scratching Gilmore behind the ears. He blinked at me, lazy, unconcerned.

"Okay, Gilmore. Keep these two in check. I'm counting on you."

Gilmore flicked his tail, as if to say, Don't push your luck.

I turned to the door, pausing with my hand on the handle.

One last look. At Mom, trying to keep it together. At Gramps, standing tall but softer than usual. At Gilmore, utterly indifferent but somehow comforting. I took a breath. A heavy, necessary breath.. The bell jingled softly as I stepped outside.

The Porsche rumbled low beneath me, steady, familiar. I rolled down Colorado Avenue, the valley floor stretching wide ahead. Telluride, shrinking behind me. I had imagined this moment so many times. Driving away. Leaving for something bigger. I should have felt free. Instead, something pulled at me.

Then—Falstaff. Right in the middle of the road. He stopped, sat down, barked. Not in greeting. Not in farewell. Something else. A warning, maybe. Or a challenge. I slowed to a stop, the Porsche idling beneath me, engine thrumming. I rolled down the window and leaned out, watching Falstaff watch me, like he knew something I didn't. I wasn't sure I was ready. I reached out, gave him a quick scratch behind the ears. His fur was warm from the sun. He blinked once, stood, and trotted off without a sound. I sat back, lifted a hand in a quiet wave, and shifted into gear.

I eased the Porsche into Reggie's station, a mile outside of town. I pulled up too fast and clipped the window-washing bucket, sending it skidding across the lot with a wet slap.

Reggie rounded the corner of the garage, wiping his hands on a rag, eyebrows already raised. He always looked like he'd stepped out of a vintage postcard—greased coveralls, work boots older than I was, and that British accent none of us had ever pinned down. England? Australia? South Africa? Nobody knew.

"Bit dramatic for a fuel stop, don't you think?"

I stepped out and reached for the pump. "She's feeling theatrical today."

Reggie grinned, leaning against the doorframe like a man with all the time in the world. "Off to new adventures?"

I shrugged. "I heard of a place with a Mai Tai the size of my head."

◎

He tipped his chin. "Well, don't forget us mountain folk when you're sipping those on the beach."

"I won't. Take care."

He disappeared back into the garage. I hooked the nozzle into the tank and watched the numbers crawl upward. And then—on the other side of the pump—a truck rattled into place. Scary Gary.

His rust-eaten Chevy coughed to a stop like it had made the trip under protest. The door creaked open. I didn't turn around. There was a beat of silence. Then—his voice, matter-of-fact and unbothered:

"Don't take that tone with me. I don't forget betrayal."

I looked over. Gary was standing beside his truck, facing the gas pump directly. Staring at it like it had deeply wronged him. Still talking. To the pump. I blinked. Took a slow breath. Then nodded to myself. Time to go.

I pulled the handle, cut the pump early, and slid the nozzle back into its cradle. Tank not full. Good enough.

I got in the car and eased it back onto the road, the mountains rising in the rearview. Behind me, Gary kept talking—to the pump, to the sky, to whatever past he was still working out loud.

Highway 145 unfolded in front of me, the road pulling me forward. But then— A flicker of silver. My breath caught.

The Honda.

Not ahead. Behind. Like Telluride. Like everything I was leaving. I had already passed her. The realization hit me like a gut punch. I pulled over, my fingers tightening on the wheel. The Porsche's engine purred, waiting.

The town was gone. But she was still there. Sitting on the hillside, like she'd been waiting for something too. I flicked my gaze to the rear-view mirror. Telluride. The past. The home I was leaving behind. Her Honda. The mystery. The girl. The unspoken words. Two things I had never quite let go of.

My pulse pounded in my ears as my hands flexed on the steering wheel. I looked down. The tachometer needle trembled, hovering at idle, as if it felt my indecision.

The engine growled, vibrating through the car, filling the silent road. I stared at the tachometer, watching it waver. A single movement away from a decision.

Every day at three, she appeared. Like clockwork. And the idea of leaving now—of missing the moment when the pattern might finally shift—made something twist in my chest. Stay. Go. Turn around. Keep driving. My foot hovered over the gas pedal.

The sun was warm on my shoulders, but a faint breeze carried the scent of rain in the distance. Inside my Walkman headphones, something soft and nostalgic played—threaded with that strange ache only old songs can stir. ♪

My hands moved in rhythm—loosen, press, smooth. The roots needed just the right amount of space, the soil just the right amount of pressure. I let the music guide me, let my body move with the kind of instinct that didn't need thinking.

♪ *"Moonshadow"* by Cat Stevens

The soil was cool and damp between my fingers, clinging beneath my nails as I pressed it gently around the base of a lavender sprout. I liked this part—the quiet work of planting, of tending, of coaxing something to grow.

There was something fitting about the song. It understood something about change. About loss. About learning to live with what's missing—and still choosing to move forward.

The house was still. Silent. Not the peaceful kind. The kind that holds its breath. The porch steps creaked beneath my weight. I knocked. Firm. Sure. Nothing. I knocked again. Louder. Still—nothing.

I exhaled, staring at the closed door. For a flicker of a moment, I thought maybe—just maybe—she was standing on the other side. Hand resting on the doorknob. Waiting. Just like I had been, all this time. The silence stretched. I looked at the door with a flicker of hope.

The world was only this garden. Only this moment. And then—something shifted. A presence. I didn't know why I looked up, only that I did. Through a gap in the wooden fence, just beyond the wild tangle of blackberry bushes, an old Porsche sat idling on the road. I stilled, my fingers resting against the soil. The sun hit its white surface, reflecting a sharp gleam of light that flickered, then settled.

It wasn't moving. Just… sitting there. The music still playing softly in my ears, a rhythm suddenly out of step with the moment. I held still, sensing something shift around me. Even with the melody threading quietly in the background, I could feel it—the low thrum of the engine, steady and waiting.

A prickle ran down the back of my neck—not fear, exactly. More like recognition. A presence brushing close, just enough to stir the air around me. The sun blinked off the car's surface again, a glint too precise to be accidental.

Something about it—the stillness, the waiting—made my breath catch. Like a question had been asked without words. Like a thread I hadn't realized was still attached had just gone taut. I reached for the next plant, but my fingers hovered above the soil. As if something had rooted itself in me instead. As if I already knew—this wasn't chance. Not this time.

I stayed like that for a long second, hand hovering over the earth, heart hovering too. Some part of me—the old, quiet part that had always believed in things you can't explain—leaned forward inside my chest. As if whatever was on the other side of that fence wasn't a stranger. As if it had been looking for me as long as I'd been looking for it.

I closed my hand around the soft green stem, grounding myself. But the world had already tilted. Just enough to change everything. When I looked up again, the car was gone—like it had never been there at all.

The road curved out ahead like it didn't care where I went next. The "Telluride 3" sign flashed past on the right in the mirror, sun-faded, quietly indifferent. I passed it without slowing. This wasn't how I imagined leaving. There was no confrontation, no final word, no dramatic ending. Just the ache of everything unfinished. In the rearview, the town disappeared swallowed by light, dust and time. ♪

Above Sunshine Mountain, the sun burned white through thin clouds, too bright to look at directly. It crowned the peak like a question I couldn't answer. I didn't know where I was going. I just knew she hadn't answered. And that I hadn't waited long enough to find out why.

♪ *"I Found"* by Amber Run

The air smelled like cut grass and change. That sharp, green scent—faintly sweet, stubbornly alive—had always done something to me. Like it knew how to tug at memory, how to fold time back into itself. I breathed it in slowly, letting it settle.

Sunlight stretched long across the soccer field, glinting off the rows of folding chairs and the glossy caps lined up in careful, fidgeting rows. The kind of late afternoon light that felt like it was trying to hold on just a little longer. Just like all of us. Somewhere, a camera clicked. Somewhere, a future had already been decided.

Allison sat to my left, bouncing her foot with restless energy, her lip gloss catching the light as she grinned toward the stage. She'd already planned her dorm decor, had a countdown to move-in day, a CU Boulder sweatshirt tied around her waist like proof she was already halfway out of here. Sarah was on my right, still adjusting her cap, murmuring something sarcastic under her breath that made Allison stifle a laugh. I barely heard them. My hands were still in my lap, fingers grazing the silky thread of my tassel like it might tether me to something.

Would I remember this moment? Not the speeches or whatever cliché someone had written about chasing dreams. But this—this stillness. This strange weight pressing down on my ribs. Like I was sitting on the edge of a dock, staring into deep water, unsure if I'd float or disappear.

On stage, Grace launched into the final lines of her valedictorian speech—something about chasing light, or dreams, or maybe both. Allison leaned toward me, stage-whispering, "If Grace sucks herself off any harder, we're gonna need a mop."

Jessica Morgan whipped around, her face pinched with indignation. 'SHHH!' she hissed, glaring pointedly. Without missing a beat,

Allison flipped her the bird, her expression cool and defiant. Jessica's eyes widened—mouth opening, then closing—before she slowly turned back around. Nobody messed with Allison unless they wanted to see the inside of an ambulance. Sarah laughed. I bit back a smile.

A name was called. Then another. Then mine. Cheers broke out here and there, uneven and sharp like little fireworks. A few rows ahead, someone had already slipped off their shoes and was fanning themselves with their program. Time moved in pieces.

The announcement echoed across the field, followed by a wave of cheers. Caps soared into the air, spinning and drifting against the wide blue sky. I didn't throw mine. I held it close, watching the others twist in the light—caught somewhere between flight and freefall.

Where would they land? Where would I?

Allison whooped, jumping to her feet and grabbing Sarah's hand. They turned to pull me with them, and I rose slowly, pulled more by their momentum than my own. My feet touched the grass. But I didn't feel like I'd stepped forward. Not yet.

Laughter rippled across the backyard deck, rising and falling like a summer breeze. Someone had strung up twinkle lights between the trees, and they blinked lazily against the deepening sky. The scent of grilled chicken mixed with lilacs from the garden, and the table sagged beneath bowls of pasta salad and pitchers of lemonade.

A folding table off to the side held a stack of cards and small wrapped gifts—envelopes from neighbors and distant relatives who already had opinions about where I'd go and what I'd do. One card had

◯

"Berkeley!" scribbled across the front in glitter pen, like it had already been sealed into my fate.

I hovered near the edge of it all, a paper plate balanced on one hand, my lemonade sweating into the napkin beneath it. My fingers drifted to a smaller note tucked under the edge of the plate, one I hadn't opened yet. It wasn't signed. Just a simple card, no glitter, no exclamation points. The handwriting was careful and slightly slanted.

Wherever you go, go with all your heart.

I read it twice. Then again. The ink had bled slightly, and I wasn't sure if it was from the condensation or something else. Someone called my name. I looked up. My mother was waving me over for a photo, her smile fixed and hopeful. Behind her, my father laughed with a neighbor, a beer in one hand, his tie loosened at the collar. I smiled. The camera clicked.

But inside, I felt like I was floating just slightly above it all. People had started using words like future and opportunity as if they were promises, not guesses. The truth was, I didn't know where I was going. Not really. Not yet. And I was beginning to understand that all their dreams for me came wrapped in quiet assumptions—about who I was, and who I would become.

The cake was cut. People cheered. The music shifted to something upbeat. Allison spun in slow circles on the grass with a paper cup balanced on her head. Sarah flirted with a boy from Dolores I didn't recognize. Everything looked like a celebration. But I stood still. The card still in my hand. Whatever came next—it had to be mine. Not theirs. Not the version that looked best on paper. Me. Wherever I went. ♪

Allison saunters over, a lazy grin curling at the corner of her mouth. She gives the backyard a slow once-over.

♪ *"Don't Dream It's Over"* by Crowded House

◯◯

"This party feels like a church potluck."

She takes a sip from her cup, winces. She holds up the cup like evidence. "This shit tastes like guilt and yeast infections."

Hawaiian 21

The hum of the engines was a low, steady drone. I leaned my head against the window, watching clouds pass beneath us like waves frozen mid-crash

Brandon's parting gift sat in my lap, wrapped in a knowing kind of silence. I tore the paper carefully, half-expecting some dumb joke— some inside reference that only made sense at 3 AM. Instead— *The Telluride Times.* The local newspaper. My breath hitched. Why the hell had he wrapped this? I flipped through the pages, half-distracted, half-dreading. And then—I saw a photograph. *Of her.*

Mid-motion, focused, powerful, graceful. Her arms outstretched, fingers meeting the ball in a perfect set.

Sophia Farraday, Setter.

Her name was right there, in print. "Sophia." I whispered, testing the way it felt against my lips. Like something I should have known all along. The cabin hummed, oblivious. My watch ticked, precise, uncaring.

3:01.

My pulse beat in time with the seconds, but I wasn't here. I was standing in the condo, breathless, staring at her through the window.

I will always be on Telluride time. *Always.*

CD

13

32:11:24:00:38:09

The propeller hummed its low, familiar rhythm—part machine, part lullaby—as the Cessna Caravan skimmed the edge of sky and sea. Below, the Pacific blurred into itself, a vast watercolor of blues: deep indigo, sunlit turquoise, soft smoke near the shallows. No lines. No borders. Just movement. Just memory. ♪

I stared down, watching the ocean smear past like paint dragged by a tired brush. It was beautiful. And unknowable. And strangely indifferent to everything I'd carried here. Then, through the haze—faint at first—a shape rose from the horizon.

An island.

Not fully formed. Not yet. Just a suggestion of green and shadow, waiting to become real. Waiting for me to see it.

♪ *"Daydream"* by Tycho

◓

I sat back slightly, breath caught somewhere between past and arrival. Almost there.

Hiva Oa. The Marquesas Islands.

Could've been worse. It could've been Gary, Indiana. It wasn't. Instead, it was timeless paradise. But I knew better than to call it paradise in my shots. That wasn't the job. The job was to see past the postcard. To look closer. To listen.

I should've felt triumphant. My first real assignment for *Wander* Magazine. A job people spent years chasing. But all I felt was the weight of the camera on my shoulder—like a question I hadn't yet earned the right to answer.

I kept running through the checklist in my head—lenses, filters, spare rolls of film, extra batteries. Had I packed enough? Had I forgotten something stupid? The kind of thing that doesn't hit you until you're miles from anywhere and the light is perfect—but your gear isn't. I told myself I was ready. But the truth was, I wasn't sure what ready was supposed to feel like.

The island appeared the way a memory resurfaces—half-formed at first, familiar before you understand why. Jagged cliffs. Emerald valleys. Waterfalls spilling like silver veins through volcanic stone. I lifted the camera, framed the shot—

But I didn't press the shutter. Not yet.

Some things aren't meant to be captured right away. Some things have to arrive in their own time.

Then I remembered why I was here. *Click.*

$$\textcircled{\textcircled{}}$$

Atuona Village

The air hung heavy with moisture as I made my way through the village, every breath thick with the scent of tropical blooms and salt. Sweat beaded on my forehead, trickling down my temples. Nothing moved quickly here—not the clouds, not the people, not time itself.

A woman sat outside her home, weaving pandanus leaves with practiced fingers. The pattern emerged without hesitation, without doubt. She didn't look up as I approached, her focus absolute.

"Ia ora na," I attempted, the Marquesan greeting foreign on my tongue.

She glanced up then, her eyes crinkling at the corners. Not quite a smile, but something close.

"American?" she asked, her fingers never pausing.

I nodded, gesturing to my camera in silent question. She returned the nod, already back to her weaving.

I raised the lens, adjusting for the dappled light through the breadfruit trees above. The contrast between her weathered hands and the fresh green leaves. The precision of movements passed down through generations. *Click.*

"You want to try?" she asked, startling me.

I hesitated, then set my camera down carefully. She made room on the mat beside her, handing me a half-finished piece.

My fingers felt thick, clumsy. The leaves bent awkwardly under my touch. She chuckled and took my hands in hers, guiding them through the motions.

"Slowly," she murmured. "Like this."

For thirty minutes, I forgot the assignment. Forgot the magazine. Forgot everything except the texture of the leaves and the quiet instruction of a stranger.

When I finally stood to leave, she handed me a small woven fish—simple but perfect.

"So you remember," she said.

I did remember. Not just the woven fish, but the feeling of being invited into something older than I could name. I wondered what else this island might ask of me.

I tucked the fish carefully into my bag, next to my extra lens caps. Something to take home that the camera couldn't capture.

Vaekahu

The trek to the waterfall took longer than the guide had promised. My shirt clung to my back, soaked with sweat and sudden, sharp bursts of rain. My boots sank into mud with every step, the path growing steeper and more treacherous.

"Not much further," Tehani, my local guide, called back. She moved effortlessly through the dense foliage, barefoot, as if the slippery ground was an old friend.

I'd hired her that morning on the guesthouse owner's recommendation. "She knows where the tourists don't go," he'd said. He was right.

The sound of the falls reached us before the sight—a distant roar swelling with every step. Then the forest opened, revealing the waterfall in all its power.

Water thundered down a black cliff face, mist curling upward like breath. Everything shimmered. Light. Sound. Motion.

And there, near the riverbank, stood a solitary white horse. Completely still. The contrast was striking—the chaos of water, the quiet of the animal. It felt mythic. Impossible.

I raised the lens. *Click.*

When I lowered it, the moment had shifted. It wasn't about capturing perfection. It was about being present for the instant before everything changed.

The horse turned, regarded me with calm, unreadable eyes, then disappeared into the brush.

"That's Hanau's horse," Tehani said. "It escaped years ago. Now it lives wild. Some say it's a spirit."

"What do you say?" I asked, my camera hanging heavy around my neck.

She smiled, the kind of smile that meant she knew something I didn't. "I say not everything needs explaining."

She led me closer to the falls. The spray soaked us within sec-

◎

onds, cool and exhilarating. I protected my camera, but felt something loosen in my chest as the water ran down my face.

Tehani climbed a slick boulder and motioned for me to follow. I hesitated, calculating the risk to my gear.

"You can't capture this place if you stand apart from it," she called.

I secured my camera and followed, clumsier than I'd like to admit. From the boulder, the view shifted—the falls weren't a backdrop anymore. They surrounded us.

I took a shot that would never make it into the magazine: Tehani, arms outstretched, face tilted to the sky, water turning her into something elemental. Something true. *Click.*

Ta'aoa Valley

"I've brought someone," Tehani called as we approached the clearing. An elderly man looked up from where he sat beneath a mango tree, his face lined and still.

"He wants to see the tiki, Papi," she explained, then to me: "This is my grandfather. He watches over this valley."

The old man studied me with a gaze that was direct but not unkind.

"You take pictures?" he asked, nodding at my camera.

"Yes," I replied. "For a magazine."

He nodded once and rose.

"Come then. Not many find this place without being shown."

We walked deeper into the valley. The path narrowed, the air thick with something I couldn't name—reverence, maybe. Or memory.

Half-buried in the earth, the tiki waited. Its surface was worn smooth by centuries of wind and rain, but the expression still held. It watched. Or waited.

I knelt beside it. My fingers hovered above the stone.

"You can touch it," the old man said. "It has known many hands."

I hesitated, then laid my palm on the cool surface. The connection wasn't mystical—it was human. Someone had carved this. Someone had believed it meant something.

Uncle Eddie used to say, "You're not taking photos. You're borrowing them."

I framed the shot. *Click.*

A face carved by hands long turned to dust. A story captured in a single breath.

"This one is called Ke'eaumoku," the old man said. "The protector."

He sat beside the tiki and unwrapped a bundle of breadfruit paste, placing some at the base. "An offering," he said. "Would you like to make one?"

I almost declined. I thought about distance. Objectivity. Instead, I reached into my bag, pulled out an energy bar, and placed it beside his.

◌

"What do you protect?" he asked suddenly.

I blinked. "I don't know. I'm not sure I protect anything."

He looked at my camera. "This captures truth?"

"It tries to."

"Then protect that. There is too little truth in the world."

That night, under the dim light of the guesthouse porch, I reviewed my shots. His words stayed with me. Protect truth. As if it were that simple. As if a photograph could do more than freeze a moment—as if it could preserve something essential.

I wondered if that's what I'd been searching for all along.

Tehueto

The sun had barely crested the horizon when Tehani arrived at my door. "Today, we go back in time," she said.

We rode in the back of her cousin's truck, bumping over roads that eventually surrendered to jungle. From there, we walked—a narrow trail known only to those who'd walked it before.

"My ancestors left messages," Tehani said as we hiked. "Stories carved in stone."

The petroglyphs were hidden deep within the forest, protected by time and shadows. Etched lines emerged from rock—human forms, spirals, symbols. Silent, enduring.

I traced one with my eyes, not daring to touch. I wondered if Sophia would have. Would she have knelt like this, in reverence? Would she have brushed her fingers along the grooves as if they meant something more? I imagined her crouched beside me, thoughtful, curious, unafraid of silence.

The thought lingered, even as I moved on. It didn't leave. *Click.*

"What does this one mean?" I asked, pointing to a complex spiral.

Tehani tilted her head. "It could be water. Or time. Or the journey of a soul."

"You don't know for certain?"

She smiled. "Is certainty so important to you?"

Before I could answer, rain fell—sudden, insistent. We ducked beneath a rocky overhang, watching the water stream down the carvings, darkening the lines, transforming them.

"Now they look different," she said. "Same carvings, different light."

I took another shot—the same petroglyph, altered by rain.

"Sometimes I think that's what photography is," I said. "Finding different light for the same subject."

"Like life," she said.

We waited out the rain, sharing a papaya she'd brought. The sweetness of the fruit, the scent of wet stone, the hush of falling water—it all settled into the moment, impossible to separate.

◑

When we finally left, I turned back once. The petroglyphs gleamed in the light, their secrets still intact.

Hanaiapa Bay

I woke before dawn, determined to catch first light over the water. The bay was still when I arrived, save for the gentle rhythm of waves curling against sand. A lone outrigger canoe rested at the shore. Beside it, a man prepared his fishing nets, his movements smooth and practiced.

I approached slowly.

"Ia ora na," I greeted.

He glanced up and gave a small nod.

"May I?" I gestured to my camera, then to him.

He shrugged—a gesture neither granting nor denying permission. I sat nearby, letting the moment unfold.

He pushed the canoe into the surf, paddling with steady grace. The sky lightened by degrees, stars fading into blue. He fished with the rising sun, casting his net in a perfect arc. Water caught the light, droplets suspended for a breath, then falling.

When he returned, his catch was modest—silver fish flapping weakly in the canoe's hull. He hauled the net ashore, every movement deliberate. There was no rush. Only rhythm. Only ritual.

I raised the camera, then paused.

Some things aren't meant to be interrupted.

☉

When I finally pressed the shutter, it wasn't to capture the fish or the light. It was to preserve the lineage in his hands.

He noticed me then, really saw me.

"You take pictures?" he asked in slow, accented English.

I nodded.

"Why this?" He gestured to the net, the fish, himself.

"Because it's real," I said. And meant it.

He considered me for a moment, then selected a small fish from his catch and held it out.

"For breakfast," he said.

I accepted it, awkward but grateful.

"Do you know how to prepare it?"

I shook my head.

"Come. I will show you."

His name was Noa. He'd fished these waters for fifty years. His father before him. His grandfather before that. As we cleaned the fish on a flat rock, he spoke of changes he'd seen—fewer fish, rising temperatures, young people leaving for Tahiti or France.

"But the sea," he said, "the sea remains."

We cooked over a small fire, the fish delicate, the flavor unlike anything I'd tasted.

"Simple is best," Noa said, watching me. "For fish. For photographs. For life."

I couldn't argue.

Cape Cabritte

On my last evening, I hiked alone to the edge of the world. The path was familiar now—my legs stronger, my body acclimated to the heat, the breath, the quiet. The island no longer felt like a place I was visiting. It felt like something I was listening to.

At the cape, the sky burned gold. The sun stretched itself across the sea, setting cliffs aglow. Shadows lengthened, and the wind stilled— as if even it didn't want to interrupt the light.

The Pacific unfolded before me, vast and unmoved. The edge of everything. I raised the camera. Framed the shot. But I didn't press the shutter. Not at first.

There was a quiet I hadn't known in years. The kind of quiet you don't hear so much as feel. I wondered if anyone else had sat here like this. If Sophia would have. Maybe she had, somewhere else. Maybe she would have seen what I was just starting to—that some truths don't need to be named. Some beauty doesn't need to be caught.

Uncle Eddie's voice echoed back to me, calm and low.

Some things are for the heart. Not the lens.

I lowered the camera. Let the moment breathe.

And then—only when it began to fade—*Click.*

As darkness fell, I stayed. Stars emerged one by one, then all at once. No city lights to drown them. The Milky Way stretched across the sky like a river made of time.

I thought about the magazine, the images I'd send back. The feature they'd turn it into. How readers would see glimpses of this place— beautiful, compelling glimpses—but never the whole. Not the smell of wet stone, the taste of fresh fish, the sound of Tehani's voice correcting my pronunciation, laughing as she did.

I thought about Sophia again—not as a fantasy or a photograph, but as someone who might understand the way a place could change you. Someone who might feel what I was beginning to feel:

That not everything is meant to be held.
Some things are meant to be witnessed.

My camera sat in my lap, quiet now. Tomorrow I'd fly back—Tahiti, then home. Deadlines. Edits. A new life I'd built, waiting to resume.

But tonight, under stars unnamed by Western charts, I was exactly where I needed to be.

Borrowed time. Borrowed place. Borrowed light.

I made no attempt to capture it.

⦿

Chimbuya - Malawi

A dust devil twisted in the distance, kicking up red earth, spinning like it had a mind of its own. I watched the children chase after it, barefoot and fearless, their laughter lifting into the bright, dry sky. Unburdened laughter—pure and infectious. The kind I'd forgotten existed until I came here.

Chimbuya, Malawi moved in a rhythm I had come to love—The sway of women balancing water jugs against their hips. The slow, deliberate steps of men guiding cattle home. The soft shuffle of sandals on packed earth. It felt natural now. Like I had always belonged here. But I hadn't. I had made a choice.

The Peace Corps sent me here three months ago after training ended. My assignment: help develop sustainable water access and assist with local literacy outreach. I spent ten weeks in a training village near Lilongwe—language immersion, community integration, basic health and engineering skills—trying to absorb everything and prepare for what couldn't be prepared for. But nothing in the binder they handed me at orientation could explain what it would feel like to arrive. To be the outsider. To be received with laughter, curiosity, and—eventually—belonging.

Yesterday, Amara had taught me to weave a basket from reeds we'd collected at the riverbank. Her fingers flew in practiced patterns while mine fumbled clumsily. Instead of frustration, her response had been joy—throwing her head back in laughter before gently repositioning my hands. "Again," she'd said, the only English word she used that day. By sunset, I had a lopsided basket and Amara had a new friend. Some connections need no translation.

The shade beneath the acacia tree was barely enough to keep the sun off our shoulders, but we huddled under it anyway, close and quiet. The children's eyes held a hunger that had nothing to do with food. They wanted stories. I passed out the books one by one, small hands brushing against mine, eager and warm. Fingers traced the pages, searching for something familiar—Something they could hold onto.

Little Beni, no more than seven, crawled into my lap without hesitation, pointing at the illustrations and whispering the English words he remembered from last week. "Tree. Sun. Boy." His pride when he remembered a word was a tangible thing, his whole body straightening with it. These moments—these small victories—they filled me in ways I hadn't expected. Ways no degree could have provided.

And I thought of the letter that had landed in my mailbox two years ago. Berkeley. A full-ride scholarship. A path. A future. My family had already seen it—lecture halls, crisp papers, the soft promise of a degree leading to a stable life. But when I held that letter, my fingers didn't linger on its words. I found something else. A folded brochure beneath it. The one that whispered something different.

Make a Difference. Change the World.

I had traced the edges of that paper like it was a door I had never dared to open. And I had felt it. That pull. The same way I felt drawn to the warmth of soil beneath my fingertips. To plants struggling toward the sun, needing only care to thrive. To things that grow.

"You're throwing away everything we've worked for." My father's voice had been steady, controlled, but his eyes betrayed him. Disappointment. Fear. Confusion. "A full ride to Berkeley doesn't just happen, Sophia."

Mom had been quieter, her silence more devastating than Dad's arguments. "We just don't understand," she'd finally said, hands clasped so tightly her knuckles whitened. "Why would you choose... this?" The way she'd gestured at the Peace Corps brochure made it clear what she thought—a whim, a phase, a mistake.

"There will be time for saving the world after you get your degree," Dad had reasoned, as if my decision were simply a matter of poor scheduling.

I hadn't argued back. What could I say that would make them understand? The words had stuck in my throat, heavy and inadequate. I'd simply folded the Berkeley letter and placed it back on the table between us, a bridge neither of us knew how to cross.

The water pump groaned as I pushed the handle down, arms aching from the effort. Then—cool relief. It splashed into the waiting containers, sending ripples through the surface.

The women beside me moved gracefully—laughter woven between them, stories exchanged between the rhythm of work. I smiled back, falling into step, feeling the ache in my muscles and the satisfaction in my chest.

Last week, we'd finished installing the pump. When the first clear stream of water had shot forth, the entire village had erupted in cele-bration. Children danced through the spray, women ululated with joy, men clasped hands and spoke blessings. That night, under stars bright enough to read by, there had been a feast. I'd been pulled into dance after dance, my awkward movements met with encouraging cheers. "Sister," they'd called me. Family found halfway across the world.

Water. It seemed so simple. So automatic. Turn on a faucet, and there it is. But here, it was different. Here, I saw what it meant. Saw the relief in a mother's face when she filled a jug that would sustain her family through the evening. Saw how something so small could be everything.

I had chosen this. Not because it was easy. But because it mattered. Because I needed to know that I could give something to the world.

Their letters came monthly, each one carrying the weight of their worry, their disappointment thinly veiled between lines asking about my health, my safety. "Your cousin Marin started at Stanford this fall," Mom wrote. "Your room is exactly as you left it," as if I might suddenly come to my senses, return home, and pick up the future they'd imagined for me.

Dad's postscripts were always the same: "The admissions office said they'd consider deferring your scholarship if you applied again next year." His way of leaving a door open, refusing to believe I'd closed it permanently.

My hands were raw from mixing cement, passing bricks, building walls. Dust clung to my curls, turning them wild, tangled. I wiped sweat from my forehead, watching as the structure took shape. A community center. A place for learning, for gathering, for shelter. One brick at a time.

Old Kondo, whose hands were gnarled with arthritis but who insisted on helping anyway, had shown me how to mix the mortar to the right consistency. He'd been a mason before his joints betrayed him, and his eyes lit up when he could share his knowledge. "Strong," he'd say, tapping the walls we built together. "Like you." The compliment had warmed me more than the African sun ever could.

The children had started learning in the center even before the roof was complete. Sitting in the shade of the half-finished walls, practicing letters, numbers, songs that they would teach their younger siblings. Their determination humbled me. Their joy in learning—pure and uncluttered by expectation—reminded me why education mattered in the first place.

I thought of all the things I had been told back home. Berkeley is the best path. You'll have security. We just want what's best for you. They meant well. But they didn't understand. Because this was what I had chosen. To build something real. To become something more than just what was expected.

"A full ride," Dad had repeated that final night, voice breaking slightly. "Do you know how many students would kill for that opportunity?"

I'd nodded, eyes burning with tears I refused to shed. I knew exactly what I was giving up. But he couldn't see what I was gaining. The divide between us had never felt so vast, so unbridgeable. I'd simply placed my hand over his for a moment before pulling away to finish packing.

And it was. But that didn't mean it was easy. Their disbelief followed me here, across oceans and continents. Their certainty that I would regret this choice lingered in the margins of every letter, every rare phone call. The weight of potential disapproval hung in the air, even here, where the air smelled of dust and possibilities.

That night the village lights flickered below me, tiny fires glowing like fallen stars. Drums beat in the distance, steady and strong, filling the night with life. I sat on the hillside, knees drawn to my chest, watching the world I had chosen unfold below me.

From this distance, I could see Nadifa's compound, where just yesterday her baby had taken his first steps. The entire neighborhood had

⦿

celebrated, passing the child from arms to arms, each person offering a blessing, a hope, a promise. They had insisted I hold him too, this child who might one day study in the building my hands had helped create. The connection between past, present, and future had never felt so tangible, so real.

Had I made the right decision? I didn't know. Maybe I would never know. But I knew that somewhere between the Berkeley acceptance letter and this hillside in Malawi, I had found something that felt like purpose. Something that felt like me. My parents couldn't understand that yet. Maybe someday they would.

For now, I had the drums, the stars, and the knowledge that tomorrow, small hands would reach for books, women would gather at the well, and I would be exactly where I was meant to be.

☾

Telluride hadn't changed. Not really. The same snow-dusted rooftops, the same scent of pine in the cold air, the same quiet hum of the town moving through the afternoon.

But today, it felt different. Because I was different. Because I was here for a reason. I turned the corner onto Colorado Avenue, and there it was—the bench. Empty. Waiting.

I took a slow breath, stuffing my hands deep into my jacket pockets. Then I walked forward, sat down, and let the silence settle around me. The Courthouse clock chimed, deep and deliberate, marking the hour.

Three o'clock.

I had spent the last year watching the world through a lens—jungles, mountains, cities draped in neon, deserts painted in gold. I had waited for the perfect light, the perfect shadow, the perfect second to press the shutter and make time stand still.

But this was different. Because I wasn't watching the world. I was waiting for her. The girl with the black curls. The one who had haunted the edges of my thoughts no matter how far I traveled. The one I had never even spoken to.

Sophia.

I didn't even know if she still lived here. Did she still come to this bench? Did she still sit here at three o'clock, flipping through books, blowing lazy bubbles of gum? Or had she left without looking back, vanishing into some other life I would never know?

I stared at the sidewalk, the people passing by in flashes of winter coats and scarves. I was just another stranger now. And maybe she was, too. The minutes stretched. Each tick of the clock another weight pressing into my ribs.

A mother walked by, tugging her child's mittened hand. A man locked up his shop, turning the sign to *Closed.* A gust of wind sent the last brittle leaves of fall skittering across the pavement.

And still—no Sophia.

I leaned back, tilting my head toward the sky. A vast, cloudless stretch of blue. Searching for something. A sign. A shift in the wind. Anything that would tell me I wasn't an idiot for sitting here, waiting for a girl who might not even remember I existed.

Nothing came. Just the deep, empty blue. Just silence. I exhaled,

◯

my breath curling in the cold air. She wasn't coming. Maybe she never would. But, still, I waited. Just a little longer. Just in case.

Kampala - Uganda

The helicopter's rotors churned up the earth, dust swirling into the air like a ghost rising from the land. I shielded my eyes, the wind whipping against my skin, gritty and relentless.

The roar grew distant as we lifted above it all—away from the dust, the sweat, the heat rising off the ground in shimmering waves. The landscape unfolded beneath us like a living map, stitched with crops and cracked roads. Fields of maize stretched out in golden rows, swaying in the rotor wash.

A farmer stood in his field, knee-deep in maize, watching us from below. His hands, rough and worn, rested on the cracked soil—soil that begged for rain.

He didn't wave. He didn't move. He just watched. I wondered what he saw. A lifeline? A disruption? Or just another machine that would come and go, leaving nothing behind but silence?

Below, the land unfolded like a slow-moving dream—rolling green hills drifting into golden haze, rivers threading the land like silver seams. Patches of farmland stretched out in soft, uneven grids, broken only by clusters of clay-colored homes, scattered like stories across the dust. ♪

I studied the landscape, my mind already cataloging what we faced. Three seasons of drought. Wells running dry. The outbreak of waterborne illness overwhelming the clinics. Children with distended bellies from malnutrition. The six-month mission was clear: establish

♪ "Dayvan Cowboy" by Boards of Canada

- 171 -

reliable water sources, treat the sick, distribute medical supplies, train local health workers.

The medical supplies sat heavy against my side. Six months to make a difference. To save those we could. To comfort those we couldn't. Six months to put my training to use in a place where even the simplest medical intervention could mean the difference between life and death.

The roads below shimmer in the heat, sun-scorched and narrow—thin, wavering threads stretching across the earth. Lines someone once believed would hold everything together. But from up here, they look fragile. Temporary.

In the distance, the foothills of Mount Elgon rise through a curtain of mist, dark and unmoving, like a sleeping god. The clouds cling to its shoulders, soft and ghostlike, as if the mountain has pulled a blanket around itself.

And then—barely visible at first—a city begins to emerge. A shimmer of tin rooftops and satellite dishes, of movement and metal. Smoke spiraling from cookfires. Motorbikes darting like minnows between buildings. A heartbeat, faint but persistent, at the edge of the wilderness.

Mbale - Uganda

It doesn't look like a destination. It looks like a question. Almost a city. Almost a beginning.

The rotors roared, a deafening, whirling storm of heat and dust. I gripped the metal bar beside the door, my knuckles white. The ground below blurred in waves of golden earth and green hills, small figures growing larger—villagers waiting, eyes fixed on us.

The world outside the helicopter felt ancient—as if it had existed long before me and would exist long after I was gone. The moment the skids kissed the dirt, my breath rushed out of me, but there was no time to think. I opened the door, and jumped.

Boots on the ground.

The heat hit next, thick and relentless, wrapping around me like a second skin. A dust storm kicked up by the blades, spinning the world into a golden haze.

I ducked, shouldering a heavy box of medical supplies, and passed it off to waiting hands. A line of us—me, the health workers, the other volunteers—moved in a steady rhythm, pulling crates from the helicopter, passing them like lifelines. One box. Then another. Bandages, medicine, bottled water, vaccines, hope.

My arms burned, sweat stinging my eyes, but I didn't stop. Because they needed this. Because I had chosen this. And this was the first real thing I had ever done.

When the last crate cleared the hold, I looked up toward the open cockpit. The pilot met my gaze through his visor. I raised my hand and gave a thumbs-up—small, simple. It was enough.

He nodded once. Then the engine whined higher, rotors slicing the air into a shrieking blur. Dust flew again, swallowing the light. The helicopter lifted, hovered, and then peeled away into the sky, shrinking fast against the sunburnt clouds.

I stood there, blinking grit from my eyes, heart pounding. And then I turned toward the village. Toward what waited. Toward the mission.

The clinic wasn't what I expected. I had prepared for a lack of resources, for broken supplies, for things held together by nothing but determination and luck. I hadn't prepared for the smell. It clung to everything. Sweat, sickness, the sharp tang of iron in the air. It crawled inside you, became part of you, a constant reminder that here, death stood closer than shadow.

I gripped my supplies tighter as I stepped inside, moving past the rows of people waiting for help. Their eyes followed me—hollow, pleading, yet somehow dignified even in suffering. Waiting for someone to make them better. Waiting for me. The weight of their hope pressed against my chest, made it hard to breathe.

A mother cradled her child in her lap, rocking slowly, whispering something only the fevered girl could hear. Prayers, perhaps. Or promises neither of them could keep. The child's skin burned with heat, her tiny chest rising and falling like a bird with a broken wing. Her lips cracked and bleeding, her eyes unfocused. So small. Too small for such suffering.

I knelt beside them, reaching for a thermometer with careful hands. The mother grasped my wrist. Her fingers dug into my skin—not out of aggression, but desperation. Bone-deep, primal. I met her eyes and saw myself reflected there, suddenly small and insufficient in the face of her need. No words. None were needed. I knew.

She wasn't asking me to save her daughter. She was begging me not to fail her. The difference crushed something inside me. I placed a cool cloth on the child's forehead, feeling the heat radiate through the fabric almost immediately. The fever wouldn't break easily. The child might not survive the night. But I had to believe she would. Because if I didn't believe that, I wouldn't last here. And I had to last.

The thermometer read *104.6*. Too high. I measured out medica-

❍

tion, my hands steady despite the tremor in my heart. As I administered the fever reducer, the little girl's eyes fluttered open. She looked at me with sudden clarity, as if death had momentarily released its grip, allowing her to see. Her hand reached up, tiny fingers brushing my cheek, leaving invisible marks I would carry forever.

I had barely finished wrapping a bandage when I felt a soft tug on my sleeve. I turned and found her. An elderly woman, skin creased with time like the dry earth outside, standing before me with hands worn but steady. She held out a small bottle of pills, her fingers trembling as she passed them to me. The bottle was nearly empty—three pills remained.

I glanced at the label—malaria medication. She pointed to her chest, then to her throat. Not words, but a message. Something wasn't right. I helped her to a nearby cot, my hands gentle under her arm. The bones beneath her skin felt like bird wings, fragile and hollow.

Her skin felt paper-thin, delicate in a way that made me afraid to hold too tightly, as if she might tear like worn fabric. I fetched a small cup of water, kneeling beside her as she struggled to lift the pill to her mouth. Her lips barely parted as she swallowed, wincing. Her body shuddered. A drop of water escaped the corner of her mouth, trailing down skin that had witnessed decades of famine, war, loss, and somehow, survival.

I reached for her hand, feeling the frailty of it in my own. She squeezed. So small a thing—just a squeeze. A silent thank you. Her eyes softened, and for a moment, I felt like I had done something right. Like I belonged here. But the next moment, another call, another need, another person waiting. I squeezed back, memorizing the pattern of lines on her palm, the quiet dignity in her eyes. And, I moved on. The weight of leaving her as heavy as the weight of staying would have been.

I washed my hands at a small metal basin, the water turning pink. The young man with the infected leg. The deep wound that smelled like rot. His clenched teeth, his bitten lip, his trembling hands. His refusal to cry. The infection had spread halfway up his calf, angry red streaks reaching toward his knee. In America, he would have been on IV antibiotics days ago. Here, I had oral medication and prayer. The moment my fingers touched the bandage, he had gasped. And I had swallowed my own gasp with it.

I hadn't been ready for that. For how real it would feel. For how wrong it was that pain like this could exist in the world and just be accepted. For how quickly I would learn to accept it too.

I scrubbed harder. Pink turned to red. The red wouldn't go away. Blood under my fingernails, in the creases of my knuckles, staining the white cuffs of my shirt. Blood that wasn't mine but somehow belonged to me now. I looked down at my hands, my breath uneven. My hands were shaking. Not from exhaustion. From helplessness. From anger. From the unfairness of it all. From the knowledge that for every person I helped today, ten more would arrive tomorrow. An endless tide of suffering I could never stem. ♪

I turned off the water and stepped outside, pushing through the heavy wooden door. The air outside was hot and thick, pressing against my lungs like wet wool. I leaned against a tree, closing my eyes. For the first time since I got here—since I made the decision to come—I let go.

And the tears came. Silently, fiercely. The sobs shook my ribs like something trying to break free, something wild and wounded. I pressed

♪ *"Love and Hate"* by Michael Kiwanuka

my hand against my mouth, muffling the sound. I wasn't crying for me. I was crying for all of it.

For the mother holding her fevered child, who had already lost two others to the same illness. For the young man who had taught himself not to cry because it wouldn't change anything, who would likely lose his leg but couldn't afford to stop working. For the elderly woman whose hands trembled as she swallowed her last hope in pill form, who had walked twelve miles to reach the clinic.

For all the suffering I couldn't stop. For all the lives I couldn't save. For the inadequacy of my training, my supplies, my hands. For the world that allowed places like this to exist while others thrived in excess.

I wiped my face with the back of my hand, tasting salt and dust. I knew what my family would say if they saw me now.

You don't have to do this.
You don't have to carry this weight.

Their voices echoed in my head, reasonable and concerned and utterly missing the point. They saw this as sacrifice. They couldn't understand it was also privilege—to be useful, to be necessary, to touch lives at their most vulnerable points. To bear witness when no one else would.

I pushed away from the tree, straightened my shoulders. Inside, they were waiting. Inside, I was needed. The tears had cleansed something in me, washed away the illusion that I could fix everything, left behind the truth that trying anyway mattered.

But someone had to try. And somewhere along the way, I decided it would be me. The ache didn't leave me. But it no longer stopped me.

I took a deep breath and went back in.

The sweater was ridiculous. My Christmas present. Bright, obnoxious red. Glitter. Actual pom-poms. I pulled it over my head with a groan.

"I feel like I could be used for target practice."

Grandfather chuckled, adjusting his glasses. "Figured you needed a little extra warmth this season."

Mom grinned, holding back laughter. "And a little extra holiday spirit."

Gilmore, sprawled lazily on the rug, cracked one disinterested eye before rolling over.

The room was warm, the fire crackling, the scent of pine and cinnamon hanging in the air. Outside, snow drifted down in slow spirals, settling on the porch railings and blanketing the silence. It should've felt like every other Christmas. The kind that gets etched into memory—mugs of cider, worn flannel, the dog's snores keeping rhythm with the radio. A tableau of comfort.

But it didn't.

There was laughter, yes. Love, even. I could feel it in the way Mom refilled my mug without asking, in the way Grandfather leaned closer to hear my answer. It was all there, and yet—something was missing.

Not a person, exactly. More like a thread. A presence. A kind of belonging I'd never had, but somehow, still missed.

Maybe that's why I loved my family the way I did. Because they kept showing up. Even in ridiculous sweaters, even in their quiet, ordinary ways. Maybe love wasn't always about what you felt in the moment—but what you chose to carry anyway.

Tamale - Ghana

Heat presses against my skin, thick and insistent, wrapping around me like a second body. The ground beneath my boots is cracked and dry, red earth split open like old pottery left too long in the sun. Overhead, the sky is endless, the sun a white-hot coin pinned in place—unmoving, unbothered.

There is no snow. No fireplace. No pine-scented wreaths or twinkling lights tangled in windows. Just the hum of voices from the village—low and musical—and the distant echo of drums rising from somewhere beyond the baobab trees. The air smells of charcoal and dust, of something alive and ancient. Earthy. Sharp. Persistent.

The sun had climbed slowly, bleeding orange over the red-dust roads. Bougainvillea spill wild over cinderblock walls, brilliant against the beige. Goats weave between cooking pots and motorcycles, undisturbed. Women balance baskets on their heads like extensions of their own grace. Barefoot children run laughing through narrow alleys, chasing plastic bottles like soccer balls.

There are no garlands. No carolers. No glitter-wrapped urgency of western holidays. Only giving. Only presence.

And still, it feels holy. This is Christmas in Tamale, Ghana.

My assignment in Ghana focused on primary health outreach and nutrition education in peri-urban and rural communities throughout the

◎

Northern Region. The directive emphasized maternal and child health, with a particular focus on malaria prevention, basic wound care, and food security initiatives. Seasonal distributions were coordinated to provide families with essential supplies—fortified staples, soap, medical basics—aimed at reducing preventable illness during the dry season.

It's not the Christmas I grew up with. But in its own way, it's something more honest. More human.

That morning, we set up folding tables under the largest neem tree in the square. The community leaders helped us organize the flow, directing people forward in neat lines, calling names in soft, clipped Dagbani. We passed out blankets, bars of soap, fortified maize meal, and in some cases, anti-malarial tablets for families with children under five.

I spent most of my time helping at the medical tent, logging vital signs and assisting Margaret, the field nurse, as she checked for signs of infection or dehydration. We treated burns from open fires, dressed wounds, rehydrated kids who came in dizzy from the heat. Some days we did vaccinations; others, we held wellness talks under the trees—teaching mothers how to rehydrate a child, or why using treated mosquito nets could save lives.

The language barrier slowed things down, but smiles helped where words failed. The children were especially curious—tugging at my sleeves, pointing at my freckles, handing me mangos sticky with juice and sand. One girl, Ama, about seven years old, insisted on braiding my hair every afternoon with quiet concentration and nimble fingers. I let her. It made her feel important, she said, though I suspected it made me feel human again.

None of it felt like enough. But it felt like something.

⦿

The line for food that morning moved slowly, each face meeting ours with quiet eyes and calloused hands. They didn't rush. They didn't reach. Just waited. And when the time came, they accepted what was offered—not with surprise, but with something deeper. Quiet gratitude. Dignity that made me look down at my own hands and wonder if I truly understood what it meant to give.

Now, I sat outside my hut, legs folded beneath me, turning a small envelope over in my fingers. A Christmas card from home. The ink was smudged from travel, the edges soft from being opened too many times.

Merry Christmas, sweetheart! We miss you so much.
Not a day goes by that we don't think about you.
Are you staying safe? Are you eating enough?
Wherever you are, we hope you know how much we love you.

My fingers hovered over the words. My breath caught. For a second, I could almost hear my mother's voice—bright and cautious. Could almost see my father's worry hiding in the spaces between the lines.

Were they proud? Or were they afraid they'd lost me to a world they didn't understand?

Behind me, the village carried on. A rooster crowed somewhere near the church steps. A woman called to her daughter in Dagbani, her voice sharp but affectionate. The air shimmered with dust and sunlight.

I wanted to write back and tell them I was okay. That I was learning what it meant to be part of something bigger than myself. That I felt useful. That I felt… home.

But as I stared at the card again, I wasn't sure if that was the truth. Because sometimes being useful still feels like being alone.

Mary Jane - Colorado

Boots hit the snow with a soft *thwump*. Overhead, the lift cables hum. Somewhere nearby, laughter rings out—sharp and bright in the cold air. It's the opening scene of a perfect winter's day at Mary Jane.

I shift my weight forward in the lift line, watching the rhythm of skiers ahead as they slide into place, the chair scooping them up and disappearing into the sky.

A figure glides up beside me, smooth and effortless. I steal a glance. She's in her late twenties, dressed in all black, her movements deliberate, confident. No hesitation. No second-guessing. She belongs here. The lift reaches us. We move in sync, gliding forward as the chair sweeps beneath us, lifting us into the air. I lean back, adjusting my gloves.

"Nice day, huh?"

She turns to face me, and for the first time, I see the full warmth of her smile. Bright. Open. The kind of smile that catches you off guard.

"Couldn't ask for better conditions!"

Her voice carries the same easy confidence as her skiing. I nod, looking out at the slopes stretching below us, sunlight bouncing off the groomed runs and the steep mogul fields that have been handing me my ass all morning.

"You ski here often?"

She pulls off one glove, flexing her fingers against the cold air.

"Yeah, as much as I can. What about you?"

◉

"First time, actually."

She tilts her head slightly, studying me like she's trying to gauge whether I know what I'm doing.

"Well, welcome to Mary Jane! So, what do you think?"

I exhale, grinning despite myself. "The moguls here are... humbling."

She laughs, a rich, melodic sound that cuts through the icy air.

"They don't call her 'No Pain, No Jane' for nothing."

I chuckle, shaking my head. "Yeah, I'm starting to get that."

Our skis dangle beneath us, Winter Park shrinking behind as we climb higher and higher, the cold wind tugging at our jackets.

She was still smiling. I turned my face toward the sun, the chill biting at the edges of my goggles. Maybe it was just the altitude, but something about that smile, that moment—felt like more than just small talk on a ski lift. I came here for snow, for stories. I didn't expect to feel... noticed. Not yet. Not here.

Pueblo Nuevo - Peru

The air clings to my skin—thick, damp, alive. Every breath carries the scent of wet earth, woodsmoke, and something sharp and green, like crushed lemongrass and rain-soaked leaves. I step out of the tent, pulling my curls into a loose knot at the base of my neck. My shirt sticks to me instantly, the fabric damp before I even move. But I barely notice anymore. The heat is constant. The wetness, a second skin.

I have been assigned to South America to oversee water sanitation and hygiene education. The mandate was clear: assess water quality, implement basic filtration systems, and train communities in sustainable hygiene practices. In practice, it meant navigating riverbanks and supply delays, language gaps and trust slowly earned.

The land here feels wide and close all at once. Jungle vines snake over the edges of worn footpaths, their leaves the size of dinner plates. Birds cry overhead in bursts of strange, melodic calls—sharp and sudden, like laughter. Somewhere deep in the trees, a machete rhythm echoes—*thwack, thwack*—cutting a trail or clearing brush. Everything is green, impossibly green. A kind of green that swallows you whole.

A few yards away, Ethan adjusts the strap of his water testing kit, the worn canvas digging into his shoulder. His faded Seattle Seahawks hat is pulled low against the sun, casting his face in shadow—but his grin is unmistakable. Easy. Steady. The kind of grin that says he's exactly where he's meant to be.

He's been with the Corps for almost two years now, like me—long days, remote villages, endless supply lists and water samples. But somehow, Ethan always moves through it like it's second nature. There's something unshakable about him—like no matter how hot it gets or how many miles we hike, he'll still have that same quiet calm, that same offhand joke waiting. Reliable. Unflustered. The same as always.

"Ready to save the world?" he calls, voice light, teasing.

It used to make me laugh. Now I just nod, the smile rising to my lips out of habit, not feeling.

I look past him to the distant ridgeline, where mist still clings to the tops of trees like a veil. The land feels untouched and tired at once.

Beautiful, yes—but also burdened. I wonder what it's like to live here, not just pass through. To belong to it, not just borrow it.

The sun is already climbing, turning the dew into steam. Somewhere nearby, a tin pan clangs, calling us back to the work ahead.

Beyond the low ridge, the river winds through the valley like a ribbon of light. Women kneel on the banks, their hands scrubbing bright fabrics against smooth stones, dark hair tied back, laughter rising with the steam. Children run barefoot along the muddy edge, their voices lifted in Spanish and Quechua, their feet slick with river silt. A dog barks. A chicken flaps wildly from under a woven basket. Life hums in every corner of this place, not loud but insistent.

This is life in Pueblo Nuevo, Peru.

It looks like something from a painting. But I know better. I see it in the little girl clinging to her mother's skirt, her tiny fingers fisting the fabric, too weak to play. I see it in the boy, coughing into his hands, his shoulders shaking, struggling to keep up.

The river is beautiful. And it is killing them.

I flex my fingers against the strap of my pack, the weight of it pressing against my shoulder. When I first came here, I thought I could help. I thought I could fix things. I didn't understand yet. Not really.

Ethan shifts, turning toward the jungle path ahead. His voice is still light, calling me forward. I take a slow breath. And follow.

The jungle breathes around us—thick, damp, alive. Every step stirs the scent of wet earth, crushed leaves, something sharp and green.

Ethan moves ahead, boots pressing deep into the jungle floor, his steps steady, unhurried. I match his pace, my own movements careful, methodical. The rhythm of our trek has become familiar—the quiet shuffle of our boots, the occasional rustle of branches overhead, the distant calls of howler monkeys echoing through the trees.

We reach the river. Wide. Still. Golden in the late afternoon light. I crouch, pulling a vial from my pack, submerging it just beneath the surface. Cool water slips between my fingers before I lift the vial, sealing the sample. I glance up—Ethan is watching me. He nods. I nod back. No words. Just understanding.

Back at camp, our makeshift testing station hums with quiet focus. The soft murmur of the river threads through the air, steady, grounding. Glass vials clink as we work—measuring, analyzing, recording.

Ethan leans over, reaching for a sample, his shoulder briefly brushing mine. The warmth of it lingers longer than it should. I don't move away.

By sunset, we're sitting on a grassy hill, the jungle stretching wide and endless below. The sky melts from gold to violet, the first stars beginning to flicker awake.

Ethan picks up a small rock and tosses it down the slope, watching as it skips and tumbles through the grass. His posture is easy—comfortable in a way I envy.

I study him for a moment, my fingers absently tracing patterns in the dirt. Strong hands. Sun-bronzed skin. That calm, thoughtful expression—like he's always watching something just beyond the horizon.

Something shifts in my chest. Soft. Unexpected. He turns suddenly, catching me mid-glance. A flicker of amusement in his eyes. A heartbeat of silence between us. Heat rises to my cheeks. I look away too fast, hoping he doesn't notice. I fix my gaze on the horizon, just as the last sliver of sun slips out of sight. Twilight settles around us. The air thickens with woodsmoke and earth.

We don't speak. We just sit—breathing in the moment. The silence between us changing shape. Becoming something else. Something I don't quite have a name for. Or maybe I do. And I just need to stop resisting.

KDFW - Dallas-Fort Worth

The *Cinnabon* line at DFW barely moves. The smell hangs in the air—syrup and cinnamon, warm and too much, like something trying too hard to comfort you. I shift forward a few inches. I check my watch.

Still time.

I scan the terminal. Not for anyone. For her. I know it doesn't make sense. She's not here. Not anywhere close. But my eyes still move across the crowd. Row by row. Gate by gate. A reflex I never unlearned.

I've done it for years—airports, markets, train stations. I know she won't be there, and still... I look. Always half-expecting some twist of fate, some cosmic glitch where she appears out of nowhere. Like the world might bend, just once, in my direction.

The truth is, the world isn't as big as we like to think. We act like it's all continents and oceans, but most of the time it's coffee lines and carry-ons, people folding into each other's orbits. Strangers brushing past one another on their way to somewhere else. We're all closer than we think—always just one gate, one intersection, one near-miss away from something we didn't know we were waiting for.

◐

I remember the first time I heard "It's a Small World"—standing in line at Disneyland with a churro in one hand and a sunburn creeping across my nose. I was eight, maybe nine. *Pirates of the Caribbean* had a line that stretched to Santa Monica, so I was stuck with a *it's a small world* instead.

The ride didn't impress me—too slow, too strange. But the song stuck. Not because it was catchy—it was quite maddening, actually—but because even then, it felt oddly true. Like maybe the world really was smaller than it looked. ♪

That tune still echoes sometimes. Usually in airports. Or today, when I passed a face I thought I'd forgotten and found a memory I didn't realize I still carried.

Too small to ignore the way some people return—again and again—even if they never technically arrived in the first place.

Someone flips through a magazine nearby. A kid rolls Hot Wheels cars across the tile, lost in his own world. Across the walkway, a girl taps the rewind button on her Walkman, eyes closed, mouthing lyrics only she can hear. People talk. Eat. Wait. I just watch.

The line creeps forward. I love this place. Always have. Some kind of heaven in a paper tray. Eventually, I reach the counter. The woman behind it hands me the roll like a ritual offering. It's warm and soft, icing already slipping into the spiral. What's not to love?

I carry the goodness to Gate D12, still watching faces as I go. Sit near the window. Eat slowly. People pass. Their footsteps echo in the high ceiling. Overhead, the PA crackles and calls out names I don't know. Still—I look. Not expecting her. Not really. Just hoping.

♪ *"It's a Small World"* by The Disneyland Children's Chorus

That's the thing about hope. It doesn't always announce itself. Sometimes it just looks like scanning a crowd for a face you'll never see.

"Final boarding call for Flight 483. All remaining passengers, please proceed to Gate D12."

One last look around. She's not here. Of course she's not. But even now, I glance back—out of habit. Out of hope. The world is small. You never know.

I toss the empty tray of heavenly delights. Pick up my bag. And walk down the jetway. The gate door clicks shut behind me—quiet, definite. A clean line between before and after.

The jetway air is humid. I step into the terminal at Gate D11, bag slung over my shoulder. The Dallas noise hits all at once—chatter, intercoms, suitcase wheels rattling over tile. Everything feels louder than it should.

Ethan walks beside me, his fingers interlaced with mine. I shift my grip on the strap of my bag. Something about airports makes me restless. The air smells sweet. Cinnamon. It tugs at something deep in my chest, something I can't quite name.

I glance toward the *Cinnabon* line. Just a flicker of curiosity. Nothing. Just travelers in line. Still—something about the scene makes me pause. I don't know why. Like a word on the tip of your tongue, like a name you almost remember. A ripple in the fabric.

Ethan gives my hand a quick squeeze, guiding me through the crowd. His touch is grounding. Familiar. But there was a time it wasn't. A time when it felt new.

O

This—this is what I think I've wanted.

Not sparks. Not unraveling. Just… that feeling when someone sees the same things I do. When I look at a broken system, a small village, a river that needs saving—and don't look away—and neither did he. That's what first held us together. Not romance. Not chemistry.

Mission. Purpose.

We both want to help. To be useful. To leave things better than we find them. And somehow, that leaks into everything else. Into laughter over supply lists. Into long afternoons testing water samples. Into sitting on the edge of a bunk bed in silence, and knowing silence isn't empty.

Ethan doesn't try to change me or pull more from me than I can give. He just shows up. Every day. With steady hands and soft jokes and eyes that don't flinch from hard things.

And maybe this is love. Or what I've always thought love should be. Not a fire, but something steady and warm. Not the rush of falling—but the quiet rhythm of building something side by side.

Brick by brick. Vial by vial. Love as devotion. Love as usefulness. Choosing someone who sees the world the same way I do. That's what I've told myself. And maybe it's true.

But something in me starts to wonder now—right here, with his hand in mine, the terminal humming around us—if I've ever really let myself want more.

Not more goodness. Not more care. But more of that unspoken something. That ache in the chest. That impossibility that makes you look across a crowded terminal for a face you've never met—and swear you'd know it if you saw it.

I don't feel swept away. I don't feel undone. I feel aligned. I am aligned. And maybe that's enough.

We move through the airport like we belong to each other. Like we're already carrying something between us worth protecting. And maybe we are.

But still—the feeling lingers. Like I almost saw something.

Or someone.

Albuquerque - New Mexico

The *whoosh* of propane burners breaks the morning stillness, a rhythmic exhale of fire against the crisp New Mexico air. All around me, colors bloom.

On the ground, massive swaths of fabric ripple and swell, stretching into shape, balloon skins shifting from crumpled silence into something alive. Their patterns—bold stripes, swirling mosaics, whimsical shapes—start to take form, catching the first light of dawn.

I adjust my camera strap, weaving through the controlled chaos. Crews tug at ropes, voices calling over the sound of hissing flames. This isn't just an event—it's a slow-motion sunrise painted in every color imaginable. A gust of wind tugs my jacket, sending a shiver through me. Above, the Sandia Mountains loom, watching as the sky fills.

A woman bumps into me, her eyes fixed upward. "Sorry," she murmurs, not looking away from the spectacle. I recognize the expression on her face—wonder mixed with disbelief. The same look I'm trying to hide behind my viewfinder.

"First time?" she asks, noticing my camera.

I nod. "Yours too?"

"Third year running," she says with a smile. "It never gets old. Wait until they all take flight."

I follow her gaze upward, where a penguin-shaped balloon bobs beside a traditional rainbow-striped one. The scale of it all is overwhelming, even to someone who's seen wonders across six continents.

Jane had been specific when she called. "Not the usual tourist shots, Michael. I want the human element. The relationship between earth and sky. What it feels like to be there."

I'd almost declined. Balloon festivals are postcard territory—too obvious, too easily reduced to cliché. But something made me say yes. Maybe it was the challenge. Maybe it was just that I'd been shooting too many empty landscapes lately. Beautiful, but hollow. Like something was missing.

A crew captain shouts in Spanish, his voice carrying over the growing roar of flames. His team moves with practiced precision, like dancers who've performed the same steps for years. I frame a shot— weathered hands gripping ropes, faces intent with concentration, the balloon above them swelling with life. *Click.*

The captain catches me watching and grins. "You want ride? We have space." He gestures to his basket—larger than most, adorned with the New Mexico state flag.

I hesitate. I've always shot from the ground. It's safer there. More controlled. I can predict the angles, the light.

"Come!" He waves me over more insistently. "Best view in the house!"

I think of Jane's directive. The human element. The relationship between earth and sky. What it feels like.

I nod, securing my camera.

The captain—Miguel, he tells me—introduces his crew, a family operation spanning three generations. His father, now too old to fly but still directing from below. His daughter, barely twenty, checking instruments with confident precision. His brother, manning the burners with a watchful eye.

"We fly this route thirty years," Miguel says as he helps me into the basket. "My father taught me, now I teach my Lucia." He nods to his daughter, pride evident in his voice.

Five others join us in the basket—tourists with wide eyes and nervous laughter. I position myself in the corner, camera ready, body tense.

A deep whoomp signals the final burst of heat. The basket shifts beneath my feet, and my stomach lurches. The ground crew releases the tethers, and suddenly—we are floating.

The sensation is nothing like I expected. Not the dramatic lift-off of airplanes, not the stomach-dropping plunge of roller coasters. Instead, it's the earth that seems to fall away. As if we remain perfectly still while the world recedes beneath us.

The desert stretches below—endless, golden, untouched. But I'm not looking at the landscape. I'm watching shadows. Hundreds of them—dark circles painted onto the earth, shifting and stretching as the sun rises. The balloons themselves are dazzling, but it's the contrast that fascinates me.

What rises and what remains behind.

I press the shutter. A perfect shot. One that tells a story. One that says something about timing. About movement. About letting go. Maybe, even, about me.

"Beautiful, no?" Miguel says, coming to stand beside me. "Like spirits leaving the ground."

I nod, unable to explain that I was thinking almost the exact same thing.

He points east, toward the mountains. "Look there. First light on the peaks."

The Sandias have turned the color that gave them their name— watermelon red in the morning sun. It happens every day, but from this vantage point, suspended between earth and sky, it feels like a revelation meant just for us.

"My father says balloons teach you everything important," Miguel continues, adjusting the burner with practiced hands. "You must respect the wind, but not fear it. You must know when to add heat and when to let things cool. You must trust what you cannot see."

The basket shifts slightly, and I grab the edge, my knuckles whitening.

Miguel notices. "First time flying?"

I nod, embarrassed. I've traveled the world with my camera, climbed mountains for the perfect shot, waded through jungles teeming with things that bite. Yet here I am, white-knuckled in a wicker basket.

"Don't worry," he says. "We all start somewhere. My first solo flight, I was terrified. Now look." He gestures to the horizon, where balloons dot the sky like colored planets in a new universe.

The experience changes me, I realize. Not just the view or the photos I'm taking, but something deeper. The surrender to elements I can't control. The trust in strangers who guide this fragile vessel. The simple act of stepping into empty air and finding it holds me.

I move around the basket carefully, capturing different angles. The other passengers—an elderly couple celebrating their anniversary, a family with two young children, a solo traveler about my age. Their faces tell different stories—exhilaration, peaceful contemplation, cautious wonder.

"Where are you from?" the solo traveler asks, noticing my camera. Her accent suggests somewhere European, maybe Scandinavian.

"Colorado," I reply.

"Beautiful mountains there," she says. "I visited once, in winter. Do you ski?"

"As much as I can," I say, then find myself adding, "Not as much as I used to. Work keeps me traveling."

"What kind of work needs this?" She gestures to my professional-grade camera.

"I'm a photographer. For a magazine."

She nods, understanding. "So you see beautiful things all the time."

I consider this. "I guess I do."

"Does it ever become... normal? To see so much beauty?"

The question catches me off guard. I think about the countless sunrises I've photographed, the landscapes that have taken my breath away, the moments I've captured and then moved on from.

"Sometimes," I admit. Then, an image rises in my mind—Sophia on that bench in Telluride, afternoon light catching in her hair, her profile turned away from me. The most beautiful thing I've ever seen.

"But true beauty?" I continue, surprising myself with my candor.

"The kind that stops your heart? That never becomes normal."

I don't tell this stranger about Sophia. About how a woman I watched from afar has somehow become my measure for all beauty. About how sometimes, when I frame a perfect shot, I'm really looking for the feeling I had when I first saw her.

"Like now," I add, gesturing to the world below us, the shadows of balloons drifting across the desert floor. A poor substitute for what I'm really thinking.

I raise my camera again. This time I focus not on the balloons or the landscape, but on the people in our basket. Miguel adjusting the burners with practiced ease. His daughter checking wind patterns with a practiced eye. The elderly couple holding hands, their faces lit by the

◎

same dawn. The family pointing excitedly as another balloon passes close by. The woman I've been speaking with, her face turned toward the mountains, a slight smile on her lips.

I press the shutter. *Click.*

It hits me then—what Jane was asking for. Not just the spectacle or the scenery, but the shared experience. The way strangers become companions in moments of wonder. The human element. The relationship between earth and sky. What it feels like to be here.

As if reading my thoughts, Miguel says, "You know why I love ballooning? Is the only way to travel where you must accept you cannot control where you go. Only how you respond to the journey."

I think about that as we begin our descent an hour later, the ground rising to meet us. About control and surrender. About capturing moments versus living them.

When we touch down, the return to earth is gentler than I expected. The crew rushes to secure the balloon, the passengers disembark with handshakes and hugs, and I stand for a moment, one foot still in the basket, feeling strangely reluctant to leave.

Miguel notices. "So? Good photos?"

I nod. "The best I've taken in a long time."

"Good." He pats the side of the basket fondly. "Sometimes we need to let go of the ground to see it clearly, no?"

As I walk back through the launch field, now emptying as balloons take to the sky or return to their trailers, I know the shots are good. I

◎

felt it in the stillness before the shutter snapped, the way the light held just long enough, the weight of instinct landing where it should.

They're technically sound, sure—but there's something else in them too. Something I haven't felt in my work for longer than I care to admit.

Presence. Connection. Life being lived, not just observed.

Alaska 365

Outside the window, the sky had gone soft and colorless—gray layered over gray, with the faintest gold just above the horizon. They were beginning to descend. The seatbelt light blinked on with its familiar chime.

Ethan sat beside me, reading something printed out on folded paper, the kind of document that had passed through too many hands. A schedule maybe. A housing checklist. I wasn't sure. His pen moved occasionally, underlining, circling. I'd barely spoken the whole flight.

The thought of home hadn't settled yet—not Peru, not Colorado, not anywhere in between. Just a shifting in the chest. Something unfastened.

Washington wasn't my home. Not yet. Maybe not ever, not in the way it was for Ethan. To me, it was the beginning of something strange and unfamiliar—coming back to the real world after years spent outside it. A world of coffee shops and traffic lights, not crumbling villages and far-off roads. A world where the urgent was often loud, and the important was often silent.

I didn't know if I belonged here anymore. Or if I ever had.

"We could look for an apartment. Something small. There's a neighborhood near Queen Anne I've always liked."

I nodded, almost before the words registered. A quiet yes. I'd never lived with anyone before. Not like that. The thought settled awkwardly—like trying on a coat that almost fit. The sleeves a little long, the shoulders not quite right. Not because I didn't care for him. I did. But that was the thing. I'd never built a life with someone. And I didn't know what it meant to be seen every morning.

I didn't know how to share space without shrinking inside it. How to let someone see the quiet parts—the ones that didn't have easy answers or polished edges. It was easier in Peru. In the field, under foreign skies, when every day was a new kind of survival.

Here, it would be different. Here, the questions would be smaller but sharper: who takes out the trash, who forgets the milk, who leaves the light on too long. I wasn't afraid of the big things. I was afraid of the thousand small ones that could unravel us without warning.

Every evening. Every in between.

Maybe belonging wasn't a place. Maybe it was something quieter—like someone knowing how you took your tea. Or what kind of silence meant sadness, and what kind meant peace. I didn't know if Ethan knew those things about me. I didn't know if I'd ever shown him.

Still, I could feel the plane tilting, the way land slowly returned beneath you. Familiar outlines taking shape. Evergreen trees like threads stitched across hills. The first smudge of coastline.

I glanced down at my hands, folded in my lap. Maybe I wasn't ready. Maybe I was. But I was going with him anyway.

(O)

12

24:03:24:00:23:56

The air is warm against my skin, but my hands are cold. I sit on the worn wooden bench at Kerry Park, staring at the view that never fails to steal my breath. The Seattle skyline rises in the distance, all glass and steel and clarity. The Space Needle stands tall, steady, certain. A landmark that belongs. That knows where it is.

A fine mist begins to settle around me—not quite rain, just Seattle's way of reminding you nothing stays clear for long. The skyline blurs slightly at its edges, the way memories do.

I twist the engagement ring between my fingers—slowly, absently. The gold band glints even in this diffused light, the diamond catching fire and then fading to glass. When did it start feeling so heavy?

Around me, life moves forward. A child's laugh cuts through the air—bright, clear, unapologetically sure of itself. Nearby, a couple leans into each other, heads tilted close, laughter low and effortless. A camera shutter clicks behind me. A tourist, probably. Trying to hold onto something fleeting.

And just like that, the memory rises.

We were sitting on a picnic blanket in Volunteer Park, just beyond the conservatory where the lawn sloped gently toward the trees. I'd made us sandwiches, Ethan had brought two of those tiny bottles of Chardonnay you get in picnic baskets—the kind with twist-off caps and little plastic cups.

It was unseasonably warm that day—one of those rare Seattle afternoons when the sun seemed determined to make everyone forget about the nine months of gray. The air smelled like crushed grass and lemon—maybe from the vinaigrette I'd packed, maybe just from the sun warming the afternoon. My skin was flushed, comfortable.

He pulled the ring from his pocket—not dramatic, just matter-of-fact. Like it had been decided for some time.

"Sophia," he said, "I want to build a life with you."

Not Will you marry me?
Not I can't imagine my life without you.

Just... that. And I'd nodded. Smiled. I think I even laughed. It wasn't grand, or overwhelming. It was warm. Safe. Familiar. That was the part that got to me—how easy it was to say yes.

The memory fades. I'm back on the bench, turning the ring in my fingers. It feels heavier now than it did then. The mist has thickened

❦

slightly, softening the hard edges of the city, making everything seem just a little less certain.

My thumb brushes the stone. Then catches on something unexpected—a small nick in the band I've never noticed before. Ethan had chosen it himself—simple, classic, elegant. He knew I wouldn't want anything flashy. He's always been good at knowing what makes sense. What fits. And maybe I thought that was enough.

The diamond flares again—bright, precise. I slide the ring down toward my fingertip, then all the way off. It sits in my palm, impossibly small for something that carries so much weight. For a moment, I imagine letting it fall. Into the grass. Into the space between who I was that day and who I am now. Between warmth and truth. Between certainty and something I don't have a name for yet.

"Excuse me?" I look up. A woman with a toddler balanced on her hip stands before me, holding out a phone.

"Would you mind taking our picture with the skyline? We're visiting from Chicago."

I close my fingers around the ring as I stand, nodding with a smile that feels borrowed. The woman's wedding band catches the light as she hands me her phone. Hers looks worn in, settled. Part of her.

"Just tap the button when you're ready," she says, returning to her husband's side.

I frame them against the skyline, this family of three. The toddler points excitedly at the Space Needle. I count silently in my head and tap the screen. They smile—unguarded, complete.

I hand the phone back and return to my bench. The family moves on, but something in their wake has shifted. I open my palm and look at the ring again. The small imperfection. The promise it holds. The question it's become. I exhale and stand.

For a long moment, I hold the ring between my finger and thumb, suspended above my ring finger. The mist has cleared briefly, and across the water, sunlight catches on the windows of the city. A thousand tiny beacons.

I close my eyes and turn my face toward the sun, as if it might whisper something certain. The skyline holds its shape. The view doesn't change. And maybe that's what scares me.

I used to think love was a decision. A choice you made and then stuck with. But now I wonder if it's also a question you're allowed to ask more than once.

I slip the ring back on. But my hands are still cold.

☾

My Boulder office is exactly how I like it—curated chaos. Stacks of photo proofs, rolls of undeveloped film, and travel trinkets from across the world cover every available surface. My camera gear is half-organized, half-forgotten, a tangled mess of straps and lenses spilling from my desk drawers.

On the wall, a framed poster of Jonny Moseley hangs—mid-air, effortless, defying gravity with a kind of reckless grace. A reminder of control in the midst of disorder.

My flip phone buzzes. I grab it, flipping it open with the ease of habit.

"Guess what?" Brandon's voice practically beams through the speaker.

"You finally landed a Wheaties box?"

"Close. Monica and I are getting married!"

I pause, letting the words settle. A slow grin spreads across my face.

"What? How's Donna taking this?"

"Devastated, obviously. But Monica said there's no room for two women in the same house—so you'd better clear up some wall space."

I laugh, leaning back in my chair, propping my feet up on an unopened travel book about Patagonia.

"So, how'd this happen? Did you bribe Monica, or did she blackmail you?"

"More like an ultimatum."

I shake my head. "And you caved?"

"Like an avalanche, my friend. But hey, that's where you come in—best man duties. You up for it?"

I glance at the poster of Jonny Moseley, frozen in time, perfectly balanced between gravity and defiance. It's that 2002 Olympic moment—the "Dinner Roll" that cost him the gold but changed mogul skiing forever. His body twisted impossibly against the blue Utah sky, breaking every rule the judges knew how to score.

He knew he wouldn't win with it. Did it anyway.

I'd framed that poster not because he was a champion, but because he'd chosen truth over medals. His own vision over validation. Sometimes I wonder if I have that kind of courage—to choose the path that feels right even when everyone tells you it's wrong.

"So, Moseley wasn't available?"

"Nope. Neither was Warren Miller or Pauly Shore, so here we are—bottom of the barrel."

I groan dramatically. "I'm behind Pauly? Brutal."

"That's why they call him 'The Weasel,' buh-dee."

I laugh, shaking my head.

"But seriously, man," I say, my voice softening, "I'm honored. I am so happy for you."

And I mean it.

After we hang up, I sit in the quiet of my office, surrounded by the evidence of my life—moments captured, frozen in time. Brandon and Monica. It makes sense, somehow. Two people deciding to build something permanent in a world that never stops moving.

I swivel in my chair, taking in the chaos around me. My life is built for motion—camera bags always half-packed, passport in the top drawer, flight schedules tacked to the corkboard. I've spent years chasing perfect light across continents, collecting moments but never staying in one place long enough to string them together.

Sometimes I wonder what it would be like—to choose one view instead of always searching for the next one. To build something that doesn't fit in a camera bag.

I stand and walk to the window, looking out at the Flatirons rising above Boulder. They've been there forever, unmoved by storm or season. I've photographed them a hundred times in different light, but never thought about what it means to choose your mountain and stay.

The thought doesn't settle easily. It shifts uncomfortably, like a pack weighted wrong for a long hike.

I turn back to my desk and reach for the Patagonia book, flipping it open to a dog-eared page. There's always another horizon. Another shot waiting to be framed.

And for now, I guess that's enough.

I watch my own reflection, studying the girl in the mirror as if she's someone else. The flowers in my hair are delicate and wild, weaving through my curls like something untouched, something free. Their subtle fragrance mingles with the scent of nerves and anticipation. The dress flows around me like water, moving with my breath. It feels light, effortless. Then why does my chest feel so heavy?

Through the window, late afternoon light spills across the dressing room floor. From somewhere beyond the door comes the murmur of voices, laughter, the quiet orchestration of a day planned for months.

Allison appears in the mirror behind me, her bridesmaid dress slightly wrinkled already, champagne flute in hand. Her third, if I'm counting correctly.

"It's not too late to run," she says. "I've got my Harley out back, full tank of gas, bottle of Don Julio in the saddlebag. We could be in Vegas by morning."

Her eyes meet mine in the mirror. I can't help but smile. Brash and honest. Exactly what I need in this moment.

I trace the embroidery on the fabric, my fingers trembling slightly as they brush over the delicate lace. So many stitches, so many small details woven together into something whole. Is love like that? A thousand small, fragile moments—stitched together, hoping they'll hold?

I exhale, smoothing the dress over my hips. This should feel different. I should feel different. Maybe I do. Maybe that's the problem. I close my eyes, listening to my own heartbeat, searching for an answer in the silence. My throat tightens around words I haven't said. Questions I haven't asked.

Beyond the mirror, life waits. I'm not rushing. I'm not hesitating. For the first time in a long time, I am stepping toward something certain. I exhale, slow and steady. Then, with quiet resolve, I turn away from the mirror and walk forward.

Allison reappears in the doorway, champagne glass refilled. She stops short, taking me in from head to toe. Her expression shifts from her usual sardonic mask to something rare—genuine awe. She nods slowly, a wicked smile spreading across her face.

"That works," she says. "If he doesn't fuck you tonight, I will."

Coming from anyone else, it would be shocking. Coming from Allison, it's the highest compliment possible. And somehow, exactly what I needed to hear.

I laugh—grateful, grounded.

Then, without warning, she pulls me into a hug. It's brief, tight, no-nonsense—very Allison. But it lands.

She leans back, her voice quieter now, just for me.

"Alright, ready to make a lifelong mistake?"

And suddenly, I'm not nervous anymore. I'm ready.

I tug at the tie again, the silk slipping through my fingers like water. I've never been good at this part—the details, the finishing touches, the things that are supposed to make a man look polished, put-together. I exhale, rolling my shoulders, trying to shake the tension creeping up my spine.

Martone's arms wrap around my waist, her touch warm, steady. The familiar scent of her perfume—peony and white tea, delicate and impossibly clean—fills the space between us. She rests her chin on my shoulder, watching me in the mirror, our reflections pressed together like two puzzle pieces that—on paper—should fit.

"Here," she murmurs, reaching forward. Her fingers brush mine as she effortlessly straightens the tie, fixing what I couldn't.

I hold my breath for a moment, caught between comfort and confinement.

Her touch lingers, a soft kiss pressing against my cheek. She is sure of us. That should be enough. Our eyes meet in the mirror. She smiles—gentle, trusting, full of quiet certainty. I want to believe I can reflect it back.

Then, just as effortlessly, she slips out of view. I don't turn to watch her go. Instead, I stare at the man left behind in the glass.

Both of us were skiing solo that day at Mary Jane—each pretending we preferred it. She made a joke about my retro Coyote skis. I laughed and said they were vintage, not old. The lift ride was too short, but somehow we ended up at the same bar at the bottom. Two beers later, we were already pretending it was fate. Maybe it was. Or maybe we were just two people tired of being alone who decided not to be. We exchanged numbers. And now—here we are.

From downstairs, I can hear the soft murmur of conversation, the occasional burst of laughter. Mom's voice is warm and eager, offering another cup of coffee, asking questions about Martone's life. I can tell she's pulling out all the stops to make Martone feel welcome—a woman she met for the first time just yesterday.

It's strange, watching them together. Thirty-four years old, and this is the first time I've brought someone home. Mom didn't say anything about that, but I caught her looking at us, studying Martone's hand in mine, as if trying to gauge how solid this thing between us really is. What does it mean that I've never done this before? What does it mean that I'm doing it now?

The tie is perfect now. But why do I feel like I'm wearing someone else's life? Somewhere else, another reflection. A different mirror. A different kind of certainty.

Cannon Beach - Oregon

The Pacific stretches endlessly, its waves rolling toward the shore in a slow, rhythmic embrace at Cannon Beach. Salt-laced air mingles with the scent of wildflowers woven into the driftwood arch standing against the backdrop of Haystack Rock—ancient, immovable, eternal.

The sky, a mix of soft gray and shifting gold, mirrors the restless tide. A gust of wind catches the delicate fabric of my gown, sending it rippling like seafoam. The wind moves through my hair, twisting it into loose curls, but I don't fight it. The ocean is always shifting, always pulling, always carrying things away.

I stare at the waves rolling toward the shore, their rhythm steady, endless. The sand is cool beneath my bare feet, and I curl my toes into it, grounding myself.

Ethan's hand is warm in mine. Solid. Certain. I glance up at him—his eyes are steady, filled with quiet joy. The same eyes that had watched me work under the Peru sun, that had found me by lantern light in village after village. He squeezes my fingers gently, as if to remind me that I'm not alone in this moment. The officiant speaks, but his words blur into the sound of the tide.

This is real.

The chairs are arranged in a crescent, our friends and family gathered close, their feet sinking into the sand. I catch my grandmother's soft smile, my mother dabbing at her eyes with a tissue. They are happy. They believe in this. Allison stands slightly apart, champagne glass mysteriously still full, her usual armor momentarily lowered as she watches us with what might almost be described as softness.

A little girl laughs as the tide sneaks up, swirling around her ankles. Her mother pulls her back, but she keeps giggling, delighted at the ocean's game.

⦿

I inhale deeply, the salt air filling my lungs. I have always loved the ocean. Its vastness, its mystery, the way it carries things away yet always returns something new to the shore.

The vows come. My voice doesn't shake. I don't hesitate. The words spill from my lips, soft but strong, carried away by the wind. Promises to stand beside him, not in his shadow. To build something together that will last beyond ourselves. To remember what brought us here—service, purpose, the belief that love does more than comfort; it transforms.

Ethan's voice is steady as he promises to honor my wildness, to never clip my wings, to build a home that is both shelter and launch-pad. The words echo the conversations we've had across continents, in moments stolen between purpose and duty.

And then, Ethan's lips meet mine.

A cheer rises, petals scatter into the breeze, and for a moment, the world feels still. I exhale, my fingers tightening around his.

I chose this. Not from fear or convention or expectations, but from the same place inside me that chose to leave Berkeley behind. From the part of me that recognizes truth when it presents itself, however unexpected the package.

Beyond us, the waves keep rolling in. The tide always moves forward.

Last Dollar Road - Telluride

The Telluride sky stretches endlessly above me, a canvas of deep blues and drifting clouds. Below it, the rugged beauty of Last Dollar Road unfolds like something untouched by time. Mount Wilson looms in the distance, its snow-dusted peak standing guard over the valley. The golden aspens sway gently in the crisp mountain air, their leaves shimmering like tiny pieces of light.

I sit near the back, watching as guests gather in a meadow at the edge of the world—a place where the earth meets the sky. A simple wooden arch, draped in wildflowers and sage, marks the spot where Brandon and Monica now stand, hand in hand. The wind carries the scent of pine and late-summer grass.

Brandon's face is open, unguarded in a way I've rarely seen. When he looks at Monica, it's not just love—it's certainty.

The officiant speaks, but the words drift past me in fragments. Love. Partnership. Building something together that time can't erode. Taking a leap and trusting that someone will catch you.

Then—cheers erupt.

Brandon kisses Monica, sealing the moment. A local bluegrass band strikes up a tune, the joyous sound weaving through the valley. Guests toss flower petals, laughter spilling into the mountain air. ♪

Brandon dips her in a dramatic flourish, and she throws her head back, eyes bright with happiness. I can't help but smile. Brandon, the guy who once swore he'd never settle down, just proved himself wrong.

As the sun begins to sink, painting the sky in violets and ambers, the reception unfolds beneath strings of fairy lights. Long wooden tables, draped in simple linens, overflow with wildflowers and flickering lanterns. Plates are full, glasses never empty, and laughter drifts through the air like an old song everyone somehow remembers.

♪ *"Red Dirt Girl"* by Emmylou Harris

⟨⟩

I sit beside Martone, a slice of wedding cake in one hand, a champagne flute in the other. Around us, people dance—slow, easy movements, soft steps, shared smiles.

At the center of it all, Brandon and Monica sway together to a bluegrass melody—something slow and warm, played live by a small quartet tucked under a string of hanging lights. Mandolin, fiddle, upright bass, and acoustic guitar, weaving a kind of quiet magic. No amplification. No flash. Just wood, string, and breath—pure and steady, like something that's always been true. ♪

They move in perfect time, like the rest of the world has dropped away—just the two of them, dancing like they've been doing it for decades. The music curls around them, soft and sincere, and something presses in my chest. A quiet ache I don't quite know what to do with. Not regret, not exactly. Just that hollow space where longing likes to sit.

Martone lifts her champagne flute, watching me over the rim. Her voice is soft, almost playful—but I hear something else beneath it.

"Does it make you want to get married?"

I turn the glass in my hands, watching the bubbles rise and break at the surface.

"It makes me want to drink more champagne."

She laughs, shaking her head. She leans in, stealing a bite of cake from my plate. She doesn't press for more. Maybe she already knows the answer. And the truth is—I have looked at someone that way. Not in a single moment. But over time. The girl on the bench. Every day at three. Always in the same spot, always still, like the world moved differently around her.

♪ *"Restless"* by Alison Krauss

⟁

The music shifts—The kind of song that settles into your bones before you realize it's there.. I never spoke to her. Never even heard her voice. But something about her presence—the way she sat with the day, the way the light touched her hair, the way she seemed to belong to some other rhythm—stayed with me. ♪

It wasn't love. Not exactly. But it was something that lived near it. Recognition, maybe. Of something I didn't know I was searching for until I saw her. A stillness I didn't know I craved. A kind of gravity that pulled at me without asking permission. And if that's not love... maybe it's the part that happens first. The part that lingers, even when everything else fades.

Martone is steady. Kind. Beautiful. She loves to ski moguls. We've built something real—habits, holidays, years stacked gently between us. But I've never looked at her the way Brandon looks at Monica. And I know she's never seen that look on my face.

I take another slow sip of champagne, eyes drifting back to the dance floor—to Brandon, to the ease in his body, to the certainty in his smile. The ache tightens. Quiet. Familiar.

Then I look at her. Martone. Right here beside me. Her laughter easy. Her presence solid. Her hand resting lightly on mine, as if it belongs there. And it does. She's real. She's present. She chose me.

But in the soft glow of lantern light, with the music still rising around us, I wonder if I'm only halfway here. If I've been holding on to something that never had a chance to begin. If I'm stringing her along without meaning to.

I want to be in it. I want to be all the way in. But something in me still looks back. Still scans the crowd. Still listens for footsteps

♪ "Angel from Montgomery" by Bonnie Raitt

that never arrives. The guilt creeps in like fog. She deserves more than a man who loves her gently, but elsewhere. I take her hand anyway. Squeeze it lightly. She squeezes back.

Above me, the mountains remain—vast, endless, unshaken. And I sit beside a woman who has always shown up. While I quietly yearn for someone I never even met.

Brandon's wedding was over, and one by one, everyone was filtering back to their real lives. Martone had to get back to work, so we hopped in the Jeep for a quick ride up to the airport so she could catch her flight back to Denver.

"It was a beautiful wedding," she said softly, staring out the window.

"Yeah," I agreed. "Perfect for them."

For them.

Not for us. The unspoken words hovered between us like a third passenger. I felt her eyes on me then, searching. The same look she'd given me when she asked if the wedding made me want to get married. I'd deflected—something about champagne—but we both knew what my silence meant.

We rolled through the valley past Reggie's station. And then I saw it.

Sophia's house.

Faded blue trim. A porch sagging just enough to be honest. Lilac bushes tangled up the railing, still green even in the heat. It stopped me—just for a second—but long enough for Martone to notice.

"Everything okay?" she asked, tilting her head, eyes scanning mine.

I nodded quickly. I gave her hand a gentle squeeze and offered a smile that didn't quite make it all the way up. She didn't press, but I felt her thumb go still.

We reached the airport a few minutes later. She adjusted the strap on her carry-on as I pulled to a stop at the drop-off zone. The good-bye was soft. Familiar.

"I'll call you tonight," she said. I kissed her goodbye, nodded like a proper boyfriend, and watched her disappear through the doors.

I slipped on my sunglasses as I headed back toward town, the late afternoon sun still high and relentless. Martone's goodbye kiss lingered on my cheek, but as the airport shrank behind me, something in my chest began to loosen. A knot I hadn't realized was there started to unravel, and in its place bloomed something I wasn't proud of—relief.

I rolled the windows down, letting the dry mountain air whip through the Jeep, tossing the thoughts out of my head one by one. Sun-baked pine. Dust. The scent of sage somewhere in the distance. It smelled like home. Or what used to be.

And then came the question I didn't want to answer:

What kind of man feels relief when saying goodbye to someone he's supposed to love?

I adjusted my grip on the steering wheel. It wasn't that I didn't care for Martone—I did. When I told her I loved her, I meant it. But I'd never looked at her the way Brandon looked at Monica. And she knew it.

The truth pressed against my ribs: I was always halfway there with her. Holding something back. Martone deserved more than a man who loved her gently —from a distance.

I told myself I'd head straight back. But the image of that faded blue house kept pulling at me. A loose thread I'd left hanging years ago.

When it came into view again, I didn't drive past it this time. I let off the gas. Slowed. Pulled onto the shoulder, gravel crunching under the tires as the Jeep rolled to a stop. For a moment, I just sat there, engine idling, hands on the wheel.

I didn't even know if it was really her house. Could've been a friend's place, or a memory I'd rewritten too many times. All I knew was that I'd stood on that porch once. I'd knocked. No one answered. I told myself I'd come back.

But I didn't. Not until now.

I pulled into the driveway and killed the engine. The silence hit instantly—just the ticking of metal and the distant call of birds. I stepped out, sun soaking into my shirt, and climbed the creaking porch steps. I remembered the sound of the creak.

I knocked.

A moment later, the door opened. A kind-looking older woman stood there, silver hair soft around her face. A ceiling fan hummed somewhere behind her.

"Afternoon," I said. "Sorry to bother you. I was just passing by and wondered—do you happen to know someone named Sophia? I think she might've lived here once."

◯

Her expression softened. "Sophia, you say?" She shook her head.

"No, I'm afraid not. I've only been renting this place a few years. Don't know anything about who came before me."

I nodded, trying to hide the flicker of disappointment. "Thanks anyway. I appreciate your time."

She studied me for a beat, her gaze sharpening. "Mind if I ask why you're looking for her?"

I hesitated, then told the truth. "She was someone I always meant to meet. I just never had the courage. I guess I'm trying to fix that now."

Her expression softened. "Ah," she said, almost to herself. "Sometimes, wondering is heavier than regret."

She looked at me, thoughtful. "Sounds like love."

I glanced away, then nodded. "It was. At first sight." I let out a dry laugh. "Feels foolish, saying that out loud."

But the moment I said it, I knew it wasn't foolish. Or at least not just foolish. It's easy to mock the idea—love at first sight. Sounds like a tagline from a movie trailer. But I remember the way my heart stalled. The way everything else dimmed around her. It wasn't logic. It wasn't even timing. It was recognition. Like something old in me woke up. Like I'd been waiting to meet her without knowing I was waiting at all.

I spent years telling myself it wasn't love. But it was actually. It just didn't look the way I thought it would.

She smiled gently. "It's not foolish. Love doesn't always announce

itself. Sometimes it's quiet. It's in the way you stay. The way you show up." A beat passed. "Took me a long time to learn that."

Her words settled over me like shade on a hot day.

"I hope I find that kind of love someday," I said.

"You will," she replied, certain as a sunrise. "Love's got a way of finding you when you're finally ready."

I smiled, thanked her, and walked back to the Jeep. Her voice echoed in my mind as I pulled away, the house shrinking in the rearview mirror— just another thread from the past I never quite picked up.

But for the first time, I didn't feel regret. Not exactly. Just something quieter. Something steadier.

Maybe hope.

We've been married awhile now, and I'm still not used to the weight of Ethan's arm draped across my waist, the rhythm of his breathing beside me. I slide out from under his embrace carefully, bare feet meeting the cool hardwood floor.

Our apartment in Queen Anne feels both foreign and familiar—a space we're slowly making our own. Ethan's humanitarian journals stacked beside my poetry collections. His utilitarian furniture softened by the pillows and throws I've added. Compromise made visible

I move to the kitchen and start the coffee, watching steam rise from the pot. The gold band on my finger catches the light. Mrs. Sophia Callahan. The name still feels like borrowed clothing I'm trying to break in.

⟨O⟩

Beyond the window, the city is already alive—people rushing to work, to school, to their own versions of ordinary life. Rain taps against the glass, a gentle percussion that reminds me of waves on sand. Not the dramatic crash of Cannon Beach, but a quieter rhythm. The everyday kind.

From our hillside apartment, I can glimpse Elliott Bay in the distance, the water gray beneath the clouded sky. On clear days, the Olympic Mountains rise beyond, but today they're hidden, shrouded in mist and low clouds. Seattle in autumn—familiar in its perpetual dampness.

I think of our wedding often—that perfect collision of elements. The vastness of the ocean, the solidity of Haystack Rock, the wind moving through everything. I had felt both anchored and free in that moment, certain in a way I rarely am.

I steam milk for my latte, watching it froth and curl while Ethan's plain black coffee brews beside it. Even here, in this small ritual, our differences surface. He takes his coffee like he approaches life—straightforward, undiluted. I prefer mine transformed, layers of flavor and texture.

I wrap my hands around the warm mug. Marriage is nothing like our wedding day. It's smaller. Quieter. It's decisions about grocery lists and whose turn it is to do laundry. Always me, it seems. It's learning that he needs silence in the mornings and conversation at night, while I'm exactly the opposite.

It's the way Ethan always squeezes toothpaste from the middle of the tube, no matter how many times I fix it. It's learning that he needs silence in the mornings and conversation at night, while I'm exactly the opposite.

I carry my latte to the small balcony and sit, watching raindrops collect on the railing. When I was younger, I always thought marriage would feel like some fundamental transformation—that I would become different, more complete somehow. But I'm still me. Just me with a different last name, a shared address, a responsibility to someone else's happiness.

Sometimes I wonder if Ethan notices how I still curl away at night, creating space between us even in sleep. How I still keep Anne Carson's *Plainwater* on my nightstand, even though I've read it so many times I could recite entire passages without turning a page. How I still struggle with the old impulse to disappear sometimes—to slip away, just for a day, maybe two, and drive west until the land runs out.

To the coast.

To that wild, ragged stretch of Oregon where the land meet the sea without apology. Where the Pacific doesn't whisper or lap politely— it roars. It crashes and hurls itself onto the shore like it's trying to remember its own name. There's nothing polite about it. No softness. Just force and rhythm and salt in your mouth. I go there in my mind when things feel too still. I think about the cold wind tearing at my sleeves, the roar in my ears louder than thought.

That kind of power makes everything else smaller. Manageable. It reminds me that the world is still moving, even when I feel stuck.

Sometimes I ache for that noise—for that honest, physical reminder that not everything needs to be folded into meaning. Some things just are.

Other times, I wish Allison would just drop in unexpectedly, kick the door open, and say, "Let's get the fuck out of here," before scooping me up on her Harley.

I wonder if Ethan would understand that. But he doesn't ask about these things. Perhaps he understands that loving someone doesn't mean possessing all their corners and shadows. Or perhaps he's afraid of what I might say.

The rain picks up, drumming harder against the balcony overhang. I close my eyes and imagine it's the ocean—imagine I'm standing on that beach again, sand between my toes, the whole world open before me. But when I open my eyes, I'm still here. In this life I've chosen. In this life we're building.

I hear Ethan stirring inside, the familiar sound of him moving through our shared space. In a moment, he'll join me with his own cup of coffee. He'll kiss the top of my head, comment on the rain, ask what I want to do today. And I'll lean into him slightly, our shoulders touching—a small gesture of connection.

I chose this. And I choose it again each morning when I wake.

Behind me, the door slides open.

"Hey," Ethan says, his voice still rough with sleep. "You're up early."

I turn and smile at him, making space on the small bench. My eyes meet his in quiet acknowledgment. No words needed.

He sits beside me, our shoulders touching. We look out at the city together, at the rain washing everything clean. For now, this is enough. This quiet togetherness, this shared moment of peace before the day begins.

The vastness of the ocean is still there, somewhere beyond the city skyline. Always shifting, always pulling. But here, in this moment, I am still. I am anchored. And there is beauty in that too.

Jensen's Photo - Boulder

I hadn't meant to stop in. But something about the sign—*Jensen's Photo & Lab, Est. 1974*—tugged at me. Part muscle memory, part something quieter. Something like grief. The kind that doesn't announce itself, just pulls you sideways without asking.

I stepped inside. The place was part camera shop, part museum. Glass display cases lined the walls like quiet shrines to the past, each lens displayed under soft light, untouched but waiting. And then the smell hit me—dust, metal, a trace of oil… and something else. Something imagined but unmistakable: fixer. Like the air itself remembered the darkroom.

I ran my hand along the edge of a counter, fingers brushing against a stack of black-and-white prints someone had left out. The edges curled slightly. Real film. Real paper. Grain you could feel.

I live in the darkroom. Hours bent under red light, fingers stained, the smell of developer sharp in my nose. There is a rhythm to it—measure, pour, agitate, wait. The stillness of it. The hush. Watching an image rise from the paper like memory made physical. You don't forget that.

"Need help with something?" came a voice from the back.

The salesman looked younger than the camera around my neck. Maybe early twenties. Ponytail, graphic tee, hands smudged from adjusting something mechanical a minute ago.

I lifted my Nikon F5 slightly. "I'm starting to feel like this isn't the future anymore."

He smiled, not unkindly. "You're right. It's the past. A beautiful past, but… past."

He walked over to the glass case near the register and unlocked it, pulling out a matte black body with practiced care. "If you're serious about going digital—this one's for real. Nikon D2. Solid. Fast. Built like a tank."

I stepped forward, my eyes locking on the familiar lettering. Nikon D2. The second generation. The kind of body made for someone who didn't want to compromise just because the world had moved on.

He slid it across the counter toward me. "Twelve-point-four megapixels. Full-frame sensor. Shoots five frames a second. Dual card slots. It'll take a beating and still keep up with you."

I picked it up. Heavy. Balanced. Purposeful. My hands wrapped around it instinctively, like muscle memory already knew how to hold the future.

"ISO range's clean up to sixteen hundred," he added. "You can push it farther, but you probably won't need to. And the autofocus? It's like cheating."

I brought it to my eye. *Click*. Not the clunk of the F5. Not the sharp slap of a mirror. Just the clean, quiet tick of progress.

Still Nikon. Still deliberate. Just faster. Sharper. Evolved. I lowered the camera, still holding it in both hands like something alive.

"You shoot?" I asked.

"Every day," he said. "Nature, mostly. Sometimes street. It's about the moment, right? Tools change, but what we're chasing doesn't."

◍

I nodded, thinking of all the years I'd spent lugging gear through airports, jungles, cities. Thirty-six exposures at a time. The long nights waiting for chemicals to do their slow, sacred work. That magic had been real. But it wasn't where the industry was headed. And the stories I wanted to tell—were moving faster now.

"I miss the darkroom sometimes," I said, half to myself. "The smell. The quiet. The red light and waiting."

He smiled. "I hear that a lot."

Still holding the D2, I looked around the store one more time.

The past was everywhere. But so was the future.

The future. Sitting in my hands.

I pulled out my wallet and placed my card on the counter.

"I'll take it."

He grinned. "You won't regret it."

Maybe not. But as I walked out with the box tucked under my arm, I knew what I'd miss—the hush of the red light. The ache of waiting for an image to appear. The alchemy of time and light and chemistry.

Still—what mattered hadn't changed. The work was the same: chasing moments, catching truth mid-motion. If this was the tool now, I had to catch up—before I became part of the past I currently document.

Because the story was still out there.

⦾

And I still had something to say.

Ban Saensam - Laos

The sun breaks late over the Mekong, mist curling off the surface like breath. Roosters have been crowing since before dawn, but the village doesn't stir until the heat begins to press itself into the day like a weight.

We've been in Laos for four months now, stationed in a small riverside community in Champasak Province. The Corps kept us together—newly married and still learning how to read each other's rhythms. Our work centers around WASH—water, sanitation, and hygiene.

Ethan's in charge of infrastructure: building latrines, mapping water lines, designing low-cost filtration systems with whatever materials we can source locally. I've taken on the education component—partnering with women's groups, developing flipbooks and illustrated guides, teaching the basics of handwashing, water safety, and waste management to children who have never seen soap in a bottle.

It's not glamorous. But it's vital.

This morning, we're back at Ban Saensam, one of the smaller villages tucked along the river's edge. The community well was contaminated during last year's floods, and Ethan's been helping install a gravity-fed system using a capped spring further up the hill. The parts arrived late. The labor never does.

Now, he's crouched beside the spring, gesturing to a group of teenage boys clustered around him, sleeves rolled, his hair darkened with sweat. His voice rises in gentle explanation—slower, clearer. He repeats a word in Lao until one of the boys grins and mirrors the movement he's shown. Ethan's always been patient. Especially with others.

I'm at the base of the hill, sitting cross-legged with a circle of children, most too young for school but curious and eager to mimic. I hold up a hand-drawn flipbook—a story of a girl who washes her hands and keeps her family healthy. They watch each page with the reverence of a bedtime story, wide-eyed and still.

Afterward, I tie a rope between two poles and hang the water jugs we brought. A tippy-tap station. I guide one girl's hands under the flow—slow, careful, deliberate. Her name is Nok. She giggles, her joy bright and sudden, like the splash of water against sun-warmed stone. The others line up behind her, ready to try—small palms outstretched, eyes bright with something that feels like hope.

The next day, Ethan kneels beside the cistern we're helping to build—a half-finished concrete square surrounded by buckets, tools, and curious children. His hands are caked in mud, shirt already soaked through. But his voice—steady, patient—carries over the hammering and the hum of cicadas as he explains something to the village chief's teenage son. Even with the language barrier, they understand each other. Purpose translates easily.

I stand a few steps away, notebook in hand, jotting down supply counts and timelines. My fingers ache. Not from the writing—but from holding onto something I can't quite name.

Everything around us is vivid. Tangible. Women pass with woven baskets strapped to their backs, filled with mangoes and small fish caught in handwoven traps. The air smells like rice, diesel, and something sweet I still haven't identified. The world here is whole. Rooted. It should be enough.

And maybe it is.

⦿

But lately, the days have started to blur. Not with boredom, but with a kind of internal stillness I can't explain. A silence that doesn't feel like peace.

Ethan calls over his shoulder, smiling as he holds up a length of pipe. I smile back, automatic. He's in his element—solving, fixing, helping. His sense of direction has always been clearer than mine. I've admired that about him. Still do.

Later, I conduct another handwashing demo with the local school kids. We've brought tippy-tap kits made from string, sticks, and old water jugs—simple things they can recreate themselves. The children gather beneath the tamarind trees, squatting in neat rows, feet bare and eyes alert.

I pull out a homemade puppet—stitched from scrap fabric with a painted-on grin—and begin the lesson. I move through the motions slowly, deliberately. They mimic each step, some giggling, others stone-serious in their focus. One small girl—Maly—tugs on my sleeve and points to her hands, holding them out like a question.

Yes, I nod. Yours too.

There's a simplicity to it all. A beauty. I watch them take turns at the tippy-tap, laughing as the water trickles over their fingers. They're proud of the act itself—of doing it right, of being seen.

That evening, we walk the edge of the rice fields, our boots pressing shallow prints into the wet earth. Ethan brushes his knuckles against mine—not quite holding my hand. Not quite letting go.

We talk about next steps—where the Peace Corps might place us after this, whether we'll request another joint assignment. Ethan speaks with ease, already dreaming ahead. I nod, but my thoughts wander.

◎

"You know," he says after a while, "they asked if we'd consider an extension. Maybe Cambodia next. Could be good. Real need there."

I don't answer. Just walk a little slower. He studies my face. I can feel it.

"This matters," he says. "What we're doing here—this is real."

I nod once. Small. Not disagreement. Not agreement. Just… noted. But some part of me wonders if I came here to find something—or to run from it.

What if I wanted a front porch and a routine? A place where laundry dried on a line that didn't also serve as a mosquito net? What if I wanted to write more, get a cat, grow herbs in a crooked clay pot? What if this kind of giving—beautiful, essential—wasn't the only way I was meant to serve?

He asks if I'm tired. I say I'm fine.

He kisses my temple anyway, brushing dirt from my cheek with a thumb worn calloused from tools. "We're doing good work," he says.

I nod. We are.

But as we cross the field, barefoot children waving at us from a cluster of banana trees, I feel the edges of something shift. Not doubt, exactly. Just a quiet wondering.

Is it okay to love this life and still want something else? I miss nothing in particular. And yet—I miss something all the same.

That night, I sit outside our small house, feet in the dust, stars unfurling above the trees like scattered ash. The frogs call to each other, relentless and full of life. Inside, Ethan sleeps curled around the breeze of a fan that barely works.

I can still smell the river in my hair—

San Miguel River - Sawpit

—I breath in the familiar scent of water on stone. The river runs clear this time of year, water rushing over smooth stones, curling into pockets and eddies before continuing its journey downward. I stand knee-deep in the cool current, feeling it push against me—persistent but not overpowering. Grandfather is upstream about thirty yards, his movements measured and deliberate as he works his line.

I watch him for a moment—the rhythmic back-and-forth of his cast, the gentle landing of the fly on the water's surface. At seventy-four, he still moves with a grace that seems to belong to the river itself. I turn my attention back to my own section of water, trying to mirror his patience.

The rod feels like an extension of my arm as I cast, the line unfurling above me, then settling on the water with a touch too heavy. Grandfather notices—he notices everything on the river.

"Lighter," he calls, his voice carrying over the water's constant murmur. "You're announcing yourself. Fish don't appreciate introductions."

I nod, adjusting my grip. The next cast is better—the fly lands with barely a ripple. Grandfather gives me a slight nod, the closest thing to effusive praise in his vocabulary.

We work the river in comfortable silence, moving upstream at a pace that feels like standing still. The mountains rise around us, indifferent to our presence, the late afternoon sun casting long shadows across the water. Time moves differently here—measured in casts and currents rather than minutes and hours.

"Getting skunked today," Grandfather says after a while, though there's no disappointment in his voice.

"Sorry about that," I reply, feeling somehow responsible for the fish's lack of interest.

He shakes his head, a small smile tugging at the corner of his mouth. "Some days the river gives. Some days it doesn't. Fishing isn't about catching fish."

He pauses, eyeing a promising ripple in the water. "Fishing is about learning to read what's beneath the surface. About understanding that what you think you see isn't always what's there."

He casts again, his line arcing perfectly before settling where the water breaks over a submerged rock. "Life's a lot like that. Most people spend their time watching the surface—the obvious things, the distractions. They miss what's happening in the deeper currents."

I consider this as I make another cast. "So what's the trick? How do you learn to see what's underneath?"

"Patience," he says simply. "Attention. And knowing when to be still." He reels in his line, adjusting the fly before casting again. "When I was younger, I was always rushing. Always pushing the river, so to speak. Took me years to learn that sometimes you just need to wait, to observe. The river reveals itself to those who pay attention."

The sun dips lower, turning the water to liquid gold. Neither of us has caught anything, but it doesn't seem to matter. This ritual has never really been about the fish.

"You're still looking for her, aren't you?" Grandfather asks suddenly, his eyes still on the water.

The question catches me off guard. "Who?"

"That girl who walked out the door. The one with the beautiful hair."

I don't ask how he knows about Sophia. Grandfather has always had a way of seeing the currents beneath my surface.

"Sometimes," I admit. A half-truth—she's always there, just beneath everything else.

He nods, as if confirming something to himself. "Some fish, you have to cast a hundred times before they'll rise to the fly. And some never will, no matter how perfect your cast." He looks at me then, his eyes clear and steady as the river. "The question is whether the waiting is making you whole or hollow."

I don't have an answer for that.

We fish until the light begins to fade, the shadows stretching across the water, the air growing cool against our skin. We catch nothing, but as we walk back along the riverbank, rods balanced on our shoulders, I feel somehow more settled than when we began.

"Remember what I said," Grandfather tells me as we load our gear into the back of the Jeep. "It's not about the catching. It's about learning to read what's beneath the surface."

◎

Delta 166

The plane shudders through turbulence. I tighten my grip on the arm-rest, watching Ethan's profile as he stares out the window. Twenty-six hours into our journey home from Laos, and we haven't really talked. Not about what matters.

Outside, darkness swallows everything except the red blinking wing light. This liminal space between worlds feels fitting somehow.

We left yesterday. The goodbyes were harder than I expected—Nok's handwoven bracelet still tight on my wrist, Maly clinging to my legs until her mother gently pulled her away. The village chief made a speech that Mr. Phoumi translated with careful dignity. Something about water bringing life. About remembering.

Ethan pulls out his journal—worn leather, pages swollen from humidity. He's been adding to a list for the past hour. I already know what it is: opportunities, possibilities, other places that need him. The world is always full of places that need someone. Lately, he can't stop talking about a mission in Cambodia—another village, another chance to help, to do good. To keep going.

I reach for my own notebook. Inside are scraps of poetry and half-formed thoughts. Observations about how light moved across the rice fields at dusk, how children's laughter sounded like water, how I sometimes stood by the river and felt both fully alive and like I was floating outside myself.

I imagine our apartment—dusty from absence. The fern in the kitchen window, likely dead. The quiet of a space without roosters, without generators, without responsibility humming in my bones.

What I crave isn't luxury—it's rhythm. Predictability. I want to plant something and be there long enough to see it bloom. Wake up in the same bed. Know the name of my neighbor's dog.

I think about a garden. Nothing elaborate—just a strip of earth along a fence, something I could tend. Basil, maybe. Nasturtiums. Tomatoes that split when it rains too hard. A chair nearby. A place where I'd sit long enough to watch something grow from nothing and know I helped it get there.

I feel myself wanting roots. They matter to me now in a way I didn't understand before Laos. Before I watched families who could name their ancestors back seven generations, all on the same piece of earth.

But there's another voice in me too—the one that wonders who I become when I stop moving. What happens to purpose when it no longer comes stamped with urgency and foreign coordinates?

I feel different. Maybe that's what happens when you leave pieces of yourself scattered across the world.

The wing light keeps blinking. Steady. Reliable. Something to navigate by. I don't regret the life we've lived. The work. The places. The people. But I'm not sure if returning means I'm done with it. Or if I'm just... shifting. The plane begins its descent. Almost home. Whatever that means now—or if it means anything at all.

I think for a minute. Okay, maybe a few luxuries:

Gelato for sure. And maybe some Bubble Yum. Something sweet. Something ordinary. Something that says: I'm still here. Still becoming whoever I'm going to be.

11

20:63:19:18:46:01

The two pink lines appeared like a plot twist I never saw coming. I sat on the edge of the bathtub, the plastic test trembling slightly in my hands.

This wasn't supposed to happen.

Not now. Not when Ethan and I had just settled back into life stateside after a year long mission, when we were still adjusting to marriage, to permanent walls instead of temporary shelters. We are husband and wife, but still feeling our way through the dark of what it meant to build something lasting outside the intensity of field work.

My hand drifted to my stomach—still flat, unchanged. No visible evidence of the seismic shift occurring beneath my skin. How could something so small rewrite our entire future in an instant?

I'd never imagined myself as a mother. Not really. In the vague someday that lived on the other side of service. After we'd completed our commitment to the communities we'd worked in. After I'd figured out what I wanted beyond the structured purpose the Corps had given me. Motherhood was a distant shore I hadn't yet decided if I wanted to swim toward.

Yet here it was. Not asking permission. Not waiting for perfect timing.

When I showed Ethan the test, his face cycled through emotions too quickly to name—shock, fear, wonder, resolve. Then something settled in his eyes—a quiet certainty I envied.

We'll figure it out, he said, his hand covering mine. Simple words that somehow felt both inadequate and exactly right. We'd figured out how to purify water in remote villages, how to implement sustainable farming practices, how to communicate across language barriers. Surely we could figure out parenthood.

Obutiti - Uganda

This was my second tour in Uganda. The first had been different. The air had still been thick with need—but it was the kind you could name. Hunger. Malaria. Access. The simple, heartbreaking math of too little care and too few hands. It had been hard work, but the kind you could measure in vaccines administered, wells dug, beds built. The kind that let you sleep at night knowing you'd done something tangible.

We hadn't planned to come back so soon. We were supposed to rest. Reset. Try, for once, to build something just for ourselves. But when the call came, Ethan read me the message out loud, and I didn't need convincing. The need was too urgent. The clinic overrun. The outbreak spreading faster than supplies could catch up. There wasn't time to hesitate.

We said yes in the quiet way we always did—with a look, a nod, a shared silence that spoke louder than debate.

But this time, something feels different. The need is still there—maybe even greater. But the boundaries between what we can fix and what we can't... they've started to blur.

Maybe it's because I'm carrying something now that can't be measured in units of medicine or hours of labor. A different kind of urgency, quieter but no less real. One I haven't said out loud yet. Not to Ethan. Not even fully to myself. It's harder to draw clean lines when your body is already building a future inside you.

Back then, I worked in a small health outpost in Mbale. The people were open. The problems felt solvable, if only we had enough supplies, enough time. Children followed me through the villages laughing, curious. The elders offered stories and tea brewed over smoky fires. It felt safe. Fragile, yes—but whole.

But that was before the conflict intensified. Before the Lord's Resistance Army began its sweep through the north with greater force. Before the villages emptied at night. Before children started sleeping in groups near town centers just to avoid being abducted. Before the camps swelled with displaced families, all waiting for something that never seemed to come.

The stories came in fragments. A cousin taken. A school burned. A brother who joined the rebels because the alternative was death. Everyone knew someone. Everyone had lost someone.

This time, I had to check in with security officers twice a week. This time, there were maps taped inside the medical tent marking red zones. This time, the Peace Corps had almost said no—but Ethan and I had insisted. I didn't tell them I was pregnant.

Not yet.

Because I wasn't ready to admit I was different now, too. That something in me had shifted. That I didn't just see suffering anymore—I felt it in places I couldn't turn off. That now, every child who tugged at my shirt reminded me of someone who hadn't even been born yet.

Ethan had been stationed in Obutiti from the beginning—a larger, better-resourced village farther from the edge. He was overseeing logistical management and coordination for the region: supply lines, staff schedules, data collection for the Ministry of Health. It was important work, necessary work. But it kept him behind the lines.

Lukome, where I'd been assigned, was different. Smaller. Poorer. Closer to the red zones. Only a few clicks from the areas where rebel movement had been reported. It hadn't been the original plan. But when the original education lead had pulled out—illness, fear, no one said for sure—the Corps had needed someone experienced. Someone who could handle isolation, instability. Someone who wouldn't panic.

So they sent me.

Ethan hadn't liked it. He argued—quietly, but with heat—under the low hum of the lantern in our tent the night the assignment came through.

"This is a bad idea, and you know why."

I didn't respond. Just stared at the floor between us, one hand drifting unconsciously to my stomach. Not yet showing. Not really. But the knowing was there. The quiet pulse of something becoming.

He watched me. Waiting. But I had no defense to offer—only the weight of a choice I'd already made. Because someone had to go. Because I could do the work. Because walking away, even now, felt like abandoning a part of myself I wasn't ready to lose.

He didn't push it after that. Just exhaled—slow, heavy—and leaned his forehead to mine. We stayed like that for a long time, suspended between everything we feared and everything we didn't want to name.

"If anything happens," he whispered, "you run. Don't think."

I nodded.

Not because I agreed. But because it was easier than saying the truth out loud. That I wasn't sure I could.

Lukome - Uganda

The air is thick with smoke and heat—the kind that clings to your skin and doesn't let go. Off in the distance, gunfire cracks. Sharp, sudden. It's supposed to be "background noise" now. That's what people call it. Like birdsong or wind. But every time it snaps through the trees, I flinch.

My hand finds my belly—barely a swell beneath my shirt. It doesn't feel real. Not with the dust, the risk, the whispers of rebels just a few villages over. But the baby is real. I can feel it—quiet and wordless, but constant. Like breath.

The camp is makeshift. Tarps stretched between mango trees. Solar lanterns swinging in the branches like strange fruit. We've been here for two weeks, trying to rebuild the health clinic that was torched in the night—no one claimed responsibility, but we all know who it was. No one says the name out loud.

I keep my head low, my movements careful. Always listening. Always scanning. This isn't Laos. This isn't Malawi. The edge is sharper here. The air more brittle. Hope thins faster.

That's when I met Emmanuel. Nine, maybe ten. All limbs and long silence. He showed up the second day, barefoot and wary, hovering near the edge of the clearing while I unpacked boxes of gauze and gloves. He wore a faded yellow soccer jersey—Pele, #10—threadbare at the collar, the number cracked and peeling but still visible.

On the third day, he peeked in again, clutching a tattered notebook like it might protect him.

On the fourth, he spoke. "I used to have books," he said. "Before."

I didn't ask before what. He didn't need to say it.

I patted the spot beside me and handed him a roll of gauze. Taught him how to fold it into tight squares. Showed him how to refill the handwashing station and where to stack the bandage wraps. He didn't smile much. But he watched everything.

I pointed to the number of his shirt. He glanced down at his shirt, tugging the hem. "Pelé is the best," he said softly, like it was a fact no one could argue with. "He made magic with his feet."

On the next supply run, I had Ethan tuck a new soccer ball between the rehydration salts and sterile gloves. It wasn't much. But it was something just for him—a little sphere of joy in a world that had taken too much.

When I handed it to him, he didn't smile. Not at first. He just

◍

held it, reverent. Like he was holding Pelé's own name. Then he ran—laughing—and the others followed.

By the end of the week, he was helping the nurse organize the first-aid shelf. He carried himself differently then. Taller. Still quiet. But less invisible.

Yesterday, as I rinsed a cut on a toddler's foot, Emmanuel sat beside me, folding cloth strips with methodical care. My back ached more than usual, and when I paused, my hand drifted to my stomach.

He followed my gaze.

"You have a baby?" he asked.

I nodded. Small. Careful. A secret shared.

"You should leave here," he said.

There was no fear in his voice. Just fact. I wanted to tell him I would. That I was going. That it was already decided. But I didn't want to lie—not to this boy who had already seen too much of how the world breaks.

That night, after the others had eaten and the clinic lights dimmed, I sat alone beneath the trees with a warm cloth pressed to my lower back. The baby hadn't moved all day. I told myself that was normal. That I'd read that somewhere.

Still—I placed both hands on the small swell of my belly and whispered into the dark. Not a prayer. Not exactly. Just a promise.

I'm getting us out of here if the shit hits the fan.

Just as I stood to head back toward camp, headlights flickered through the trees.

An army transport rolled through the village—flatbed, camo, maybe a dozen soldiers packed tight in the back, rifles slung but eyes alert. One of them nodded at me through the haze as they passed, boots thudding softly against the wooden truckbed.

They didn't stop. Just kept moving. But it was enough.

I let out a breath I hadn't realized I was holding. Not safety exactly. But presence. A reminder that—for now—we weren't alone.

The courthouse clock's chimes fade into silence, the recital now complete. The reverberations seem to hang in the thin mountain air for a moment before dissipating completely.

3:00. I settle onto the wooden bench, the same one I've sat on a dozen times before. I love the sound of that clocktower ritual and what it's come to mean to me—a marker of consistency in a life where little else remains the same. Three o'clock. My time. Her time. Our time, though she doesn't know it.

The mountains stretch before me, their familiar silhouette etched against the blue Colorado sky. A couple passes by, hands entwined, lost in conversation. Two dogs chase each other across the street, their owners calling after them. Normal moments on a normal afternoon. Everything as it should be.

Except her.

3:07. The sun is warm on my face, the air clear and thin at this altitude. I try to recall Grandfather's words. About patience. About attention. About knowing when to be still.

Three days in a row I've come here now. Always at three. Always to this bench. Always looking for a woman from the past, whose name I only know from a newspaper article.

Like a whisper I wasn't meant to catch.

3:12. A flicker of movement catches my eye from the path on the left. But even before I fully turn, I know it's not her. Sophia moves with a grace that's unmistakable, a lightness I could recognize from a mile away.

This woman's steps are hurried, purposeful—nothing like Sophia's unhurried rhythm. I watch her pass, not even bothering to entertain false hope. When it's Sophia, I'll know. Her presence announces itself like nothing else.

I lean back, trying to relax the tension in my shoulders. What am I doing here? What am I hoping for? That she'll appear, sit beside me, and somehow the universe will arrange itself perfectly? That the woman who never noticed me before will suddenly see me now?

Grandfather would call this "pushing the river."

3:20. Maybe she's not coming. Maybe she never comes here anymore. Maybe she moved away, got married, found a different bench in a different city. Maybe I missed my chance back then. Maybe that's all it ever was—something beautiful meant to be observed, not lived.

I should leave. Do something—anything—that makes more sense than sitting here waiting for a stranger who may never appear.

◎

And yet I stay.

3:35. The shadows have shifted slightly, the light warming toward late afternoon. A hawk circles overhead, riding thermals, patient in its hunting. I watch it glide, effortless and attentive, reading the invisible currents of the air the way Grandfather reads the river.

I close my eyes for a moment, feeling the sun on my face, the gentle mountain breeze. The sound of distant laughter, leaves rustling, life continuing around me. When I open them again, I half-expect to see her there, as if my momentary surrender might conjure her into being.

But the space beside me remains empty.

4:00. The courthouse clock begins to chime. A full hour of waiting, of watching, of hoping. Each resonant tone marks another sixty minutes spent chasing a ghost.

Maybe tomorrow. Maybe never. Either way, I've cast my line upon these waters one more time, and once again, nothing has risen to meet it.

4:15. As I walk away, I glance back at the bench—at the empty space I've left behind. The question echoes in my mind, Grandfather's voice steady and clear:

Is the waiting making you whole or hollow?

I still don't know.

Lukome - Uganda

I was hanging bandages to dry when the first shots cracked through the trees—short bursts. Close. The cloth slipped from my fingers, fluttering to the ground. I froze, blood icing in my limbs before instinct shoved me into motion. I didn't move. Just listened. One heartbeat. Then another.

Then the ground shook.

An Army gunship tore across the sky, low and fast—its rotors screaming, drowning out everything else. I ducked instinctively as it passed overhead, the blades slicing the air, the downdraft slamming into the tents like a fist.

Another burst of gunfire cracked through the trees—closer this time. The gunship opened fire, its cannons roaring so loud it felt like the sky was tearing itself apart. From where I stood, I could see the brass casings raining down—tiny flashes of gold tumbling through smoke, clattering against rooftops and dirt. The sound wasn't just loud. It was final.

Then the unmistakable *chop-chop-chop* of another helicopter—low, fast, urgent. I looked up just as the Red Cross helicopter crested the ridge. It dove hard into the clearing, no ceremony, no grace—just necessity. Dust exploded around it like a detonation. The rotor wash tore through the trees, ripped tarps from their lines, sent papers spiraling into the sky like frightened birds.

Somewhere behind me, someone screamed. Another voice shouted over the din: "Go! We have to move—now!"

I was already running.

The camp looked smaller in motion. A blur of faces and boxes, fabric straining on lines. Nothing tethered. Nothing still. The med tent flapped wildly at one end, half-collapsed. I scanned for him through the haze of dust and kicked-up ash.

◐

Emmanuel stood near the edge of the clearing, under a broken shadow of the acacia tree. Alone. He clutched the notebook tight to his chest. His eyes tracked the helicopter, but he didn't flinch. Didn't move. Like he'd been expecting this moment. Like he already knew.

I crossed the distance fast, breath burning, the weight of the baby and the truth of everything pressing down on my ribs. My boots skidded in the dirt as I dropped into a crouch in front of him.

His face was calm. Too calm. I reached for his hands. He didn't pull away. I pressed my scarf into his palm—the red one I'd worn every day, faded now, soft with sweat and time. He looked down at it, then up at me. There were a thousand things I could've said. Should've said.

But he already understood.

The *thump-thump* of the rotor blades blurred into the rhythm of my heartbeat. Behind me—*crack-crack-crack*. Gunfire. Closer now. Short bursts. Automatic. Barking from the treeline, echoing off stone and sand. A second later, the *pop* of return fire. Then screaming. Not words. Just noise.

I stood. Emmanuel didn't speak. He just tightened his grip on the notebook and the scarf and gave the smallest nod. Not goodbye. Just... *go.*

Don't think, Sophia. *Run.* So I ran.

The heat from the exhaust slapped my face as I stepped onto the skid of the Huey, the roar of the rotors deafening, wind whipping hard across my skin. I turned to look at Emmanuel one last time— but before I could find his face again, someone yanked me inside. The doors slammed shut. I dropped into a seat by the window, legs shaking, breath shallow. My hand fell instinctively to the curve of my belly. Still small. Still secret.

"Go!" someone shouted.

I pressed my palm to the window, uselessly. I was already too far—sealed inside, moving on, whether I was ready or not.

The pitch shifted—higher, sharper—as the Huey strained against gravity. The rotors bit into the heat, blades screaming as the ground dropped away beneath us. Dust swirled in violent spirals. Tarps snapped. The village blurred.

The sky tilted. My eyes filled up.

Below us, the village blurred—tents, trees, smoke, Emmanuel. He hadn't moved. He looked up as we lifted. From above, we could see the rebels entering the far end of the village. Emmanuel was waving the scarf. Just once. Just enough.

My hand stayed on the glass. A useless gesture. A goodbye too small for what it meant. Tears spilled hot and fast, streaking my dust-covered cheeks. I didn't wipe them away. I let them fall. When I finally pulled my hand away, a faint print remained on the window—smudged, imperfect, clinging. I stared at it, feeling something tighten in my chest. A mark no one else would see. A proof that I had been there. That I had stayed as long as I could. That even leaving, I had tried to hold on.

The Huey shook slightly as we banked east towards Obutiti, rotors roaring above us. The air inside was thick with heat, sweat, and something quieter. Something raw. I looked around.

Across from me, Mara sat with her head bowed, clutching the

sat phone like it might ring with different news. Her eyes were wide, unblinking, rimmed in red. But when she looked up and saw me watching her, she gave the smallest nod—barely there, but steady.

I'm okay. You're okay. We're still here.

Next to her, Anil stared down at his hands—blood on his sleeves, dried and flaking off like ash. He hadn't spoken since we left the ground.

One of the medics sat with his forehead pressed to his knees, lips moving silently, some prayer or plea too private to say aloud.

No one spoke. No one smiled. The fear hadn't lifted. It just changed shape. From adrenaline to aftermath.

We'd made it out. *Barely.*

I looked down at my hand resting on my thigh.

It was shaking. Trembling so badly I hadn't even felt it until that moment—like my body had held everything in too tightly and now couldn't hold anything at all.

I curled my fingers into a fist, slow, deliberate, trying to remember what still belonged to me.

Then I pressed that same hand to the curve of my stomach. The baby didn't move. But I was still here. And I wasn't sure how to carry that.

Not yet.

I thought of Emmanuel—with my scarf in his hands, the way he didn't flinch, even with the world coming apart.

⊙

Please let that be enough. Please let him be one of the ones who makes it. Please let something we did still matter.

KSLC - Salt Lake City

My father was already waiting when I stepped outside the terminal in Salt Lake City, leaning against his orange International Scout like no time had passed at all. Same North Face jacket. Same faded Utah Jazz cap. Same truck—dented, scratched, and still running like it knew the roads better than anyone else.

I've been thinking about him more and more lately. About how time has a way of slipping past when you're not paying attention. It's too easy to get wrapped up in your own orbit and let the people who matter most fade into the background noise.

I keep telling myself I'll make the time. Go visit. Take a few runs together. Sit and actually talk. But somehow, the days stack up, and the call never gets made. I know better. I just forget sometimes. So here I am, trying to do better.

We hugged—solid and familiar—and I let myself lean into it for a second longer than I meant to. It felt good to see him.

He gave me that look—half grin, half squint. "Took you long enough."

I dropped my bag in the backseat. "Traffic."

"Uh-huh," he said. "Twenty years of it, apparently."

I held up a box of *Cinnabon.* "Peace offering."

◎

He cracked a grin. "You're forgiven."

The drive up Parleys Canyon was quiet—the kind of silence that used to feel like comfort, but now carried weight. Not awkward, just… older. We didn't talk much. We never really needed to.

But even quiet has shape when time has passed unspoken.

He finally broke it.

"How's your mom?"

I knew that was coming. He always asks. I think he has regrets, but he never talks about them. I can just tell.

"She's the same. Out of control."

He chuckled. "Sounds about right."

As we headed up Park Avenue, the old blue Victorian came into view—paint peeling a little, porch sagging just enough to creak under your boots. Everyone in my family has always loved Victorians. Big rooms, drafty windows, too many stairs. I think I'm starting to lean that way too. Maybe it's learned. Or maybe it's in the blood.

I've just never been into anything modern. Not houses, not cars, not skis, not much of anything. I like things with wear. With memory. Things that rattle a little when they move. Things that creak when you walk across them. There's something comforting about that—a kind of truth.

Give me the growl of an old Scout over one of those sleek new Lexuses or Land Rovers any day. I don't trust a car that's too quiet. Same goes for houses.

People though—that's different. Some silences carry weight. Sophia's did. Not empty. Just deliberate. Like still water that runs deep and pulls you toward it without ever making a sound.

Maybe it's just nostalgia. Or maybe I've always needed to feel the history in the things I keep close. Something that proves it's lasted. Something that says: I've been through some shit. And I'm still here.

At the door, my dad handed me the key with a knowing look. "You know the drill," he said. I smiled—muscle memory. The lock had always been temperamental, more suggestion than mechanism. I gave it the right twist, the familiar bump with my shoulder, and it gave way.

"Thirty years of sticking, and you still haven't fixed it?" I asked, stepping inside. He shrugged, already kicking snow off his boots.

"Why would I? Then it wouldn't be our door."

I laughed. It made a strange kind of sense. In this house, if something didn't work exactly right, it just became tradition.

Inside, not much had changed. Same photos on the mantel— snapshots of past ski trips, us in jackets two decades too old, sunburned and grinning into windblown film. And tucked between them, the one I always notice first: my stepmother holding a thermos and wearing that ridiculous knitted hat she refused to retire.

She's not here—off visiting her mother in California—but somehow her presence still is. In the framed note by the door reminding me to keep Dad off the moguls. I smiled at that one. In the throw blanket she crocheted, still draped over the arm of the couch.

She never treated me like a stepchild. Not once. She loved without

◯◯

disclaimers, without needing to prove anything. She just made room for me and filled the quiet spaces with kindness. She held this house together in ways no one ever asked her to, stitching it into something whole with her steady hands and quiet faith. There were no grand speeches, no demands—just the kind of love that shows up every day and stays. She made it feel like home. Like we were already enough. I won't ever forget that. I couldn't if I tried.

Deer Valley Resort

The next morning, we hit the mountain early. He still insisted on first tracks. Said the snow always told the truth before the crowds covered it up.

"You up for some bumps?"

He shook his head and tapped one knee with his pole. "Those days are over, son."

I frowned. "I guess it's groomers with the 'experts' from Newport Beach, then."

I glanced at my dad, already pulling on his gloves with the easy rhythm of someone who didn't need to think about it. The mountain was stitched into him by now—every turn, every break in the trees. He wasn't moving like he used to, and I wasn't either, not really. But maybe that was the point. You don't come to Deer Valley to prove something. You come here when you've got nothing left to prove.

He grinned, clipped into his skis with that same old-school precision—one click, then the other, like muscle memory. There was something steady in it, something that made everything else seem unchanged. But it wasn't. He moved slower now. Just a beat. But I noticed. The pause before he leaned forward. The deeper breath at the top. The way his hands hovered over the poles, like he was checking for something that used to come easy.

I didn't say anything. He wouldn't have wanted me to. But it landed harder than I expected—how easy it is to forget that the people who raised you aren't permanent.

As we slid into the lift line, I looked around—immaculate corduroy, designer jackets, not a mogul in sight. And then it hit me.

Deer Valley.

No bump runs. No edge-of-death cliffs to tumble down. Just endless, manicured groomers and complimentary tissues at the bottom of every lift. And then—like a warm beam of divine grace—one glorious truth:

No damn snowboarders allowed.

A blessing. A relic. A sanctuary for the two-plank faithful.

I followed him down, carving turns behind him, watching his shape move across the slope. It felt like watching a photograph develop in reverse—familiar becoming something... softer. Or maybe something fading.

For lunch, we skied down to Silver Lake and grabbed two seats out on the deck. Dad grabbed a coffee. I got a Coke with ice. Coke just tastes better on the mountain—kind of like ginger ale on an airplane. No idea why. Maybe it's psychological. Probably is. Or maybe it's just one of those weird little truths that doesn't need explaining.

"How long you staying?" he asked.

I hesitated. Not because I didn't know, but because I did. And because the answer felt heavier now than it used to.

"I don't know," I said. "I should probably turn my phone off."

He nodded, not pushing. But I saw something flicker behind his eyes. Not disappointment. Not relief, exactly. Just… presence.

And that's when it landed.

I needed to show up more. Not just for a few days. Not just in post-cards or phone calls or polite holiday visits. But for these moments—the chipped tables, old lifts, and Coke that tastes like memory.

Family doesn't ask loudly. It waits.

And I'd left mine waiting for too long.

Later, we stood in the garage, looking through the racks of skis like we were flipping through old yearbooks. He pulled out a pair of old Coyotes—scratched, scarred, but still solid. Back in the day, everyone skied on these.

"You should take these back with you," he said. "They've still got a few runs left in them."

I ran my hand along the edge. "I will," I said. "But not this trip."

He smiled, but there was something else in it.

"Try not to be such a stranger."

I met his eyes. "I won't. Promise."

And this time, I meant it. I wanted to freeze the time I'd just had with him—hold it in my hands like a photograph I'd forgotten to take. Some things don't last. But showing up? That's the part I can choose.

I barely made it out. Not just from the village, or the rebels, or the gunfire that still echoed behind my eyes when I tried to sleep. I mean all of it. The weight. The risk. The blind hope I'd carried like armor.

I hadn't known how close I was to losing everything. Not until I was in the air, dust still in my teeth, watching Emmanuel disappear into smoke with my scarf in his hand. I had always said I would give everything. And I meant it.

Until I had something I couldn't afford to lose.

My days in the Corps were over. Not because I didn't believe in the work anymore—but because I couldn't ask this child to pay for the promises I'd made before I knew my baby.

The months that followed blurred together—my body changing in ways both miraculous and unsettling. The first flutter of movement inside me sent me to my knees in the kitchen, hands pressed against the cool tile floor, overwhelmed by the reality that I was no longer alone in my own skin. The journal I'd kept throughout my service was filled with observations, questions without answers. Writing had always been my way of processing what I couldn't articulate aloud—this transformation happening both to me and within me was no different.

Ethan approached the nursery on weekends, his careful precision both comforting and maddening. He tackled parenthood preparation like our community projects—researching, planning, preparing for every contingency. I watched him assemble furniture with methodi-

◐

cal focus, the same concentration he'd shown when building irrigation systems in the highlands.

What if I'm terrible at this?

The question followed me like a shadow, growing longer as my due date approached. In Uganda, Peru and other countries, I'd known my purpose, had clear objectives, measurable outcomes. Motherhood seemed more nebulous, more permanent, with no completion date or evaluation metrics.

His methodical approach to impending parenthood highlighted the fundamental difference in how we approached the unknown—his faith in systems and preparation, my preference for intuition and adaptation based on need.

Then came the birth—thirty-six hours of labor that stripped away every pretense, every carefully constructed narrative I'd built about who I was. Pain became my world, narrowing my existence to breath and endurance. Time lost meaning. My body became both stranger and more intimately known than ever before.

"You can do this," the nurse kept saying, her voice a lifeline through the fog of exhaustion.

I wanted to scream that she was wrong. That I couldn't. That I'd made a terrible mistake thinking I was strong enough for this. But some deeper wisdom kept me breathing, kept me pushing toward the inevitable.

At least until my inner Allison broke through the pain—furious, foul-mouthed, and completely uninvited:

◐

"Unless you're gonna reach in there and yank it out yourself, shut the fuck up, you rabid bitch!"

I didn't say it out loud. But oh, I wanted to.

When they finally placed Gray on my chest—red-faced, wrinkled, impossibly small yet somehow complete—the world recalibrated. She looked at me with unfocused eyes, and I recognized something in her gaze. A question, maybe. Or a challenge:

Who are you going to be for me?

The first weeks passed in a sleepless haze. Breastfeeding was a battle neither of us seemed equipped to win—each feeding a negotiation between my raw, aching body and her desperate hunger. I cried more than she did some days, overwhelmed by the relentlessness of her needs, by the disappearance of my former self beneath the title of "mother."

We named her Gray the morning after we found out I was having a baby girl. The sky had been that perfect shade between night and dawn, full of possibility. Not black or white, but something more complex, more beautiful. Ethan had wanted to name her after my grandmother, but I'd shaken my head. This child was something new, something entirely her own. She deserved a name that wasn't borrowed, that didn't carry expectations. Gray—like the color of clouds before rain, like the space between certainties. A name that could become anything.

Ethan took paternity leave, moving through our apartment with quiet efficiency—changing diapers, washing dishes, fielding calls from our Peace Corps friends scattered across the country. He seemed to adapt to fatherhood with an ease I resented and admired in equal measure.

But sometimes, in the pauses—when Gray finally settled and the apartment fell into rare stillness—I'd catch him staring out the window. Watching the rain bead down the glass like it was tracing a map he couldn't follow.

I don't know who I am anymore, I thought one afternoon, Gray asleep after hours of fussing. In the Corps, I had purpose. Identity. Clear goals. Now everything feels undefined.

My mother came to visit a week after Gray was born. She brought lemon muffins from a place back home, a stack of dish towels I hadn't asked for, and that particular brand of calm that used to drive me crazy when I was younger. Now it felt like oxygen.

She sat beside me on the couch, hands wrapped around a chipped mug of tea. The living room was quiet—Gray finally asleep in the next room. She didn't say much at first. Just looked at me. Really looked, in that way she always did, like she already knew the answer I hadn't figured out yet.

Then, softly, "Maybe the point of becoming a mother is… you don't stay the same. You become someone new. Someone you couldn't have imagined before."

She reached out, brushing a curl from my cheek. Her hand was warm. Steady. "It's not about having it all figured out. It's about growing into it. Like anything that matters."

I turned her words over slowly, like the smooth river stones I used to collect along the Sacred Valley in Peru. Was that transformation beautiful—or terrifying? A loss, or a becoming? Maybe both. Simultaneously.But as her words settled, another question surfaced: How long could Ethan sit still in this version of our life before the field called him back? Before the stillness became too much?

Slowly, imperceptibly at first, something began to shift. Gray and

I found our rhythm. My body healed. Sleep, while still fragmented, became possible again. I started to recognize myself in glimpses—in the way I hummed the Peruvian lullabies to her while changing her diaper, in the stories I whispered against her fontanel when no one else was listening, in the fierce protectiveness that rose in me when she cried.

And then came the night, somewhere in that third month, when I realized I'd been sitting in the rocking chair for hours—not from obligation, not from necessity, but because I couldn't bear to put her down. Because watching her sleep had become its own form of meditation, its own kind of prayer.

The weight of her in my arms no longer felt like burden but like anchor. Keeping me present. Keeping me real. Perhaps this was what it meant to be a mother—not the loss of self I had feared, but an expansion. A widening of my heart to accommodate this new, unbreakable love. A love I never knew I was capable of until it was required of me.

KATL - Atlanta

Another trip. Another airport. The escalator hummed beneath my boots as I rode down into the concourse. The light here was always clinical—flat and too clean—but somehow, it still managed to catch the dust in the air just right. Made the ordinary feel like a photograph waiting to happen.

I slung my camera bag a little higher on my shoulder and stepped off into the terminal. Same layout. Same soft jazz leaking from unseen speakers. Same smell of coffee, plastic, and whatever cleaning product the janitorial crew was addicted to. ♪

I always scan the crowds. Habit, I guess. Muscle memory. Faces, posture, movement. I watch people the way some folks count exits in a restaurant. And half the time, I don't even know what I'm looking for.

♪ *"Take Five"* by Dave Brubeck

◍

Not danger. Not the nearest exit like I'm Jason Bourne. Just... a flicker. A shift. Something that might mean something.

Once, I would've said I was looking for a story. Now? Maybe I'm just looking for her. There's always a moment—brief, but sharp—when I see someone from behind and think maybe. The right hair. The right dress. The right pause in the middle of a step. My chest always tightens before my brain catches up. And then the head turns, and it's not her. It never is.

But I still look. Every airport. Every concourse. Every time.

I found a seat near a row of windows and dropped into it with a soft grunt. Across from me, a kid in a puffer jacket played a game on his Nintendo, face lit in flickering color.

His mom sat beside him, ankles crossed, thumbing the corner of a paperback. *The Light Between Oceans* by M.L. Stedman. I'd read it once, years ago. Someone had left a copy tucked into the seatback pocket on a flight from Lisbon—dog-eared, underlined, the kind of book that had clearly meant something to someone. I was too jet-lagged to sleep, too restless to think, so I read it cover to cover somewhere over the Atlantic.

It was the kind of story that stayed with you—not because of what happened, but because of what didn't. A book full of silences and choices that couldn't be undone. People doing the wrong things for the right reasons. Or maybe it was the other way around.

She didn't look up. Just kept reading, line after line, like she was trying to outrun something soft and sad. And I got it. I really did. There's a moment in that book where the truth finally breaks the surface—and it doesn't bring peace. Just clarity. The understanding that love doesn't always look like rescue. Sometimes it looks like letting go.

❂

I shifted in my seat and looked out past the glass at the runway—engines humming, carts rolling, the slow choreography of departure. People leaving, people arriving, no one really staying long enough to mean it.

I watched the automatic doors open and close in rhythm—like the place was breathing. People moved with that dazed kind of urgency airports tend to inspire. Always late, always lost, always clutching their carry-ons like they might fall through the floor at any moment. And still, I watched. Out of habit. Out of hope. Out of something I don't name anymore.

The glass beside me reflected a distorted version of myself—older than I expected, even though I knew the number. Salt at my temples. Eyes a little more tired than I'd left them. I rubbed the back of my neck and thought about my last trip to see my dad.

He was probably out on the porch right about now, feet up, glass of Dewars in hand, making mental notes about which part of the roof he was going to ignore fixing this spring. I definitely inherited his procrastination. No question.

Fuck the roof. When does the Jazz game start?

I should be there. Or calling. Or doing something other than sitting in an airport like I'm waiting for something I already missed. That's the trouble with people like me—we're always arriving or departing. Never just being.

I think of the old Scout, the creaky front door, the smell of pine, ski wax and cinnamon. I think of how quiet the garage had been that last night, both of us pretending we weren't counting down time. Maybe that's what I'm chasing these days—not the photo, not the headline, not even Sophia. Maybe I'm just trying to figure out how to stay still long enough to matter.

The intercom buzzed. Another flight announced. Another wave of movement. I stayed put. Watched. Right now, I'm not missing anything. I'm not moving, not hunting for a shot or an angle. I'm just sitting here, letting it all drift past like it doesn't need me to catch it. Maybe lightning isn't something you wait for. Maybe it's something you have to chase. Or become.

That's the problem, isn't it? I keep thinking the sky owes me something. That if I stand still long enough, the universe will send down some bolt of clarity or love or forgiveness and it'll all make sense. I should call Martone. Tell her I love her. Which I do. Instead, I'm here—watching for Sophia. Waiting for lightning to strike. Like always.

I feel like a hot mess. Actually, I am one. Maybe I should just lean into it—get a good bottle, pass out on the floor every night, forget all my troubles. I've heard it works.

The freezer door slams behind me, and Gray lets out a soft grunt against my chest. I shift my weight instinctively, bouncing slightly as I move into the checkout line. One hand on the cart. One cupped around the back of her fuzzy little hat. She settles almost immediately, a warm weight pressed into me like a second heartbeat.

We're out of wipes. Low on diapers. I haven't eaten anything that required a fork in over a week. I glance at the conveyor belt—formula, frozen peas, oatmeal, a pack of toilet paper. There's no version of this that doesn't scream new mother trying to keep it together.

I glance at the candy rack without meaning to. And there it is. Bubble Yum. Watermelon. The bright pink packaging stops me cold. I used to love that stuff—when I was ten, maybe eleven. I'd spend entire afternoons trying to blow bubbles the size of my face. Laughing when they popped. Picking sticky bits of gum out of my hair. It was loud, obnoxious, sugary as hell. I used to chew two pieces at a time. Minimum.

I haven't thought about it in years. I grab a pack and place it on the belt before I can change my mind. The cashier doesn't say anything—just scans it like it's any other item. But it feels different. Not like an impulse buy. More like a small rebellion. A quiet reminder. I slip the gum into my jacket pocket. I'm not even sure I'll chew it. Not today, anyway.

My grandmother never let me have gum. Said it was tacky, undignified. Maybe that was just her generation. She kept peppermint Altoids in her purse and handed me one whenever I asked for something sweet. I think she believed discipline was a kind of elegance. I used to think she was right. Now… I'm not so sure.

Maybe elegance has nothing to do with restraint. Maybe it looks more like joy. Like laughing too loud. Like bright pink gum at the checkout line. Like being fully yourself, even when no one's watching.

I wonder if one day I'll slip a piece of gum to Gray when we're in a store just like this—no lecture, no warning about how it looks. Just the sweetness of it. Just the fun. Maybe we'll blow bubbles in the car with the windows down, and I'll tell her how I used to do the same thing when I was her age. And maybe—if I do it right—she'll never have to unlearn the idea that joy and dignity can live in the same body.

Maybe later—just for a moment—I'll see if I can still blow a bubble. Just to remind myself that I'm still in here, too. Not because I want to be anywhere else. I love this little girl more than I ever thought possible. But even inside this all-consuming, beautiful love, there's still room for the girl who once laughed with gum stuck in her hair.

She hasn't gone away. She's just been quiet for a while.

10

19:07:23:16:53:27

The mobile spins in slow, weightless circles above me—tiny stars and crescent moons drifting in endless orbit. Their shadows stretch and shrink across the nursery walls, shifting with every quiet creak of the rocking chair.

In my arms, six-month-old baby Gray breathes in tiny, steady puffs against my chest, her warmth seeping into me. I cradle her closer, feeling the weight of her, the small but undeniable presence of her existence pressing into mine.

She is mine.

That thought should feel more natural by now. But it still stuns me, still settles in my bones with a quiet, trembling weight. I never understood how much space love could take up inside a person. How it could be both heavy and infinite at the same time.

Gray stirs, her tiny fingers brushing against the fabric of my shirt, searching for something, maybe nothing. Her mouth makes a soft, breathy sound before she settles again, a small sigh that feels older than she is. I press my palm to her back, fingers spanning most of it, and wonder how something so small can carry the full force of my heart.

My heartbeat adjusts, instinctively matching her rhythm. I never thought about these things before—about how a child rewrites the very code of who you are, how your body becomes attuned to theirs, how their needs become the compass that dictates every movement, every breath.

I tilt my head back against the chair, exhaling slowly. This is forever now. The weight of that truth presses into my chest—not with fear, but with something deeper, something unnameable. It is not just love. It is devotion. It is knowing that I am no longer just me. That every choice I make, every step I take, will shape the world that Gray grows up in.

I wonder if she knows yet, in some deep, instinctual way, that I would give anything to protect her. That I already have.

She lets out a tiny hiccup, a sound like a whisper caught mid-laugh, and I smile. There are whole languages we speak now without words— just breaths and touches and knowing.

A shift in the doorway.

I glance up and find Ethan standing there, arms crossed loosely over his chest, leaning against the frame. The dim glow from the hallway edges his face, casting shadows that soften his expression—but I can still see it. That look in his eyes. Something between awe and hesitation. Like he's watching something sacred. Or something he doesn't quite know how to enter.

☉

He smiles—just barely—but doesn't move. Doesn't come in. I wait for him to say something, but the silence stretches out like a thread pulled too tight. I wonder if he feels the weight of this the way I do. If he lies awake at night, realizing the world will never be the same. That we are not just two people anymore.

He shifts his weight, one hand braced lightly against the doorframe. Like he's still deciding whether he belongs inside this picture. Or just outside it.

We are responsible for something greater.

But sometimes I wonder if he's still catching up. If part of him is still on the other side of this threshold we crossed the moment Gray was born. And if so—how long can I hold us both here, inside this moment, before it passes? I think he thought he could adapt. And maybe he did—for a while. But Ethan isn't wired for walls and rocking chairs. He's built for movement. Purpose. Fieldwork. And I'm starting to see the ache of that in the quiet spaces between us.

The mobile creaks overhead, still spinning. I run my fingers over Gray's back, slow and steady, memorizing the way she fits in my arms tonight, knowing she'll never be quite this small again. I press my lips to the top of her head and close my eyes.

Sometimes I think this is what eternity looks like—not a stretch of time, but a single night like this. A heartbeat syncing with hers. A chair that keeps moving even after you stop thinking about it. The quiet knowledge that even if the rest of the world forgets this moment, I won't. I can't. Because this is the night I understood what forever really means.

And I just keep rocking.

⟨O⟩

The Sink - Boulder

The warm, worn-in energy of *The Sink* wraps around me like an old leather jacket. It's the kind of place where stories linger in the woodgrain of the bar, where every scribbled message on the walls and ceiling feels like a secret between strangers. It smells like beer, charred burgers, and the unmistakable scent of Boulder history.

Brandon and I sit at the bar, the hum of conversation folding around us. A group of college kids play pool in the corner, their laughter cutting through the classic rock playing overhead. ♪

I swirl the amber liquid in my glass before asking, "Have you and Monica thought about kids at all?"

Brandon shrugs, taking a sip of his beer. "We talk about it sometimes. I think we'll probably wait a while, but who knows? Life has a funny way of changing plans."

I let out a wry chuckle. "Indeed. One minute you're living the dream, and the next, you're up to your elbows in shit."

Brandon grins. "Exactly! So, for now, we're thinking about getting a dog."

I arch an eyebrow. "Dogs come with shit too, ya know."

We both laugh, the kind of easy, familiar laughter that comes from years of knowing exactly how the other thinks.

Brandon takes another swig of his beer before shifting the conversation. "So, how are you and Martone doing?"

♪ *"Simple Man"* by Lynyrd Skynyrd

◎

I hesitate for a beat, then shrug. "Oh fine, but I think she's frustrated with all my traveling."

Brandon smirks. "Well, she knew who you were when she met you."

"I don't think she sees it that way."

Brandon shakes his head.

"Nope. She's gonna try to change you, no matter what."

I glance at him, curious.

"Really?"

He nods knowingly.

"Yep. It's just a matter of time before she has total control."

I chuckle, leaning back in my chair. Another song drifts lazily from the old speakers, like even the music had nowhere better to be. ♪

"So you know this from experience?"

"Yep. I just do what I'm told. Women have all the power, my friend."

I smirk. "So you're saying I should just get a leash and save myself the trouble?"

Brandon clinks his beer against mine. "That's exactly what I'm saying."

♪ "Old Man" by Neil Young

I shake my head, amused. "Well, then. I'm surprised Monica actually let you out."

Brandon leans in, lowering his voice conspiratorially. "She didn't. She thinks I'm working."

We laugh, the sound getting lost in the bar's noisy hum. It's moments like these—easy, ridiculous, unfiltered—that remind me why Brandon's been my closest friend for years.

The laughter fades, and for a moment, I just sit there, staring into the swirl of my drink, watching the light fracture across the glass. A group of students shout near the dartboard, full of life and fire and unearned confidence. I used to be like that. Or maybe I just wanted to be.

I think about what Brandon said. About dogs. About Monica. About the possibility of kids. And I realize—I want that.

Not in a dramatic, cinematic way. Not tomorrow. But someday. I want the clutter. The noise. The kind of chaos that builds a life instead of tearing one apart. I want the tiny socks on the stairs and drawings stuck to the fridge. I want the questions, the wonder, the late-night pacing with a crying baby and the quiet thrill of someone depending on you entirely.

But then I think of Martone. Of hotel rooms and departure boards. Of trying to write captions from airport lounges while pretending I'm not missing anything. And I wonder how any of that fits into what I've built.

Or maybe that's the problem. Maybe I've built something so carefully around solitude and motion, there's no space left for stillness.

Brandon's talking again, something about fantasy football, but I'm still somewhere else. Somewhere in a house I've never seen, with someone I've never quite had, and a child with eyes I recognize. And for the first time in a long time, I wonder if chasing stories has kept me from writing my own.

My phone buzzes on the bar beside me. I glance at the number.

I answer, my voice soft. "Hey, Jane."

There's a pause as I listen. My posture shifts. The background fades.

"Yeah… yeah. Of course I can."

Another pause. My mouth tightens slightly. A beat.

"Alright. I'll take the next available flight out."

I hang up, heart starting to race in a different way now.

The sunlight spilled across the hardwood, warming the floor where Gray pressed her palms flat against the grain. She rocked gently on her hands and knees, brow furrowed in concentration. Her little fists curled and uncurled like she was negotiating with the floor itself.

She'd been trying for days—lurching forward, sliding back, collapsing into tiny frustrated heaps. But this time… she moved. Just a few inches. A half-crawl. Then another. The movement was clumsy, off-center, full of grit.

And suddenly, she was across the room. I didn't say anything. I didn't clap. I just watched. Let it land. There's something sacred in a first. The silence around it. The way it reshapes the air. Gray sat back on her heels and looked at me, cheeks flushed with effort, eyes bright and waiting for approval.

I smiled. My heart did something soft and sharp at the same time. She was changing right in front of me. Becoming.

I glanced at the clock on the wall. It was morning in Paraguay. Ethan might be teaching by now—standing in front of a dusty chalkboard in a village school, or biking down a dirt road with lesson plans bouncing in his backpack. He wouldn't know. Not yet. Maybe not for weeks.

He'd send a call or send a letter when he could, eventually. Long and warm and full of good intentions. He always meant well. He hadn't planned on missing everything. But life doesn't slow down for promises. It just… keeps going.

I ran a hand through my hair, still watching her. Gray reached for a book, missed, then scooted forward again with sheer willpower. No hesitation. No permission asked. Just forward.

And that's what I was doing too, I realized. I'd stopped waiting for Ethan to become a father in the way I'd imagined. The kind who knelt down in moments like these and said:

You did it, baby girl.

I stopped waiting for letters to land in time. For guilt to turn into presence.

For shared weight.

It was just us. Me and her. She looked up again, toothless grin

◐

wide. I scooped her into my arms, kissed the top of her head, and whispered words she didn't understand yet but someday would. We were okay. We were more than okay.

She'd remember love—*not absence.*

Claiborne Avenue - Lower Ninth Ward

The water is up to my knees already, and I'm not even halfway down the block. It's slow-moving, thick with debris—bottles, roofing tiles, what looks like a soaked teddy bear drifting past. The air smells like mildew and oil and the inside of an old refrigerator that's been left in the sun. Everything feels warped—too quiet, too still.

New Orleans is holding its breath under the weight of Hurricane Katrina.

I step up onto a strip of raised concrete that used to be a median. The camera's already out, but I haven't taken a shot in twenty minutes. I'm not even sure what I'm waiting for. Something that doesn't feel like ruin porn. Something real.

Then I see him.

He's about thirty yards out, wading through the water like it's nothing. Shirt plastered to his chest, face half-shadowed by the light. He's holding a plastic grocery bag with both hands, like it's made of glass. He doesn't look around. Doesn't call out. Just moves slow and steady, each step sending ripples out into the broken world.

I lift the camera, more on instinct than intent.

He stops. Right there in the middle of the street.

Then, with this strange, deliberate care, he reaches into the bag and pulls something out. A photograph.

I can't see what's on it from here. Could be a child. A wife. A Sunday morning in better light. It's waterlogged—edges curling, color already running—but he stares at it like it's all he has left. And maybe it is.

I adjust the lens. My breath catches. He holds it against his chest. Not to save it. To feel it.

Click. One frame.

He never sees me. Never looks up. Just slips the photo back into the bag and keeps going—chest-deep through a city that barely remembers how to stand. I don't move.

There are stories you chase. Assignments. Names on a clipboard. And then there are the ones that find you standing in the middle of a flooded street, watching a stranger hold the past like it still means something.

This one found me.

And I know, right then, I'll never take another photo like it again.

Gray sits in the middle of the living room rug, legs sprawled like a sleepy starfish, a board book propped against one knee and her beloved stuffed elephant tucked under one arm. She babbles softly as she flips the pages—tiny syllables that rise and fall in rhythm with her curiosity. Most of it doesn't make sense, but all of it makes me smile.

From the couch, I watch her. A grocery list rests half-written in my lap, the pen idle between my fingers. The light from the window catches in her curls, a little halo of late afternoon gold. One sock is missing. There's yogurt crusted on her sleeve.

I can't imagine anything more perfect.

She turned another page, pointed at something—maybe a duck, maybe a shoe—and then paused. Her eyes lifted, scanning until they found mine. We held that gaze for a moment.

Then her mouth opened.

"Mama."

A single, clear word. No buildup. No warning. Just... there. The pen dropped from my fingers. I didn't move. I couldn't. She said it again, with the same wide-eyed innocence, testing the sound on her tongue. "Mama?"

I slid to the floor without thinking, knees against the rug, hands trembling slightly. I reached for her, pressing a hand to my heart, then to hers. I nodded.

Yes. Yes, my love.

She grinned, delighted by my reaction, and clapped her hands like she'd just discovered something extraordinary.

"Mama!" she said again, louder this time, the word bursting from her like joy.

I wrapped my arms around her and held her close, kissed her cheek, her hair, her forehead. She rested one small hand against my cheek, the way she always did when she was trying to understand something. Her fingers were warm, her skin soft.

She didn't understand what that word meant to me. Not yet. But she would someday.

And for now, that was enough.She whispered it one more time, barely louder than a breath. "Mama…"

I closed my eyes and let it settle deep. It was the most beautiful sound I had ever heard.

The glow from my laptop screen flickers against the walls, casting restless shadows across the room. The cursor blinks in the MySpace search bar, waiting. Waiting for me to make a choice.

I hesitate. I shouldn't be doing this. Then—I type it anyway.

Sophia Farraday.

A moment passes. Then another. The screen fills with profiles— rows of strangers with the same name, but none of them her. I scroll, my chest tightening with something I don't want to name. Click. Scroll. Click. Dead end.

I sit back, rubbing a hand over my face. What am I even looking for? No. I know.

It's been years, and yet she's still there—tucked into the spaces between things I don't say out loud. Always lingering just beyond reach, just beyond the next search result.

And I'm in a relationship. With Martone. Someone who's here. Real. Present. But still, I keep looking.

Last weekend, Martone left a toothbrush at my place. She didn't say anything, just slid it into the holder next to mine and kissed my shoulder like it was the most natural thing in the world. A small gesture of permanence. I should have felt something more than panic.

I've imagined Sophia's voice. The way she might laugh, lean forward mid-conversation. I don't even know her—but there's a version of her that's lived in my mind for years. Not love. Not really. But something that feels close. Something that feels possible.

My fingers hover over the trackpad. Maybe this is the moment I stop. Close the laptop. Move on. Instead, I scroll again. Another dead end.

"What are you doing?"

Martone's voice slices through the quiet, and my whole body tenses. Too late to make it look natural. Too late to pretend this isn't exactly what it looks like.

I snap the laptop shut—too fast, too guilty.

She leans against the doorway, arms crossed, framed in the dim hall light. Her silhouette is soft around the edges, but her eyes aren't. They're fixed on me, waiting.

I stretch like I'm just shaking off a long night.

"Oh, nothing," I say. Casual. Easy.

Her gaze flicks to the laptop.

CO

"Nothing, huh?"

I force a crooked smirk. "Yeah. Just... killing time."

The lie tastes bitter. I've never given Martone a reason not to trust me—at least not one she knows about. But this feels like a betrayal anyway. Not because I've touched someone else. But because I'm chasing the idea of someone else. Chasing a memory that was never even mine.

Martone doesn't push. She just watches me for a second too long, then disappears down the hall without another word.

I wait. Listening. Her footsteps fade. Only when I'm sure she's gone do I let out the breath I've been holding. I stare at the closed laptop. I shouldn't open it again. But I already know I will.

Because somewhere in the back of my mind, there's a life I keep imagining. One where I find Sophia. One where our paths cross and something clicks into place like it was always meant to. And some nights—like this one—that fantasy feels more honest than the life I'm actually living.

Martone deserves better. She deserves someone all in, someone here. But I don't know how to tell her the truth: The man she's falling for is chasing the ghost of someone he's never even met.

I reach for the laptop again. Hesitate. Then pull my hand back. Not tonight. But I'm just postponing the inevitable.

How the hell did I get here? Obsessing over a woman from a newspaper article. A name I shouldn't even remember—but do. And I know I'll never forget it.

It doesn't make sense. And yet—here I am.

The morning air is filled with the soft hush of waking streets. Morning light spills across the pavement, stretching long shadows that shift as Gray bounces beside me, her small fingers wrapped around the strap of her backpack. I kneel, adjusting the straps so they sit snug against her tiny shoulders.

Too tiny, I think. Too soon.

Gray giggles, rolling her eyes. "Mama, it's fine."

I smooth down a stray curl, letting my fingers linger for a moment longer than necessary.

The low rumble of the school bus grows closer, and my heart tightens around itself. It pulls up in front of us, exhaling a long breath of steam as the doors creak open.

Flo's warm voice rings out from the driver's seat, her usual grin waiting for my daughter.

"Good morning, Gray! All ready?"

Gray beams. No hesitation. No fear. "Hi, Flo! I am ready!"

Ready.

I nod, my arms stiff at my sides as Gray takes the first step up. She turns, just once, throwing her arms around me in a quick, tight squeeze. Then she's gone.

I step back as the doors fold shut. The bus lurches forward, kicking up a soft cloud of dust. Through the rear window, Gray waves—

bright-eyed, fearless, already looking ahead to whatever's next. I lift my hand and wave back, but she's already turned around.

I used to be the horizon she ran toward.
Now I'm the place she leaves behind.

The bus disappears down the street. The morning quiet settles again. I stand still. Watching. Waiting. As if she might suddenly change her mind, come running back, arms wide, saying Mama, I'm not ready after all.

But she doesn't. I press a hand to my chest, breathing through the ache. This is what love does. You pour everything into them—your time, your heart, your very breath. And then, one day, you have to let them go. Even when they are ready—and you're still learning how to be.

St. Johns - Antigua

The Grumman Goose bobs lazily in the sun-dappled waters of Antigua, its polished aluminum skin reflecting the Caribbean light. The scent of salt and warm diesel drifts through the open hatch as the seaplane sways, waiting.

Then—the engines sputter to life. A cough, a shudder, a reluctant roar before they settle into a steady, throaty purr. The Goose lurches forward, slicing through the harbor's gentle waves, leaving a ribbon of white foam in its wake.

As the pilot increases throttle, the pontoons skip over the surface, bouncing once, twice—until with a final surge, the aircraft breaks free.

The moment of weightlessness hits—the transition between sea and sky, where gravity releases its grip and the world tilts into something wider, something untethered.

Through the window, turquoise shallows unfurl like a painting, vibrant coral gardens visible beneath the glassy surface. Shadows of sea turtles drift lazily over the reefs. The white curves of untouched beaches stretch toward the horizon, where the water shifts from sapphire to indigo.

Higher now, the Goose cuts through the golden light, skimming the edges of the world. And then, rising from the haze, an island appears—untouched, waiting.

Route 518 - SeaTac

Rain pounds against the windshield, thick and relentless, blurring the road ahead. The wipers push back and forth, clearing just enough to glimpse the glowing Departures sign at SeaTac before the downpour swallows it again. I don't want to stop. I just want to keep driving. Straight through. And maybe I should.

Ethan sits beside me, silent, staring out at the sheets of rain. His hands rest in his lap, fingers twitching slightly with nervous energy. Maybe he knows I'm angry. Maybe he doesn't care. In the back seat, Gray clutches her Peace Corps teddy bear—the same one Ethan gave her the last time he left. The same one she's kept close ever since.

I tighten my grip on the wheel. This should be the last time. It should have been the last time a long time ago. Ethan said this trip was different. Said it would only be a few months. Said he'd come back and settle down. Find a real job. Be the kind of father Gray needs—the kind who stays. I could use a loving husband, too. Not just one who comes home every now and then like a guest. But here we are. *Again.*

The terminal lights appear ahead, glowing through the rain, haloed and distant. My stomach twists, a familiar ache rising in my chest—one

I thought I'd learned to live with. And maybe I had, until Gray came along.

I put the Audi into park and sit for a moment. Ethan turns toward the back seat, forcing a soft smile.

"Hey, sweetheart. Come here, let me hug you."

Gray doesn't move. She knows what's coming. We all do. Her arms tighten around the bear, pulling it close. She shakes her head, her bottom lip trembling.

"Please don't go, Daddy," she whispers.

The words are small and broken, but they land like a punch to the chest. Ethan exhales slowly and reaches for her, trying to soothe. "Look at your bear, sweetheart," he says, his voice gentle. "He's helping people all over the world, just like Daddy."

Gray lifts her chin and meets his eyes in the mirror. Her voice is even softer this time, barely a breath.

"But I need help too."

The silence that follows is immediate and crushing. I stare straight ahead, my throat tight. Gray doesn't understand why he keeps leaving. She can't grasp the pull, the mission, the way it burrows into your soul and whispers that you matter more when you're far from home.

But I do. I used to be him. I used to chase purpose across borders and time zones, chasing the high of helping. Until I made a choice. Until I realized that Gray wasn't something I could leave behind. I made peace with that. Ethan hasn't.

He looks at me then, searching my face for something—understanding, forgiveness, maybe permission. But I don't give it. My hands stay on the wheel, knuckles tight against the leather. I won't stop him. But I won't pretend it's okay, either.

The terminal doors slide open, casting light onto the wet pavement. Ethan turns back to Gray, still hoping for one more moment before he goes. "Come on, sweetheart. Just one hug before I go."

Still, she doesn't move. Her arms remain locked around the bear. The moment stretches out until finally, Ethan exhales, opens the door, and steps out into the storm.

Cold air rushes into the car, sharp and immediate. Rain lashes the interior, soaking the edge of the seat and floor mat. He hesitates at the door—just for a second—but then he walks away. The doors close behind him, sealing us in again.

Gray stares ahead, unblinking. She doesn't cry. She doesn't call after him. She doesn't ask when he'll be back. The bear slips from her fingers, landing in a heap beside her.

After a long beat, she unbuckles her seatbelt and climbs into the front seat. She curls into my side, pulling her knees up, pressing close. Her hands fist into my sweater, gripping tight, her face buried in the space beneath my arm.

Ethan never looks back.

Through the rain-slicked windshield, under the glow of the terminal lights, I see a family huddled beneath a single umbrella. A father wraps his arm around the mother, pulling her close. Their little boy bounces between them, splashing in puddles, holding tight to both their hands.

A sharp contrast.

I let the ache settle in. This should have been the last time. I should have asked him to stay. Maybe I should have demanded it. But I didn't. So maybe this is on me, too.

I buckle Gray in, shift into drive, and leave the airport behind.

Montserrat - Lesser Antilles

The Goose drifted lower, its twin radial engines purring like something half-asleep. Warm air curled against the windows, and below us, the sea shimmered—teal, then jade, then the pale blue of breath held too long.

I watched our shadow slide across the surface, a dark shape skimming the water like it belonged to something ancient and slow. It rippled over the waves, warped and stretched, always just ahead—just out of reach. ♪

Up ahead, the island emerged. Not sudden, not dramatic—just rising, steady and solemn. The floats skimmed the water once. Then again. A light kiss, then drag. Then we were down—part sky, part sea, part something else entirely..

This was the island of Montserrat in the Lesser Antilles.

The first time I saw a photograph of this place, I thought it was something out of a dream. A city buried beneath ash. A modern-day Pompeii. But nothing about this felt dreamlike now—only unsettlingly real.

♪ *"Ascension"* by Tycho

◐

The Soufrière Hills Volcano loomed in the distance, sending thin ribbons of steam curling into the sky, the earth still breathing beneath its wounds. As the Goose skimmed the waves and came to a gentle stop, I braced myself. I wasn't here for paradise. I was here for what came after destruction.

The pilot—a weathered man with skin tanned to leather—helped me unload my gear. He introduced me to Joseph, a slender local man waiting beside an aging Land Rover. Joseph would be my driver, taking me where I needed to go.

Plymouth - The Buried City

The heat pressed in around me, thick and inescapable. Even through my boots, the ground radiated warmth—a reminder that what slept beneath the surface had not been vanquished, only resting.

Joseph drove in silence for most of the journey, the Land Rover bouncing over roads that seemed more suggestion than reality. Occasionally, he'd point out landmarks—places that meant something in a landscape that had been rewritten by disaster.

"My uncle had a shop there," he said, gesturing to what looked like nothing but jungle to me.

"Sold the best saltfish and johnny cakes on the island."

I searched for any sign of a building but saw only creeping vines and the occasional glimpse of concrete.

"When did you leave?" I asked.

"After the big eruptions." His knuckles whitened on the steering wheel.

⓪

"Had no choice. Government evacuated everyone. Some went to England. Some to other islands. My family stayed on the north side. Safe zone."

I thought about that—what it would mean to watch your home become uninhabitable. To be forced to decide what to take and what to leave behind. What objects could hold the weight of a life abandoned.

"Do you ever go back?" I asked. "To see what's left?"

Joseph's eyes met mine in the rearview mirror. "Every Sunday. My mother is buried there. The cemetery is... mostly covered now. But I know where she is."

I fell silent, suddenly aware of the presumption in my questions. This wasn't just a fascinating ruin to him. It was loss given physical form.

Ahead, what was left of Plymouth emerged from the haze. I had seen the old photos—a town bustling with life. Streets packed with fishermen selling their morning catch, children kicking soccer balls down narrow roads, music pouring from open doorways. A place that had once pulsed with stories.

Now, silence had swallowed everything whole.

Joseph parked at the edge of the exclusion zone. "I can take you as far as the checkpoint. Beyond that, you'll have a guide from the Disaster Management Coordination Agency. Two hours, then we head back before dark."

My guide turned out to be a middle-aged woman named Eliza with sharp eyes and a no-nonsense demeanor. She checked my permits, my protective gear, and issued rapid-fire safety instructions.

◎

"The volcano has been quiet lately, but that can change. When I say move, you move. Understand?"

I nodded, adjusting my mask against the fine volcanic dust that hung in the air.

"And don't wander off," she added. "Some buildings look stable but aren't. Ground can shift. Things collapse."

We moved through the outskirts of what had once been a thriving colonial port. The destruction wasn't clean or complete—that was what struck me first. Some structures stood almost intact beside others completely entombed. A gas station sign poked through layers of ash, its faded colors advertising prices from another time.

I moved carefully, my footsteps disturbing thin layers of ash that had settled like a second skin over the ruins. The rooftops of houses barely peeked above the surface, windows hollow and unseeing. An old streetlamp leaned at an unnatural angle, half-buried, its glass shattered.

"This was Parliament Street," Eliza said, pointing to what looked like a narrow canyon of gray. "Main shopping area. That building there—" she indicated a structure more intact than its neighbors, "—was the bank. Built stronger than most. Still standing, more or less."

I framed several shots, trying to capture the surreal quality of a street that was no longer a street. The layers of history visible in the strata of ash and mud.

"You're looking for the pretty shots," Eliza observed, watching me work. It wasn't a compliment.

"I'm looking for the truth," I countered.

⦿

She made a sound—not quite a laugh. "Truth isn't pretty."

"It doesn't have to be."

Eliza's expression softened slightly. "This way then. I'll show you truth."

She led me deeper into the ruined city, past what had been a school, a hospital, a hotel. Each structure told its own story of the day everything changed. Some buildings showed signs of hasty abandonment—personal belongings still visible through broken windows. Others had been methodically emptied, their owners clearly believing they would someday return.

Then—the clock tower. It rose like a defiant monument from the wasteland, its face frozen at the exact moment the volcano had taken everything.

I lifted my camera, framing the shot. I have traveled the world capturing places untouched by time. But here, time had been stolen, trapped beneath layers of earth.

The shutter clicked. And then, something caught my eye. A scarlet hibiscus, blooming in the ash. The red was almost violent against the gray, a wound or a promise—maybe both.

"Life finds a way," Eliza said, following my gaze. "Nature doesn't know how to give up."

The deeper I walked into the ruins, the more I saw. Vines twisted through the shattered windows of an old café, curling around the rusting metal of chairs and tables. A bananaquit bird—small, yellow, full of life—flitted between the green tendrils, as if the jungle had already begun whispering the town's eulogy.

The earth reclaims what man abandons.

"My husband and I had our first date there," Eliza said suddenly, pointing to the café. "Every Saturday after that, same table by the window. For seven years."

I looked at her, really looked for the first time. The lines around her eyes, the set of her jaw. The wedding band she still wore.

"He didn't make it out?" I asked softly.

"He made it out," she said. "But something in him never left this place. He's in Manchester now. With our daughter." She touched the ring briefly. "Some losses can't be photographed."

Her words stayed with me as we continued our tour. I found myself shooting differently—not just capturing the visual drama of destruction, but looking for the human echoes. A child's toy half-buried in mud. A sign outside a shop still advertising a sale that never concluded. A calendar on a wall, pages forever frozen on the day evacuation was ordered.

And yet, even among the wreckage, life had found a way back. I knelt, my hand brushing against the cracked pavement beneath me. It had split open, fractured by heat, by time, by loss. But pushing up from the break was a single green leaf. Small. Unshaken.

I didn't raise my camera immediately. I just looked at it—really looked. I exhaled, steadying my hands, and pressed the shutter.

◎

Because the world ends. And then, it begins again.

"You should see more than just ruins," Eliza said as we made our way back to the checkpoint. "This island isn't only about what we lost."

I thought of the assignment parameters—ruins and devastation, the dramatic narrative of nature's power. But she was right. The story wasn't complete without what came after, what remained, what continued despite everything.

"I'd like that," I said.

Joseph was waiting with the Land Rover. After a brief conversation with Eliza in local patois too quick for me to follow, he nodded.

"We have time for two more stops before sunset," he told me. "Places you should see."

Community Lunch - Capitol Hill

The hall smells like onions, warm bread, and something faintly metallic from the old coffee urns near the back. Steam rises in soft curls from the soup pots, fogging the lower panes of the tall windows that line the wall. Folding chairs scrape against scuffed linoleum as the room fills with voices—quiet ones, tired ones, a few lifted in bursts of laughter.

Gray stands beside me on a stool someone dragged over from the break room, her apron too big and tied in a loose knot at her back. A strand of hair slips from behind her ear as she concentrates, ladling vegetable soup into a chipped ceramic bowl with more care than most adults I've seen.

"Carrots," she says softly, satisfied. "Lots of them."

◯◯

I nod and hand her a chunk of cornbread wrapped in a paper napkin. She places it on the tray with a kind of reverence, like each plate is a gift. Her small fingers tremble a little from the weight, but she doesn't complain. She takes it to the front of the line, where the man waiting doesn't look up at first.

He's thin beneath his worn army jacket, hands raw from the wind. The stubble on his chin is silver-gray, like the wool peeking from his sleeves. Gray stands in front of him for a beat too long, tray held high. When he finally lifts his eyes, they soften.

"Thank you" he says, voice rough but kind.

Gray doesn't say anything at first. She just studies him, then offers the smallest smile. "Do you like cornbread?" she asks.

He blinks, then lets out a surprised laugh. "I love cornbread."

"Me too," she whispers, before hurrying back to me.

I reach out and squeeze her hand. She doesn't look up, just picks up the next bowl and begins again.

I glance toward the line—toward the man now seated near the radiator, holding the tray like it matters. Maybe it does.

Gray will never know what this night will stay in my memory as. Not the food or the people. But the way she looked at him. The way she waited, as if dignity was something best offered in silence.

Later, we wipe down tables together, her small fingers darting between salt shakers and baskets of crumpled napkins. She hums to herself—a tune I almost recognize. Something steady. Something

⦿

brave. It takes a moment, but then I catch it. Fleetwood Mac. It's *always* Fleetwood Mac with her. ♪

She doesn't ask why we do this. She already understands.

Runaway Ghaut

The narrow ravine cut deep into the mountainside, a slash of vibrant green against volcanic stone. Water trickled down its center, gathering in natural stone basins before continuing its journey to the sea.

"Runaway Ghaut," Joseph announced, pulling the Land Rover to a stop at a small clearing. "One of the island's gifts that even the volcano couldn't take."

The air changed as we walked toward it—cooler, damper, alive with the scent of moss and ferns. After the ash and dust of Plymouth, it felt like stepping into another world.

"Legend says," Joseph explained, leading me along a stone pathway, "if you drink from these waters, you will always return to Montserrat."

I raised my camera, capturing the play of light through the canopy, the way it dappled the flowing water.

"Many people did return," he continued, his voice softening. "After the evacuations. Even knowing the danger. The pull of home is strong."

I framed another shot—water droplets suspended in sunlight, ferns unfurling at the edges of the stream.

"Would you like to drink?" Joseph asked, gesturing to a small stone cup chained to the rock beside the clearest pool.

♪ *"Dreams"* by Fleetwood Mac

◎

I hesitated, thinking about superstitions and promises. About places that mark you, that call you back.

"It's just water," he said, noting my hesitation. "But also not."

I filled the cup and drank. The water was cool and sweet, tasting of earth and stone and something I couldn't name.

Click. I photographed the cup returning to its place on the rock. A simple object, worn smooth by thousands of hands, thousands of returns.

"Now you'll come back someday," Joseph said. It wasn't a question.

I wiped water from my lips, feeling it like a seal, a contract. "Seems like I've promised."

"The island remembers," he replied, looking up at the canopy where birds darted between branches, unconcerned with the volcano looming in the distance or the human dramas below.

Little Bay

The sun was already low in the sky when we reached Little Bay. Golden light washed over construction sites, temporary government buildings, and freshly painted homes. Cranes stood like mechanical sentinels against the darkening sky, promising something still taking shape.

"Our new beginning," Joseph said, parking on a hill overlooking the development. "Not what we would have chosen, but what we've made."

Below, children played soccer on a newly laid field. Market stalls lined a waterfront still raw with recent construction. Fishing boats bobbed in the harbor, their day's work complete. It wasn't Plymouth—

nothing would ever be Plymouth again—but it pulsed with present-tense life.

"Two-thirds of the island uninhabitable," Joseph said, "but we adapt. We continue."

I photographed a group of women laughing outside a small restaurant, their faces lit by both the setting sun and something from within. I captured construction workers ending their day, hard hats in hand, looking out at the sea from the framework of what would someday be a new government building.

"This matters too," Joseph said, watching me work. "Not just what was buried."

"I know," I said, and meant it.

As the sun dipped behind the peaks, the sky turned gold, stretching long shadows across Little Bay, the new capital still becoming itself. Below, lights began to flicker on—in homes, in businesses, in lives being rebuilt.

I took one last shot—a panorama capturing both the volcano in the distance and the new settlement in the foreground. Destruction and creation in the same frame. The island's past and future coexisting. For now, the volcano slept. But life didn't. And that was the story I had come to tell.

Later, as Joseph drove me back to the small guesthouse, I scrolled through the day's shots on my camera. Plymouth's clock tower frozen in time. The hibiscus blooming in ash. The leaf breaking through concrete. Eliza standing before the café where her life had once been

〇〇

ordinary and happy. The sacred waters of Runaway Ghaut promising return. The builders of Little Bay looking toward the future.

"Did you find what you were looking for?" Joseph asked, breaking the long silence.

I thought about Sophia for some reason. About missed connections and second chances. About life finding its way through cracks in what we thought was solid.

"Something better," I said. "I found what I wasn't looking for."

Joseph smiled slightly, nodding as if I'd finally said something he understood.

Back at my guesthouse that evening, I sent a handful of images to Jane—the expected shots of devastation and abandonment. But I held back the others. The ones that showed resilience. Rebirth. The persistence of life.

Those, I saved for a different story. One I wasn't ready to tell yet, but someday would.

Page & Puddle

Inside a bookstore, the world softens. The wood floors creak just enough to remind you you're somewhere meant to be lingered in. The air smells like old paper, dust, and something warm from the café—maybe cinnamon, maybe vanilla. Light filters through tall windows, catching on the spines of well-loved books and making them glow like quiet invitations.

Gray moved ahead of me with quiet purpose, fingertips skimming along the lower shelves. She didn't ask for help. She never did. She liked the search, the discovery. It reminded me of someone else I used to know.

She stopped at the children's section, crouched low, and pulled a small, green book from the shelf.

Goodnight Moon by Margaret Wise Brown.

My chest tightened—not with sadness, but something softer. Recognition. Memory. She opened it carefully, her lips moving as she read the first lines in a whisper only she could hear. "In the great green room…"

I stepped closer, slow, and crouched beside her. She didn't look up. She didn't have to. She knew I was there.

She clutched the book to her chest, nodding once—small, certain. This was the one. I reached out and brushed a bit of hair from her forehead, my hand resting there for a moment longer than it needed to. Her eyes lifted to mine, bright with that quiet certainty that lives in children who know they've chosen well.

She didn't say anything. Neither did I. But something passed between us all the same.

That book had been mine, once. Its pages worn from years of bedtime readings, the moon always there, always watching. A world where nothing bad ever happened. Just a bunny. A quiet room. A gentle goodbye to everything.

And now, she had it too.

The moment stretched between us—still, golden, almost sacred.

A hand-me-down kind of magic. She loved books. Like I did. Like I still do. I let myself feel that joy. Let it settle in my chest like warmth.

This was enough.

I chose *Braiding Sweetgrass* by Robin Wall Kimmerer, drawn first by the cover, then by the way the author spoke of plants as teachers, as gifts. Something in me needed that. Not instruction, exactly. More like permission—to slow down, to tend to what's still growing.

I trail my fingers along the shelf beside her—not really looking for anything, just enjoying the weight of being here. The smell of paper and ink. The warmth of wood floors and soft lamplight.

And slowly, my thoughts drift—back to when I was her age.

There wasn't a bookstore back home—just a squat brick library near the post office, with foggy windows and creaky radiator heat. I used to walk there after school, boots scuffing the sidewalk, mittens stuffed in my pockets. It wasn't grand, but it felt like it held the whole world inside.

An old-school library. Not the clean, algorithm-fed clicks of today. The real kind. Where the carpet was always too thin and smelled faintly of pencil shavings and book glue. Where finding a title meant a journey—not a keyword.

You had to want a book in those days. Had to hunt it.

Sliding open the long oak drawers of the card catalog, flipping past yellowed index cards typed with faded letters. Author. Title. Subject. Dewey Decimal numbers penciled so faintly they already looked like memory. Sometimes it took longer to find the book than to read it—but somehow, that made it feel more earned. Like you were chasing something. Like the search was part of the magic.

I remember the hush of the stacks. The rustle of pages turning behind heavy wooden tables. The way the quiet wasn't empty—it was full. Charged. Like all the stories were waiting just beneath the surface, ready to be discovered if you knew how to look.

Sometimes I'd pull books at random, just to check the card tucked inside. I wasn't looking for a title—I was looking for names. Classmates. Neighbors. People I knew who'd touched the same pages before me. There was something strange and comforting about it, as if the story had already passed through someone else's hands, and now it was mine to carry next.

Once, I found Anderson Brooks' name in a paperback with a cover that left very little to the imagination—a woman in torn lace, clutched dramatically by a man whose shirt seemed to have lost its will to exist. I'd sort of had a quiet crush on him up until that point. He was tall. Polite. Had decent handwriting. But after that day, I couldn't look at him the same way. Some stories change how you see people. Even the ones they didn't mean to share.

Everything changes. Card files give way to search bars. Hardcovers to screens. But some things stay. Like the feel of a new book in your hands. Or the look in your child's eyes when they find a story that feels like theirs.

And maybe that's enough.

The bell jingles as Gray and I step outside, our books warm in our arms. She clutches her book holding it tight against her chest like it's something precious, something meant to be kept close.

◎

As we walk past the window display—stacked spines and little paper snowflakes strung from fishing wire—Gray pauses to adjust the bag slung over her shoulder. Her fingers curl protectively around her book, and for a moment, I see myself in her. Not in any dramatic way. Just in the quiet reverence of the gesture.

Queen Anne moved at its usual rhythm. The scent of espresso drifts from a sidewalk café, laughter spills from a nearby boutique, and golden leaves flutter down like confetti from something recently broken but still beautiful.

Then—a guitar. A familiar melody floats through the crisp autumn air. Gentle. Nostalgic. My breath catches before I even place it.

"Moonshadow."

The world continues around us—strangers brushing past, a barista calling out a name—but I've gone somewhere else. Somewhere warmer. Simpler. A moment long gone: dusty air, sun-stained skin, a girl with salt on her lips and this song under her breath like a quiet prayer. She believed in its hope, its strange humor, its promise that even loss could be met with grace.

Gray spins. Just a little. An effortless twirl on the sidewalk, like her body is answering the music before her mind can catch up. The musician grins, catching the movement, and leans into the rhythm, strumming brighter. She twirls again, curls bouncing, cheeks flushed with joy. She doesn't know the song. Doesn't know what it meant—to me. What it still means.

I step forward and tuck a folded bill into the open guitar case. The musician nods his thanks, never missing a beat.

Gray bounds to my side, breathless and bright, her small hand finding mine. I brush a stray curl from her forehead, my fingers lingering for a heartbeat longer than necessary.

We keep walking. The music trails behind us like a shadow that doesn't want to be forgotten. Then—something stops me.

A "FOR LEASE" sign, taped inside a dusty storefront window.

The shop is empty. Sunlight filters through the large pane of glass, catching floating dust motes, stirring the ghost of something that once existed. Or maybe something that still could.

Gray notices a few steps later. She tugs at my sleeve, following my gaze. Her palm presses gently to the glass, nose almost touching.

"What's in there?" she asks.

I don't answer. Not because I don't want to. But because I don't know. Maybe it's nothing. Or maybe it's the beginning of something I haven't dared to name yet.

She tugs at me again, and I let her pull me back into the light.

Behind us, the guitar fades into the distance, but the melody stays, curling somewhere deep inside. And for the first time in a long time, I don't just wonder what I'm still searching for—I wonder if I've already started to find it.

That night, after Gray had gone to bed, I found myself standing at the kitchen counter, staring at the grain of the butcher block. My hands were wrapped around a mug I'd already forgotten to drink. The house was quiet. Still. But something wasn't.

I kept thinking about that empty storefront. The way the light hit the floor. The dust in the window. The shape of possibility. Not purpose in the way I'd known it—fieldwork and flashlights, clipboards and water filters. But something smaller. Softer. Still vital.

A place for people to come in from the cold. A place to sit. To be. A place where the world could slow down for a moment. Where names were remembered, and stories were shared, and you could taste something warm and know it had been made by hand.

I didn't need the old kind of mission anymore. Maybe now, I needed to build something rooted. Something that stayed.

I set the mug down, turned off the light, and walked toward the window. The street was empty, quiet in that particular way only late nights can be. But something stirred in me—a flicker of possibility. Not a plan. Not yet. But a pull.

The cursor blinks. A small, pulsing thing, waiting. Waiting for input. For permission. For truth. I type:

Sophia Farraday.

The Facebook search bar fills with endless names, faces, lives. A scroll of strangers—some close, some impossibly far. None of them her. I scroll. And scroll. Profiles blur together. Different eyes, different smiles, different lives I have no connection to. But no Sophia. No trace of her in this digital sprawl of existence.

I lean back in my chair, rubbing a hand over my face. Exhale. How many times have I done this? How many times have I hit refresh, scanned through names, let myself believe—for just a second—that I'd find her?

A knock at the door. I straighten, blinking away the quiet frustration curling at the edges of my mind. Andy stands there, easy grin, a stack of papers in one hand.

"Hey, Jane is ready for an update on next month's feature shoot."

"Okay," I nod. "I'll be right there. Thanks."

Andy disappears down the hall. I don't move right away. Instead, I stare out the window. The city moves fast—too fast. Buses blur past, cyclists dart between cars, people rush through the crosswalks like their lives depend on it. And then—stillness.

A girl on a bench. She's alone, reading. The world moves around her, but she doesn't seem to notice. Fingers idly brush the edge of the pages, lost in some other world—somewhere untouched by the rush of everything around her. ✳

A flicker of something sharp and familiar cuts through me. For a second, it's not Boulder. It's not now. It's Telluride. It's then. Sophia. Sitting on the bench. Still. Unaware. A book in her hands. The afternoon light softened her face, her curls shifting as she turned a page.

I inhale, slow. The city rushes on. The girl turns another page. The memory fades. I drag a hand through my hair, pushing the chair back. My eyes flick to the Facebook screen still open in front of me. A name with no answers. "Where are you?"

☼

We were stuck in traffic, the late summer sun slanting through the windshield, casting long strips of light across the dashboard. Gray sat in the passenger seat, legs swinging above the floor, scuffed sneakers dusty from the park. She leaned against the window frame, watching the car beside us.

✳ *"The Secret Garden"* by Frances Hodgson Burnett

⦿

A teenage girl sat in the front seat, hair in a messy bun, sunglasses perched on her head. She blew a massive pink bubble, let it pop against her lips, then laughed with her friends like it was the best thing that had happened all day.

Gray turned to me with a look that was all question and delight. I reached into the glove compartment and pulled out a pack of Bubble Yum—Watermelon, flattened from the heat. Her eyes lit up. I wondered if this would become one of those stories she'd tell someday— about the bubble gum, the traffic, the sun in her eyes.

I handed her a piece, then tore one off for myself. We chewed together, slow and exaggerated. She mimicked my rhythm with the kind of fierce determination only a child learning something sacred can have.

The first bubble didn't go far. The second collapsed. But the third— round and wobbly—hovered for a second before bursting across her nose. She shrieked with laughter. I wiped her cheek with a tissue, still chewing. She beamed up at me like we'd pulled off a miracle. The radio played something soft. The windows were down. The breeze smelled of hot pavement and cut grass. I leaned back in my seat. Gray looked over, eyes shining, pink gum stuck to her front teeth. ♪

There wasn't anywhere to be. No urgency. Just the sun sliding lower, the hum of the engine, the occasional bump of the breeze against our arms. We were suspended—between destinations, between her childhood and whatever comes next. Not a milestone. Not a lesson. Just a perfect, ordinary moment that asked nothing of us except to be in it.

I smiled. And I hoped she'd remember this. The wind. The gum. The joy of trying. And the mother who once taught her how to make magic—without ever saying a word.

♪ "Tupelo Honey" by Van Morrison

09

17:01:10:03:13:38

The key stuck at first. Old lock. Stubborn. Like the place wasn't quite sure if it was ready to be opened again. I jiggled it once, then again. The metal scraped, caught—and turned.

The door gave way with a soft groan, hinges dry but still willing. Light spilled in from the street behind me, pooling across the scuffed hardwood floor like it had been waiting.

I stepped inside, and the air shifted. Dust. Old wood. Something faint and citrusy from a candle long since burned out. It smelled like memory and maybe—just maybe—possibility. Like something waiting to begin again.

The door closed behind me with a *click*.

After a few weeks of quiet negotiations, second-guessing, and rereading the lease more times than I care to admit—

This was mine now.

The space was still empty. Bare walls, dust settling in the corners. The faint scent of old wood and possibility lingers in the air. Light filters through the front window, spilling across the scuffed hardwood floor—the only thing that remains of whatever existed here before. I move slowly, sketchpad in hand, pacing the length of the room. The echo of my footsteps follows me. Empty, yes.

But not for long.

I press the tip of my pencil to the page, and in a few quick strokes, the emptiness begins to take form. A counter here, bathed in warm light. Booths lining the wall, worn but inviting. Shelves filled with books, poetry, stories waiting to be discovered. I glance up, eyes tracing the blank canvas before me. No warmth.

No color. No life. Not yet. But I see it.

I sit at the small wooden table I dragged in from home, flipping to a fresh page. The tip of my pencil glides, bringing soft curves and swirling lines to life. The name comes naturally, like it has always existed— just waiting to be found.

The letters spill across the page, looping into a design as natural as breath. A name that feels like home. I turn, imagining the light catching the logo as it sits proudly in the window. Inviting. Warm. A promise of something different.

I can almost hear it. The soft hum of conversation, the quiet clatter of cups against saucers, the hiss of milk steaming into something rich and golden. A place where words linger in the air. Where poetry is more than just what's written—it's what's felt. What's shared.

I sketch faster now, adding details, flourishes, bits of life. A hand-painted menu. A vintage record player in the corner. The lines on the page blur as my mind races ahead, pulling me toward what could be. It's real. It just doesn't exist yet. I stand, holding up my sketch, picturing it coming to life.

And in my mind. It does—

Cafe Sonnet

—Dawn breaks with gentle insistence through the windows. I arrived before sunrise, finding comfort in the quiet ritual of opening—the methodical click of lights, the gentle hum of the espresso machine warming up, flour dusting my hands as I shaped the day's first batch of scones. These solitary morning moments center me, before the world filters in.

The air is thick with the scent of coffee and fresh pastries, warmth curling through the space like an embrace. The once-empty walls now breathe with life—lined with poetry, old book pages, and paintings by local artists. Sunlight spills through the window, catching flecks of flour on the counter, swirling them like tiny stars.

I glance at the window. The logo I sketched now etched in glass, bold yet soft. *Café Sonnet*. A name. A home. A dream brought to life.

Outside, the sky darkens suddenly—a spring shower approaching. The light changes, casting the café in a soft blue glow that makes every-

◎

thing feel slightly underwater. I adjust the dimmer switch, compensating with warm lighting that makes the wooden tables glow amber.

The bell above the door chimes as the rain begins to fall, bringing with it a sudden rush of customers seeking shelter. I move faster now, a practiced dance between coffee grounds and steamed milk, between oven and counter. A small spill of coffee becomes a quick wipe, a dropped pastry immediately replaced. The controlled chaos of a morning rush feels electric in my veins.

An acoustic melody drifts from the café speakers—gentle, golden, familiar. It moves like morning light across a kitchen floor: easy, unhurried, quietly certain of its place in the world. It doesn't demand attention. It just fills the space with something warm and steady. The kind of song that feels like fresh coffee and bare feet. Like the beginning of something that already knows it's going to last. ♪

"The scones are even better today," a voice calls out from the community table. It belongs to Marcus, who comes in every Thursday with a stack of papers to grade. He's been here since the beginning, since the days when I wasn't sure if anyone would come at all. His approval feels like validation.

And for the first time in a long time, I feel completely awake. I move through the café, my café, my hands steady and sure. A careful pour of coffee, steam curling into the air. A gentle swirl of milk, the foam forming delicate shapes beneath my touch. A plate of fresh scones, set down before an elderly man who greets me with a knowing smile.

"Another cinnamon latte today?" he asks, already reaching for it.

I nod, my lips curving into a small smile. I know his order by

♪ *"Sunrise"* by Norah Jones

⦾

heart. I know he lingers a little longer over his coffee on rainy days and always tucks an old book beneath his arm.

As if on cue, he pulls out his book—a different one today. The cover is faded red fabric, no title visible. He notices me noticing and pats the book gently. "My late wife's favorite," he offers, a rare personal detail that feels like a gift. ✳

The crowd ebbs slightly as the rain intensifies, drumming against the roof in a soothing rhythm. I breathe in the petrichor drifting in from the briefly opened door, mingling with coffee and cinnamon.

Near the window, a woman with tired eyes sits alone, staring out at the rain. The kind of silence that feels heavy, full of things left unsaid. The ache in her expression lingers with me. I know that look—I've worn it myself on days when the weight of memory becomes too much. I place a warm lemon muffin beside her coffee, a quiet offering, and move on. She startles slightly, then looks up, blinking.

"Oh," she breathes, touching the edge of the plate. "Thank you." There's a tremor in her voice, a fragility that suggests this small kindness might be the first she's received today.

I nod, but don't linger. Because sometimes, comfort isn't words. Sometimes, it's the weight of a warm cup in your hands, the scent of lemon lingering in the air, the knowledge that someone sees you—even when you don't ask to be seen.

The rain begins to ease, light breaking through clouds, casting long shadows across the wooden floors. I reach up to adjust the hanging plants, their vines trailing down toward the communal table where a group of students have spread out their laptops, creating their own

✳ "A Tree Grows in Brooklyn" by Betty Smith

little ecosystem of productivity. One catches my eye and raises her mug in silent thanks.

At a corner table, a young girl sits, her nose buried in a book far too advanced for her age. She has the same deep focus that Gray has— the same quiet intensity. I slide a hot chocolate onto her table, setting it down without a word. She doesn't look up right away, but when she does, her small smile says everything. ✳

"I'm at the good part," she whispers, as if sharing a secret. Her fingers are stained with ink—she's been writing in the margins again. I nod in understanding and move away, giving her space to dive back into her world.

Through the window, I can see the first rainbow of spring arching over the buildings across the street. Inside, the café hums with gentle conversation, the clink of spoons against ceramic, pages turning, lives intersecting in this space I've created.

The bell above the door chimes softly as someone new enters, shaking raindrops from their umbrella. I turn, my heart full, my hands steady.

I built this place with love. And in return, it gives love back, not just to me, but to everyone who walks through that door seeking warmth, connection, or simply a moment of peace in their day.

Beast + Bottle

The restaurant glows with a quiet intimacy—soft candlelight flickering against exposed brick walls, a hum of conversation blending with the slow, steady notes of jazz in the background. *Beast + Bottle* is the kind of place that makes you want to stay awhile.

✳ *"A Wrinkle in Time"* by Madeleine L'Engle

◍

But I have the sinking feeling that tonight, something is coming that I won't be able to outrun.

Across from me, Martone's eyes catch the low light—dark, thoughtful, searching. She reaches across the table, her fingers tracing the back of my hand. The gesture is warm, but there's a nervous energy underneath it, a kind of hesitation that makes my chest tighten.

I know this moment. I've photographed it before—not with us, but in the expressions of people all over the world. That fleeting second before something shifts.

She exhales slowly, forcing a smile.

"This place is stunning," she says. "I've been looking forward to this all week."

I nod, mirroring the smile, trying to smooth over the edge creeping into the space between us.

"Me too. It's nice to slow down for once."

The words feel like a placeholder. I don't slow down. Not really.

Martone studies me for a beat, then drops her gaze, running her fingertip along the rim of her wine glass. "You've been so busy lately," she says carefully. "Every time I see you, it feels like I'm catching a shooting star—here one second, gone the next."

A sharp pang of guilt stirs, but I smother it with humor. "Always up in the air. I should start calling myself Ryan Bingham." ♪

She laughs, but it doesn't reach her eyes.

♪ "The Snow Before Us" by Charles Atlas

- 313 -

◉

Then, she takes a deep breath—one of those steadying breaths people take before stepping onto uncertain ground.

Here it comes.

"Michael…" she hesitates, her fingers tightening around her wine glass. "There's something I need to say. It's been weighing on me for a while."

A prickle of unease crawls up my spine.

I set my glass down and meet her gaze. "Okay… what's on your mind?"

Martone shifts, pressing her lips together, then exhales. "We've been together for a long time, and I love you. I love what we have. But… I'm not sure where we're going."

She pauses, watching me carefully.

"It feels like we're stuck, always waiting for something—your next trip, your next flight. I need to know if we're heading toward something real."

The words land like a slow-moving avalanche, pressing down, filling the space between us with something heavy. I want to give her certainty. I wish I could. But I can't. Not yet. Maybe not ever.

I shift in my seat, my hands curling around my napkin, buying myself a few seconds I already know won't be enough.

"I love you too, Martone. I really do." The words aren't a lie. But the next part…

"But… I don't know if I'm ready for that next step."

Her face softens for a moment, but there's something else behind her expression now. A glimmer of sadness. Of realization. She already knows what I'm going to say.

"Maybe it's because I'm gone so much," I continue. "It's not fair to you."

Martone leans back, looking down at her hands, then back at me.

"I get it, Michael." Her voice is steady, but her fingers tighten slightly around her wine glass.

"I've always known your work is important, and I admire that. I have my own career too, and I'm not asking you to change who you are. But I've made sacrifices…" She trails off, then takes another breath.

"I've put things on hold, thinking we'd figure it out together. I just can't keep waiting in limbo."

I reach for her hand, squeezing it gently, trying to anchor her to me. But her sadness is turning into resolve. And that terrifies me.

"I wish I could give you the answers you deserve," I admit. "But right now… I just don't know."

Martone exhales, nodding slowly. For the first time all night, I feel her pulling away. Not physically. But in that way people do when they realize they might be reaching for something that isn't there.

She gently pulls her hand back, tucking it in her lap. "I understand that you don't have all the answers," she says, her voice careful, measured. "But Michael, I want more. I want stability, a home, maybe a family someday."

The word family sits between us, heavy as stone. She looks at me, her expression unreadable.

"I need to know that's something we're moving toward—together."

The weight of it settles deeper. She swallows, blinking once, then continues. "I can't live in this space where I'm always wondering if your next flight will take you away for good."

Her voice is so calm, so even. But the way she's gripping her napkin tells me everything. She's already made her decision. She just needs me to make mine.

I look down at the flickering candle, watching the way the wax drips, pooling at the base, hardening as it cools.

I know the answer she wants. I know the answer I should give. But all I have is silence. And the longer it stretches, the more final it feels. Martone watches me, waiting. Hoping. Then—slowly, like something breaking—her hope fades.

She leans back, her lips pressing into a thin, sad smile. "I don't want to walk away from us," she says softly.

"But I have to be honest with myself. I can't keep waiting for you to figure it out."

Her words cut, not because they're cruel, but because they're true. She doesn't say "yet." She doesn't say "someday." And that's when I know—this isn't just a conversation. This is a crossroads.

She smiles at me, but it's not the same as before. Not open. Not full of possibility. Just sad. Resigned. Final.

"I love you, Michael." She pauses, then exhales. "But love isn't enough if we're just going through the motions."

She stands, reaching for her purse. Then—she hesitates. Leans in. And presses a soft kiss to my cheek.

It's not romantic. Not pleading. It's something quieter than that. A goodbye wrapped in kindness. In grief. Her voice is barely above a whisper, meant only for me.

"I'm sorry, Michael. But time has run out on us."

She straightens. Offers a small, sad smile. One more glance. And then she turns, heels tapping gently across the floor as she walks away.

I don't stop her. I just sit there, staring at the empty place across the table, the untouched wineglass, the flickering candle between us.

And I do nothing. Because I know—This was the moment. And it's already gone.

The kitchen at *Café Sonnet* was quiet, the kind of quiet that hummed beneath fluorescent lights and the low purr of refrigeration. Steam curled from a pot on the stove, the scent of rosemary and roasted garlic settling into my sweater. I stood at the prep table, spreading out stacks of to-go containers like cards, each one labeled in neat block print with black Sharpie.

Meatloaf. Mashed potatoes. Green beans.

⊚

Behind me, banana bread cooled on the rack, already sliced and wrapped. Granola bars, bagged. Fruit, sorted. The kind of meal that didn't fix anything, but maybe made the night a little easier. A little softer.

I sealed another container and pressed it into the growing line. It was always like this—quiet, methodical. A rhythm I didn't have to think about. My hands moved, but my thoughts drifted.

I used to believe I had to go far away to make a difference. Across oceans. Into villages where everything felt foreign and extraordinary. Maybe it was the way Ethan spoke about his time—like the only lives that mattered were the ones in distant time zones. He meant well. We both did. But somewhere along the way, he'd missed the truth I'd come to understand here, in this small kitchen, in this town.

This place—these four walls—had become a new kind of mission. Different zip code, same heartbeat. A space to serve, to feed, to listen. Not because it made headlines, but because it mattered.

Need isn't always wrapped in the exotic. It doesn't always come with stamps in a passport or stories that impress at dinner parties. Sometimes, it lives just down the street. Sometimes, it waits at the edge of a park bench or lingers in the pause before someone asks for help.

I reached for another container, wiping a smudge off the lid before pressing it closed. There was always something to do. Someone to feed. Someone to see. And I didn't have to leave the country to do it.

It turns out, you don't need to cross an ocean to serve. Just a door-

⦿

frame. The café wasn't just mine—it was a way back to the kind of purpose I thought I'd left behind with the Peace Corps.

Here, no one asked for a grand gesture. Just a warm meal. A steady hand. A kind face that stayed.

And for the first time in a long time, that felt like enough.

Gross Reservoir - Boulder County

The lake stretches wide and glassy, mirroring the pale blue sky. Gross Reservoir always has this stillness to it—like time doesn't touch it, like everything slows the moment you push off from shore.

Brandon and I drift in a canoe, rods propped lazily against the side, beer bottles wedged between our knees. The air smells like pine and water, the occasional ripple breaking the surface. It should feel peaceful. It always has before. But today, my thoughts are too loud.

I let my hand skim the surface, trailing through the cold, dark water. The ripples spread outward, vanishing into nothing. Then, without looking up, I say it.

"So, Martone left me."

Brandon snaps open his beer, takes a sip without missing a beat.

"What? You two seemed inseparable. What happened?"

I exhale, watching a dragonfly skim the surface before darting away. I envy its freedom.

"She couldn't wait for me to commit."

Brandon reels in his line, checking the bait.

"Okay. So, why didn't you?"

I should have an answer by now. I've been asking myself the same thing for weeks. Martone was everything I should have wanted. Smart, beautiful, steady. She grounded me in ways I never knew I needed. She fit into my life so easily. So why couldn't I give her what she deserved?

I don't answer right away, just watch as the canoe drifts, the water parting effortlessly around us. Finally, I say the only truth I have.

"To be honest, I could never look at Martone the way I looked at Sophia."

Brandon groans, exasperated. "Sophia from Telluride? Are we talking about the same person? That was, what, twenty-five years ago?"

I roll the beer bottle between my hands. "Yeah, I know it sounds crazy."

Brandon shakes his head, casting his line again. The lure skips across the water before vanishing beneath the surface.

"Michael, Sophia is a fairy tale. An idealized version of perfection. In reality, she could be that chick from Fatal Attraction."

I try to deflect. "Alex Forrest? Great."

Brandon leans back slightly, resting an arm on the side of the canoe. "You know what Monica told me when we first got together? She said, 'I don't want to be someone's perfect dream. I want to be someone's beautiful reality.'"

⦿

I take a slow sip of beer, the bitterness settling on my tongue.

"And that worked for you?"

"Yeah, because I stopped chasing the idea of perfect."

A fish jumps nearby, sending ripples across the surface. I watch the water swirl, then flatten back into glass.

"I loved Martone. I really did. But thinking about another woman felt like betrayal."

But it wasn't just that. It was the way my chest felt tight whenever she talked about the future. The way I stalled whenever she brought up moving in together, buying a house, marriage. She thought it was my job, my travel schedule. And maybe that was part of it. But the truth was simpler.

I was never all in. And she deserved someone who was.

Brandon shrugs, his voice quieter now. "Nobody is perfect. Don't be so hard on yourself."

I shake my head, casting my line without much thought. "It still doesn't make it right."

Brandon doesn't argue. Just watches his own line, the tip of the rod barely twitching.

Then, after a long pause, he says, "Listen, when I met Monica, I was hung up on this girl from college. I thought she was the one that got away. Monica knew it too."

I glance at him, studying his expression.

"What changed?"

Brandon exhales, watching the sky. "Monica said something I'll never forget. She said, 'I'd rather be your messy reality than compete with a perfect memory.'"

I roll that over in my mind, feeling the weight of it. Messy reality. Perfect memory. I take another sip of beer, letting the words settle.

"I just... haven't seen anyone like Sophia—before or since."

Brandon chuckles, shaking his head. "Funny thing—I can't even remember that girl's name now. But what Monica and I built? The real stuff, the hard stuff? That's what matters."

I think about that. Would I have ever built something real with Martone, if I had just let go of the past? Or would I have still been chasing a ghost?

Brandon reels in his line—no fish, but no disappointment either.

"You can't let this cloud your judgment, or you'll end up alone."

I stare out over the water, watching the sun glint off its rippled surface.

"That thought keeps me up at night."

Brandon gives the canoe a gentle nudge with his paddle, adjusting our drift.

"You deserve something real. Monica and I didn't have a story-book romance, but we fought for it. Still do."

I sigh, tipping my beer toward him.

"Yeah, but you make it look easy. You're my idol, Brandon."

Brandon grins, raising his bottle. "To finding what's real."

We clink bottles. A comfortable silence stretches between us, broken only by the occasional plunk of water against the hull.

Then Brandon shakes his head, amused.

"Am I really your idol?"

"Not really."

I slide on my sunglasses. A pause.

"Bob Dylan is."

☼

The house is silent except for the ticking of the kitchen clock. The kind of silence that isn't peaceful, but heavy—thick with all the words we haven't said.

I stand at the window, arms crossed, watching the yard. Gray's soccer ball lies forgotten in the grass. Her bicycle is tipped over near the porch, the front wheel still slightly spinning from the wind. Little things. Ordinary things. But today, they feel like something else. Like remnants of a life Ethan is walking away from.

⦿

I turn, my fingers brushing over the table until they land on a photograph. Gray's last birthday. In the picture, she's wedged between us, beaming at the camera, two front teeth missing, hands still sticky from cake. Her smile is big, unshaken, unknowing.

I hold the photo a moment longer, then turn it toward Ethan. Our eyes meet across the room. The weight between us is unbearable. Ethan exhales, rubbing a hand over his face.

"Of all people, you should understand." he says.

I don't move. His words are meant to explain, maybe even absolve, but all they do is push me further into silence. Because I do understand. I understand in a way he never had to. I know what it means to walk away from something you love for something greater. But I also know what it means to stay.

My gaze flickers to his Peace Corps jacket—the same one he's worn through jungles, over dusty roads, through villages where his name doesn't matter but his work does. The fabric is soft, worn thin in places. Like an old friend he chooses, over and over. And over.

His bag is already packed, waiting by the door like it's always been. Like it knew before I did that he was leaving.

I set the photo back down carefully, my fingers lingering on Gray's face. A piece of her childhood, captured—frozen, untouched by what's happening right now.

A part of me is relieved she's away this weekend, snowboarding with friends at Mt. Baker. Relieved that she doesn't have to witness this. That she's not in the back seat, clutching that bear, pleading with him again. That she doesn't have to hear another goodbye.

◉

Ethan shifts, hesitating in the doorway. Waiting. Maybe hoping. For what? That I'll turn? That I'll stop him? That I'll tell him I understand and let him go without feeling like he's abandoning us? I let my silence be his answer.

The door clicks shut. The sound is final. Like a punctuation mark at the end of a sentence I never got to write.

I stay frozen in place, listening for the familiar scrape of his boots down the steps. Then—the crunch of tires, the low idle of the cab waiting at the curb. The front door clicks shut behind him. Quiet settles in its place.

I move to the window again. Pull the curtain back just enough to see Ethan emerging, dragging his bag behind him. He doesn't look up. Doesn't glance back. Just opens the door, slides into the backseat, and the cab pulls away. I watch until it turns the corner, until the taillights vanish behind the trees.

And then I stay there. Still. Quiet. Not because I'm waiting for him to come back. But because I need a minute to feel it. All of it. The grief. The failure. The strange, hollow relief. Love is never supposed to end this way. But sometimes it doesn't end at all—it just... runs dry. Fades into silence. Disappears in the rearview.

I press my hand to the cold glass, breathing in the quiet that's left behind. Let it go, I think. Let him go. And for the first time, I do.

My reflection stares back—blurred by breath, haloed in lights from the street behind me. Just a shape now. A version of myself I'm finally ready to stop chasing.

The glass shifts. So does the reflection—

(0)

Zulu Queen - Telluride

—The mirrored surface of my goggles reflects the slope ahead—clean, untouched, waiting. The wind bites against my face, sharp and bracing, but I barely feel it. Up here, at the top, the world is silent. Just me, the sky, and the mountains stretched out like something ancient and infinite. ♪

I lift my goggles from my helmet and let them rest on my forehead. My breath curls into the air in slow white puffs, and I squint into the sun, scanning the ridgeline. The snow catches the light in fractured diamonds, blinding and perfect. Everything looks smaller from up here. The problems. The noise. The life I keep trying to untangle.

I shift my weight, adjusting the bindings, the familiar click of boot against ski echoing against the wind. My poles dig into the snow—light, instinctive. I glance down at the line ahead of me: steep, untouched, a narrow ribbon of ruts still waiting for its first carve of the day.

I lower my goggles again. The world tints amber, edges sharpening, everything narrowing to the slope and the sky.

The cold stings my nose, sneaks into my gloves. My thighs already hum with the familiar ache of altitude and anticipation. A raven cuts across the horizon in a silent arc, winging its way toward the lift station.

I take one long breath, the kind that settles deep into the ribs. There's something about these mountains that still hums in my bones, even after all these years. They don't care who I am. They don't care where I've been. But they've kept me company through it all.

Gravity takes hold, and for a fleeting second—weightlessness. The

♪ *"Age of Man"* by Greta Van Fleet

rush of wind, the sudden quiet just before the world tilts forward. Then—momentum.

The first turn is clean, my skis carving deep into the zipperline. The mountain moves beneath me, guiding, not resisting. Everything sharpens—the cold air, the scrape of steel edges against snow, the sheer drop below, daring me forward.

I pick up speed. The slope is steep, unforgiving. The kind of terrain that doesn't tolerate hesitation. I lean in, letting instinct take over.

Turn. Compress. Breathe.

The wind roars past my ears, drowning everything else. Nothing exists but the descent—the rhythm of movement, the pulse of adrenaline, the absolute clarity that comes when you're fully inside the moment.

The world narrows into motion, into now. Not the regrets. Not the questions. Not the girl I can't stop thinking about. For the first time in a long while, I'm not thinking about anything. Not the past. Not the future. Just the mountain beneath me, the snow flying in my wake, and the rare, elusive feeling of being exactly where I'm supposed to be.

Just this. The rhythm of descent. The clean arc of a turn. The mountain under my feet...

Gray stands beside me behind the counter, sleeves rolled to her elbows, a dusting of flour on her cheek she hasn't noticed. She moves with more confidence these days—tucking pastries into the case, refilling napkin holders, rinsing espresso cups without being asked. On weekends, she insists on helping. She says it's "just something we do," like it's always been this way.

And maybe it has. I don't remember the exact day she stopped playing café and started showing up for it. I only know that I love these mornings. The quiet rhythm of our hands moving in sync, the unspoken dance of mother and daughter working side by side.

There's something about her in this space—something settled. Grounded. She hums under her breath sometimes, still Fleetwood Mac, usually off-key. I let her run the register when it's slow, and she makes the lattes a little too foamy. But she's good with people. She notices things. I watch her out of the corner of my eye sometimes and think: she's becoming someone I'd want to know, even if she weren't mine. ♪

The bell above the door gave its usual soft jingle—light, almost shy. I looked up from wiping the counter and saw him shuffle in. Same coat. Same tired eyes. He always moved the same way—cautious, like he didn't want to be noticed. But by now, he was part of the rhythm here. I didn't know his name. He'd never offered it, and I'd never asked.

Before I could move, Gray stepped beside me, wiping her hands on her apron, eyes fixed on him.

"He likes cornbread," she said softly, leaning in.

I blinked, surprised. I hadn't realized she'd been paying attention that closely. But of course she had. Gray always sees what matters.

She turned and pulled a plate from the stack, already moving. "I'll take it to him," she added, voice low, certain.

I poured the coffee—dark roast, splash of cream, no sugar—while Gray cut a thick square of the still-warm cornbread. She added a small packet of butter, tucked it neatly on the plate, and took both from the counter with careful hands. For a moment, I just watched her. The

♪ *"Silver Springs"* by Fleetwood Mac

steadiness in her step. The quiet, instinctive grace of someone who understood more than she should have at her age.

The man had chosen the table by the window again, as he always did. Shoulders hunched, eyes cast low. But when Gray approached, his gaze lifted—not wary, just surprised.

"I remember you," she said gently, setting the plate and coffee down in front of him.

He looked at her for a long moment. Then nodded once, slow and deliberate. His eyes crinkled just slightly at the corners. Not a smile, not quite—but close. The kind that says thank you without saying a word.

Gray didn't linger. Just gave a small, respectful nod and turned back to the counter. She didn't rush, didn't glance over her shoulder to check on him. She just resumed wiping down the espresso machine, humming quietly to herself like nothing out of the ordinary had just happened.

But it had.

Behind the counter, I folded napkins and watched Gray move from task to task, deliberate and calm. There was so much of the world she didn't know yet. But this part? The part where we see each other, where we give without asking anything in return? She already understood that. And somehow, just watching her... I did too.

As he sat at the window, I caught the way his shoulders sagged, then slowly began to settle. The sunlight drew out every line, every tired crease. I recognized that look—the quiet calculation of someone used to weighing how long they can stay in one place before they're asked to move along.

It wasn't so different from the faces I saw years ago, in the villages where I first learned the language of need. Malawi. Uganda. Ghana. The names still lived inside me, even if the dirt roads and dusty courtyards were far behind. There, I learned how poverty could take on different shapes. Hunger didn't always show itself in bones—it showed in eyes, in silence, in the way someone carried their hands when they didn't know what they were allowed to touch.

Here, in the café, it showed in how slowly he sat. How carefully he ate. Like it might all be taken back. He ate with both hands on the cornbread, elbows tucked in close. Careful. Grateful. He never stayed long. But he always finished the coffee. And I never charged him.

It wasn't a transaction. It never had been.

We both looked over once more, just to make sure he looked warm enough. Settled enough.

The scent of rosemary, sage, and something slightly untraditional drifts through the dining room, curling into the warm air like a promise. Thanksgiving at our house never follows the rules. We always eat early—no real reason. It's just the way it's always been.

I glance over the spread on the table—sure, there's turkey, but next to it, I spot something unexpected. Something with a little too much flair for your average holiday meal.

"I see tradition has taken a back seat again." I smirk, reaching for my wine glass.

Grandfather leans back in his chair, his usual air of wisdom laced with mischief. "They say variety is the spice of life. And with your Mom's cooking, we certainly get a lot of spice."

Mom shrugs, a playful smile tugging at her lips as she tops off my wine. "What can I say? Thanksgiving doesn't have to be predictable."

We all laugh, the sound rich and easy, folding itself into the warmth of the room. This is what I miss most when I'm away. The effortless banter. The teasing that never veers into cruelty. The way home feels like a place where I don't have to be anything but me.

I glance at Grandfather, watching as he carefully carves into the turkey, his movements slow, deliberate. His hands, once so strong, now tremble slightly with age. A flicker of emotion catches me off guard. Time is moving, always moving.

Mom moves around the table, fussing over details, adjusting the centerpiece, refilling glasses. She's always in motion, always creating, always making something beautiful.

I watch her and Grandfather, feeling that familiar warmth settle in my chest. No matter how far I travel, no matter what stories I capture through my lens, nothing compares to this. Except maybe that first moment on the sidewalk—a stranger whose face somehow changed everything.

Later, the warm water runs over my hands as I scrub the last of the Thanksgiving dishes, the scent of leftover turkey and spiced cider lingering in the air. Soap suds swirl down the drain, disappearing like the years that have slipped past me.

Outside the kitchen window, the quiet street is dusted with fresh snow. Rooftops glow under the late afternoon light, and bare trees sway in the wind. Everything here feels still—unchanged. Familiar.

Then—the chime. The courthouse clock. My breath catches. The sound rolls through the valley, deep and deliberate. The same chime I used to race against.

I remember the rhythm of those runs—boots pounding the sidewalk, dodging tourists, weaving through crowds. My lungs burning, my heart louder than the bell. Not just from the sprint, but from the possibility that she'd be there. That I'd make it in time. That I wouldn't miss her.

I was always running toward her. Always.

My grip tightens on the dish towel. For a second, I feel it again. The pull. The urgency. The ache in my chest that had nothing to do with exertion and everything to do with hope.

When the chime ended, she'd either be there—or she wouldn't. I glance down at the soapy water. The last bubbles vanish. The chime fades.

This time, I don't run.

The Telluride wind carries the sound of the courthouse clock as Gray and I step up to my brother's front porch. The chime settles into my bones—low, familiar, steady. A reminder of all that's changed, and all that hasn't.

Daniel used to say he'd never move back. City life suited him then—fast-paced, anonymous, full of motion. But even that lost its shine. He came back a few years ago, quietly, like the decision had always been waiting. This house tucked just off Colorado Ave, walking distance to everything and nothing. He says the pace makes sense now. That the quiet doesn't feel empty anymore.

Gray hugs herself against the cold. I wrap an arm around her shoulders, and she leans in with a small sigh. For a moment, we just stand there. Listening. She glances up at me. I squeeze her shoulder, and she steps forward to ring the bell.

The door swings open, and warmth spills out—laughter, light, the smell of roasted turkey and sage.

Daniel grins at us from the doorway, his smile just as I remember.

"Hey, look who finally showed up!"

He pulls me into a hug, and I let it happen. I didn't know I needed it until it landed. Gray ducks beneath his arm and disappears inside, already peeling off her coat, drawn by the sound of her cousins in the next room.

I linger in the doorway. Inhale. Rosemary. Bread. The scent of home. Daniel nudges me gently. "Come on in," he says, his voice softer now. I step inside, and close the door behind me.

Candlelight flickers across familiar faces, catching the shimmer of cranberry sauce and the rising steam from a basket of bread. My mother fusses over the gravy boat, my father carves the turkey with the same quiet confidence he once used to steady me on ice skates. Daniel pours another round of wine. Gray laughs with her cousins, cheeks pink from warmth and belonging.

My mother catches my eye from across the kitchen. She's wiping her hands on a dishtowel, her hair silver now, sun-kissed from retirement in Arizona. She opens her arms without a word. I cross the room, let myself be held. Her hug is soft but certain—familiar in a way I didn't realize I'd missed.

Behind her, my father waits with a quiet smile. He smells like cedar and warm spice, like every Thanksgiving I remember. I wrap my arms around him, too, and he presses a hand gently to my back. No words. Just that steady reassurance I grew up with. Their winters are warmer now, but they've flown up anyway. For this.

I let my eyes drift over all of them, and feel it—The press of something unspoken. All the years I spent chasing meaning. Distance. Answers. And somehow, I've landed here. In this moment. In this room.

Daniel raises his glass. "Mom, you outdid yourself."

She waves him off, but her eyes soften. "You say that every year."

"Because it's always true."

Their easy rhythm flows around me, and for the first time in a long while, I feel the shape of something I used to know. Family has always been here. Even when I ran from it. Even when I disappeared.

Daniel meets my gaze across the table. His eyes hold the question.

"Are you okay?"

I nod. Just enough. He doesn't press. He never has. My constant. Gray leans against my arm, resting her head there before drifting back into conversation. I rest my hand on her back. A silent promise.

Ethan isn't here. He should be. But at least I'm not alone.

KSEA - Seattle-Tacoma

The jet engines howl as a 737 descends, streaking across the steel-gray sky. I watch through the terminal window as it nears the ground, the wheels skimming the tarmac before making contact. Thud. A heart-beat later, the thrust reversers engage, a deafening roar shaking the runway as the aircraft slows. Another arrival in the Emerald City. The exact moment of arrival. An ending. A beginning. A choice.

Inside, SeaTac is alive with motion—families reuniting, business travelers rushing, voices layered over the occasional boarding call. I move through it all, my camera bag slung over my shoulder, my eyes scanning faces out of habit. Or maybe out of hope.

Then, I see her. Curly black hair. A book balanced in her hands, her fingers absently brushing the pages. Waiting.

My breath stills for half a second—an instinctive hitch, a flicker of something old, something worn but not yet faded. My pace slows. The air in my chest feels suddenly fragile, like glass about to crack. I step closer.

Not her.

The girl turns a page, unaware of my mistake. A sharp disappoint-ment bites the back of my throat, but I push it down.

I move on. Like I always do.

I weave through the crowd, past the endless rows of chairs, past the fluorescent glow of departure screens flashing names of places I could disappear to. Then—a voice from the past.

I glance up at a television mounted above the gate seating, tuned to MTV News. The ever-serious face of Kurt Loder fills the screen.

"In celebrity news, Downtown Julie Brown, our beloved MTV VJ, has announced her engagement to longtime fan, Robert Hannay. The couple met at a fan event and have been inseparable ever since."

A photo flashes beside Loder—Julie, still radiant, still unmistakably Downtown Julie Brown, smiling beside Robert in a fan-club t-shirt.

I let out a quiet, disbelieving laugh. Robert actually pulled it off. A reminder that life moves forward, that people chase what they want— and sometimes, against all odds, they catch it. It makes me wonder if maybe that's what I'm doing too. Hoping there's still time to find her.

I keep walking. Gate B7. Gate B9. Gate B11. Then, I stop. The scent hits me first—warm, sweet, nostalgic. I can already taste the melted icing, the perfect balance of cinnamon and sugar.

Cinnabon.

I smile. Maybe, just this once, I'll stay in one place long enough to enjoy something simple.

The damp Seattle air clings to my jacket as I slide into the back of the yellow cab. The scent of old leather and lingering spice lingers in the warm interior, mixing with the faintest trace of rain-soaked pavement.

I drop my camera bag beside me and stretch my legs, rolling my stiff shoulders. One day in Seattle, one quick assignment— in and out before I can even settle in.

The cabby, a middle-aged man with sharp eyes and black hair streaked with gray, adjusts the rearview mirror before meeting my gaze.

"Where to?"

◍

I exhale. "Pike Place Market, please."

The engine hums as we pull away from the curb, merging into the steady pulse of city traffic. The streets blur past in streaks of neon and headlights, reflections smearing across wet pavement.

"Are you a local?" the cabby asks, his voice warm, curious.

I shake my head slightly. "I'm never home long enough to call anywhere home."

He chuckles knowingly, his hands steady on the wheel. "I know that feeling all too well."

His words settle into my chest like an unexpected weight. I stare out the window, watching the city slip by, but my mind drifts elsewhere. Never home long enough. Always on the road. The truth of it stings more than I care to admit. Martone had said the same thing, just in different words.

I feel like I'm always waiting for you.
I need something real, Michael. I need to know if I'm a priority.

She was right. I never let myself land anywhere for too long. Always moving. Always chasing the next story, the next photograph, the next fleeting moment that wasn't really mine to keep. It had cost me.

I tighten my grip on my bag, shifting in my seat as the cab winds through the hilly streets of Queen Anne. The city looks different every time I come back—like I'm seeing it from the outside, like I don't quite belong to it.

Up ahead, the traffic light shifts from green to yellow. The cabby

steps on the gas. The engine growls as the cab surges forward, pushing over the crest of the hill. My stomach dips slightly from the momentum, but I barely react. Just another rush through another city, another fleeting moment in a life full of them. The light flicks to red just as we pass through the intersection.

A yellow cab blurs past, tires hissing against the wet pavement. The air is damp with rain and espresso as I step off the curb, my bag pressed close against my side. Thanksgiving was nice—loud, full, a little chaotic in that way only family can be. And still, I'm ready to get back to the café. Back to the quiet rhythm of my own space. My own choosing.

The street is mostly empty, the sky still the soft gray of early morning. My focus narrows as I reach the door—the small café that is mine. The place that owns me. The key slides into the lock, the metal cool beneath my fingers. I turn it, push open the door, and step inside.

The warmth greets me, thick with the scent of old wood and yesterday's roast. But I don't feel it. Not yet. What I feel is the weight of everything waiting inside—the to-do list written in sharpie on the back of a paper cup, the napkin order I forgot to place, the humming silence that fills the room before the first customer walks in.

Family always leaves me thoughtful. It's the way they hold your past so plainly—like it's nothing, like it doesn't ache. They ask questions I don't always want to answer, offer help I rarely know how to accept. And still, I love them. Fiercely. Quietly. The way I love this place. It's all tangled together somehow.

I move behind the counter and set down my bag. The light flickers on overhead. I breathe it in—the space, the stillness, the familiarity of

it all. I press my palm against the edge of the counter and let it steady
me. Let it hold me up while I find my place again.

This is home, too. In a different way. And for today, that's enough.

The coffee grinder hums from its overnight timer, the scent of
old grounds lingering in the air. A half-empty donation jar sits next to
the register, its handwritten label curling at the edges. A stack of fundraiser flyers clutters the counter, alongside the list of vendors I haven't
called back yet.

The unopened stack of mail waits near the untouched cup of
coffee from yesterday. I don't have time for breakfast. I didn't have
time for lunch. But I had time for everything else.

The bell on the door jingles. A volunteer drops off a few more
canned goods for tonight's food drive, and I murmur my thanks with a
tired smile. The door swings shut again, and I turn toward the kitchen.

The soup pot is on the stove. Ladle, portion, pack. The routine is
second nature now. I don't need to think, just move.

The phone buzzes. I glance down.

Poetic Pulse meets at 7 PM! Hope to see you!

My chest tightens. Poetry. I can barely remember the last time I
sat down with my journal. The last time I let myself breathe without
worrying about invoices, event planning, or making sure someone else
had what they needed.

I want to go. I should go.

But the fundraiser needs finalizing, the bakery order hasn't been picked up, and I still need to call the bank about the café's lease renewal. I swipe the notification away and pull the fundraiser ledger toward me instead. Another chime. Another message. Allison.

I miss you bitch! When can I visit?

A real smile tugs at my lips, but it vanishes almost immediately. I can't even remember the last time I sat down with a friend. Instead of replying, I reach for the donation jar, shaking it slightly.

Not enough. It's never enough.

I exhale, pressing my fingertips to my temples. The espresso machine hisses. The rain taps against the window. A half-eaten granola bar I left on the counter this morning stares back at me.

I should eat. I should text Allison back. I should go to poetry night. Instead, I pick up a stack of flyers and force myself to keep moving.

Later in the afternoon the café had gone quiet. The last of the mugs were rinsed and drying in their racks, the chairs flipped upside down on tabletops. I moved slowly through the room with a rag in hand, wiping down the last table by the front window—the one the man always sat at, the one that caught the best light in the morning.

That's when I saw it.

A book, left behind. It was old. The spine cracked, the cover soft and faded, like it had been carried through years and across continents. *The Little Prince* by Antoine de Saint-Exupéry I knew the title before I read it. I'd seen it before—in bookstores, in the bottom of backpacks worn by travelers who never stayed long. I'd never read it. But I knew it.

I picked it up gently, turning it in my hands, and that's when I noticed the napkin tucked beneath the cover. Just a corner sticking out. I slid it free.

In pen, a few words were scrawled in a slanted hand:

You reminded me of this.

No name. No signature. Just that.

I stood there for a moment, napkin in one hand, book in the other, the hush of the empty shop settling around me like snow.

Back behind the counter, I flipped the book open. The pages were yellowed, some of them dog-eared. I ran my thumb along the edges until one stopped me. Folded at the top, worn from being read too many times. I smoothed it open and read the line.

It is only with the heart that one can see rightly;
what is essential is invisible to the eye.

My fingers brushed the words again, slower this time. As if I could feel them rather than read them.

I don't know how long I stood there. Long enough for the espresso machine to let out a final settling hiss. Long enough for the windows to fog just slightly with the breath of the quiet inside. Long enough for that line to settle into me like something I hadn't known I was waiting for.

The book sat on the counter for days. I couldn't bring myself to shelve it or move it too far. It stayed beside the register, near the tip jar, where I could glance at it without trying to.

⦾

You reminded me of this.

Who had written it? One of the regulars? A stranger? The corn-bread man? Had they meant me?

The mystery pressed lightly against my chest. Not uncomfortable. Not demanding. Just there—like a presence. Like the gentle weight of something left behind on purpose. And every time I passed the book, I thought of that line again. *What is essential is invisible to the eye.* I didn't know what it meant. But I wanted to.

Queen Anne Community Center

The room hums around me, voices overlapping, folding into one another like ocean waves. Warmth radiates from the people filling the rows of chairs—volunteers, neighbors, familiar faces, all gathered together.

Beside me, Gray's fingers tighten around mine, her quiet excitement vibrating through her grip. She's beaming, eyes shining as she glances up at me, oblivious to the weight pressing against my ribs. I squeeze her hand back.

Up front, Councilwoman Hayes speaks, her voice steady, full of warmth. "Some people talk about making a difference. One person lives it."

The words drift toward me, but they feel distant, as if they're meant for someone else. I shift slightly in my chair, fingers curling into my lap, bracing myself.

"She turned a simple idea into something much more—a place where people felt seen, where creativity thrived, and where kindness was always on the menu."

A flicker of movement in the crowd—nodding heads, soft smiles, hands folded in quiet appreciation. People who have passed through her doors, who have found comfort there, who see something in me I don't always see in myself.

"Some people talk about change. Others make it happen. She didn't wait for someone else to step up—she became the person others could count on."

The words settle over me like a weight, too heavy, pressing down on my chest. I never set out to be anything special. I just filled the spaces that needed filling. Stepped in when no one else did. Poured the coffee, stocked the shelves, listened when someone needed to talk. One thing at a time, one choice, then another. It never felt like enough, but maybe, somehow, it was.

"The Queen Anne Community Service Award celebrates those who lift us all higher. This year's recipient, has done exactly that, one cup of coffee, one kind word, one moment of grace at a time."

Gray nudges me, practically vibrating now.

"Please join me in celebrating Sophia Callahan from Cafe Sonnet!"

The room bursts into applause. I blink, pushing up from my chair, my legs unsteady beneath me. The faces blur together—smiling, expectant, full of something I can't quite name.

Gray's hands shove me forward, her excitement a sharp contrast to the hollow ache expanding inside me. A standing ovation.

I walk to the podium, the claps rolling over me, swallowing me whole. The award is warm in my hands, heavier than I expected. I meet Councilwoman Hayes' gaze. She smiles—genuine, steady, believing.

I should feel something. I should feel proud. I press my lips together, nodding once, my hands tightening around the award. The applause swells. And I stand there, holding something I'm not sure I deserve.

The Four Seasons - Orlando

The ballroom hums with quiet anticipation. Glasses clink softly, silverware scrapes against fine china, and the low murmur of conversation fills the air. At the front of the room, a large screen displays one of my photos—the photo—the one that, for a brief moment, made the world stop.

A man wades through chest-deep floodwater in New Orleans, clutching a soaked photograph to his chest. Around him, the streets are unrecognizable—houses submerged, trees uprooted, remnants of lives scattered in the current. His face is turned away, but his posture, the way his fingers tighten around that single, fragile memory, says more than words ever could. I shift in my seat, fingers lightly tapping against the base of my wine glass.

"And now," the presenter says, stepping up to the podium, "for his powerful and unflinching coverage of Hurricane Katrina's aftermath, we are proud to present the National Press Photographers Association Award for Excellence in Journalism to Wander magazine's Michael Connelly!"

Applause swells. I exhale, standing as the crowd rises to their feet. A few familiar faces—editors, colleagues, mentors—nod at me as I make my way to the stage. The weight of a hundred assignments, a hundred shutter clicks, a hundred stories untold presses against my chest.

I shake hands with the presenter, the award now firm in my grasp. But my eyes flicker back to the photo on the screen. The floodwaters. The man holding onto the last piece of a life he would never get back.

I step to the microphone.

"When I took this photo, I was filling in for another photographer on a broken levee, watching an entire city fight to stay afloat. Another magazine needed someone on short notice when the floods hit - normally I shoot landscapes, travel features... not disaster or war zones. People had lost everything—homes, memories, their sense of normal." My voice is steady, but the unfamiliarity of that assignment and the weight of what I witnessed still sits heavy in my chest.

"And yet, in the middle of all of that, this man—he wasn't clinging to food or money. He wasn't holding onto a bag of belongings. He was holding a photograph. A single, waterlogged piece of paper that meant more to him than anything that could be replaced."

The room is silent now, the weight of the moment settling over the crowd.

"That's what photography does. It reminds us of what we fight to hold onto. It gives people back the moments that time, disaster, or history tried to take from them."

I pause, glancing at the photo again.

"I don't know who this man was. I never got his name. But this image—it's his story, not mine. And I hope, wherever he is, he knows that people saw him. That he wasn't just another face in a storm."

I grip the podium for a second longer, the applause growing again,

though my mind is still lost in the floodwaters, in the weight of what's been lost and what remains. I step back from the podium, nodding in thanks, and return to my seat. The award feels heavy in my hands, too solid, too real.

I stare at the plaque, tracing the engraved letters with my thum. But was it really excellence? Or was I just there? Right place, right time. Right shutter speed. Right angle. That man in the floodwaters—he did the hard part. He survived it. All I did was press a button.

The photo lingers on the screen for a moment longer before fading to black. I let out a breath I didn't realize I was holding and take a sip of water. The glass trembles slightly against my lips.

The gravel crackled beneath the tires as I eased the car to a stop, dust rising in the rearview. The stables stretched out in front of us, all wood beams and soft morning light, the scent of hay and earth already finding its way through the vents.

Whispering Creek Stables, the sign read—hand-painted and crooked, like something pulled from a storybook.

Gray was out of the car before I'd even cut the engine. Her boots hit the ground with a confidence that felt too big for her small frame, her eyes scanning the paddock like she was already choosing a future.

I stepped out slower, giving her the space, but close enough to feel the tug. The way she moved—purposeful, direct—reminded me she wasn't a baby anymore. She hadn't been for a while.

Robin met us at the gate, her face soft, a weather-worn ball cap shading her smile. She gave a small nod and disappeared around the corner, returning with a tall, dark gelding. He was beautiful in a quiet way—broad-chested, gentle-eyed, with a pale scar running along the side of his face like an old riverbed.

"Scar," she said. "Gentle as they come. Carries a story, like most of us."

I took a small step forward to guide Gray closer, reaching out instinctively for her hand, ready to help her approach the horse. But she shook her head, eyes locked on Scar, and said it plainly.

"I can do it, Mom."

Not with defiance. Just certainty. I froze. Then slowly lowered my hand. Gray walked forward alone, one step at a time, reaching up toward his face. Scar didn't flinch. Just lowered his head like he already knew her. Like he'd been waiting. She touched his scar with the gentlest graze of her fingertips. He blinked, calm and still, then leaned just slightly into her hand.

I stayed near the fence, arms crossed, holding myself there—quiet, proud, aching in a way only mothers know. There was something in the way they stood together—this small girl and the horse marked by time. An unspoken understanding. No fear. No hesitation.

There's something about horses—something ancient and kind. They're all power, all grace, but they move like they're holding the world gently. Even the big ones, with hooves the size of dinner plates, walk like they know how breakable we are. They carry our burdens without complaint—our weight, our histories, our dreams of conquest and freedom. For centuries, they've pulled our plows and carried our soldiers, built our cities and connected our distant lands.

They've bent their wild spirits to human will not because they

◯◯

had to, but perhaps because they chose to bear witness to our stumbling progress.

I never rode much myself, but I've always loved them. Their presence. Their silence. The way they breathe, deep and steady, like they're drawing strength from the earth itself. The way they seem to look right through you, not unkindly, just... clearly. As if they've seen all of humanity's glory and folly, and decided to stay anyway. There's wisdom in those liquid eyes—patience earned through generations of partnership with a species far more reckless than their own. When a horse stands beside you, you feel both humbled and protected at once, in the presence of something that understands burden in ways we never could.

Gray looked over her shoulder, grinning. I could feel her heart from here. It filled the space between us. The saddle came next. She didn't ask for help. Not even a glance. She just climbed, awkward but determined, settling into place like she'd done it a hundred times before. I exhaled slowly, fingers tightening around the fence rail. I hadn't expected this feeling—this mix of awe and grief. The growing away, even as she grows into something strong and shining. Into herself.

Scar shifted under Gray's weight, adjusting, patient. She patted his neck like she already belonged to him.

"I'm ready," she said.

I used to think readiness meant control—being sure of the outcome, steady on your feet. But maybe it's simpler than that. Maybe it's just the willingness to step forward, even when your heart is pounding. Gray had that. Has always had that. She reminds me what it means to be brave in small, quiet ways.

And for the first time in a long while, I didn't worry about what came next. I just watched my daughter find her seat in the world, one step at a time.

The buzz of my phone rattles the desk, sharp against the steady hum of the office. I glance down. Mom. A familiar warmth flickers in my chest as I lean back, stretching my legs out. I swipe to answer, my voice easy.

"Hey, Mom. What's up?"

But the moment she speaks, everything shifts. The air feels thinner. The background noise of the office dulls, fading into something distant—the chatter, the ringing phones, the rhythmic tap of fingers against keyboards. Someone laughs across the room. The sound is all wrong.

I sit up, my free hand gripping the edge of the desk.

"Wait—" I start, but my throat tightens. I press my fingers against my temple, exhaling slowly, forcing my breath steady.

The office suddenly feels too bright, too cold, too far from where I need to be. The city moves outside my window, oblivious, taxis honking, people rushing, life continuing without hesitation.

But something has stopped. Something that matters. I close my eyes, grounding myself, feeling the weight settle deep in my ribs.

"Tell me everything."

ꙮ

08

11:09:27:23:36:54

The wind carries the scent of pine through the cemetery, weaving between bare branches, rustling softly like whispered goodbyes. The mountains rise in the distance, snow clinging to their peaks, watching over everything the way they always have.

The funeral is over.

Everyone has left besides me and Mom. I stand near the freshly turned earth, my hands shoved deep into my coat pockets. My breath curls in the cold air, disappearing before it even has the chance to linger.

My grandfather's name is carved into stone—a beginning, an end, and everything in between reduced to a simple dash. I stare at it, waiting for it to mean something. Something more than just finality.

That dash. His entire life, shrunk to a pause between two dates.

But I remember the sound of his laugh echoing off the river. His worn flannel shirts. The way he always carried butterscotch candies in his coat pocket, like some quiet magic trick he never announced. The way his hands were always warm, no matter how cold the world got.

That dash held all of it. The small things. The quiet things. The things no one else would know from looking.

I shift my weight, the crunch of frost beneath my boots breaking the stillness. Beside me, Mom dabs at her eyes with a tissue. She doesn't say anything. Neither do I. There's nothing to say that can fill the space he left behind.

The courthouse clock chimes in the distance, steady and familiar. The same sound I grew up hearing every hour. The same sound he always paused to listen to, even when it had long since stopped being remarkable. I close my eyes. Let it settle inside me.

I wonder if he knew. That the reason I became a photographer wasn't about adventure. Not really. It was about the way he saw things—slowly, carefully, reverently. The way he noticed what others missed. How he taught me that the quietest parts of life were often the most important.

I never told him that. Not in words. Maybe he knew anyway. Or maybe I just want to believe he did.

I think of all the questions I didn't ask. The stories he never got around to telling. It's strange—the longer someone is gone, the more they start to take up space in you. Like their absence grows roots. Like the missing becomes its own kind of presence.

I find myself sitting on a nearby bench. Mom joins me, her hands folded in her lap. We don't talk. Not because we don't want to—but because we don't need to. Her grief is quiet, like mine. It doesn't need translation.

I exhale slowly, curling my fingers inside my gloves, holding on to whatever warmth is left.

And for a moment, I imagine him here—standing just behind us, arms crossed, nodding like he does when he's trying not to cry. Like he's proud. Like he sees us.

I don't believe in ghosts. But maybe I believe in echoes.

And maybe that's enough.

☾

The house feels different without him. The air is still heavy with the quiet that grief leaves behind, the kind that lingers in the walls, settles into the furniture. I sit on the couch, staring at nothing, the weight of the day pressing against me.

Mom walks into the room, cradling a small wooden box in her hands. It's old, the corners worn smooth with time. She hesitates before handing it to me, her eyes full of something unreadable.

"Michael, there's something your Grandfather wanted you to have." Her voice wavers, but she doesn't look away.

I take the box carefully, running my fingers over the lid before lifting it. Inside, legal documents and an envelope, the handwriting unmistakable. I swallow hard as I read the letter.

To my dearest grandson—In the spirit of adventure and the pursuit of beauty, I bequeath to you my retreat in the islands. May it be a haven for your soul, as it has been for mine.

I blink, reading it twice, maybe three times, waiting for it to make sense.

"His house in the islands?"

Mom nods, her voice softer now. "He believed you should always have a place to find peace and inspiration. It's yours now."

I close my eyes for a moment, letting the words settle.

On the mantle, a framed photo of him catches my eye—fishing in Mexico, sun-worn and smiling, like he always did. I pick it up, studying the man I thought would always be here. He taught me how to fish, how to tell a story so well that people swore they'd lived it. He told me the world was bigger than just myself.

The fire crackles beside me, its glow reflected in the glass. For a second, the flames blur his face. Then, just as quickly, he comes back. But he's not really here. Not anymore.

I set the photo back on the mantle, carefully. The frame makes a soft sound as it touches the wood—barely audible, but final somehow. My fingers linger for a breath longer than necessary. Then I let go—

—The photo frame is cool in my hands, but the weight of it feels different now. He's smiling in the picture—Ethan, frozen mid-laugh, sun catching in his lashes like a halo. We were young. We thought that meant we had time. That the future would stretch out in front of us like some open road we'd always walk together.

For years, this picture was my proof. That I wasn't alone. That I had a partner, a father for Gray, a life we were building—albeit across time zones and shaky phone calls. I told myself the distance was temporary. That the Peace Corps was just a chapter. That love meant enough to bridge the silence. But love isn't a bridge when only one of you is walking toward the other.

I trace the edge of the glass slowly, my fingertip catching on a small crack in the corner. I hadn't noticed it before. Or maybe I had. Maybe I just didn't want to see it.

How long did I wait?

How many birthdays, holidays, parent-teacher conferences, nights alone on the couch with the baby monitor buzzing beside me? How many promises that he'd be back soon, that the next mission would be closer, easier, different?

Too many.

I press my lips together, the ache rising in my throat fast and sharp. There was a time I made excuses for him. Told myself what he was doing mattered—that his absence was noble. That saving the world was more important than being here. But what about this world? What about me, holding the weight of it all? What about Gray, asking when he'd be home, forgetting the sound of his voice?

I blink, but the tears don't fall. Not yet.

I look around the room. Our room. Still half-filled with things that once meant permanence. His coat still in the closet. His books collecting dust on the shelf. His toothbrush tucked behind mine. Markers of a man who came and went, always with purpose, always with reasons. But never with roots.

And the thing is... I don't hate him. Not really.

I just can't do this anymore.

My arms fold tightly around my body, trying to keep the anger in. Or maybe trying to hold myself together. I believed in him. I believed in us. I believed that love meant staying, even when it hurt. Especially when it hurt.

But now? Now I believe in me. I believe in Gray. And I believe that being alone isn't the worst thing.

Being forgotten is.

I stand, breath steady, heart sore but clear. I walk to the window, pressing my palm against the glass. The city stretches out in glittering patterns—cars threading through the dark, porch lights glowing in rows. Lives unfolding. People showing up for each other. ♪

I want that. I deserve that.

The reflection in the glass shows a woman who has waited long enough. Ethan will come home eventually. And when he does, I'll be gone. Not out of anger. Not out of punishment. But because I'm done waiting to be chosen.

This is me choosing myself. The world keeps moving forward. And this time, I'm going with it.

♪ *"Hey Now"* by London Grammar

I look at my wedding ring. It slips off my finger too easily. A small, perfect circle that should have meant forever.

And maybe that's the thing no one tells you—if you stop applying pressure long enough, even a diamond remembers it used to be coal. Hard doesn't always mean strong. Sometimes it just means compressed. Contained. Waiting to break.

Some loves leave you polished and shining. Others leave you marked—scratched in places no one else can see. What we had was both.

"Diamonds and Rust." ♪

There was value in it. Weight. Sparkle, even. But there was corrosion too—the slow wearing down of something once meant to last. I used to carry it all like treasure. Proof that it meant something. That I meant something. But even diamonds can lose their shine when held too long in the dark.

And rust? Rust spreads.

So I set it down. Carefully. Finally. Not with bitterness. Not with regret. Just with the quiet knowledge that it's no longer mine to carry.

☾

The last of my things are packed. Everything I need, everything I don't, all shoved into the Porsche like some kind of puzzle. I stand beside the open door, taking in the view one last time. The mountains rise in the distance, unchanged, unmoved—just like they always have been.

I should feel more. A clean break. A bigger ache. But mostly, what I feel is the weight of goodbye—quiet and steady, like snowfall that doesn't ask permission.

♪ "Diamonds and Rust" by Joan Baez

- 357 -

These mountains are in my bones. They always have been. Every ridge and pass. Every line I ever carved into snow. They're part of the rhythm of me. I know their moods, their seasons, their silences. I'll miss them. More than I probably even realize yet.

Washington has mountains too. Beautiful ones. And the ocean— that vast, endless hush I've never quite learned how to listen to. But they're not these mountains. Not home.

Still—something's pulling me forward. Not away from this place, exactly. Just toward something else.

I've never put much stock in that old saying—everything happens for a reason. It always felt like something people said when they didn't know what else to say. A way to dress up uncertainty and call it fate.

But maybe there's a version of it that's true. Maybe it's not about fate at all. Maybe it's just about timing. A pull you can't explain. A door you didn't know you were standing in front of until you see the knob turn.

And right now, something's turning. I can feel it.

My reflection stares back at me in the rearview mirror, eyes tired but clear. There's a flicker there. Something like purpose. Something I haven't seen in a while.

I should feel something more. A greater sense of finality. Instead, there's just this strange, quiet anticipation. My reflection stares back at me in the rearview mirror, eyes bright with something I haven't felt in a while—purpose.

I've been driving this same old car for decades. People never stop

giving me shit about it. You still driving that old fossil? Like I'm holding onto it out of habit, or stubbornness, or because I don't know better.

But it's not about the car. Not really. It's about what it feels like to sit behind the wheel of something that doesn't apologize for being exactly what it is. No digital brain guessing what I might want. Just me, the road, and the growl of an engine that still speaks in analog.

It's imperfect. A little noisy. It makes you work for everything. But that's the point. That's what I love about it. Driving it feels like having a conversation with time—like the road and I remember each other.

And maybe that's the truth of it. I don't keep the Porsche because it's fast, or rare, or nostalgic. I keep it because it still fits. Rough around the edges. Doesn't always start on the first try. But honest. And I don't know... maybe that's me too.

I turn the key. It starts on the first try. I am almost disappointed.

The road home curls in long, familiar turns—just wide enough for my thoughts to wander. I've done this drive so many times it barely requires attention. The clouds are layered low, the sky a soft gray that seems to hush everything beneath it. On the passenger seat, Gray's forgotten water bottle rolls slightly as I slow for a stoplight, the soccer field already fading in the rearview mirror.

Her voice still echoes in my head. "Love you, Mom!" Bright, simple. Like it always is.

Sometimes I catch myself in moments like this—driving back from practice, the car still smelling faintly of grass and fruit snacks— and wonder how I got here. I never imagined I'd become the stereotype. The "soccer mom." The one who keeps a foldable chair in her trunk and knows the offside rule. The one who cheers too loud and always remembers the orange slices. I don't have a minivan. Yet. But I've caught myself eyeing one more than once—and that's the part that really gets me.

It's not that I resent it. Not at all. I love showing up for Gray. I love watching her run—fierce and focused, her curls bouncing, her face flushed with joy. But still, there's this quiet flicker inside me sometimes, asking if this version of my life is the only one I get. If I've traded something essential for something expected. If there's a version of me I've left behind without realizing it.

The light turns green. I ease forward.

I exhale, letting the quiet settle around me. No plans tonight. No conversations waiting. Just a little space. Just me.

And that's when I see it.

Off to the left, in the corner of a used car lot, tucked between a dented Subaru and a tired-looking minivan, sits a convertible with a tan rag top. Low to the ground. Slightly curved at the edges. The paint dulled by time but still striking.

It doesn't belong there—too stylish for a lot like that. Too full of some half-forgotten kind of personality. A crooked *For Sale* sign is taped inside the windshield, the numbers sun-bleached but legible.

I smile before I even realize I'm doing it.

It's not a car for hauling groceries or picking up kids from soccer. It doesn't scream practicality, doesn't ask for permission to make sense.

◎

It's the kind of car that invites second glances, not because it's flashy, but because it doesn't apologize. It's the kind of car someone drives when they've decided—quietly, stubbornly—that they're allowed to want something just because. No explanation. No justification.

It's a little rebellious. A little romantic. Definitely inconvenient.

In other words... it suits me.

Or maybe it suits the version of me I've been trying to get back to— the one who used to do things just because they felt right, not because they checked the right boxes.

I don't stop. Not yet. But I slow as I pass, glancing once, then again. It's classy, but unexpected. A car with a little grit under the polish. A car with character. And for a moment, the thought flits across my mind, uninvited but insistent: Maybe I need something different. Not a new beginning exactly—but a shift. A choice that's mine alone.

The kind you don't ask permission for.

A few years ago—maybe even a few months ago—I would've dismissed it immediately. Too risky. Too much. What would Ethan have said? But Ethan isn't in the picture anymore. Not in the ways that matter. The divorce was quiet. Clean on paper, messier in the heart. We said all the right things. Stayed kind. But the distance had been growing for years. I just finally stepped away from the edge of it.

Now the silence belongs to me.

I tap my fingers on the wheel as the car disappears behind me. Still smiling. Maybe it's nothing. A passing thought. A flicker of color on an ordinary drive. Or maybe it's something more. A nudge. A whisper.

⦾

Not everything has to be practical. Not everything has to make sense. Maybe I'm allowed to want something different. Something just for me. And maybe—just maybe—that's where everything starts.

I should turn around.

Interstate 25 - Colorado

The sun breaks low over the horizon as I merge onto I-25 north, the asphalt stretching ahead in long, empty lines. The city fades behind me in the rearview mirror—smudged glass, thinning skyline, the last gas stations and fast food signs giving way to wide, open country.

This part of the drive always feels like exhaling. Like the land's finally letting go of something.

I watch the mountains slide slowly into the distance, those familiar peaks softening with every mile. There's a tug in my chest I've learned to ignore—grief's quieter cousin, the one that doesn't cry or shout, just sits with you in the silence.

Leaving Colorado feels like leaving a version of myself behind. The younger one. The one who thought home was a place you could always come back to. But I've circled back enough times to know: home changes. And if you stay still too long, it changes without you.

I drive with the window cracked, letting the cold morning air pour in. It smells like sage and frost. Like farmland and thawing earth. I've made this drive before, too many times to count—but this time feels different. Not like escape. Not like chasing something, either. Just... moving forward.

I pass a faded green road sign: *Cheyenne 93*

Thirteen hundred–something miles. A long way to move when you're not sure what comes next. But I'm going anyway. It's a new chapter. And it's time.

The road hums beneath the tires, steady as a heartbeat. And for the first time in a long time, I let myself believe that maybe—just maybe—I'm heading toward something that matters.

The radio fades in and out as the miles tick by. When it catches a clear signal, a voice fills the cab—a raw, honest sound that always cuts through the noise. I turn it up. The song speaks to something I've felt but couldn't name: the quiet rebellion of choosing your own path when society keeps trying to sell you something different. ♪

For years, I collected the things I thought would make me complete—the right job, the right address, the right connections. But none of it filled that hollow space inside. Funny how leaving it all behind feels more like freedom than loss.

The bell above the shelter door gave its usual jingle—thin and a little tired, but still one of my favorite sounds. There was something welcoming about a door that rang when you opened it, like it wanted you to be there.

Inside, the familiar scent of sawdust and antiseptic clung to the air, part vet office, part old classroom—clean, utilitarian, but softened by the undercurrent of fur and warmth.

The woman at the front desk looked up and offered me a small, knowing smile—the kind that didn't need words. I'd been in enough times that she didn't ask if I needed help. Her nod was approving, as if she knew I wouldn't be leaving empty-handed forever. I returned it with a quiet one of my own, slipping past toward the back, where the

♪ "Society" by Eddie Vedder

real heart of the place lived—cages lined in neat rows, full of rustles and breath and possibility.

There was no rush. I didn't come looking for anything in particular. Just… something soft. Something alive. Something else to care for.

The room was filled with rustling and mewling. A tabby stretched lazily in a sunbeam. A ginger persian curled into the crook of a blanket. None of them looked my way. I wandered the aisle, pausing here and there, my fingertips resting against the cool metal of each cage, feeling the hum of quiet lives all around me.

Then—movement. Barely a sound. A flicker of shadow near the far corner of the room. A small black kitten—more fluff than form— had squeezed through the open edge of her crate and was padding toward me on uncertain legs. Her fur was smoky gray in the light, nearly black when she stepped into shadow. I crouched, slowly, not wanting to startle her.

She didn't pause. She came right to me, like she already knew. Tiny paws against my boots. A blink of green eyes. Then she climbed— bold and clumsy—right into my lap, curling there like she'd been waiting all along. I froze, unsure whether to laugh or cry.

The shelter worker peeked around the corner. Her eyes softened.

"Looks like she's picked you."

I nodded once, still looking down. Shadow. The name came without effort. Soft but not fragile. Quiet, but full of presence. I stroked the kitten's tiny spine with one finger, and she gave a soft purr, small as a whisper. I felt something loosen in my chest—something I hadn't realized was still wound tight.

⌀

I had plants at home that leaned toward the light when I opened the blinds. I had Gray, grown and blooming into her own kind of wild. And now—I had this little thing in my lap, trusting me already. A new rhythm. A new need. And I would love her like everything else that had found its way to me and stayed.

Highway 191 - Jackson Hole

The Porsche eats up Highway 191 through Wyoming, tires humming a steady rhythm against the asphalt, matching the quiet churn of thoughts in my head. Colorado is long behind me now—shrinking in the rearview like a chapter I stopped reading mid-sentence.

The Tetons rise in the distance, jagged and indifferent beneath a sky that can't decide if it wants to be blue or gold. I've photographed them a dozen times—maybe more. Usually, I'd pull over. Frame the moment. Catch the way the light drapes over the ridgelines like silk. But not today.

Today, I keep driving.

Because this isn't about the shot. This isn't a story I'm trying to capture. It's my life. And for once, I'm not stopping to curate the moment. I'm letting it pass—unfiltered. Unclaimed.

I flick on the radio, scanning until I land on something quieter—acoustic guitar, a warm voice layered with ache. Not lyrics I know, but it stops me. The song flows easy, but it's not soft. It's the kind of song that settles into you—not with answers, but with recognition. The kind that walks beside you, not ahead. ♪

It sounds like the road I'm on. Like the weight I've carried. Like the exact kind of quiet I didn't realize I needed.

♪ "Like a River" by Ocie Elliot

⦿

I never bothered installing a tape deck. Never made the jump to CDs. No Bluetooth, no playlists, no carefully curated soundtrack. Just FM radio—scratchy, inconsistent, a little stubborn. Which, if I'm being honest, sounds a lot like me.

But there's something about it I've always liked. The randomness, maybe. The surprise of a song finding you instead of the other way around. It's not polished. It's not predictable.

It feels nostalgic in a way I can't quite explain.

Jackson Hole rises out of the valley like a memory you didn't expect to run into. The road curves around it, and for a moment, I think about the first time I came here with my dad. We'd driven up to ski, bundled in layers that never felt like enough. I remember the cold—how it wrapped around your bones and stayed there—but I also remember how he taught me to lean into it. To slow down. To stop chasing the summit and just enjoy the turns. Not every journey needed a destination, he said. Sometimes you go just to remember you still can.

I glance toward the edge of town, where a stretch of weathered wooden signs point toward ski lodges, local diners, trailheads. I've skied here. Slept here. Stood waist-deep in snow on powder days so cold I couldn't feel my face. Part of me wants to turn off and stay the night for old times sake.

But I don't.

Because it's about the road ahead. The music continues—river-like in its rhythm, in its quiet strength. No urgency. Just presence. Just movement.

The road stretches forward—long, empty, full of maybe. I don't know what's waiting for me in Washington. But I know I'm done circling. I'm not chasing ghosts anymore. I'm answering something I've ignored for too long. The Porsche hums along, engine warm, tires carving their rhythm into the road like a heartbeat. Maybe the road knows more than I do. Maybe it always has.

The café hummed in its usual rhythm—steam hissing from the espresso machine, the low clink of mugs behind the counter, a quiet playlist threading through the warmth of conversation.

Gray sat at the corner table near the window, hunched over her geometry homework, pencil tapping a restless beat. Her curls were pulled back in a messy knot, but a few had escaped, curling like vines around her cheeks. Every now and then, she glanced at the door, pretending not to be watching it. She was always watching.

I wiped down a table with slow, practiced motion, cloth in one hand, thoughts in the other. The bell above the door jingled, and I looked up. A man stepped in—broad-shouldered, maybe mid-thirties, with wind-roughened skin and the kind of posture that belonged to someone who worked with his hands. He paused in the doorway for a moment, as if he wasn't quite sure he'd come to the right place.

Then he smiled. He didn't smile at anyone in particular, just at the room—as though it reminded him of something.

He ordered a black coffee. No hesitation, no modifications. He paid in cash, folding the bills neatly. Then he turned, scanning for a seat. There were a dozen open ones, but he made his way toward the far end of the counter—close enough to speak, far enough to give space. He nodded once in my direction. Not polite. Familiar.

⓪

I refilled the creamers. Checked the lids on the sugar jars. Noticed the way he watched the room, how he noticed things quietly. He didn't look like the type who needed to fill silence with words.

Neither was I.

Gray's intent gaze burned into my back. I could feel it without turning around. This wasn't the first time. For months now, she'd been doing this—pointing out customers, suggesting I "accidentally" give them my number with their receipt, even leaving a dating app open on her phone where I could see it. The irony wasn't lost on me. My thirteen-year-old trying to resurrect my love life.

"You need someone besides me," she'd said last week, so matter-of-factly it had caught me off guard. "Someone who makes you laugh." As if rebuilding a heart was as simple as geometry—just connecting the right points, finding the correct angle.

I never told her how those casual suggestions twisted something inside me—fear and maybe guilt about the divorce, intertwined like old roots. Moving forward always felt like leaving something behind. Someone behind.

Gray perked up when she saw me watching him. She grinned, tapping her pencil to her lip like she was plotting something. Later, when I came to check on her, she leaned in and whispered, "You should talk to him."

I raised an eyebrow.

She smirked. "You know. Talk." Her tone was teasing, but her eyes were curious. I ruffled her hair as I passed. She swatted my hand away but didn't stop smiling.

She didn't understand that some silences become comfortable. That alone doesn't always mean lonely. Or maybe she did understand. Maybe she saw what I couldn't—that I'd been hiding in the safety of routine, in the predictable rhythm of coffee pours and pastry orders.

I turned back toward the register, restocking sleeves and lids with steady hands. I glanced over my shoulder at the man—Cal, I'd learn later. He hadn't moved. Just sat there, sipping his coffee like it meant something. Like it gave him a moment to breathe.

I knew that feeling.

Gray had gone back to her homework, but she kept stealing glances, her foot bouncing under the table like it was connected to the pulse of the room. She wanted something for me. Something more than routine. More than reliability. She wanted proof that love could be rebuilt.

Maybe I did too.

I just didn't know what that would look like anymore.

When Ethan and I signed the papers, there hadn't been a breakdown. No shouting. No grand betrayal. It ended the same way most quiet things do—slowly. A series of missed moments and conversations that never quite reached the center. I didn't cry. Not once. Not because it didn't matter. But because by the time it ended, the grief had already settled in too deep to spill out.

I folded our life up like a fitted sheet—clumsy, uneven, done more from muscle memory than intention. People asked if I was okay, and I said yes. And they believed me. Most days, I believed me too.

But there are days—still—when I wonder if I missed something.

⦾

If I should've tried harder. If I'd failed at something essential. And even when I remind myself that no one walks away for no reason, that peace is sometimes quieter than pain, the doubt lingers in the corners. Soft, but present. A weight I've learned to carry.

I know I didn't do anything wrong.

And yet… sometimes, it still feels like a kind of loss you don't get to mourn out loud.

I've built something since then. A café. A daughter who sees the world with more clarity than I ever did at her age. But even with all of it, there are nights when the silence wraps a little too tightly around me. Nights when I fall asleep with a book open beside me, just to feel like someone is still talking.

And maybe that's why I kept watching Cal, the man who didn't say much, who looked around like he was trying to find something he'd lost. Because I know that search. I live it, quietly, in the spaces between espresso shots and half-finished conversations. I know what it is to sit still and hope the world finds its way back to you.

The café hummed around us. Safe. Familiar. But something had shifted. I didn't know what yet.

Just that it had.

Gray caught my eye again, then offered a sly, knowing look. The kind that made me want to laugh and cry all at once.

And this time—I didn't look away.

I looked at the man at the end of the counter. And I let myself

◎

wonder. Maybe it was nothing. A Tuesday. A stranger. A cup of coffee that would go cold.

Or maybe—not. Maybe something had just begun.

Highway 410 - Mt. Rainer

Mount Rainier rises ahead—massive, unmoved. Its snowcapped peak cuts clean into the sky like something older than language, older than time. The mountain doesn't just sit on the horizon—it owns it. Commands it with the quiet certainty of something that has outlived everything else.

I ease off the gas, letting the curve of Highway 410 carry me forward. The road winds through walls of evergreen, the mist threading through the branches like breath.

Washington feels different. Not just in color, but in weight. It's heavier here. Wetter. Wilder. The green presses in from all sides—ferns crowding the shoulder, moss crawling up trunks like it's trying to reclaim what was lost. The air smells like cedar and rain and something deeper—like earth that remembers things.

I crack the window. Let it in.

It's cold. Bracing. But good. And for the first time in a long while, I don't feel like I'm chasing something. I just... exist. Suspended between what I left behind and whatever's waiting up ahead.

The mountain hovers in my periphery—steady, indifferent, like it knows I'm not sure what I'm doing. I've passed through towns without stopping, watched the gas gauge dip low, let the radio go quiet. It's been a long time since I've sat with silence this willingly.

I don't know if I'm driving toward something or away from it.
Maybe both. Maybe that's always been the problem—I never stayed
long enough to tell the difference.

I keep going. I'm almost there. Wherever there is.

The next bend opens into a stretch of road where the trees fall back
and the mountain comes into full view. It's so sudden—so immense—
it feels almost mythic. The way the light shifts over the peak, catching
in the ridgelines, it looks less like a place and more like a reckoning.
The kind of landmark that asks you to answer for the person you've
been up until now.

I flick the radio back on. A low hum rolls in—his voice, rough
around the edges, like gravel under bootheels. It's the kind of song
that doesn't push its way in. It settles. Quietly. Slowly. Like rain on
old wood. ♪

Not mournful. Just weathered. Like someone who's seen too
much and still keeps moving. There's dust in it. Moonlight. A weight
that doesn't ask to be named.

It's not trying to impress me. It doesn't need to. The melody winds
through the car like memory—worn and familiar, even if I can't place
it. It sounds like leaving something behind without slamming the door.
Like staying soft, even after the world tried to make you hard.

There's a tension in it that mirrors something in my chest—something
I've been carrying without knowing it. A quiet ache I haven't had words
for. It stays with me, just under the surface, as the road pulls me forward.
Not toward closure. Not toward answers. Just the next mile. The next
breath. The next version of me—whoever he's about to become.

♪ *"The Stable Song"* by Gregory Alan Isakov

⦿

The mountain never looks back. It just stands there, unconcerned with whether I'm ready or not. I press the gas a little harder. Let the road take me. For once, that's enough.

Interstate 5 - Tukwila

The hum of the freeway fills the car, steady, predictable. Gray is home, safe. The café is taken care of. For once, there's nowhere I need to be, nothing pulling me in a hundred directions.

I glance at the road sign—almost to my exit. Almost home. Then something catches my eye: an old white Porsche just ahead, gliding through traffic. I frown, something tugging at the back of my mind. Something familiar. The Colorado plate:

POWLIFE.

The grip on my steering wheel tightens. My heart stutters—not in panic, not in fear, but in faint recognition. I flick my eyes toward the driver, but just as I do—my exit appears. I hesitate. Just for a second.

Then, I turn the wheel, veering right. The Porsche continues straight. A moment later, it's swallowed by the sea of cars. I exhale, shaking my head, willing my pulse to steady.

Just a coincidence. That's all.

I guide the car through the neighborhood, tires humming softly over the smooth pavement. The streets are lined with old trees, their branches reaching toward each other in a kind of secret conversation overhead. Dappled sunlight flickers through the leaves, casting shifting patterns across the windshield. The houses here are well-loved—porches with

◯

creaking swings, flower boxes spilling over with late-summer color, chalk drawings on sidewalks fading from last week's rain.

When I turn onto my new street, something in me settles a little. It's quieter here. Slower.

I pull into the driveway—paved and slightly sloped, edged with a row of untrimmed grass pushing up from the cracks. The house is tucked back from the street just enough to feel hidden, its wide porch framed by overgrown hydrangeas and a low stone wall that's starting to lean. A craftsman, worn but proud. The paint's a little faded. One shutter hangs crooked. But it stands like it belongs. Like it's weathered things and stayed standing anyway.

I cut the engine and sit for a moment, palms resting on the wheel, staring at the front door. The porch light sways slightly in the breeze, even though it's not on. A ceramic planter sits cracked near the steps, half full of trailing ivy that hasn't decided whether to flourish or give up. Still, there's life here. In the plants. In the air. In the silence.

I step out and close the door behind me. The pavement is warm beneath my feet. The wind smells like cedar and coffee from somewhere nearby. The city hums in the distance, soft and manageable, like background music I don't need to turn down. This isn't just a place to live. It's a beginning. I let out a breath. This is home now:

Ballard.

The name settles into me slowly, like steam rising from a cup—quiet, persistent. It doesn't feel like mine yet, but it might. One day soon.

I open the front door revealing a house still caught in transition—boxes stacked high, furniture in disarray, a space waiting to become a home. But for the first time in a long time, the sight doesn't feel over-whelming. It feels like possibility.

A soft meow greets me from below. I glance down as Shadow winds between my ankles, her green eyes blinking up at me. I scoop her up, feeling the warmth of her small body against my chest. She purrs as I press a kiss to the top of her head before setting her down near her food bowl. Her name is printed on the side in neat, swirling letters—something stable, something permanent.

When I first brought Shadow home, Gray—naturally—lobbied hard to name her Rhiannon. She stood in the kitchen, arms crossed, eyes fierce with purpose, and said, "Mom. She's a mystical witch god-dess. It's literally the only name that makes sense." ♪

I pointed out the cat had just tried to eat a hair tie and got stuck behind the bookshelf for three hours.

"Exactly," Gray had replied. "Mystery. Power. Chaos. She is Rhiannon."

But the cat had other ideas. She kept to the shadows for days, hiss-ing at loud noises, only emerging when no one was watching. When I finally said the word Shadow aloud, she came right to me.

Gray had sighed, dramatically. "Fine."

She still calls her Rhiannon sometimes, especially when she wants something. And honestly? She's not wrong.

The hallway is lined with pieces of my life—snapshots of moments frozen in time. A photo of Gray, grinning wide, her two front teeth missing. A group picture from the Peace Corps, sunburnt faces, arms slung over shoulders, dusty but alive. A family photo from years ago,

♪ *"Rhiannon"* by Fleetwood Mac

my parents, my brother, and me, all standing close, all still whole. And then—the cross-stitch.

Everything Happens for a Reason.

I pause, my fingers ghosting over the frame. For years, I held onto this phrase like a lifeline. A way to make sense of loss, of sacrifice, of the choices that led me here. I used to believe it. I want to believe it. Maybe I will again.

I move deeper into the house, my eyes drifting toward the lush greenery scattered in every corner. Potted plants of every kind perch on makeshift tables or rest directly on the floor, still waiting for a proper home. It's chaotic, but not in a bad way—more like something just beginning. Despite the disarray, they bring the space to life, breathing quiet color into the stillness.

My books are everywhere—stacked in uneven towers, half-unpacked from cardboard boxes. Some teeter on the edge of shelves, others spill across the floor like they've claimed the space before I could. Their weight is familiar, comforting. Stories waiting to be returned to, or discovered for the first time. I don't know where they'll go yet. But I will. Eventually.

I knock softly on Gray's bedroom door and peek inside. She's sprawled across her bed, headphones on, one foot dangling off the side, completely immersed in whatever universe she's built inside her Pandora playlist—she somehow inherited my love for the oldies, though she'd never admit it out loud. When she notices me, she lifts a hand in a lazy wave, a smile tugging at the corner of her mouth. I smile back, something warm and familiar settling in my chest—the kind of moment you know won't last forever, so you let it linger a second longer. ♪

♪ *"Over My Head"* by Fleetwood Mac

◯

She's okay. We're okay. That truth never stops surprising me.

The move, the divorce—I had braced for fallout. For slammed doors. For silence. But Gray adapted the way she always has, like water—finding the shape of her new life and pouring herself into it. She still calls Ethan. Still loves him. But she stopped asking when he'd be home a long time ago. I think she realized before I did that some absences aren't temporary.

She never said it out loud, but I saw it in the way she looked at other kids with their dads on the sidelines, or the way she stopped setting aside the last piece of banana bread like she used to when he was supposed to come back.

She doesn't carry resentment—not exactly. Just… understanding. The kind that comes too early. The kind kids shouldn't have to learn.

I linger a moment longer, watching her eyes flicker across whatever story is unfolding behind those headphones. She's so much her own person now. But still mine, too. Still the one thing I got right.

I gently close the door, leaving her to her music.

I fill the watering can from the sink, the steady stream of water a quiet backdrop to my thoughts. Outside, a ferry horn sounds in the distance, the low, familiar hum settling over the neighborhood like a reminder that life is always moving.

I step toward the potted plants scattered across the windowsill, their leaves stretching toward the light. With careful hands, I tilt the watering can, letting the water soak into the soil, watching as the earth drinks it in. A simple ritual. A moment of care. A promise to keep growing. I exhale, a slow, steady breath.

◎

New house. New car. New life. New beginning. And for the first time in a long time, I feel ready.

MV Elwha - San Juan Island

The ferry cuts through the steel-gray water, the cold wind threading through my jacket as I watch the island draw closer.

San Juan Island.

I hadn't been here since I was a kid, chasing seagulls along the rocky shore, my grandfather's laugh echoing behind me. Now, the dock rises ahead, weathered and waiting.

I roll the Porsche off the ferry ramp, tires crunching over the apron into town. The drive then winds through evergreens and open fields, past farms with split-rail fences and red barns. The smell of salt lingers in the air, mixing with pine and earth. Then, the road bends, and there it is—his house.

A Victorian beauty, perched on the hillside, watching over the water like it always has. I pull into the driveway and kill the engine. For a long moment, I just sit.

The house feels the same—like it belongs to another time, another world. The circular porch wraps the front door with a wide embrace, paint peeling slightly on the railings. The second-story windows blink down at me, unmoved by my return.

I grab my bag and step out into the Salish Sea air. Gravel shifts beneath my boots as I cross the yard toward the house. The worn wooden porch stairs creak under my weight as I ascend them, each step familiar in its particular song. At the top, I pause, my fingers brushing over the key, cool and familiar. The lock turns smoothly. The door creaks open. I step inside.

Everything smells like cedar and dust, like an attic filled with forgotten things. The kitchen is exactly the same. The old cross-stitch still hangs by the door—

Kwitchyerbellyakin.

Grandfather's motto for just about everything. I used to think it was a joke. A funny word stitched in crooked thread. But it was more than that—it was his entire worldview boiled down into a single, backhanded piece of wisdom.

He said it when the Jeep broke down on Imogene Pass. When the winter storm knocked out power to my darkroom for three days. When I came home sulking after a breakup with Heidi in high school. 'Kwitchyerbellyakin, kid,' he'd mutter, barely looking up from whatever he was repairing with his precise, methodical hands—a camera lens, a watch movement, anything that required patience and care.

It wasn't about toughness, not really. It was about perspective. About getting on with things. Life hands you what it hands you— weather, heartbreak, flat tires, loneliness. You deal. You don't sit around complaining about it.

Of course, as a kid, I hated it. It felt dismissive. Like he didn't care. But now, standing here with dust motes swirling through the shafts of late afternoon light, I understand. He wasn't saying not to feel it. He was saying don't get stuck in it.

Move forward. Adjust. Keep going.

⟲

Kwitchyerbellyakin wasn't just a shrug—it was a challenge. A push toward resilience.

I brush my fingers over the frame, the thread faded with time. Crooked as ever. But it holds. Just like he did. Just like I still want to.

The clocks in the parlor haven't stopped. Their steady tick-tock keeps time with something deeper, something unshaken. The family photographs on the walls haven't moved either—my mother as a girl, Grandfather beside a freshly caught marlin, my own face younger, freer, unaware of what time could take. And in one corner frame, a woman I never really knew—my grandmother, smiling faintly beneath a wide sunhat, already halfway to memory even then.

I trail my fingers along the wooden banister as I climb the stairs. The floorboards groan under my weight, but the house doesn't protest my return.

It's been waiting.

The bedrooms remain untouched—beds still made, books still stacked neatly, the scent of old paper thick in the air. I linger in the doorway of the room I used to stay in, looking at the window where I once sat counting the stars. Somewhere deep in the house, a clock chimes, out of time with the rest.

The attic door resists at first, swollen with time, but then it gives. Dust swirls in the slanted light coming through the small round window. The air is thick with the scent of old wood and forgotten things. Trunks, boxes, stacks of yellowing letters.

I move carefully, stepping over memories—some known, some

waiting to be uncovered. Then, something catches my eye. A black guitar case, half-buried beneath a pile of books and faded quilts.

I kneel, brushing off the dust, my fingers hesitating before unlatching the rusted clasps. The lid creaks open, revealing a Martin guitar. The wood is warm beneath my touch, smooth from years of playing. I press my fingers against the frets—just a test, just a memory.

A slow, instinctive strum. The sound is soft but rich, filling the empty attic like a voice finally breaking the silence.

In the trunk beside me, something else waits.

I lift out a folded American flag. The fabric is stiff, carefully preserved. Beneath it, a black-and-white photograph. Grandfather, impossibly young, standing on the deck of an aircraft carrier. I turn it over.

USS Enterprise CV-6, June 25, 1943.

I flip the photo back over, studying his face. A man who had seen the worst of the world but somehow still looked steady. Certain. I exhale, the weight of it settling in my chest. I don't know what I expected to find here. Maybe I thought coming back would bring clarity, some kind of direction. Instead, all I feel is time pressing in from all sides.

My iPhone rings. It's Jane. I already know what that means. Back to work. I swipe to answer. "Hey, what's up?"

Her voice crackles through, and I sit up a little straighter, the tone in her voice already flicking something on in my brain—something I haven't felt in a while.

"A special assignment?" I repeat, eyebrows lifting.

There's a pause as I listen—just long enough for my pulse to pick up speed. Curiosity sharpens into something else: Excitement.

"Yes," I say, already standing. "Absolutely. Count me in."

I close the guitar case gently. The house exhales around me, quiet and still, like it's waiting for me to decide what comes next.

I stood behind the counter, restocking cups, moving slowly, methodically—my mind elsewhere. Outside, the trees had just begun to turn. Gold. Rust. The first signs of letting go. The espresso machine hissed softly in the background, its warmth a stark contrast to the crisp autumn air that slipped in each time the door opened.

Cal was in his usual spot. Third stool from the end. Black coffee. No sugar. No cream. The kind of man who didn't need anything extra. He had a book open—something old, spine-worn. But he wasn't really reading. His thumb traced the edge of a page, his eyes drifting. Watching the way the light moved through the window. Watching me. ✳

When I brought over the fresh pot and tilted it toward his cup, he looked up and smiled. Not the kind that asked anything. Just... acknowledgment. "Thanks," he said. His voice was always soft in here, like he understood this place had a different kind of quiet. He waited a beat, then closed the book gently.

"I was thinking," he said, tapping his fingers once against the cover, "if you ever felt like taking a break from this place... I know a little gallery that has these hand-tinted black-and-white prints. Mountain landscapes. Old film. Thought you might like it."

He didn't push. Didn't call it a date. Just left the offer there between

✳ *"East of Eden"* by John Steinbeck

us, like a leaf settling on still water. My hands stilled. The warmth of the coffee pot seeped into my palm. It had been nearly two years since the divorce—longer since I'd even let myself consider someone. There was still a bruise beneath the surface—not fresh, but not healed either..

I thought of Gray waiting at home, probably sprawled across our couch with her homework. My daughter who saw too much, understood too well. She'd noticed Cal. Had even teased, gently. "He only comes in on your shifts, Mom." But she didn't understand—not yet—that letting someone in again comes with weight. With risk. And me? I wasn't sure I had the room.

I didn't nod. Just let a small breath out, steady and slow, and gave the smallest smile. A maybe. A not-today. He seemed to understand. The next customer walked in, and I turned away, hands already moving. But the offer stayed with me. Quiet. Unrushed. Like him. Like something that could wait.

And maybe that was the truth of it—I wasn't ready. Not for gallery walls or new beginnings. Some doors don't close all at once. They ease shut. Quietly. On their own time.

There was a part of me—small, stubborn—that wanted to step toward something new. But another part held back. The part that remembered the midnight arguments, the silent dinners, the gradual emptying of our shared life until nothing remained but echoes. The part that didn't know if it could risk the quiet life we had rebuilt, fragile and whole in its own way.

When I got home, Gray was curled on the couch, textbook forgotten beside her, scrolling through her phone. The scent of the microwave dinner she'd made herself still lingered in the air. She looked up, studied my face with that uncanny perception of hers. "Cal asked you out, didn't he?" she said, not really a question. I shrugged, tried for casual, but she just smiled that knowing smile.

"Mom, you know it's okay to want things again."

She went back to her phone, the subject apparently closed. But her words stayed, settling somewhere between my ribs. When had she grown wise enough to remind me of things I'd forgotten? And when had I become the one afraid to step forward?

Ghost 207

The ocean stretches in every direction, endless and glassy beneath us. From my seat behind the pilot, the canopy wraps overhead like a bubble, the world outside tilting as we bank left into final approach. The Pacific horizon slants at a hard angle—clean, blue, and sharp as a blade. I grip the edge of my harness as the jet dips and flattens out. ♪

Flaps drop. The nose dips. My whole body tenses against the pull of gravity. Every sound inside the cockpit sharpens—gear lock thuds into place, wind screams over the canopy, the jet trembles under the strain of deceleration.

Ahead, whitewater churns in the distance—an arrowhead of wake slicing through the ocean. Then it appears. A floating city rises from the sea like a steel monolith, growing larger with every second. The deck gleams in the sun, a slab of scorched gray with cables stretched across its width like tripwires.

The pilot—callsign PAIL—keeps his voice level, relaxed.

"Ghost 207, three-quarters of a mile. Call the ball."

♪ *"Outro"* by M83

He keys his mic. "Ghost 207, Growler, ball, 4.8."

I glance to the left, just beyond the HUD, and catch it—the "meat-ball" hovering on the Fresnel Lens. Glowing amber, bracketed by green datum lights. Steady. Still. The only thing I'm supposed to watch. Pail's eyes stay locked forward, reading the deck like a riddle. My stomach tightens as the carrier rushes up to meet us, growing with every breath.

This close, the ship is alive. Figures wait on the deck in color-coded vests—yellow, red, green—moving with precision, timing their steps like they've rehearsed this scene a thousand times.

And they have. *I hope.*

Fifty feet. Forty. Thirty.

The deck fills the frame, stripes and lights and movement blurring together.

Then the wheels hit—*hard.*

A violent slam. The hook grabs one of the arresting wires and the Growler snaps to a brutal stop, the G-force slamming me forward into the harness before snapping me back.

Trapped.

Everything shudders. The engine howls as the nose dips and steadies, and then we're not flying anymore—we're back on Earth, even if Earth is made of steel and floating in the middle of the Pacific.

I exhale. Slowly.

The jet taxis forward. Our wings fold skyward, as if the aircraft itself is breathing again. I feel my pulse in my throat, in my fingertips. The deck crew guides us in with glowing paddles, their gestures sharp and certain. No words. Just motion and trust.

I've photographed glaciers calving into Arctic waters. I've stood in war zones and hurricane paths. But nothing—absolutely nothing—compares to this moment. This machine, this sky, this ship. The madness of catching a fighter jet like a fastball on a postage stamp in the middle of nowhere.

And I'm here for it. Not just to capture it. But to feel it. All of it.

The jet shutters down around us, the cockpit still and warm from the sun. The deck hums with life outside—chains clinking, engines starting, distant voices calling out to each other in a language that only works here, in this world.

And I sit there for just a second longer, hands still tight on the straps, heart still thundering.

Gray bursts through the front door like a gust of late winter wind—cheeks flushed, boots stomping, backpack thudding to the floor in its usual spot just left of the rug. I hear the familiar tone of a phone unlocking, the rapid click of thumbs moving with purpose. She hums under her breath—something new. Not Fleetwood Mac this time. The kind of tune that loops on a crush-fueled playlist. ♪

I'm standing at the end of the couch, folding laundry from a basket that's been giving me judgmental looks all afternoon. A fitted sheet dangles from my hands, halfway to tamed. The tea I made earlier sits untouched on the side table, probably already cold. I don't move.

♪ *"You Make My Dreams (Come True)"* by Hall & Oates

◌◌

I don't speak. I just watch her cross the living room—like a girl who's not quite here, her body arriving ahead of her mind.

She sinks into the armchair across from me and immediately checks her phone again, trying not to smile. Failing. She bites her lip. Her cheeks pink deeper. The light from the screen softens her features, and for a brief moment, she looks so young. And also, somehow, not at all.

The name appears at the top of the screen. Lucas. A tiny red heart sits next to it. I don't recognize the name.

Gray holds the phone to her chest and stares at the ceiling like it has something to say about all this. Then she lets out a sound—half sigh, half laugh—and wraps both arms around the pillow in her lap. I catch the bounce of her foot against the chair leg. Nervous energy. The kind I know too well. I've worn it. I've buried it. I've missed it.

She glances over, notices me watching. "What?" she asks, defensively—but there's no edge to it.

I shake my head gently. Nothing.

Her eyes narrow. "You're giving me a look."

I arch an eyebrow.

She rolls hers and mutters, "He's just a friend."

That's new. Not the crush—I saw that coming a mile away. The way she lingers a little longer at the mirror, the half-smile that shows up when she thinks I'm not looking, the sudden interest in which days we wash her favorite hoodie. I've seen the signs. I'm not that far removed from being her age, even if my knees would beg to differ.

I want to ask a dozen things. What does he listen to—actual music, or just noise and bravado? Has he made you laugh until your stomach hurt? Has he made you cry yet?

Can I get Aunt Allison to beat the living crap out of him?

But I don't ask.

She smiles at something on the screen. Something—or someone—texting back. Then she tucks the phone under her leg like it might say too much if I see it again. She steals another glance at me like I might press. I don't.

I watch her for a moment longer, feeling the ground shift ever so slightly beneath us. She's growing up. She's keeping things. And I want to protect all of it—even the parts I'm not invited into.

I glance down at the soft cotton in my hands. A T-shirt with a faint stain from last weekend's much needed raspberry gelato run. She doesn't know I never got it all out. Doesn't know how many little things I've saved without her noticing.

I don't say anything. I just keep folding. And let her keep this moment. She's not quite a child anymore. But not yet grown. Somewhere in between. Floating in that strange, golden hour of girlhood where everything feels too much and not enough.

My chest aches. Not with fear. Not even sadness. Just... awe. How did we get here already?

I reach for my tea, but I don't drink it. I just hold it. Let the warmth anchor me while the rest of the world changes quietly in front of me.

She hums again. The song is back. The blush still lingering on her cheeks. There's something beautiful about it. This first small unfolding. This sweet, reckless step into wanting.

I watch her longer than I should. And I think: Where does she get all of this? This knowing. This soft bravery. This light. She's just a girl. But she already knows things I still haven't learned how to name.

I close my eyes for a breath. Let it pass through me. I don't need to have the right words. Not tonight. I just need to show up. And stay.

Gray accidentally hums the lyrics. "Oh yeah, you make my dreams come true."

Hall and Oates. *Oh shit.*

USS Carl Vinson - The Marshall Islands

There isn't much wind, so the Vinson is pushing hard—thirty knots, maybe more—just to keep enough air moving over the deck. I can feel it in the soles of my boots, the way the steel hums beneath me.

The air doesn't howl like I expected. It rushes, steady and urgent, thick with jet exhaust and salt, wrapping around my shoulders and rat-tling inside the helmet. The sky stretches wide and white-hot above us, and everything out here feels sharper. Closer. Like the whole world's been stripped down to speed, steel, and sky.

Just ahead, a yellow-vested shooter stands at the edge of power and consequence. One hand raised, fingers circling overhead—spool it up. The F/A-18 behind him snarls to life, its engines roaring higher until the pitch cuts straight through your chest. It doesn't just vibrate—it shakes the air, the deck, your bones.

The Hornet hunches against the holdback bar, afterburners blooming in twin cones of searing blue, the exhaust warping everything behind it like heat bending time. The aircraft isn't waiting—it's straining, barely leashed, daring the catapult to let go.

I don't breathe. I just watch. Then the shooter drops into his stance, a crouch so fluid it could be dance. His right arm slices forward. The deck shakes beneath my boots. But I've already raised my camera for the cat shot.

Click.

The shutter's whisper is absurdly quiet against the chaos. But I hear it. I always hear it. It's the sound of being exactly where I want to be.

The Hornet slams forward, pulled by the catapult in a blur of fury and control. A thick white plume of steam explodes from beneath the aircraft, enveloping the launch area in a sudden fog—rising, roiling, then vanishing just as fast. The jet punches through it, slicing the sky clean, and lifts in a single, decisive motion—up and gone, trailing the last of the mist behind it like smoke from a fuse.

The jet-blast fence thuds down as the flight deck resets.

This isn't the kind of beauty I'm used to. I don't shoot conflict. I shoot light. Stillness. Stories etched into stone, or mountains that haven't changed in centuries. But this ship is a living thing. Built for force. For precision. For *war.* And yet—even here, inside this engine of destruction, there's grace. The flight deck is a kind of dance floor.

◐

Loud, brutal, but choreographed down to the second. Every motion is discipline. Every launch a ritual.

It hits me harder than I expect. Because even in places designed for power, there's still poetry. It's just sharper. Stripped down. Earned. I've spent my whole life chasing beauty. But maybe I've misunderstood where to look. Maybe it's not just in what's peaceful—but in what's necessary.

In what's endured.

Another sound rises behind me—a lower rumble, different in shape—and I turn just as an E-2 Hawkeye drops into view. Wide wings. Dome-like radar dish. It looks like it belongs to another era, but here it is, lining up for the deck.

I raise the camera again. My fingers are ready before I am.

The Hawkeye touches down hard, the twin props screaming like something alive. Its tailhook snags the arresting wire with a brutal snap, yanking the plane to a stop in a heartbeat.

Trapped.

A second later, the cable recoils—snapping back into place with a violent whip, hissing as it resets on the deck. It's like watching a muscle contract, fast and deadly. I feel it in my chest, even from behind the camera. My hands flinch instinctively, even though I'm behind the safety line, shielded by layers of protocol and experience I don't yet understand.

I lower the camera for a second. Just breathe.

The deck crew doesn't flinch. Yellow vests guide the aircraft clear with curt gestures, eyes locked, bodies braced. Someone in green waves the taxi signal. Another bolts across the deck, ducking beneath the wing like it's second nature. No one hesitates. No one stands still for long.

I've read that the flight deck of an aircraft carrier is one of the most dangerous workplaces on Earth. Now I know it. The noise alone is relentless—more than sound, it's pressure, rattling through my ribs, thick in my throat, like the whole ocean's screaming at once.

The heat rises in waves off the steel, mixed with jet exhaust and sun-scorched metal. The air stings with fuel and sweat and something else—something volatile. These planes aren't just machines of speed. They're armed. Fully loaded. Missiles slung beneath wings. Bombs locked beneath hatches.

The deck isn't just dangerous. It's primed. Tense. A slip of timing, a missed signal, a wrench where it shouldn't be—and the whole rhythm collapses. Out here, precision isn't a virtue. It's the only thing holding the chaos back.

And still—they move. With trust. With instinct. Like this is just another morning.

I raise my camera again and catch one of the green shirts wiping sweat from his brow with a sleeve, eyes scanning the horizon for the next inbound. There's a wild dignity in the way he stands. Not flashy. Not heroic. Just necessary. And I feel something shift in my chest.

I don't belong here. And I need to stay the fuck out of the way.

These aren't people performing for the camera. They're surviving it. Living it. Owning every inch of this floating battlefield with the quiet certainty of those who understand its rules better than they understand their own breath.

Normally, I shoot mountains, temples, windswept ruins. Places the world forgot. I wait for golden hour, for perfect symmetry, for nature to hand me its magic. But out here? Out here, there's no waiting. No perfection. Just movement and consequence. Noise and risk. Human hands taming impossibility. A sense comes over me:

I'm a tourist in a helmet and borrowed gear. But my camera feels different now—less like a tool for collecting and more like one for witnessing.

Not for beauty. For truth.

The Hawkeye is taxiing out of view. The next launch team is already forming. The deck crew shifts like a tide, reconfiguring, resetting. I step back, give them space.

Somewhere beneath the roar of jet engines and the thrum of tension, I feel it: a thread pulled tight between fear and awe. And for the first time, I don't reach for words or metaphors. I just take the shot.

The café is silent. Too silent. The kind of silence that hums beneath your skin, that makes every sound feel louder just for daring to exist. I sit at my desk, staring down at the FINAL NOTICE stamps that scream in red across the stack of unpaid bills. The ink is thick, unforgiving. My fingers trace the lines as if I can erase them just by willing them into softness.

Electric. Rent. Suppliers. All overdue. All loud in their own way.

Above me, the first dollar I ever made still hangs in its crooked frame. The glass is dusted over, but I can still see through it—to her. The younger version of me with sleeves rolled up and hope clutched in both hands. I remember that morning—how proud I felt. How sure I was that this place would thrive. That I would.

Now, the café feels like a memory I'm still living inside.

The chairs are stacked on the tables, legs sticking up like wings folded in surrender. The espresso machine—the one that once hissed and purred like a living thing—sits cold. Still. A relic.

I drift through the room, trailing my fingers along the countertop. The one smoothed by years of elbows and stories and small kindnesses exchanged over caffeine and cinnamon. How many hands reached for comfort here? How many secrets were shared over oat milk lattes?

The walls are still full of color. Photos from community nights. Storytime flyers. Posters for coat drives and poetry readings. A mosaic of all the ways I tried to make this more than just a coffee shop. I built this space to hold people. To give them a place to land.

Above it all, the old wooden sign still hangs:

Every Cup Served With Love.

It wasn't branding. It was a promise. And maybe that was the problem. Love isn't profitable. Heart doesn't balance a ledger.

I should've paid more attention to margins, to spreadsheets, to the slow bleed of overhead. I should've said no more often. To late hours. To free coffee for the kid who always forgot his wallet. To baking extra muffins for the shelter around the corner.

But I didn't. And now… now this place is drowning under its own compassion. I only have myself to blame.

I stop at the community board near the door. It's cluttered with old flyers, hand-scrawled thank-you notes, kids' drawings faded from the sun. One stands out:

"Thank you for making this more than just a café.
You made it a home."

My hand rests on the paper longer than it needs to. A home. That's what it became for so many. But for me… it was everything. It still is. And I'm losing it.

Back at the desk, I press my palms to my eyes. The exhaustion isn't new—it's been building for months—but tonight it feels unmanageable. Like it's no longer just tiredness. It's surrender.

My phone buzzes. A message from Dad.

I stare at the screen, thumb hovering. He'd help me. No question. I wouldn't even have to ask twice. But to ask is to admit failure. To say the words out loud: *I can't do this anymore.*

I type: *Dad, I really need help.*

But I don't send it. Not yet. I stare at the blinking cursor. My thumb trembles. And then I delete the message.

The phone slips from my hand, lands facedown on the desk. The screen goes dark. Just like that—like maybe if I can't see it, it won't be real.

◎

I push back from the desk. Let the silence stretch.

Then, without thinking, I reach below the counter—past the stack of faded menus and the crumpled apron I've worn too many times—and pull out the teacup.

It's chipped on one side. The floral pattern worn soft by time. But I've kept it here since the beginning. It belonged to my grandmother. She used to drink from it when I was small, always careful, always quiet—like the cup itself held a kind of dignity. I never let it out on the floor. It wasn't for customers. It was for me. For the moments I needed to remember why I started.

I turn it over slowly in my hands, my thumb tracing the worn gold along the rim. It's more than ceramic. It's memory. Weight. Love in its most ordinary form.

And now, as everything begins to slip through my fingers, I hold it like it means something. Because it does.

☾

I step out onto the porch with a mug of coffee and my black leather bomber still faintly smelling of jet fuel. The trip to the Marshalls was everything it should've been—sharp, vivid, unforgettable—but now, back on solid ground, all I feel is how heavy my legs are. The kind of tired that doesn't come from one flight, but from all of them.

The fog clings low to the trees, drifting in from the water like it hasn't decided whether it's coming or going. I get it. Below, gulls cry into the stillness, and the tide pulls back to reveal dark rocks slick with seaweed, tide pools catching the first light like scattered pieces of glass. It's beautiful. And for once, I'm not reaching for the camera.

From the living room behind me, the soft crackle of the record player filters out through the open window—Dylan's voice, worn and familiar, murmuring over a fingerpicked guitar. It's not loud. It doesn't need to be. It just hums there—steady, tired, a little frayed at the edges. Like the island. Like me. ♪

The lyrics aren't trying to be profound. They just are. Like someone admitting their life aloud for the first time, without needing to dress it up.

Island mornings are different. Quieter, but not in the same way as the mountains. The stillness here isn't vast or epic—it's intimate. Closer. You don't wake to the roar of wind across peaks or the rush of pine-scented air. You wake to the rustle of madrone leaves in the breeze, to the soft chatter of birds threading their way through the morning light. The air smells like salt and damp earth, like things growing slowly. It's a slower kind of breath.

I wrap my hands around the mug and lean against the railing. From here, I can see sailboats drifting out in the channel, their white sails catching the pale light like small prayers whispered to the wind. Beyond them, the Olympic Mountains rise faint and blue across the water, distant but watchful. In the mountains, I always felt like I had to rise to meet the world—up, up, always up. But here, the island doesn't demand anything. It just... holds still. Steady. Enduring. It doesn't care how you show up. It lets you arrive as you are.

And maybe that's what I need now. Not a challenge to conquer. Not a mogul to chase. But a place to land. A place to let the questions settle.

Roots.

Dylan keeps singing. His voice falters a little at the edge of the

♪ "Buckets of Rain" by Bob Dylan

verse, but that's part of the magic. It sounds like he means it. Every note. Every line. Like he's been through all of it and came out with a shrug and a smile that still knows how to hurt.

The Church of Bob.

I belong. No pews. No sermons. Just a man with a harmonica telling the truth sideways.

There's no explaining Dylan to someone who doesn't get it. I've tried before—played him for friends who just frowned and asked why he sounds like that. They hear the voice, but miss the wisdom underneath.

Dylan taught me more about life than any classroom ever could. How to see beauty in imperfection. How to acknowledge that the world is broken without losing hope. How sometimes the most important truths come disguised as riddles, wrapped in metaphors that take years to fully understand.

I was nineteen when I first really heard Dylan– not just listened to him, but heard him. That admission that certainty is the enemy of growth, that we can look back at our younger, more rigid selves with a kind of compassionate understanding. It hit me like revelation. Changed how I saw myself, how I judged others.

That's what Dylan does. He drops these nuggets of hard-earned wisdom into your life, and suddenly you're seeing everything differently. You learn that love isn't what greeting cards say it is – it's messy, complicated, sometimes painful. You learn that justice doesn't always look like victory. You learn that questions matter more than answers.

I lean back, letting the music wash through me. Each album has been a different teacher at different points in my life. When I was lost, his wandering songs gave me permission to not know where I was going. When I was heartbroken, his breakup songs taught me there was something valuable even in endings. When I felt alone, his voice was like finding someone who understood.

You either get Dylan or you don't. There is no in-between. And I'm grateful, every day, to be among those who do – those who found not just music but a way of moving through the world, eyes open, heart bruised but beating, always asking the next question.

The track changes. Another song begins. I smile to myself, recognizing the opening notes. This one taught me about finding safety in a chaotic world, about the healing power of connection when everything else falls apart. About how sometimes the people who save us appear when we least expect them, offering refuge when we're battered by life's storms. And yet, within that same song, there's the acknowledgment that even the deepest shelter is temporary, that we all eventually step back into the rain. Dylan never offers simple solutions - just profound recognition of what it means to be human. ♪

I think about my grandfather—how he ended up here after everything. The war, the loss, the years that changed his body but never seemed to touch his core. Maybe he understood something I'm only just starting to. That the world doesn't always need to be captured or explained. Sometimes it's enough to live inside it. To take a walk at dusk. To eat the peach while it's ripe. To sit still and listen to the tide go out.

It reminds me of the prior track where he talks about accepting life's sadness and just doing what you need to do to get through. My grandfather and Dylan—different men from different worlds, speaking the same truth in their own languages. One through calloused hands and quiet mornings on the porch, the other through poetry and that voice that sounds like time itself. Both teaching me that wisdom isn't about

♪ *"Shelter from the Storm"* by Bob Dylan

having all the answers, but about making peace with the questions. verse, but that's part of the magic. It sounds like he means it.

I sit with that thought for a while, letting it settle. The breeze shifts, carrying the faint scent of cut grass and something sweet blooming nearby. The sun has climbed higher, casting everything in that sharp, honest light that morning always brings.

I tilt my head back, staring up at the blue sky overhead—wide, endless, untouchable. "Yeah," I murmur to no one, to Dylan, to the ghosts of old versions of myself still clinging to the past.

"I'm tangled up in blue, all right."

And for once, I don't try to untangle it. I just let it be.

I pull into the crowded parking lot of the multiplex, maneuvering around groups of teenagers moving in packs toward the bright lights of the theater entrance. Gray has been quiet most of the drive, her attention divided between her phone and her reflection in the passenger window. Every few minutes, she runs her fingers through her hair or adjusts the collar of her jacket—small, nervous gestures I pretend not to notice.

Lucas stands waiting, headphones around his neck, a dark blue jacket with a snowflake pattern down one sleeve. I pull up to the curb and Gray unbuckles with surprising speed.

I touch her arm lightly, raising an eyebrow.

She sighs. "Yes, I'll be careful. Lucas said his mom can drive me home."

I nod but don't drive away as she approaches him. Her walk changes—more measured, more conscious. When Lucas spots her, something shifts in his posture—a straightening, an alertness that wasn't there before.

Through the windshield, I watch their silent choreography—the careful distance between them, Gray tucking her hair behind her ear, Lucas listening with his whole body turned toward her. He pulls out pre-purchased tickets. She looks surprised, then pleased. He says something that makes her laugh—a real laugh, not the careful one she uses at school.

I sit for a moment, my hands still on the wheel. A tightness forms in my chest—not fear exactly, but something adjacent to it. This is more parts of motherhood no one prepares you for: the slow, necessary letting go.

The first crush. The first heartbreak waiting somewhere down the line.

I can't protect her from any of it. Wouldn't want to, really. These small, beautiful hurts are how she'll find herself.

I remember my own first movie dates—the magnificent torture of wanting to be both seen and invisible at the same time. I wore too much eyeliner and pretended not to care what he thought of my laugh. I did, though. I cared about everything.

I smile and put the car in drive.

The radio hums low, an old song I only half remember, and for a second I let myself feel it—this quiet joy threaded through with the ache of time passing. ♪

She's growing up. And I'm still learning how to let her.

♪ *"The Only Living Boy in New York"* by Simon and Garfunkel

◎

07

10:01:26:21:57:16

The Retirement Sale sign flutters slightly in the mountain breeze, its edges curling from too many cold nights and too much sun. I stand on the ladder, carefully unscrewing the bolts that have held the *Charm & Whimsy* sign in place for as long as I can remember. It doesn't come down easily. I grip the edges, feeling the weight of it—not just wood and paint, but history. My history.

I step down from the ladder, running my fingers over the worn lettering. A name, a place, a piece of us.

Mom's gaze lingers on the sign in my hands. "I used to think retirement would feel like freedom," she says softly. "But it feels more like… surrender. And somehow, still, the right kind."

I glance at her. "Does that scare you?"

She smiles, but it's thinner now. "Less than I thought. Maybe it's not about stopping. Maybe it's just about choosing a different kind of pace."

I nod slowly, tucking that away. Because that's what this is, isn't it? For both of us. Letting go of the familiar so something else can have space to begin.

Below me, Mom watches with a wistful smile, arms folded across her chest. The door to the shop stands open behind her, a hollow space where shelves once overflowed with trinkets, candles, and the kind of things people never knew they needed until they found them here. I step down from the ladder, running my fingers over the worn lettering. A name, a place, a piece of us.

We step inside for the last time. The store is too quiet. No soft hum of conversation, no scent of cinnamon and lavender lingering in the air. The walls are bare, the floors scuffed in places where customers once gathered, where I used to sit behind the counter flipping through photography magazines, listening to Mom help someone find the perfect gift.

She exhales softly beside me.

"It feels like yesterday that I first opened these doors."

Her voice is steady, but I can hear the ache underneath. I nod, scanning the empty space.

"Every corner of this place has good memories."

Somewhere between now and then, I see it—Mom arranging holiday displays in the front window, Grandfather chuckling as he fixed a wobbly shelf, me, years ago, helping restock while dreaming about

the world beyond these walls. Everything changes. But standing here, it doesn't feel real.

Mom reaches for the light switch. I follow her to the door. The bell above chimes softly. For the last time.

The café still smells like coffee. Even with the shelves cleared, the tables gone, and the espresso machine sold off to cover the final bills, the scent lingers. It's in the floorboards, the walls, the worn wood of the counter—like it doesn't know the story is over. Or maybe it's just waiting for the next chapter.

Gray and I work quietly. We've boxed the last of the mugs. The chairs are stacked against the far wall. The air feels too still. Too big for a space that used to hold so much life.

I glance around and try to see it the way customers once did—the tiny bookshelf by the window, the framed poems, the crooked jar of dog treats by the door. All gone now.

The truth is, this place became more than a café. It became an anchor. A way to stay grounded when everything else was shifting. But anchors can start to weigh you down. And lately, I've felt something loosening in me. Maybe letting go isn't the same as giving up. Maybe I'm ready for something different.

Gray is folding the last of the linens when the bell above the door chimes. It's habit, I suppose—that instinct to smile at whoever walks in. Only now, there's no one left to serve. Then we see him.

The cornbread man.

But he's not the same. The coat is different. His hair is neatly trimmed. His posture, straighter. The hollowed-out look in his eyes has softened into something brighter—calmer. He steps inside with a kind of reverence, his gaze moving across the bare walls like he's remembering what used to be here.

Gray's face brightens. "Hey," she says, stepping forward. "You look different."

He smiles, and it transforms him. "I am different."

He tells us he's working at the library now. Shelving books. Six months strong. Says he has a small apartment of his own. Clean clothes. A soft chair. A space that's his.

I just listen. I don't interrupt. I let the warmth bloom quietly in my chest. She asks if he still likes cornbread, and his laugh fills the empty room—a sound I've never heard from him before. He says he can make his own now, and something clicks into place.

I walk to a small box on the counter—the one holding the few personal items I've decided to take home. Inside is my grandmother's cornbread recipe, handwritten on a card so old the edges have softened like cloth. I've kept it in the café all these years, thumbed it so often the ink has begun to fade. I've memorized it by now—don't need the card anymore. But someone else might.

I hand it to Gray with a nod toward our visitor. She understands immediately.

"My mom wants you to have this," she says. "It's her grandmother's cornbread recipe. The one she always made for you."

◎

He takes it slowly, like it might crumble if he moves too fast. His eyes scan the card, then lift to mine.

"Thank you," he says. The gratitude is written all over his face. That smile again—soft, steady, full of something real. He folds the recipe carefully and slips it into his coat.

He looks around the café one last time—the empty walls, the quiet air, the absence of what once was. And then, with that same soft smile, he turns and walks out.

The bell rings once more. A last note. And then he's gone.

Gray turns to me, eyes bright with something I can't name. She leans her shoulder against mine, not looking up.

"Thunder only happens when it's raining," she says, almost like she's quoting a prayer. She doesn't explain it. She doesn't need to. I feel the truth of it settle in my chest.

In the midst of this ending, here is proof that what we built mattered. What we gave returned, somehow. The café may be closing, but its impact lingers—in the cornbread man, in us, in countless small kindnesses that rippled outward in ways we'll never fully know.

I exhale slowly, pressing my palm to the glass of the front door, watching him disappear down the sidewalk.

Behind me, Gray pulls the handwritten sign from the counter. I take it from her, fingers smoothing the edges.

Thank You for the Memories.

◯

I open the door, step outside, and crouch to tape it to the glass. My hand lingers against the window longer than it needs to. People pass by, caught in their own lives. No one sees what's ending here. But I do.

Gray joins me. She doesn't say anything. She doesn't have to. She just wraps her arms around me and holds tight. I press a kiss to the top of her head and let my eyes close.

It's over. And somehow—it's not. Not really.

She leans back, studying the empty window for a second. Then she bumps her shoulder against mine and says, soft but certain, "I think this calls for gelato."

A laugh bubbles up—small, surprised, grateful. Of course she's right. She always is. When in doubt: gelato.

We turn away from the shop together, the door clicking closed behind us. Some endings deserve something sweet.

Baked in Telluride

The scent of fresh bread and roasted coffee wraps around me the moment I step inside the bakery. Warmth, conversation, the low clatter of plates and cups—it's all the same.

Nothing has changed. And yet, everything has.

I remember when Telluride was just a forgotten mining town turned ski village—all weathered wood and brick buildings, locals in faded flannels. We'd spend afternoons at the *Sheridan*, where everyone knew everyone, and a round of beers cost less than the latte I'm about to order. Back then, each day came with unfiltered conversation and something else—connection. Real and unpolished. Now, I hardly recognize anyone.

The mountains haven't changed. Still towering. Still indifferent to the transformation below. The powder is still perfect, the trails still exhilarating. Everything is still beautiful—always extraordinary. But it's a different kind of extraordinary now.

Maybe I'm just being nostalgic. Romanticizing a past that had its own cracks. Probably. Still—there was something honest about the old town. A kind of realness that can't be manufactured. And once it's gone, you feel it everywhere.

I step up to the counter, scanning the menu even though I already know what I want. Some habits never break. The barista, bright-eyed and full of the kind of morning energy I've never understood, smiles at me.

"Hi! What can I get started for you today?"

I hesitate for half a second.

"Hey, I'll have a double shot latte. And, um, a black coffee too. Thanks."

Her hands move fast, pulling espresso shots, steaming milk. I glance around, taking in the color and noise, trying to find something I recognize.

A group of ski bums huddle over a newspaper, probably talking about the latest snowfall. A father and daughter share a massive cinnamon roll, her fingers sticky with icing. The kind of moment that makes time feel slower.

In the corner, I spot someone familiar. An old-timer.

Scary Gary.

Deep in conversation—with his bagel. His hands gesture wildly, his expression intense, as if debating philosophy with the sesame seeds. I smile, shaking my head. Still Gary. And still scary. I smile. Some things always stay the same.

"Here you go! Enjoy!"

I blink, snapping back.

"Thanks," I say, grabbing both drinks.

I turn to leave, drinks in hand—but I pause. The kid's laughter drifts across the room, icing smeared across her cheek, the father leaning in with a grin as she pulls apart the cinnamon roll like it's treasure. The kind of moment you don't plan. The kind that stays. I glance back at the pastry case.

Cinnabon. Or something close enough.

I step sideways, clearing my throat. "Actually—sorry, one more thing. That cinnamon roll. Yeah, the big one."

The barista beams, already reaching for the tongs. "Great choice. It's our best seller."

Of course it is. Because frosting and nostalgia are hard to beat. As she bags it, I feel something loosen in my chest—something small and dumb and good. Because why not? Life's short. Eat the damn cinna-

mon roll. Some things are worth remembering. And some things are worth tasting again.

My gaze drifts back to Gary and his breakfast companion. He points a dramatic finger at the bagel, then sighs, as if deeply disappointed by its silence. I take a sip of my latte and push open the door.

Gray's bedroom is a disaster. I stand in the doorway, arms crossed, surveying the battlefield of discarded clothes, open textbooks, and half-empty Starbucks cups. The comforter is halfway off the bed, pillows buried beneath a tangle of hoodies. A bottle of nail polish sits uncapped on the desk, dangerously close to spilling onto a pile of crumpled homework. I exhale slowly, shaking my head.

Above the chaos, a Speed Racer poster still clings to the wall, its corners curling from time and tape. It's been there since she was nine—bright, bold, utterly out of place among the teenage clutter. But she won't let me take it down. Says Speed has wisdom.

Sure, I guess. Her idolizing Stevie Nicks or Shaun White—I can understand. But Speed Racer? Still, there's something weirdly comforting about it. Like an anchor to a version of her that lingers beneath the sarcasm and Dr. Pepper. Softer, smaller—but still in there somewhere, driving fast and thinking deep.

Teenagers.

A part of me wants to yell for Gray to clean this shit up right now—but another part, the part that's spent years juggling responsibilities, just feels… tired. I close the door instead.

Out of sight, out of mind.

⟪⟫

Downstairs, I settle into my usual spot at the kitchen table, pulling my laptop toward me. The glow of the screen flickers over my face as I scroll through endless job listings:

Barista. Marketing Assistant. Retail Associate. Accountant.

I rub my temple, frustration simmering beneath my skin. None of these feel right. None of them feel me. The scrolling slows.

Greenery Assistant.

I pause, my finger hovering over the trackpad.

Urban Roots — Community Garden Project.
Just a love of plants and community required.

The job description expands, filling the screen with an image of a garden in full bloom—lush greenery spilling over brick pathways, wildflowers bursting with color. Beneath it, the words:

Help revitalize neglected green spaces in Seattle neighborhoods. Hands-on work with plants, planning garden layouts, and engaging with local volunteers.

Something tugs deep in my chest. I glance toward the window, where my own neglected plants sit on the sill, their leaves reaching for light. How long had it been since I tended to them the way I used to? Since I let myself get lost in the simple rhythm of caring for something?

My eyes drift toward the bookshelf. *Braiding Sweetgrass* is still there, the corners dog-eared, a dried flower pressed between the pages. I remember reading it slowly, savoring the way the author spoke about plants—not just as objects, but as teachers. As gifts.

There was something in those pages I hadn't realized I needed—an idea that staying in one place, nurturing what's around you, could be just as meaningful as saving the world. That tending isn't failure. It's a kind of love.

I rest my head against my hand, fingers gently pressing into my temple. The weight of closing the cafe, the uncertainty, the endless worrying—it doesn't disappear, but for the first time, it shifts. Just a little. A faint smile tugs at the corner of my lips. It's not much. But it's something.

The walk up to Lone Pine Cemetery is always quiet. My footsteps crunch along the gravel path, the wind threading through the pines, whispering through the valley. The mountains are watching.

I reach my Grandfathers final resting spot and stop, staring down at the weathered stone. I set the black coffee beside it. The steam curls into the cold air.

I kneel, running my fingers over the carved letters, the name that feels like a permanent part of my own history.

"Miss you, Gramps."

The words feel small, insignificant, not nearly enough. The wind picks up, rattling the branches overhead. Or maybe, answering me. I sit back on my heels, the town stretching below in the distance, alive with the movement of people, of life continuing. For a while, I just stay.

Discovery Park - Seattle

The evening air carries the scent of the ocean as I walk, my boots crunching softly along the dirt trail. Everything feels still, yet rest-

⓪

less—like the world is waiting for me to make a decision I don't know how to make.

I reach the fork in the path and stop, my chest suddenly tight. My fingernails dig into my palms, leaving crescent moons in their wake. My body seems to know what my mind doesn't—that this decision matters more than I'm willing to admit.

The fork in the path feels like a mockery of my life right now. Right leads to the beach—wild, unpredictable, constantly changing. Left leads to the lighthouse—stable, purposeful, enduring.

I swallow hard, surprised by the thought I can't quite finish.

I follow the path toward West Point Lighthouse, the sound of waves rising through the trees, threading between branches like wind-borne thread. With each step, the scent of salt air deepens—clean, familiar. Below, the Sound glimmers beneath the soft evening light, its surface shifting silver. Restless. Reflective. Always moving. Always changing.

I stop at the bluff, arms wrapping around my knees as I sit. The lighthouse stands before me—constant, unwavering, everything I'm not. I run my fingers over the worn cover of *Plainwater* in my bag, the book that's traveled with me longer than it should have. Some things we carry not because we need them, but because we can't let them go.

A ferry glides across the Sound, cutting clean lines through the water. Its passengers have somewhere to go. I don't. I close my eyes, listening to the waves crash against the rocks—relentless, unchanging. A heartbeat that isn't mine but somehow echoes inside me.

Somewhere in the back of my mind, a melody stirs—a voice, smoky and familiar. A song I used to play late at night, when the house was quiet and I didn't know what I needed, only that I was missing something. It always made me feel both untethered and held. Like drifting could be sacred. Like the fog might eventually lift. ♪

I remember dancing to it alone in my kitchen once, barefoot on cool tile, the light from the oven clock blinking 2:14 AM. No audience. No reason. Just the music and me, trying to feel something solid. I'd forgotten that until now.

When did certainty become so elusive?
When did the path forward become so unclear?

A flock of seabirds shifts course midair, circling uncertainly before finally settling on a direction. I follow their movement, envying their collective decision. Then stop. What if I keep waiting for certainty, and it never comes? What if standing still is just another way of choosing?

The sun slips lower, turning the sky into something bruised and burning. I feel exposed out here, as if the fading light might reveal what I've been hiding even from myself—that what terrifies me isn't making the wrong choice, but making any choice at all. Choosing means closing doors. Choosing means admitting what I really want.

The last of the sunlight touches the water, soft and smoldering, before disappearing below the horizon. Gone. The lighthouse beam begins its steady rhythm, sweeping across the darkening water. Revealing what was hidden. Guiding what is lost.

I exhale, pulling my jacket tighter around me. I don't know where I'm going. But I can't stay here forever. I reach down and pick up a smooth stone, turning it over in my palm, feeling its weight—the culmination of years being shaped by forces bigger than itself. With a

♪ *"Into the Mystic"* by Van Morrison

⦾

sudden movement, I hurl it toward the darkening water. It disappears without a sound, but I've made something move. It's a start.

☾

The porch swing creaks softly beneath us as we sway in unspoken rhythm, the ice in our glasses clinking against the glass as we sip our tea. The air smells like pine and fading sunlight, the last warmth of the day slipping over the mountains of early spring.

Mom exhales, settling deeper into her seat, watching the sky go gold and violet. For a moment, everything feels suspended, like time itself is holding its breath. Then, she speaks.

"So, are you ever going to settle down?" She nudges me with her elbow. "I really want grandchildren, you know."

I huff a small laugh, shaking my head. "I mean, sure. I just... well, you know."

She gives me a look—one of those motherly looks that could see straight through steel. Arms folded, voice playful but edged with something else.

"I thought for sure you would marry Martone."

The name hangs between us for a second too long. I look down at the tea swirling in my glass, the ice slowly melting.

"Yeah," I say finally. "I really blew that one."

Mom doesn't push, just watches me carefully. She's known her fair share of heartbreak. More than I ever have.

"Well, that's life," she says after a moment, her voice softer now. "Not every love story lasts forever. Something I learned more than once."

The sky deepens to indigo, and I hear the distant chime of the Courthouse clock rolling through town. Mom places her hand on mine. Warm, steady.

"Just don't let the past keep you from finding what's next, dear."

The morning light slants low through the trees, soft and golden—the kind that makes everything feel both temporary and important. I tighten the scarf around my neck as I step out onto the gravel path past the sign that reads *"Urban Roots – Growing Together"*, the hum of voices already drifting up from the garden below. Laughter. The slap of rubber boots in wet dirt. The sharp rustle of wheelbarrows being dragged over stone.

It's still strange, sometimes, to think of this is me now—this job, this rhythm. I hadn't expected to find something that fit so quietly, so completely. But I said yes to *Urban Roots*, and somehow, they said yes to me. Most days, it feels like luck. The good kind. The kind you don't question.

I make my way down the hill, arms full of seedling trays—spinach, lettuce, snap peas. The kind of green that promises spring. Damp earth clings to my boots, and somewhere nearby, someone starts music low on a speaker—old soul, mellow and familiar. I don't recognize the track, but it settles into the background like it belongs here.

Theo's already in the center of it all. I met him my first week here—part lead gardener, part unofficial chaos wrangler. He has a way of making everyone feel at ease, like there's no wrong way to learn.

Now, he's kneeling by the raised beds with a group of kids, showing them how to space out carrot seeds using a string line and popsicle sticks. One of the boys is patting the dirt like it's a sandbox. Theo doesn't correct him. He just adjusts the line and smiles, patient. I pause a few steps away. Watching him.

There's something unhurried in the way he moves, something grounded. Like the rest of the world runs on noise, and he just doesn't subscribe to it. I'm not used to noticing men. Not lately. But I notice him.

He stands and spots me, lifting a gloved hand in hello. I nod, shifting the weight of the trays in my arms. He jogs over to meet me halfway.

"I was wondering when the quiet magic would show up," he says, taking the top tray without asking. "These yours?"

I nod again. He already knows. He glances down. "Spinach, huh? Bold move. You're trusting the weather more than I do."

I shrug and tap the tray gently. Maybe. Maybe not. But it's worth the risk. We move toward the beds without speaking. The kids are focused now, digging and dropping seeds, burying them too deep or not at all. Theo lets it happen. He walks the line, encouraging, adjusting, laughing.

I kneel beside a girl tangled in her hoodie. She doesn't ask for help, so I don't offer. But I hand her a new spool of twine, and she lights up like I've given her something rare. Out of the corner of my eye, I see him watching. Just for a second.

We'd just finished planting the last bed for the day—snap peas, butter lettuce, a few rows of radish. My gloves were still damp, soil clinging beneath my fingernails, knees aching from crouching too long. The spring sun hovered just above the rooftops, throwing long shadows across the beds, and the garden had gone quiet in that satisfying, tired way—like the earth was taking a breath along with us.

I was brushing dirt from my pants when Theo reappeared, two paper cups in hand. He crossed the flagstone path with the easy kind of confidence that didn't ask for attention but didn't avoid it either. He handed me one of the cups without a word. I blinked, caught off guard.

"Almond milk latte," he said, voice low. "I think I remembered right."

I took it, fingers closing slowly around the warmth. I hadn't asked. Hadn't said much of anything, really. But he remembered. I glanced at the cup, then back at him, searching for something to say. I settled for a small nod. It was perfect.

He looked toward the others gathered at the edge of the garden— someone had brought pastries, another a thermos of something too sweet. Laughter moved easily between them. I usually slipped away after planting days, tucked out the back, unnoticed. I didn't like long goodbyes or lingering questions. But Theo was still standing there.

"You always slip out," he said, eyes still on the others. "Wasn't sure you'd stay today."

I hesitated, the cup held close to my chest. I hadn't decided yet.

Theo sat on the edge of a raised bed, motioning to the spot beside him but not insisting. I sat, slower, brushing my palms against my thighs before settling. The latte was still too hot to drink, but I liked the feel of it in my hands. I liked that he hadn't asked me anything more.

We sat there for a while, the garden breathing around us—dirt tilled and tidy, plants just beginning to root. Across the street, wind moved through the trees, catching the edges of the neighbor's laundry line. Somewhere, a dog barked twice and then fell quiet.

I snuck a glance at Theo. His elbows rested loosely on his knees, hands wrapped around his coffee like it was something more important than it was. He didn't fill the space with small talk. He just sat, present, unhurried. And I didn't want to move.

It wasn't love. Not anything close. But it was something. A flicker of possibility. A softness I hadn't allowed myself in a long time. Maybe I didn't have room for more. Maybe this wasn't the right season of my life. But something about the way he'd remembered my coffee, the way he didn't ask for more than I could give—that stayed with me. I took a sip. I didn't get up right away. And I guess that should tell me something.

☾

I approach the long-standing hot dog stand. From his post behind the cart, the ever-grumpy Hot Dog Man squints at me, arms folded, head shaking in something between disapproval and amusement.

"Well, well," he calls out. "If it isn't Mr. Magoo."

I grin, giving him a wave. Yep. Some things never change. And I like that.

I cross the street as the courthouse clock begins its recital—three o'clock, like always. The bench waits. I sit, right side as always, stretching an arm along the backrest. And I wait. I don't know why I still come here. Or maybe I do.

The street breathes with its usual rhythm—tourists strolling past, shop doors chiming, bicycles whirring. The world moves around me, and yet I sit, stuck between yesterday and tomorrow.

⦾

Footsteps approach. A woman, mid-40s, with a quiet confidence about her, pauses nearby. She takes in the town, the bench, and then me.

"Hello," she says, voice warm but unobtrusive. "Mind if I sit down?"

I blink, slightly caught off guard.

"Hi," I say, shifting slightly. "Please do."

Blythe—that's what she introduces herself as—settles in beside me, and we sit in comfortable silence, watching the world go by.

After a beat, she tilts her head. "Do you come here often?"

I hesitate. My gaze drifts down the street, to where something—someone—should be. "Oh... as often as I can," I admit.

She nods, understanding more than she should. "I can see why."

I glance at her, surprised by the way she just gets it.

"Yeah," I say. "It's... a good spot to just take everything in."

She studies me. "You seem like you're waiting for something."

I exhale, rubbing the back of my neck.

"Yeah, I guess you could say that. This bench is special to me."

Blythe smiles, a knowing kind of smile. "Funny how certain places hold memories like that. It's like they wait for you to come back, even if the moment has passed."

⦵

Her words hit somewhere deep. Am I still waiting for something that's already gone?

I shake my head, letting out a soft chuckle. "I keep asking myself why I come back... like I'm stuck chasing a shadow that's already gone."

Blythe leans back slightly, considering. "Maybe it's not about the past. Maybe it's about finding something new in what's familiar."

I sit with that for a second. The thought presses against something inside me I don't quite know how to name.

"I've spent so much time waiting," I murmur, mostly to myself. "Waiting for something to happen. I guess I forgot how to move forward."

The silence that follows isn't heavy. If anything, it's freeing. Blythe shifts, looking over at me again. "How do you feel about coffee?"

"Well... I'd say coffee is more essential than air."

She grins. "I know a place. Care to join me?"

I hesitate only a moment. Then, I smile back. "Sure," I say, standing. "Why not?"

And just like that, I take a step forward.

Bruno's - Edmonds

The smell of grilled meat and sweet syrup drifted through the warm air like a promise by the ferry line. The stand itself looked like it hadn't moved in decades—an old red trailer with sun-faded trim and peeling stickers from minor league baseball teams and long-gone political campaigns.

Gray marched straight up to the window like she'd been here a hundred times. "Two hot dogs, please," she said. "Ketchup only."

Behind the counter, a man with forearms like tree trunks and a jaw carved out of granite narrowed his eyes. His nametag read *Bruno*, which felt about right. "Ketchup?" he said slowly, leaning forward like he hadn't heard her correctly. "Ketchup, young lady?"

Gray didn't miss a beat. "Yep. Ketchup. The red stuff."

Bruno squinted, sizing her up like she'd just insulted his grandmother. "You don't put ketchup on a hot dog."

She shrugged, cool as ever. "Well, we do."

Bruno crossed his arms. "Listen, I've been running this stand longer than you've been alive. There are rules."

Gray didn't flinch. "Rules?" she shot back. "It's a hot dog, not the Ten Commandments."

Bruno stared at her. She stared right back—defiant, unbothered, entirely herself. With a dramatic sigh, he reached behind him and slapped a bottle of ketchup on the counter like it betrayed his very soul.

"Go ahead. Ruin it."

Gray grinned. "Gladly."

I stood off to the side, pretending to be very invested in the sno cone flavors. But inside, I was laughing. *Loud.*

This girl. Definitely my daughter.

06

09:11:29:20:23:55

Kathmandu is alive in a way few places are. The streets don't just move—they pulse. Voices spill over each other, rising in a symphony of barter and laughter. The air is thick with spice and incense, a weight that clings to my skin.

I move through the market, my camera raised, framing the fleeting beauty around me. A monk in saffron robes, fingers gliding over his prayer beads. A woman balancing a basket of marigolds, her walk measured, effortless. A young girl spinning through a cloud of Holi powder, her dress blooming around her like something out of a dream. I capture her mid-spin, suspended between chaos and light.

The deep chime of temple bells rolls through the streets, cutting through the noise like something ancient. Above, the Boudhanath Stupa watches me. Its painted eyes, unblinking, seem to know something I don't. I lower the camera.

For years, I've chased the perfect shot. The light, the framing, the fleeting second that says something real. I've crossed continents for it—stood before mountains, monasteries, jungles, and winter fields—always behind the lens. Removed. Observing.

But standing here, beneath those eyes, something shifts. And I wonder—for the thousandth time—if I've spent too much of my life capturing moments instead of living them. Maybe I've been collecting beauty without truly holding it. Maybe I've been looking in the wrong places—or from the wrong distance.

I keep walking, letting the city fall into step beside me. The noise fades behind a quiet turn. The rhythm slows.

Then I see it. A painted wooden sign hangs crookedly over a doorway, its letters faded by sun and time:

Sherpa Services – Treks & Expeditions

I pause beneath it, snow melting from my boots onto the stone step. The window beside the door is clouded with age, revealing only a blur of warm light inside. For a second, I hesitate—then push the door open.

Inside, the air is warm with the scent of yak butter tea and old wood. The walls are crowded with faded photographs of Everest expeditions—faces frozen in time, weathered and unshaken. I step inside fully. The bell jingles softly, swallowed by the stillness of the room.

At a wooden table near the window, Tenzing, a Sherpa in his 40s, sits in quiet observation. His fingers roll a string of worn prayer beads, as if tracing something only he can see.

"Namaste," I say, offering a slight bow.

⦾

Tenzing sets his tea down, his dark eyes steady, unmoving.

"Namaste," he replies, studying me.

Tenzing sets his tea down, his dark eyes steady, unmoving.

"I need a guide," I say, adjusting the strap of my camera. "I want to photograph the mountains. The monasteries. Capture the people, the life—"

Tenzing tilts his head slightly, cutting me off with silence.

"You seek the mountains… but do you understand what they will ask of you?"

I hesitate. The weight of his words lingers in the space between us. He picks up his prayer beads again, rolling them once between his fingers before speaking.

"The Himalayas do not reveal their truth to those who come only to take," he says. "They will ask you to leave something behind in return."

Something in my chest tightens. I hold his gaze.

"I'll give whatever they ask of me."

"Then let's see if the mountains find you worthy."

A slow, knowing smile tugs at the corners of his mouth. He stands, extending his hand.

◎

Dudh Khosi River - Phakding

The trail along the river unfolds like a secret whispered between the mountains—narrow, ancient, carved into the hillside by centuries of footsteps and prayer. We follow its winding path through dense rhododendron forests, their gnarled branches heavy with mist and moss.

The air is rich with the scent of damp earth and woodsmoke, and always, the low, constant murmur of the river below. Suspension bridges sway above deep gorges, flapping with strings of tattered prayer flags. As we climb higher, the Himalayas begin to reveal themselves—first as glimpses between trees, then rising fully into view, sharp and white against the blue. They don't just tower—they loom, eternal and indifferent.

The path grows steeper, quieter. Each step feels like an offering. The monastery is still ahead, nestled on a ridge where the world narrows to sky, stone, and the low chant of wind. I fight for breath with every step. Tenzing moves effortlessly, his boots barely leaving prints in the mud. He glances back at me, amused.

"You rely too much on your legs," he says. "The journey is not about the body. It is about the breath."

I slow my steps, matching my breath to the rhythm of my boots crunching against the earth. Tenzing nods, approving.

Then, at last, we reach the ridge. A stone cairn marks the highest point—weathered, draped in faded prayer flags that flick and snap in the wind. The clouds roll below us like restless waves, hiding and revealing the world in pieces. I raise my camera. But again, I don't take the shot. I don't know why. Or maybe I do, and I just don't want to admit it.

◎

Tengboche - Khumbu

Tengboche rises like a dream at the edge of the world—perched on a high ridge where the sky feels closer than the ground. Its crimson and gold facade stands in vivid contrast to the snow-draped peaks behind it, most notably the towering presence of Ama Dablam.

Prayer wheels line the entrance, spinning softly in the wind, while the scent of juniper smoke drifts from the courtyard. Bells chime faintly, and the low hum of chanting monks echoes through the still, thin air. It's not just a monastery—it's a threshold between earth and something greater.

Inside the monastery, the flickering glow of butter lamps casts long shadows against the walls. The air is thick with centuries-old incense. I sit cross-legged before a monk. His gaze is patient, knowing.

"You capture beauty through your lens," he says. "But what is it you truly seek?"

The answer is immediate, but I hesitate to say it. Finally, I exhale.

"I've been searching for someone… have been most of my life."

The monk nods, as if he already knew.

"The mountains do not mourn what they release. Each season brings new snow."

His voice is gentle, but the words hit like an avalanche. I look down, fingers tightening around my camera.

"Let go of the shadow," he says. "And perhaps you will finally see the light."

A memory comes without warning. Unbidden. Unshaken. In slow motion. Or maybe that was just how it felt.

Sophia, moving through the sunlight like it was parting just for her, a golden halo spilling across her shoulders. Barefoot.

A long sundress catching the wind, swaying around her ankles. Her midnight curls wild and unbound, twisting as if they had a life of their own. My whole world stopped. She wasn't real. Couldn't be. And yet—she was.

I didn't know her name. I didn't know anything about her. But I knew this—she was already written into my story before I had the sense to read the words. But I turned. I turned because something in me already knew—this wasn't just another stranger passing by. This was something else. Something I wasn't ready for.

The monk watches me, silent, waiting.

"You chase the perfect moment through your lens," he says.

I nod, throat tight. I always have.

"Sometimes… the perfect moment finds you."

I exhale, my breath shaky, my grip tightening around my camera. Maybe that moment—that first moment on the sidewalk—was the only one that ever really mattered. And I had let it slip past.

The morning was still damp from last night's rain. The sidewalk held the cool scent of wet pavement and cedar mulch, and the clouds overhead moved slow, like they hadn't made up their mind yet. I walked beside Theo toward the neighborhood nursery, a canvas bag slung over my shoulder and my hands tucked deep into my sleeves.

We didn't call it anything. Just said we needed a few more starts for the late-season beds. But when he offered to come with me, I said yes. And I didn't overthink it. Not much.

The nursery was quiet at this hour, the usual weekend crowds not quite awake yet. Wooden tables lined with trays of herbs and vegetables stretched out under misted greenhouse roofs. The scent of rosemary and warm dirt drifted through the air, grounding, familiar. We walked slowly, pausing to run fingers across leaves and whisper names to each other—basil, sage, lemon balm.

He lifted a pot of mint and held it toward me with a crooked smile. "Smells like summer, right"

I leaned in, letting the scent bloom beneath my nose—sweet, sharp, alive. I nodded, offering a small smile. It did smell like summer. And something about the way he looked at me in that moment—open, a little amused—sent a flutter low in my chest that I wasn't expecting.

We wandered past rows of lavender, the kind with soft gray-green stems and buds like tiny violet bees. He asked questions sometimes—about light, about spacing, about how long it took certain things to grow. I answered the best I could.

Eventually, we found a bench near the potting shed, half-shaded by a tangle of ivy climbing the fence. He pulled a paper bag from his coat and offered it to me without a word. Banana bread. I took a piece, letting the steam curl around my fingertips before breaking it in half and handing him the other.

Theo told me a story about trying to grow cilantro in college—how it wilted within days, how he kept watering it long after it had clearly given up. The way he told it—dry, self-deprecating, with just the right pause before the punchline—caught me off guard.

I laughed. Quiet, but real. The sound surprised even me. It slipped out before I could stop it, like sunlight breaking through after days of gray.

Theo looked over, eyebrows lifting just slightly, but he didn't say anything. He just smiled, wide and easy, like he'd been waiting for that moment all morning.

We sat like that for a while. Not touching. Not rushing. Just sipping coffee from mismatched mugs. Mine was chipped. His had a faded sunflower on one side. The silence between us felt easy. Not empty.

As the wind stirred the ivy above us, I thought of a different bench, in a different season—Gray, maybe six years old, curled beside me with scraped knees and a dandelion crown, chattering about worms and the secrets they knew underground. Her fingers had been dirty, her curiosity endless. That memory drifted up like mist—brief, soft, and suddenly close.

I looked down at my hands. The same hands that had held her then. The same hands that now rested beside a stranger.

I wasn't sure what this was. What it could be. But I didn't pull away from it either. And maybe, for today, that was enough.

$$\odot$$

The Karakoram Trail - Skardu

The wind is a living thing. It snakes between the jagged peaks, howling through the valley, pulling at my jacket, clawing at my face. My breath comes fast, clouding in the thin air. Each step is slow, deliberate—one foot in front of the other, measured, controlled.

Tenzing moves ahead, a steady presence in the white silence. He knows this terrain like a second language. I, on the other hand, am an outsider, a visitor in a place that does not welcome visitors.

A few hundred feet back, my footing faltered. A patch of unstable ice gave way beneath my boot. For a split second, gravity betrayed me—my body pitched forward, my fingers clawing at the snow before Tenzing's iron grip locked around my wrist.

His voice was calm. "Do not fight the fall. Find your balance."

Now, as I press forward, my muscles burning, I can still feel the phantom sensation of weightlessness—the brief, stomach-churning moment of knowing that one wrong step means oblivion.

Up ahead, something catches the wind—a piece of fabric, shredded and half-buried in ice. A tent. No movement. No footprints. Just the remains of someone who didn't make it down. A sobering reminder: this place does not remember names.

Tenzing doesn't slow as we pass. He doesn't have to. He's seen this before. I swallow, tightening my grip on my camera strap. I raise the lens, framing the stark contrast of torn red fabric against endless white.

This time I take the shot. *Click.*

☾

The wind picked up as the trail narrowed, its sharp breath tearing through the valley and up the ridge. Our boots crunched into the hardened snow, the path zigzagging endlessly through rock and ice like a scar etched into the earth. ♪

Step. Breath. Step.

My legs ached with every motion—slow, deliberate movements against the rising grade. The thin air clawed at my lungs, each inhale more fragile than the last. Tenzing moved just ahead, steady as ever, his silhouette framed by sky and stone.

We had been climbing for hours. Now the world felt thinner. Emptier. And somehow more alive. Up ahead, the trail crested in a jagged line of fractured stone and glacial wind. Tenzing reached it first, pausing at the top. His hand rose—not in triumph, but in quiet recognition. A gesture meant not to summon me, but to prepare me.

I climbed the final few feet, legs trembling with fatigue. My hand brushed against the cold rock as I pulled myself over the ridge. Then—
There it was.

K2.

Rising from the clouds like something forged from myth, not stone. Massive. Impossibly still. The second-highest mountain on Earth, yet somehow more remote, more unknowable than any peak I had ever seen before.

The sky behind it glowed with a thin, pearlescent light, the kind of light that felt borrowed from another world. Snow whipped off its summit in long, silver ribbons, the wind howling in silence I could somehow hear.

♪ *"Adrift"* by Tycho

⓪

For a long moment, I didn't breathe. I just stood there, my camera forgotten, my mind blank. There are moments when the world does not ask you to understand it. Only to witness it. This was one of them.

Tenzing said nothing. He didn't need to. We stood together in the cold, the summit stretching before us at the edge of forever.

K2 Base Camp - Kashmir

At base camp, tents huddle together like fragile bones beneath an unrelenting sky. The wind whips through, testing their resolve. Inside, climbers sit hunched over steaming bowls of food, their faces wind-burned, their hands cracked from cold.

A crampon-clad boot crunches into the ice, sending fractures racing across the surface. The climber steadies himself, the weight of the mountain pressing down. *Click.*

A tent flaps violently in the wind. Nearby, a man checks his oxygen canister, jaw tight—calculating if he has enough. *Click.*

An ice axe slams into frozen earth. Another climber tightens a carabiner, his frostbitten knuckles raw, bleeding, but he doesn't stop. *Click.*

A lone figure stands at the edge of camp, touching a row of prayer flags, his lips moving in silent prayer. *Click.*

The wind shifts, and for a moment, the world is still. I adjust my settings, exhaling slow. My breath curls into the air, freezing before it disappears. Through my mirrored sunglasses, K2 towers above me—a cold, ruthless deity.

◍

A crack in the lens warps the summit—just slightly, just enough to suggest that some things can't be captured, or conquered. Only survived.

And not everyone does.

Later we sit out of the wind, tucked against a ridge where the howling storm softens to a distant whisper. The glow of tents lit from within casts shifting colors against the snow, flickering like dying embers. Tenzing pours steaming butter tea from a dented thermos into a tin cup, passing it to me. The warmth bleeds through my gloves, grounding me.

For a long time, neither of us speak. Just the crackle of ice shifting, the whisper of wind threading through camp. Tenzing looks up at the mountain—a dark, hulking shadow against the star-filled sky.

"She does not care if we are here."

I nod, watching steam curl from my cup. "You are chasing something," he says, his voice quiet but knowing. "But you do not know if it is real or a ghost."

I don't answer. I look away, staring at the firelight flickering against the ice. But her memory is always there, unbidden, like a prayer flag caught in the wind. The fire casts warm flickers against Tenzing's steady face as he watches me

"Do you remember what the Monk said?"

I stare down at the cracked lens in my hands.

"He told me to let go of the shadow."

Tenzing nods, satisfied.

⊙

"Then why are you still chasing it?"

The words are simple, but they land like a fault line splitting open. I don't have an answer. Because I already know the truth. I have spent years searching for the perfect moment. Chasing memories. Holding on to something that no longer belongs to me. Maybe it never did. And maybe… it's time to stop. But, I've said that before.

Tenzing sips his tea, watching the fire. Above us, K2 looms—unforgiving, unconquerable, untouched. For the third time, I don't try to capture it. I just sit. And let it go. The thing about mountains is they don't yield to desire. They don't bend to your will or reshape themselves for your comfort. Unlike memories, which we mold and retouch until they become something entirely different—something we can live with.

For years, I've carried her with me like equipment: necessary, heavy, familiar. I've climbed with the weight of her absence strapped to my back. I've framed every shot with the negative space she left behind.

But photographs can't capture gravity or cold or fear. They can't hold the thunder of an avalanche or the silence that follows. Just like memories can't truly hold a person. They're just fragments, distorted by time and distance—a warped lens showing me what I wanted to see.

Maybe that's what I've been climbing toward all along. Not the summit, but the understanding that some things remain beyond reach. That letting go isn't failure—it's the only way to keep going.

I don't need the photograph to remember. Her face is every-where—in the silence between shutter clicks, in the way light moves through a doorway. I didn't come here to forget her. I came to remember who I am without her. And maybe… I'm starting to.

⦿

05

07:05:04:17:28:22

Are you Annie?

The words linger in the air, as the final moment of *Sleepless in Seattle* settle deep in my chest. The credits begin to roll, accompanied by the soft, sentimental soundtrack. The glow of the TV flickers across the living room walls, casting shifting shadows in the dim light. ♪

Gray is curled up against me, her head resting lightly on my shoulder, a blanket wrapped around us both. The warmth of it is familiar, comforting. She sighs, tilting her face up toward me. Her voice is soft but certain.

"See, Mom? There's a perfect person out there for everyone. You just have to believe you'll find each other."

My breath catches. She's not just talking about the movie. I glance

♪ *"Make Someone Happy"* by Jimmy Durante

- 439 -

down at her, but she's still watching the screen, her fingers absently twisting the edge of the blanket. There's no teasing in her voice. No playful nudge. Just quiet expectation. *She means me.* I shift, forcing a small smile as I brush a curl from her face.

Perfect doesn't exist. I used to believe in it, once. Before. But Gray does. And maybe that's what matters. She sighs again, curling tighter against me, her fingers finding mine under the blanket. Her heartbeat is steady, slow, trusting.

I stare at the screen as the list of names scrolls by—producers, directors, key grips. The people who made something beautiful. Something that still makes people believe.

I saw *Sleepless* in the theater when it first came out. Back when movies were an event. You planned for them. Picked a time, waited in line. Paid actual cash for a ticket, committed to your choice. Popcorn in a crinkly bag, Milk Duds sticking to your molars. You stayed until the end—whether the film was magic or mediocre—because you were in it. Invested. A shared hush in a dark room with strangers all hoping for the same thing:

To feel something.

Now it's just a button. One click and the story vanishes. Too slow? Too quiet? Not enough action in the first five minutes? People turn it off before it even finds its rhythm.

Something about that feels sad to me. Like we've forgotten how to sit still and let something unfold. How to wait for the good parts. How to stay.

Gray doesn't say anything, just leans her head on my shoulder, content in the glow of the credits. And I think—I'm glad we watched it this way. All the way through. *Together.*

But Gray's words linger with me, waiting. For an answer. For something I'm not sure I know how to give. Or for that matter, find. Or maybe just for proof that I still believe, even if I'm not sure I do

Suddenly, Shadow leaps onto the coffee table, knocking over an empty glass and staring directly at us with those unblinking green eyes. She sits perfectly still for a moment, tail swishing with deliberate slowness, before suddenly batting Gray's phone off the table and disappearing into the darkness of the hallway.

Gray raises an eyebrow at me. "See? She is Rhiannon."

I can't help but laugh. Maybe Gray has a point. Maybe we're all a little bit of who others see in us, even when we think we're hiding in the shadows.

Outside, the rain taps gently against the window, misting the glass with its quiet, endless rhythm. The city stretches beyond it—lights reflecting on wet pavement, people moving through the night, searching.

The soft blue glow of the screen flickers against the dimly lit office.

Sophia Farraday Telluride.

The cursor blinks, waiting. I hit Enter. Pages upon pages of search results unfurl before me—fragments of a life, but never the right one. A Sophia who ran marathons. Another who wrote an obscure academic paper on botany. A LinkedIn profile with no picture. A Facebook page long abandoned. None of them her.

◯

I scroll. Click. Backtrack. Try again. Each search is a dead end, a loop that brings me right back to nowhere.

A deep sigh escapes me as I rub my forehead, the dull ache behind my eyes intensifying. My desk is cluttered with coffee-stained notes, old film canisters, and the remnants of past assignments. But beneath it all—beneath the mess of my life—is the one thing I've kept undisturbed.

The newspaper clipping.

Sophia, frozen in time. Caught in motion, but somehow effort-less. The light in her eyes, the energy in her stance, the way she seemed untouchable—unstoppable. I run my fingers over the faded ink, trac-ing the outline of her form. This is the only version of her I have. The one that hasn't disappeared.

A lump rises in my throat, unexpected and unwelcome. My vision blurs for half a second before I swipe a hand across my face, shaking it off. This is ridiculous.

I lean back in my chair, dragging both hands through my hair, exhaling sharply. What am I even looking for? A name on a screen? A sign? A chance that after all these years, she's still out there, waiting in the same way I am? I never even met her.

The clock on the wall ticks forward. The room feels heavier, smaller. I set the clipping down carefully, smoothing the edges before pushing it away. Then, without thinking, I close the browser tab. The screen goes dark. For the first time in years, I wonder if maybe—just maybe—it's time to stop searching and let go of the shadow like the monk said.

Maybe the past isn't meant to be found.

The garden doesn't ask much of me today. Just my hands. My breath. A little patience. I sink into the old Adirondack chair near the back fence, boots still muddy, gloves in my lap. The air smells like damp soil and lavender. Everything is soft with the hush of late afternoon—golden light brushing the tops of the raised beds, bees still working the salvia like there's no such thing as quitting time.

Plainwater rests open on my thigh, spine cracked in the best way. I've dog-eared half the pages, but one line stops me cold:

"To live past the end of your myth is a perilous thing."

I read it again, slower this time. I know that feeling. I've lived it.

There was a time I thought I knew exactly who I was. Wife. Café owner. Someone people could rely on—for warm bread, clean answers, predictability. That life was built on rhythms: baking before dawn, Gray's lunches packed by seven, the lights of the café flicking on while the rest of the world still stretched its arms.

But stories shift. My marriage ended. The café closed. And the myth—whatever it was—burned down slow and quiet, like the last candle in a room no one's speaking in anymore.

I thought starting over would feel louder. Messier. But the truth is, it's quieter than I expected. It's pruning roses before they go leggy. Learning the Latin names for plants I've known since childhood. Drinking tea alone and not calling it loneliness. It's mornings at *Urban Roots*, dirt under my fingernails, coaxing life from stubborn soil.

That used to feel like failure. Now… I'm not so sure.

◎

I close the book and let it rest beside me on the armrest. A breeze stirs the rosemary, and a hummingbird zips past like it's late for something. I watch the garden breathe around me—this small, living thing I get to tend. Not own. Just care for. That feels like enough.

Maybe the danger isn't in outliving the myth. Maybe it's in believing your story only mattered while the myth was intact.

Because right now, in this chair, with mud on my boots and sweat at the back of my neck, I feel more myself than I ever did in the marriage or the café. I'm not who I was. But I'm still here. And that has to count for something.

I worked a double shift yesterday—two school groups, one community class, and a soil delivery that arrived two hours late. Somewhere in the middle of it, I laughed. I also nearly cried. It's been that kind of week. There's comfort in the work, most days. Something steady in watering schedules and pruning cycles. The plants don't care how you feel. They grow or they don't. They need what they need. It's honest.

But lately… I've been wondering.

What happens when your passion becomes your job? When your home and your work both smell like compost and basil? When you find leaves in your bra at the end of the day? When even your dreams taste like mint and wormwood?

Do what you love, they say.
If you love your job, you'll never work a day in your life.

That's the lie, isn't it? The quiet trick of turning joy into obligation. Because when your passion is your work, it doesn't clock out with you.

❃

It follows you home. It lingers in your shoulders, in your laundry and your sleep. It becomes everything.

I love this—this life I've built in the dirt. But sometimes I worry I'll wear it out. That I'll grow tired of green things. That lavender will stop calming me. That I'll wake up and not want to dig anymore.

And what then?

I reach for *Plainwater* again. I've been rereading it slowly, like she's speaking in code only I'm meant to understand. There's a line I underlined yesterday before work, but now I can't find it. Something about the danger of over-naming. How naming is a kind of taming. A way of owning. Maybe that's what I'm afraid of. That I've tamed my love for this too much.

I run my fingers through the thyme growing between the flagstones. Its scent releases instantly—earthy, sharp. Familiar. It still smells like safety. Like the café kitchen before the rush. Like Gray's childhood. Like myself.

Still, I can't ignore the whisper that's been stirring again lately.

Writing.

It's been years since I really tried. Decades, even. Since I sat at the dining table before sunrise, tea in one hand, pen in the other, scribbling half-thoughts and memories disguised as fiction. I told myself I didn't have the time. Or the audience. Or the right to speak when so many others said it better.

But the stories are still here. In the way the sun hits the blackberry canes. In the overheard conversations at the garden center. In the rhythm of pulling weeds and remembering who we were, who we're becoming.

Maybe it doesn't matter if anyone reads it. Maybe writing isn't about being heard—it's about hearing yourself. Having one place that's just yours. Not for tending. Not for teaching. Not for harvesting.

Just for being.

A rustle draws my eyes—Shadow slips through the lilacs like a rumor. The wind shifts. The garden exhales, carrying the scent of damp earth and the last breath of summer.

I close the book and hold it to my chest.

Tomorrow, I'll be back at the greenhouse, teaching middle-schoolers about root systems. I'll haul compost. I'll explain how sun and patience and pruning can change everything.

But maybe tonight, I'll write something. Just a line. A paragraph. Something that doesn't have to bloom to matter.

The quote comes back to me. Not exactly, but close:

"To name a thing is to try and hold it still."

It wasn't a comfort. It was a warning. About how names become cages, even when they sound like poetry. Maybe I don't need to name everything right now. Maybe being in it is enough.

Maybe growth isn't loud. Maybe it's quiet. Invisible at first. Like roots threading through the dark, reaching for something they can't even see yet.

◎

KSFO - San Francisco

The voices of air traffic controllers filter through my mind like an old radio frequency, disembodied and steady, guiding planes through the endless stretch of sky. Somewhere out there, unseen but perfectly timed, another jetliner breaks through the night, descending in a ballet of navigation and trust.

The cabin hums with a quiet intensity as my flight makes its final approach into San Francisco. I sit in my seat, adjusting my grip on the armrest, watching the city unfold below through the small oval window.

The city glows beneath us—an intricate map of headlights threading through the dark streets, the bridges like golden veins stretched over black water. Even from here, the city pulses, moving, breathing, alive.

The aircraft dips lower, the runway lights stretching toward us in a perfect line. The pilots up front work seamlessly, their hands moving across dials and controls, guiding us toward the ground with practiced precision.

A slight jolt. Tires kiss the pavement. Touchdown. The reverse thrust roars as we slow, the weight of the journey settling into my bones. I exhale. Another city. Another arrival. Another moment where I expect to feel something different and don't. This feeling is becoming all too frequent.

The automatic doors glide open with a quiet hiss, spilling me onto the arrival curb. The air is sharp with jet fuel and sea salt, buzzing faintly with the restless hum of the city.

I shift my bag over my shoulder, balancing the warm *Cinnabon* box in my other hand—airport tradition, maybe. Or superstition. A small, sweet thing to hold onto.

Around me, life unfolds in reunions. A child barrels into his mother's arms. Someone cries against someone else's neck. A driver waves a cardboard sign, hopeful and half-asleep.

I stand there for a moment, not moving. And then I see her.

Blythe.

A silver Lexus eases up to the curb, headlights catching in the edges of her smile. The window glides down, and there's Blythe—her expression soft with recognition, her presence grounded and easy. A kind of stillness in the rush.

I hesitate. Not because I don't want to see her. But because I don't know how to carry this weight without showing it. Still, I smile. Toss the bag in the back. Climb in beside her. The door closes with that familiar thunk that always makes a car feel like shelter.

The city rises around us in red taillights and blur, the skyline braced against the night. She glances over, fingers drumming lightly on the wheel.

"How was the flight?"

"Long," I say, rubbing my face.

"You look like it," she teases gently.

I laugh—small, real. She always knows how to do that. Blythe is sharp. Steady. The kind of person who doesn't ask for more than you can give—but somehow makes you want to try.

I watch her profile as she navigates through traffic, her face catching the shifting light from passing storefronts. I should reach over. Touch her hand. Tell her I missed her. It would be easy. True, even. But something holds me back—a hesitation I can't explain, or perhaps don't want to explain. The simplest gestures of affection feel complicated, weighted with something I refuse to name

I tell myself it's about work. The relentless travel. How much I despise the city. The jet lag. The way my life isn't built for connection. All the convenient explanations that point outward, never inward. I've gotten good at this kind of misdirection—crafting perfectly reasonable excuses that protect me from the truth about why I hold back. It's easier to blame circumstances than to examine choices.

And I like her. I do. But sometimes, even in her presence, I still feel like I'm waiting. For something that's not coming. For someone who never did. And I've been trying to convince myself ever since that it's enough. That she's enough. That the past doesn't matter. That I can move forward. That I can build something real. But as we drive deeper into the city, I feel the truth settle inside me—quiet, heavy, immovable. I'm still waiting.

Tacoma - Washington

The dull roar of Interstate 5 presses down like a weight. I feel it in my bones, in the spaces between my ribs. Above, cars blur past—warm, oblivious, full of people on their way to somewhere else. People who don't have to think about what's beneath them. Down here, the air is sharp with cold, thick with the scent of damp cardboard, burnt coffee, and exhaustion. The smell of forgotten humanity.

◎

I stand behind the folding table, my gloves stiff with condensation from the food trays, fingers aching from hours in the damp cold. The line in front of me never seems to end. Faces blurred by hunger, by fatigue, by the particular kind of invisibility that comes with living in the shadows of a city that rushes past overhead. A man with sunken cheeks clutches his coat tighter, the fabric worn threadbare at the elbows. A woman with a baby tucked inside her jacket rocks side to side, humming something only she can hear, her eyes fixed on some distant point as if looking at anything too directly might break her.

A little girl steps forward. She can't be older than six. Her coat is too big, swallowing her arms, and she clutches a stuffed animal so worn I can't tell what it used to be. The fur matted and gray, one button eye missing, stuffing leaking from a seam. She stares at the food like she isn't sure if it's really for her. Like she's learned already that gifts come with conditions.

I place a meal into her hands. She hesitates, then takes it, her fingers gripping the edge of the container like it might disappear. She looks up at me. Her eyes are too old for her face. Eyes that have seen adults fail her, seen promises broken. I want to say something. Anything. Words that might matter, that might convince her the world isn't always this hard. Instead, I kneel slightly, just enough to exist in her space. Just enough to let her know I see her. That someone sees her. She clutches her stuffed animal tighter and disappears into the crowd. I swallow, my throat tight with all the things I didn't say.

Further back, a family huddles beneath a sagging tarp, the parents curled around their kids, shielding them from the wind that bites through everything. Their camping stove flickers weakly, the blue flame barely visible in the gathering dusk. The mother stares at nothing, her hand automatically stroking her child's hair, a gesture of comfort that seems to comfort her more than the sleeping child.

◍

I've seen that look before. The thousand-yard stare of someone who has run out of options but keeps going anyway.

A few feet away, a boy, maybe ten, balances his meal on his lap. He doesn't eat. Instead, he breaks off small pieces, passing them quietly to his younger siblings first. Making sure they get enough before he takes a bite. His movements careful, practiced. This isn't the first time he's been the parent.

My chest constricts. Something cracks open inside me, raw and aching. I step back, my boots crunching over damp gravel. I press my back against the nearest concrete pillar, trying to breathe through the weight crushing my ribs. My eyes burn, and I blink rapidly against the threat of tears. Not here. Not where they can see my weakness when they have no luxury of showing their own.

I can't do this anymore.

I pull my phone from my pocket, my fingers stiff from the cold. The screen glows, bright against the dimming sky, illuminating the exhaustion etched into the lines of my face. I type a message to Gray without thinking, the words spilling out before I can censor them:

I don't know if I can keep doing this work. It feels hopeless. Like trying to empty the ocean with a teaspoon.

I stare at the words. My thumb hovers over the send button, then presses down. A few seconds pass. Then—

Mom, for once, you need to take care of yourself. You can't always pour from an empty cup. And you taught me that hope isn't about fixing everything—it's about showing up anyway.

I blink. My fingers tighten around the phone until my knuckles turn white. Gray is right. My daughter, who once needed me for everything, now offering wisdom I should have learned decades ago. I tip my head back against the pillar, exhaling slowly. A cloud of vapor in the cold air, proof of life. Around me, the camp shifts—new people trickling in, shoulders hunched, searching for warmth, for relief, for something to hold on to.

The need never stops. It's a tide that never recedes.

I close my eyes, and for a moment, I'm not under the freeway. I'm back in Uganda. A different kind of ache, a different kind of hunger. That slow, wasting kind. The kind that hollowed out entire villages until there was nothing left but silence and flies.

I remember a girl with cracked lips and quiet dignity, who offered me half of her maize cake even though she hadn't eaten in two days. The way her fingers broke it carefully, precisely, an act of generosity that humbled me to my core. I remember the boys who tried to make soccer balls out of trash bags and twine, laughing louder than the weight of the world should've allowed. Their joy a defiance, a rebellion against circumstances that should have crushed them.

And I remember how I used to believe I could fix things. That enough heart, enough hands, enough love could mend the fracture in the world. That if I just worked harder, cared more deeply, sacrificed more completely, somehow it would be enough.

But love doesn't stretch that far. Not always. Not across systemic failures, entrenched poverty, political indifference. Not across the chasm between intention and impact.

It stings to admit, but the kids under the overpass—they're not starving. They're not injured. Not in the same way as those in Uganda. But their eyes… the dull, unblinking way they scan the line, like they already know life doesn't owe them anything—that's what breaks me. It's not the hunger. It's the absence of hope. The quiet acceptance that this concrete underpass might be as good as it gets.

Still, that boy sharing with his siblings—the tenderness in that. It gives me something to hold onto. A reminder that even here, even now, love finds a way to exist. In scraps. In silence. In the careful division of a meal that was never enough to begin with.

But Gray is right. I can't pour from an empty cup. I can't save everyone, and the weight of trying is crushing me slow and sure as the traffic overhead.

I've spent so long tending other people's gardens. Feeding strangers. Staying too long in a marriage that didn't have room for me. Helping everyone but myself. Maybe it's time I learned how to stay with my own heart. To plant something in soil that's mine. To nurture my own roots instead of always reaching for others.

Even if it scares me. *Especially* because it scares me.

I wipe my eyes with the back of my gloved hand, take a deep breath that tastes of exhaust and damp earth, and push away from the pillar. There's still a line. There are still hungry people. I can't fix everything.

But I can serve one more meal. I can see one more face. I can be present for this moment, and then—maybe—I can learn to be present for myself.

The sun is just beginning to dip behind the low hills, casting long shadows across the lawn. Blythe's voice drifts from the back porch—something light about how the fog keeps killing her tomatoes and how she's switching to succulents.

I'm on my knees in her small garden, tugging at weeds that seem to be held in place by a personal grudge. The earth is warm beneath my palms—crumbly, stubborn, honest.

I kind of respect that. It doesn't pretend to be anything it's not. Unlike me, who definitely pretended to enjoy yardwork when I agreed to help. I hate yardwork. Always have. But I do it anyway, mostly because I care about her, and partly because I haven't figured out how to fake a back injury convincingly.

"Blythe? Have you ever thought about getting a condo? You know... something without ground-level responsibilities."

She just laughs.

Hard to believe this started on the bench in Telluride. Sophia's bench. Then Blythe sat down—asked if I came there often—and something in her tone, open and unhurried, made me say yes. We got coffee that day. Exchanged numbers. I wasn't sure I'd ever use it. But a few weeks later, I had a vineyard shoot in Sonoma, and San Francisco was on the way. So I reached out.

That was four months ago.

Since then, we've walked along the Embarcadero, browsed used bookstores in the Mission, shared dumplings in Chinatown, and spent slow mornings in mismatched pajamas arguing over who makes better coffee. It's me. She disagrees. But I let her make the coffee anyway.

And now we're here.

Behind me, Blythe laughs—one of those low, unhurried laughs that sneaks up on you and stays awhile. She moves like someone who knows who she is, and doesn't apologize for it. There's something grounding in that. She doesn't try to impress. She doesn't try to save. She just is. And it's... good.

I should be more present. I should be soaking this in. Instead, I'm in my head again. I reach for another stubborn weed and pull harder than I need to.

Blythe appears beside me with a glass of lemonade and a tired smile, handing it off without a word. I take it, our fingers brushing, and she sits down in the grass beside me, knees drawn up, her eyes scanning the evening sky like she's tracking something I'll never see.

"You know your laces are coming undone again," she says without looking at me. "I swear, they've been rebelling since the day I met you."

I glance down. Of course they are.

"At least some things in my life are consistent," I say.

"So is gravity," she murmurs. "Doesn't mean you have to trip over it."

She isn't wrong. We sit in the quiet for a while. She doesn't fill it with questions. She never does.

"I like this," I say finally, surprising myself. "All of it. Just... this."

Blythe turns her head toward me, waiting. Not expectant. Just open. I drain half the glass and set it beside me.

"But sometimes I wonder," I continue. "If I'm here because I'm choosing to be. Or because I'm tired of being everywhere else."

She doesn't flinch. That's something else about her. She doesn't shrink away from the hard stuff. She just nods, like she already suspected this would come up eventually.

"It's okay not to know yet," she says. And I believe her. Mostly.

I glance down at my hands—dirt under my fingernails, a smear across my forearm. I've always been the one chasing light in far-off places. Now here I am, pulling weeds with a woman who makes the world feel smaller—in a good way. Like it fits. Or could.

But the truth? I don't know if this is love, or just the first soft thing I've let myself fall into since Martone. I don't know if I'm healing, or hiding.

What I do know is that Blythe deserves more than someone halfway in. I feel like this is my relationship with Martone all over again.

She reaches out, brushing the back of her fingers against my arm. A gentle, quiet touch. No demands in it.

"You don't have to say anything," she says. "Just... don't lie to yourself."

I nod slowly, my eyes fixed on the horizon. The sky's starting to turn.

"I'm trying," I say. And I mean it.

$$\textcircled{0}$$

But even as I sit beside her, I wonder why Sophia's name still lives in the corner of my thoughts like a song I can't skip. That's the thing about moving forward—it doesn't always mean you've stopped looking back.

Second Act - Capitol Hill

We step into a consignment shop that smells faintly of lavender, old cedar, and someone's long-gone grandmother's perfume. The floor creaks under our feet. Everything inside seems to hum with forgotten stories—trinkets and teacups, mismatched boots, and jewelry tangled in itself like time knotted up.

Gray moves ahead, pulled toward the rows of clothes like they're calling her by name. I trail behind, slower, letting the quiet pull me sideways toward a bin of vinyl records near the front.

I flip through them absently. America, Joni Mitchell—my heart softens. Then—Bob Dylan. I pause. Shake my head, just once. A quiet, familiar no. Even the cover looks smug. I slide him to the back of the stack, like I'm doing the rest a favor. ♪

That's when I see it—tucked in behind a milk crate labeled *Vintage Cords*. A beige IBM Selectric typewriter.

My feet move toward it before I even realize I'm doing it. I stop just short, looking down at its wide, boxy frame. Still solid.

A handwritten note is taped to the carriage arm: *Still works!*

I flip the switch. It hums faintly, like it remembers what it was made for. I reach out and press one of the keys. It bites back—not soft, not forgiving, but decisive. A clean, mechanical snap. Then I run my hand gently along the return lever and push.

♪ "Coyote" by Joni Mitchell

⦿

Ding.

That sound. It's always the same. Clear. Confident. Like a sentence knowing it's done. There's no illusion here. No blinking cursor waiting for indecision. You write, you mean it.

There's something about a typewriter. The finality of the keys. The certainty of the sound. You write, and it stays written.

Gray appears at my side, flannel shirt tucked under one arm. She spots the typewriter immediately.

She grins. "That guy in Sleepless was obsessed with these things, remember?"

I nod.

She taps one key, smiling at the feel of it. "It makes everything sound important. Even if you're just writing a grocery list."

She's not wrong.

I rest my hand on the space bar. That dull, weighty quiet of some-thing waiting to speak again. It's not practical. Not even necessary. But the tug is there.

And we both know—that's the point.

I linger for one more heartbeat, then press both palms to the top of the machine. It doesn't move easily—solid, stubborn, heavier than it looks. The kind of weight that says: You don't just take me. You commit.

Gray watches me, one eyebrow lifted, curious.

☉

I run my fingers over the keys one more time. There's nothing convenient about it.

But maybe that's the point. Some things aren't meant to be easy. Just meaningful.

Battery Spencer - San Francisco

The wind cuts sharp and salty off the bay, carrying the distant hum of traffic from the Golden Gate Bridge below. I sit on the weathered concrete ledge of Battery Spencer, my boots scuffing against the stone as I press my phone to my ear.

"How does an epic, all-expense-paid ski trip next season sound?" I say, grinning.

"I told the Mag I need an assistant, and somehow, they bought it!"

Brandon's laughter crackles through the line. "That's insane! But… I'll have to run it by the boss first."

I shake my head, eyes flicking to the bridge stretching endlessly before me. The towers cut through the sky, their burnt-orange steel unwavering against the wind.

"Do you need a permission slip?" I tease.

"Hey," Brandon says, defensive but amused. "Happy wife, happy life."

"But this is the Pow Life trip we've been dreaming about," I press.

He groans dramatically. "Maybe I can do the dishes for a month… or buy those expensive organic vegetables she likes."

I laugh, already picturing the negotiation. "Just make it happen."

"I'll practice my puppy-dog eyes," he sighs.

I lower the phone, shaking my head as I take in the sweeping view. The Golden Gate Bridge—unchanged, unmoved. I breathe in the crisp air, feeling the weight of something shifting inside me. Maybe I've spent too much time chasing moments, waiting for life to line up the way I imagined. Maybe it's time to just go.

Brandon hangs up, a grin spreading across his face as he spins his chair around—And freezes.

Monica stands in the doorway, arms crossed, one eyebrow arched in that way that tells him she had heard everything.

"Oh, Hey honey..."

Delancey - Ballard

The scent of pizza drifts from the kitchen, mingling with the salty breeze rolling in from the Sound. Afternoon light spills across the bistro's tiny patio, glinting off our wine glasses as Allison settles into another story—full of dramatic hand gestures and exaggerated expressions that make the older couple at the next table smirk into their menus.

She's been like this as long as I've known her. Animated. Alive. A force of nature wrapped in a sundress and a knowing smile. And yet, I haven't been the best at being a friend in return. Allison flew all the way from Florida for this. For me. A five-hour flight, a whirlwind of time zones and airport chaos, just to sit here, sip wine, and remind me of who I used to be.

And when was the last time I had done the same for her? Guilt tugs at the edges of my thoughts, but before I can grab hold of it, something else catches my attention.

A couple walks by, their fingers brushing before effortlessly twining together. No hesitation. No second thought. A quiet connection that needs no words.

My chest tightens. When was the last time I had that? Since I had reached for someone and knew, without a doubt, they would reach back? I take a slow sip of my wine, watching them disappear down the street.

"If you undress them with your eyes any slower, they'll finish without you."

I laugh, nearly spitting out my wine.

Allison doesn't flinch—just lifts her glass and shrugs. "What? I'm just saying what we're both thinking."

And this—this is what she does. She says the one thing no one else would dare to, and suddenly the weight lifts. No one makes me laugh like Allison. Not the polite kind. The real kind. The kind that sneaks up on you and reminds you you're still alive.

"Hey, dreamy! Smile!"

A sudden click. I blink, pulled back into the present. Allison grins from behind her phone, tilting the screen toward me.

An image of me, caught mid-thought—wine glass hovering, the ghost of a smile still lingering, my eyes distant, somewhere between content and wistful. I shake my head, setting my glass down.

- ☾ -

"You need to start collecting happy moments," Allison says, nudging my arm. "Not just for other people—for yourself, too."

Her words settle deep. For so long, I've given everything to the community, the café, to the people who needed me. And I don't regret that. Not for a second. But I haven't made the same effort for my friendships, for myself.

Lately, I've been trying. Saying yes to small things that aren't obligations. Taking walks with no destination. Answering calls instead of letting them go to voicemail, promising myself I'll call back later.

Because friendship—real friendship—deserves as much effort as anything else worth keeping. Allison clinks her glass against mine, her expression knowing.

"The universe isn't done with you yet," she says.

Maybe, for the first time in a long time, I believe her. And maybe, this time, I won't let too much time pass before I make the effort, too.

She leans back in her chair, eyes on me over the rim of her wine glass.

"And for the love of God, next time someone makes you feel something—don't overthink it. Just sit on his face and figure out the details later."

This time I nearly choke, the wine going down the wrong pipe.

She grins, completely unbothered. "What? Healing looks different on everyone."

Late summer in Telluride always brought it back—the stillness, the ache, the sense that something was about to happen even if nothing ever did. The valley didn't change much. But something in me always did.

Mom was on the porch, barefoot, cheeks flushed, a smudge of ochre paint on her forearm. Retirement looked good on her. There was a lightness to her that I hadn't seen in years—maybe ever. Her garden had exploded since the last time I visited. Roses along the fence. Tomatoes in neat rows. Herbs tumbling out of planters like they couldn't help themselves.

She talked about compost and watercolor techniques, flitting between the garden and her latest canvas like the two were just versions of the same thing. I nodded, smiled, listened. But part of me was already elsewhere.

Maybe it was the quiet. Or the way the wind moved through the porch rails. But I found myself asking if she ever got lonely, being on her own so much.

She didn't even pause. Just tucked a lock of hair behind her ear, eyes bright and sure. "Been there, done that," she said, with a small shrug. "I like my own company. I know how to be happy with it."

She meant it. There was no bitterness, no sadness—just certainty. She'd figured out what most people spend years trying to learn: how to belong to yourself.

I smiled back, but something in me twisted. I admired her steadiness, her ease—but I didn't have it. Not yet. There was still something in me that reached, that waited, that couldn't quite settle.

⊙

While she disappeared into the kitchen to make iced tea, I slipped into the backyard. The roses were wide open—lush and fragrant, their petals soft as breath. I chose one carefully. Pale pink. Just enough green left in the stem. I broke it off with a quiet snap, glancing toward the house, half-expecting her to scold me like I was twelve again. But the kitchen window stayed quiet.

I was looking forward to the walk to town. So I took the long way, past the places that still remembered who I used to be. The rose sat in my hand, stem wrapped loosely in my fingers, petals brushing against my jacket as I walked.

Telluride hadn't changed much, at least not in the places that mattered. Same boardwalk storefronts. Same faded signs. Same uneven sidewalks that still caught your boot if you weren't paying attention.

And then—of course.

The Civil War Guy.

He was older now, a little grayer around the edges, but still fully committed to the cause. Long wool coat, and a canteen slung across his chest. That same droopy cavalry hat pulled low like he'd just returned from Appomattox. No explanation. Never had been. Just part of the town.

As we passed, I gave him a mock quick-draw with my finger gun. Just a flick of the wrist and a smirk. Too slow, my old friend.

He didn't miss a beat. Just narrowed his eyes like he was weighing whether I was worth the duel, then shook his head slowly, solemnly, and kept walking.

I smiled. Yep. Some things never change.

The bench was a few blocks further, waiting in its usual place on the corner. I tightened my grip on the rose and kept walking.

I'd stopped coming for a while. Told myself it didn't matter anymore. That rituals were for people who couldn't let go. But here I was, heart doing the same thing it always did at this hour.

I walked slowly, the sidewalk warm beneath my boots. The bench came into view, unchanged. Waiting, like it always was.

The recital begins. Three o'clock.

I sat.

The rose rested in my hand—a ridiculous thing, really. Fragile. Out of place. But I brought it anyway. For her. For the most beautiful girl in the world. The one I still couldn't seem to forget. The girl with the quiet gravity.

When the courthouse bell chimed four, I stood.

No note. No message. Just the rose, left in the center of the bench, petals already catching the breeze.

This was the last time. I told myself that as I walked away. Maybe I even believed it.

I kept my eyes forward. Kept walking. And then I looked back. Just in case.

⦿

The University of Washington - Seattle

The cherry blossoms drift from the trees, catching the sunlight as they spiral toward the ground. They land on stone walkways, on empty benches, on the shoulders of passersby who barely seem to notice. Petals scatter like snow, soft and aimless, stirred by the faintest breeze.

Everything smells faintly of rain and earth and spring trying to assert itself. The trees arch overhead, full and blooming—briefly brilliant, already beginning to let go. It's beautiful in a way that feels almost cruel.

A quiet reminder that time moves forward whether I'm ready for it or not. That nothing—no matter how vivid or full—gets to stay.

Gray walks ahead of me, her pace light, unburdened. She turns in a slow circle, taking it all in—the towering buildings, the students sprawled across the grass, the quiet hum of something new and unknown. Her eyes shine with the kind of excitement that makes my chest ache.

I should have known it would feel like this. The beginning of the end. The end of the beginning.

A breeze stirs through the pathway, lifting the scent of spring— fresh-cut grass, warm pavement, the faint trace of coffee from somewhere nearby.

Gray doesn't notice the way I slow my steps, letting her pull ahead, giving her space to exist in this moment without the weight of my watching. She stops suddenly, her hands on her hips, her gaze fixed on something in the distance. I already know what she's thinking. She turns, her expression full of something so pure, so open, it steals my breath. Her lips move. "Mom, look!"

She gestures toward a group of students beneath a stone archway, deep in conversation, their books open on the grass. Her excitement spills over, bright and uncontainable.

I take her in—the way she stands with one foot slightly forward, ready to move, ready to go. She's already halfway here. A deep inhale.

The lump in my throat stays.

Gray loops her arm through mine, resting her head briefly against my shoulder before pulling away. I hold onto the feeling. She lifts an eyebrow at me, questioning. You okay? I nod, offering a small, reassuring smile. She grins, rolling her eyes. I haven't even done anything yet. But she has. She's become her.

We keep walking, the future unfolding in front of us like the tree-lined path ahead. I let her lead.

For now, she's still mine.

Tadich - San Francisco

The glow of *Tadich* spills onto the rain-slicked sidewalk, casting flickers of red and gold across the passing cars. Inside, the energy is relentless—forks scraping plates, voices rising in overlapping waves, the open kitchen hissing with steam and citrus. San Francisco doesn't pause for anything.

I flew in from Denver a few days ago. Part of me just wanted to go home. But I'm trying. Trying to show up for Blythe. To be present. To give her the steadiness she deserves, even if some part of me is still turned in another direction.

We sit outside beneath a rusted heat lamp. The small patio table wobbles slightly every time someone walks past. The lamp casts a soft amber glow across Blythe's face, highlighting the edge of her cheekbones, the corner of her mouth. She looks calm. Strong. The kind of person who knows her own weather.

She tucks a strand of hair behind her ear and gives a small smile. "I've been thinking. You could really do something here. With your photography. With your eye. The city's alive—it moves fast, and I think that kind of energy might pull something out of you."

I nod, running my thumb along the side of my glass, tracing a droplet of condensation. A streetcar rattles past behind her, its reflection sweeping like a flicker of memory across the window. In the glass, I catch a glimpse of myself—tired, a little older, caught somewhere between two lives.

She watches me for a beat, but doesn't push. Then she sets her drink down with a soft clink.

"I can't do long-distance, Michael. Not just cities. Emotionally, I mean. I've done it before, and I know myself. I need someone who's here. Who's all in."

I look up. She's not angry. Just steady.

"You deserve that," I say quietly. "And I've tried to be that person."

Her eyes shine just slightly before she blinks it away. Not with resentment—just quiet resignation.

"I've built everything here," she says. "My home. My life. I thought maybe you'd want to build something too."

I nod slowly, heart low in my chest.

A pause opens between us, wide enough to feel final. Then she tilts her head, voice gentler now.

"Michael... your heart's somewhere else, isn't it?"

I hesitate. Then I nod.

"Yes."

She doesn't flinch.

"Were you waiting for someone when I met you on that bench in Telluride?"

There was someone," I say, my voice quieter now. "A long time ago. I never met her. I just saw her—from a distance, and then once, up close. Only for a few seconds. But something about that moment... it stayed.

Blythe looks down at her drink, her thumb smoothing the edge of the napkin beneath it.

"And she doesn't know?"

"She doesn't even know I exist," I say. "We never spoke. Just... passed each other. But it rooted somewhere. I've tried to forget. I've tried to move on. But it's like part of me has been waiting for something I can't quite explain."

She lets out a small breath, half a laugh. "And you've been holding space for a ghost."

"Not chasing," I say. "Not exactly. Just... not ready to let go."

Blythe turns her glass slowly in her hand, then looks up at me. There's no bitterness in her eyes. Just clarity.

"You're still on that bench in Telluride, aren't you?"

I swallow hard. "Yeah. I think I am."

The city continues around us—horns echo down the block, a protest chant rises and fades, a man laughs loudly from inside the restaurant. But at our table, it's quiet. Still.

"You're not wrong for waiting," she says softly. "Some people are worth that. I just hope when you finally stop waiting, it's because she turned around—and not because you gave up."

The words land with quiet grace. Gentle. Devastating.

I stare at her for a long moment. How is it possible to feel both seen and released at the same time?

"I don't know what I did to deserve this kind of understanding," I say. "But thank you. For seeing me. For not asking me to lie. For letting me be honest."

I reach across the table—not to change her mind, not to hold on, just to say goodbye the only way I know how. My fingers find hers. She lets them stay there for a while.

"You're remarkable, Blythe," I say. "Somewhere out there, someone's going to be smart enough to stay."

Her hand gives mine one final, quiet squeeze. Then she lets go.

I sit there after she lets go, hands folded now in the silence she left behind. There's something strange about being let go with kindness. We expect breakups to come with sharp edges—fights, tears, final words flung like warnings. But this one didn't. It just eased open and let the truth in. And somehow, that makes it ache more.

Most people talk about love as if it's all or nothing. Stay or go. Fight or flee. But sometimes love shows up for a season—not to last, but to teach you something you couldn't have learned alone. Blythe did that. She held space for me, not as a placeholder, but as a mirror. And when it was time to let go, she didn't look away.

I wonder if this is the real kind of courage—not chasing the impossible, but sitting across from someone who deserves more and telling the truth anyway. I didn't want to hurt her. But I couldn't pretend. Not when I'm still shaped by a question I haven't yet answered.

Relationships ask a lot of us. Not just presence, but clarity. A willingness to name where your heart really lives, even when it's not where you are. I used to think love meant holding on. But maybe sometimes it means stepping aside. Letting someone walk away, not because you don't care—but because you do.

I don't know what will happen next. I just know I told the truth tonight. And for the first time in a long time, I feel something settle in me. Not relief, exactly. But alignment. Like I'm finally facing the right direction.

The light above us shifts from warmth to flicker. The night leans in around the buildings, and I feel the moment settle—not as regret, but as truth. It's over. Not because there wasn't something real. But

because love—the kind that lasts—asks you to show up with your whole heart. And mine still belongs somewhere else.

The late afternoon sun spilled across the garden in wide, honey-colored bands, catching in the tall grass and turning everything gold. I stood at the edge of the raised beds, a hose coiled loosely in my hand, water trickling slowly into the soil. The kids had gone home for the day. The tools were put away. The garden had fallen quiet.

Theo was leaving.

The words sit quietly in my chest, like they were waiting to be felt.

Hawaii. A community permaculture project just outside Hilo. He'd told me over coffee that morning—same bench, same chipped mugs. His eyes lit up when he talked about it. The soil, the native plants, the way the land spoke if you were willing to slow down and listen. I was happy for him. I said so with a smile and a soft nod. And I meant it. But something lingered beneath the surface, warm and unspoken.

I always liked Theo. More than I admitted, maybe even to myself. He was kind. Steady. The sort of person who showed up when he said he would, who knew how to listen without pressing. There were times—quiet moments, shared jokes, long silences filled with ease— when it felt like we were on the edge of something more. And maybe we were. But I never stepped forward.

I told myself the timing wasn't right. That I was still healing. That Gray needed me.

But the truth was simpler.

I never made room. I let everything else—work, community service, memory, distance—take up the space where love might have lived. I built my days around purpose and caretaking, until there was nothing left over. I told myself that was noble. That it meant I was strong. But maybe I was just hiding.

Something in me was always holding back.

As if I believed love had to come from somewhere else. From someone else. Someone louder. Braver. More certain than I ever let myself be.

I was waiting for a sign. For the universe to tap me on the shoulder and say, now. But maybe I'd been saying no all along—and just didn't know it.

I watch the last of the water soak into the bed, the earth darkening and drinking it in. Then I shut off the hose, letting it coil into itself.

Theo waved from the greenhouse as he packed up a box of seed trays and notes. I lifted a hand in return. He wouldn't leave tomorrow or even next week. There would be goodbyes, a farewell lunch, maybe even a card. But I knew this was the real ending. The quiet one. Something might have bloomed—but didn't. Not because the soil was wrong. But because I never planted anything there.

Not because it couldn't. But because I never let it.

Theo had become a kind of steady in my life I hadn't realized I needed until he was already part of it. He showed up without asking for anything. No expectations. No pressure. Just a presence—warm, patient, consistent. He made space for silence, for odd jokes, for muddy boots and garden soil and banana bread on rainy mornings.

He was a friend. A good one. Maybe more, if I'd let it be. But love, the real kind, asks for risk. For letting someone see the fragile places you've tried to keep hidden. For opening a door and not knowing what's on the other side.

And I couldn't do it. Because love doesn't wait on safety. And I've spent too long choosing safe over uncertain. Guarded over vulnerable.

Maybe what I want now—what I didn't even know to ask for before—is a different kind of love. The kind that stays. That listens when you don't have the words. That makes space for the stories you only tell once. The hard ones. The quiet ones. The ones you've tucked away because no one ever asked the right question.

Someone to share the late garden hours with. To sit in silence with and know it means something. Someone who sees past the strength and into the soft places I've tried to keep hidden—even from myself.

I used to think love would take me somewhere. Now I think the right kind of love brings you back. Back to yourself. Back to softness. Back to the version of you that still believed in joy.

Maybe that's what I've been waiting for all along—not a person to chase, but a kind of coming home. I thought love would come when I was ready. But love doesn't always wait for readiness. Sometimes it waits for courage. But still—he mattered. He always will.

Alaska 1289

There's a strange kind of silence you only get at 35,000 feet—dull, constant, like the inside of a shell. I'm pressed against the window, elbows tucked in tight, watching the city dissolve beneath a wash of clouds. San

⓪

Francisco shrinks behind me—glass, light, motion—becoming smaller, more manageable, the farther away I get.

I never wanted to hurt Blythe. She didn't deserve that. She offered me something rare—clarity, warmth, presence—and I gave her honesty. Not answers. Not a plan. But the truth.

It was the one promise I knew I could keep.

The truth is, I respected her too much to pretend. And I cared enough to let her go.

I'm not sure I would've done that a year ago. With Martone, I tried to be someone I wasn't. Smiled at brunches. Nodded through gallery openings. Spoke in futures I didn't believe in. Blythe never asked for that. She just asked for me—the version that didn't dodge eye contact or tuck the past into polite silences.

And I gave it to her. Not everything. But enough.

It didn't make the goodbye easier. But it made it cleaner. Quieter. It didn't feel like failure. It felt like grace.

The truth is, I don't compromise well. Not when it comes to place. Or love. Or whatever strange, silent engine has kept me moving all these years. It's never been about settling down—it's been about trying to outrun the feeling that I don't belong anywhere. That maybe I wasn't built to stay. But something shifted tonight. Not because of what Blythe said. Not even because it ended. But because it didn't feel tragic.

It felt inevitable.

Or maybe I just use the excuse that I'm a dude. We're allowed to be emotionally confused and commitment-adjacent. That's our whole brand, according to *Vogue* magazine.

Whatever.

I lean my head against the window. The engine drones on, steady and hypnotic, like it's been humming the same note since takeoff. A contrail drifts beside us, sharp and silver in the late sun. I sip from the plastic cup in my hand. Ginger ale. Ice. My usual. Except it's only my usual up here.

I never drink ginger ale on the ground. Never order it in a restaurant. Never keep it in my fridge. But the moment I sit in an airplane seat, buckle in, and hear the rattle of the drink cart, I ask for it—some quiet reflex reaching for comfort. Tradition. Something sweet and sharp that makes the altitude feel like permission.

The smallest rituals, it turns out, are the ones that stay. Longer than cities. Longer than people.

Or maybe it just tastes better up here—the altitude dulling everything else so that something sharp and sweet suddenly feels like clarity. Or maybe it's the illusion of control. It's ridiculous, really. But also... kind of telling.

A couple rows ahead, someone laughs. A deep, unguarded kind of laugh—the kind that only comes when you're sitting next to someone who really knows you. I envy that. Not the sound. The certainty.

Blythe wanted a life she could build—blueprints, foundations, futures you can map. I wanted something quieter. A window seat. A garden that doesn't need explaining. Maybe a tree out front. Something that felt like choosing, not surrendering. A life you don't perform. Just live.

I still think about kids. Not in the traditional way anymore—not with soccer games and PTA meetings and carefully packed lunches. It's softer now. Imagined moments, not imagined milestones. Laughter echoing from another room. A second toothbrush beside the sink. Boots at the door that aren't my size.

That life would've had to happen with Martone, and it didn't. I couldn't give her what she needed, and by the time I figured out what I wanted, the timing was gone.

It's not about legacy. It's about belonging.

And love? I used to think it would arrive once I'd finally figured myself out. But maybe that's the lie. Maybe love doesn't need you to be finished. Maybe it just wants you to show up. Mess and all.

I thought Martone might be that future. Then Blythe. But neither were mine to keep. Not because they weren't enough. But because part of me was always somewhere else.

Someone else.

I close my eyes for a moment, resting them in the hush of recycled air and fluorescent light. I see her again. Sophia. The shape of her framed by memory. Soft and certain. I've never heard her speak. And still—I've been listening for her ever since.

The plane banks gently north. Lights shimmer below, scattered gold and amber. I wonder if she'd even recognize me now. Or if I've

imagined the whole thing bigger than it ever really was. I shift in my seat. Watch the sky turn steel. And I think—

Maybe I didn't leave the city for the island. Maybe I left for a chance at something honest. Something whole. Maybe I should stop waiting. And start searching.

I step out of my brother's house, coffee warming one hand, bag slung over my shoulder, letting the quiet of Telluride settle into my bones. The mountains loom like old sentries, their peaks dusted in white, unchanged and unmoved by the passing of time.

The town itself holds the same steady presence—brick and stone storefronts lining Colorado Avenue, their weathered facades worn by decades of sun, wind, and snowfall. The same street lamps, the same distant chime of the courthouse clock, the same quiet hum of a place that never needed to chase the world—because the world always found its way here.

Telluride has a way of making you feel both insignificant and essential at the same time—dwarfed by mountains that will outlast civilizations, yet somehow exactly where you're meant to be. It's why I keep returning, despite Seattle and the life I've built there. The familiarity of this place doesn't diminish its beauty; it simply reveals new layers, like reading a beloved book for the second or third time.

I walk without direction, just letting myself exist, my boots clicking softly against the sidewalk. Then, something catches my eye. A single feather, pale and delicate, drifting downward, caught in the slow rhythm of the breeze. It lands in front of me, resting lightly on the sidewalk.

I stop, crouching to pick it up, twirling it between my fingers. It's impossibly soft, weightless—like it doesn't quite belong to this world. Like it's meant to keep moving.

A small smile tugs at my lips. How many times had I believed in signs? Looked for them in everything—falling leaves, a certain song on the radio, the way the ocean moved? I turn it over in my hands. Maybe it's nothing. Or maybe it's something.

I tuck the feather into my journal, between pages filled with thoughts I rarely share aloud. Some people spend their lives in motion, constantly seeking the next place, the next experience, the next moment worth capturing. I've always been different—finding infinity in stillness, in returning, in the quiet spaces between words. The feather reminds me of that somehow—how something so light can choose to land, can make contact with the earth before the wind carries it elsewhere. How presence, however brief, leaves its own kind of mark.

I tip my head back, looking up at the sky—vast, endless, impossibly blue—

The Kootenays - British Columbia

—A sky is so blue it doesn't seem real, an endless stretch of color so crisp it feels like I could fall right into it.

Below, the world is nothing but white—untouched, endless, waiting.

Then— the rhythm begins. A deep, low *thump-thump-thump*, like the heartbeat of the mountains themselves. It builds, growing stronger as the sound echoes off the ridgelines.

A shadow sweeps across the snow. Then—a helicopter bursts into view. A big Bell 212 hangs just above the ridge, its rotors kicking up a storm of powder—swirling white mist curling through the air like smoke. The sound is deafening, alive. The snow blurs everything but motion and light.

The side door slides open with a metallic clatter, and the wind rushes in—sharp, electric, full of adrenaline. Brandon and I exchange a grin. I lean out, crouched low against the howl, boots sinking into the snow. I glance back at the pilot—his face barely visible beneath the visor. Thumbs up. He nods once.

The chopper lifts off, banking away, disappearing back down the mountain. And just like that—silence. Not the empty kind, not the kind that feels like something is missing. The kind that makes you realize just how big the world is.

Brandon exhales beside me, hands on his hips, soaking it all in. I pull out my camera, frame the shot—pure wilderness in every direction, peaks rolling like frozen waves into the horizon. *Click.*

I lower the camera, grinning as Brandon clicks into his bindings.

"Nothing like fresh powder and a clean canvas," he says, shaking his head in awe. "Unbelievable."

"Pow Life, baby," I laugh. "This one's for the history books."

We tap knuckles, a ritual we've done a hundred times before. But this moment? This one feels bigger. ♪

We push off—and the world tilts forward. The first carve is like slicing through silk. The powder explodes behind us, a cloud of white trailing in our wake.

♪ *"Club Foot"* by Kasabian

I pick up speed, weightless, gravity pulling me faster as the slope steepens. Brandon's just ahead, cutting clean arcs through the snow, his movements effortless, fluid—like the mountain has been waiting for him all along.

We weave through spines of untouched snow, dodging wind-sculpted ridges, the valley sprawling out below us like a painting come to life.

This. This is why we do it.

For the feeling of motion and weightlessness, of control and surrender, all at once. For the way the mountain accepts you, but only if you respect it. For the moments like this—when nothing else exists but you, the snow, and the sky.

I let out a whoop as we hit an open stretch, the rush of speed roaring in my ears. Brandon glances back, laughing, his eyes alive.

Pure joy. Pure freedom.

The snow falls softly, swallowing the world in quiet. Ajax Mountain looms down the street, its peak lost in the heavy white veil, standing as it always has—silent, steady, unchanged. My last day in Telluride.

The bench remembers me.

Every day, I'd come here at three o'clock—like clockwork. It wasn't planned at first. It just became routine. This was where I'd catch my breath before heading home. Where I could think without interruption. Where I could just be.

Sometimes I had a book. Sometimes my journal. Sometimes I

brought nothing at all—just whatever was circling in my mind. I'd sit with the town moving gently around me, the courthouse clock ticking like it was keeping time for my thoughts.

Every summer, it was strawberry ice cream every Friday. I'd walk to the corner shop after school, then come straight here, trying to eat it before the sun melted it faster than I could keep up. One time I dropped the whole thing on the ground mid-laugh and nearly cried, even though I was too old to cry over ice cream.

Allison looked at the mess, shook her head, and said, "That's it. Childhood's over. Next thing to drop is your panties."

We laughed until we couldn't breathe. Not because it wasn't true, but because it was. It was just a bench. Just three o'clock. And some-how—it became the place the world made the most sense.

I take a slow sip of coffee, letting the warmth linger against the cold. The bench beneath me is familiar, worn in all the right places. It belongs to me. Or maybe, after all these years, I belong to it.

The courthouse clock chimes three. I reach into my bag, fingers brushing the familiar, dog-eared cover of *The Alchemist* by Paulo Coelho. The spine is soft, creased by years of being opened and reopened, searched for meaning over and over again. I turn to the passage, the words waiting for me like an old friend.

When you want something, all the universe conspires in helping you to achieve it.

I close the book gently, pressing the feather I found between the pages. A bookmark. A reminder. A whisper from the universe.

The courthouse clock sounds again, half-past. A softer note. A reminder I won't get this moment back. My gaze lingers, but the details blur—the past slipping back into the snowfall.

I glance around—at the quiet shops, the snow-draped lampposts, the slow rhythm of this town that once felt too small to hold me. And yet now, it feels impossibly vast. Brimming with meaning I couldn't see before.

When you're young, you think these things will always be here. The bench. The mountain. The slow drift of snow through the same old streets. You chase what's next, certain that the small moments are just filler for the big ones.

But then you grow up. And the things that seemed so trivial— quiet mornings, old buildings, familiar chimes—become the things you ache for. The ones you carry with you. The ones that mean home.

It's not that I didn't love this place before. I just didn't understand how much. Not until I was older. Not until now.

Across the street, an elderly couple walks arm in arm. The woman stumbles slightly on the ice—not enough to fall, but enough to remind her of time. The man catches her without hesitation, his hand steady, instinctual. Like he has spent a lifetime doing just this. They exchange a look. Not just affection, not just love—understanding. A language built between them, spoken without words. Her fingers find his. Decades in that touch. A whole life, held between them. Something tightens in my throat.

I lift my free hand, letting the snow fall into my palm. One flake lands alone—perfect, tiny and elaborate, delicate as lace. I stare at it, holding my breath. How does something so fleeting hold so much detail? It melts slowly, vanishing into my skin. Gone, just like that.

But for a moment, it was *mine*. Like memory asking to be held.

The wind shifts, carrying the sound of the clock's half hour chime as it echoes down the street. My gaze lingers, but the details blur—the past slipping back into the snowfall. I pull my coat tighter around me.

Whistler-Blackcomb - British Columbia

The camera lifts to my eye, but the image is blurred—just color and motion. I adjust the focus slowly, and the shape sharpens: five inter-locking rings, standing in the snow like a monument to dreams that once had edges. *Click.*

I lower the camera and exhale into the cold. The Olympic Rings gleam in the late-winter light, framed by snow-dusted evergreens and the sharp outlines of distant peaks. A soft crunch of footsteps in fresh snow echoes nearby, muffled by layers of fleece and down.

A plaque beneath the rings reads *Whistler Olympic Plaza*, though the world stage packed up long ago. What remains is something quieter, more local. The kind of space that remembers—but doesn't need to prove anything.

Children climb the rings, their boots slipping against the slick metal, while their parents linger nearby, sipping hot cider from paper cups, steam curling into the crisp afternoon air. There's a trace of cinnamon on the breeze.

Fireball.

For a moment, I consider grabbing one. To warm my hands, I tell myself. Which is, of course, a lie. Sometimes the middle of the day just calls for questionable decisions and spiced liquor. I resist. Barely.

Or maybe I just want to be part of this small scene unfolding around me—boots scraping metal, kids laughing, the low murmur of conversations floating on cinnamon-scented air. But I stay where I am, fingers still tingling from the chill, the camera strap a familiar weight against my chest.

This is what I chase, isn't it? The quiet, in-between moments. The way life keeps going after the banners come down. I don't move. Just stand there, hands tucked into my coat pockets, watching. Holding the moment before it slips away.

Brandon steps up beside me, hands tucked into the pockets of his down jacket, his breath curling in the air.

"You get your perfect shot?" he asks, half-teasing.

I glance at the display screen. "It'll do."

Whistler is its own kind of postcard—wood-beamed chalets stacked shoulder to shoulder, fairy lights strung across every eave like it's always December. The pedestrian village thrums with people— skiers clomping in boots, couples bundled in wool, the faint sound of jazz drifting from an open patio.

Everything here is curated but alive. High-end gear shops beside cozy bookstores. Coffee houses beside designer boutiques. Mountains rising like myths at the end of every walkway. We wander without talking much, letting the rhythm of the place carry us.

Cool air brushes my arms, scented faintly with woodsmoke from somewhere down the street. The rest of the house is dark—only the lamp on the side table glows, soft and golden, casting long shadows across the hardwood floor.

I should be in bed.

Instead, I'm here. Barefoot, in my nightgown, elbows on the dining table like I've been summoned and don't know why.

The Selectric sits in front of me. Beige, boxy, stubborn in the way only something mechanical and meaningful can be. I carried it home awhile ago, still unsure why. It had tugged at something quiet and unnamed inside me. And now—tonight—it waits.

I run my fingers over the keys. There's a click, then a hum as it wakes up, the carriage shifting slightly like it's stretching after a long sleep. I thread in a sheet of paper, smooth it flat, and stare at the blankness.

I don't even know what I want to say. I just know I want to try. The silence in the room isn't empty. It's waiting. So I begin. Not with a plan. Not with structure. Just a pulse of something that needed out.

I walk through fire with nothing to say,
The smoke in my lungs won't drift away.
Love and pain both call my name,
Two sides of silence, playing the game.

The sun comes up but I don't feel warm,
It lights a world that's a weathered storm.
Some fight for power, some fight for peace,
But all I want is the smallest of release.

They ask me why my eyes look tired,
Why I don't burn with the same old fire.

❀

It's hard to shine when the sky's gone gray,
But hope feels like just a breath away.

Love lifts me up, then sets me down,
Pain builds a throne and hands me the crown.
I wear it heavy, I wear it low,
Still searching for a place to go.

But deep in the dark, a voice remains—
Not loud, not proud, but it still sustains.
It hums a truth I can't forsake:
You can break a heart, but not its ache.

I stop. Reread it once. The page is filled now, edges curling slightly from the warmth of the lamp. The words feel both too small and exactly enough. Like stepping barefoot into a tide and realizing it knows your name.

I reach up, press the return lever gently. *Ding.*

The sound lands with weight and clarity. A full stop. A kind of final breath. My hands rest on the keys for a long moment. This part of me—the writing, the rhythm, the quiet truths—had almost slipped away. Not on purpose. Just slowly. Forgotten under the noise of days that demanded everything else.

Outside, a moth flutters against the screen. A car passes with headlights low, then disappears again. The silence folds back in—unbothered. Still waiting. But not for me.

I exhale and ease the page from the typewriter. It's nothing extraordinary. Just a poem. Just a piece of me, pinned in place by ink and click and weight.

Tomorrow there will be weeds to pull and seedlings to water. Compost to turn. People to teach. But tonight, I remembered something that was mine—before the café, before Gray, before the quiet grief I told myself didn't count. The kind that settles in slowly, without ceremony. I never cried. Not once. But that doesn't mean it didn't hurt.

I made something. It didn't need to bloom to matter. And for now—for this one quiet, midnight breath—that feels like enough.

Just a poem. Just me. And the soft mechanical hum of something finally coming back to life.

Araxi

By nightfall, the cold has deepened, and the sky presses low with snow that hasn't started falling yet. The windows of *Araxi* glow gold against the dark. Inside, it's warmth and wood and soft conversation. Candles flicker across polished glassware. Waiters move like shadows—efficient, unobtrusive. There's a fireplace tucked into one corner, and Brandon and I sink into the plush chairs beside it like we've been on our feet for a decade.

I glance at the wine list, letting my eyes drift over the page without really reading it. I already know what I want. An Old-Fashioned—just the way I like it, with a splash of Grand Marnier. Warm, complex, and unapologetically strong. Like memory in a glass.

Brandon leans back in his chair, arms stretched behind his head, eyes half-lidded in that signature ski-lift bliss. "You know," he says, gazing out the window at the snow-dusted peaks, "if heaven has an après scene, I'm pretty sure it looks like this."

I let out a low laugh, the kind that starts deep in the chest. The fire snaps beside us, heat licking the edges of my tired limbs. For a moment—just one—everything else fades. The miles, the ache, the unanswered questions. Here, wrapped in firelight and woodsmoke, it's easy to pretend life isn't pulling at me from all directions.

But I never forget for long.

The waiter approaches setting our drinks down with the kind of reverence reserved for small rituals. Mine glows amber in the low light, citrus oils shimmering on the surface. I lift the glass, the chill pressing into my fingers, and take a slow sip.

Brandon raises his glass in a silent toast. "To mountains. And what we leave at the bottom of them."

I clink mine against his, the sound small but sharp. "And the powder we find at the top."

The warmth of the drink settles in my chest, softening the edges of the day. Outside, the mountains glow with the last light of sun, their shadows stretching long across the valley. For a second, I think maybe this—this exact moment—is what peace feels like. A fire, a drink, an old friend.

"So," Brandon says, swirling his glass, eyes flicking toward me with that familiar mix of curiosity and mischief, "I forgot to ask what happened with the city slicker?"

Blythe. Smart. Steady. Present in a way that felt rare. She asked for truth and nothing less. And I gave it to her—every messy, uncertain part of it. We had coffee in San Francisco. Walks through farmers markets. Late nights with records and good wine. There was something there. Not built on fantasy. Just presence. And maybe, for once, I showed up honestly.

⦾

"She wanted me to move to the Bay Area," I say. "But I couldn't do it."

Brandon chuckles, shaking his head. "She had to know the island would've called you back."

"Yeah. She did." I sip. The whiskey burns just enough. "We ended as friends. Just two people being honest about who they really were."

He studies me for a beat, then leans forward. "Let me ask you something—would you move to the city for Sophia?"

The question hits harder than I expect. I don't even hesitate.

"In a nanosecond."

And I mean it. That's the thing about Sophia—she was never just a moment. Never just a maybe. She's the gravitational pull I haven't been able to walk away from.

Blythe was right—she deserved someone who loved the city the way she did. Who wanted the blueprint. The calendar. The glass of wine by the fireplace after work. But Sophia? With her, I wouldn't care where we lived. A cabin in the woods. A shoebox above a pizza shop. A tent, if it came to that. If it meant waking up to her—every day— I'd do it.

Because that's what love is. It doesn't require negotiation. It invites rearrangement. It's taken me too long to learn that real love doesn't fit into the life you already have. It asks you to build something new.

Together.

With Martone, I played the part. Smiled on cue. Gave just enough to keep the peace but never enough to feel at home. With Blythe, I didn't pretend. I told her the truth—that I was still carrying someone else in the quiet parts of my mind. And she didn't shrink from that. She didn't try to change me. She just nodded and let me go.

That kind of grace doesn't leave you.

Brandon exhales. "Still no clue where she is?"

I shake my head. "None."

I stare into the fire. "Finding her feels impossible—like trying to pick out a single star in the night sky."

He leans back, thoughtful. "Sometimes, you've got to search the whole sky before one shines through."

"I'd trade everything for just five minutes with her."

And that's the truth. All the years. All the countries. All the images. None of it has mattered the way that one moment did. Watching her walk past, like time had slowed just long enough for me to notice something important.

Brandon raises an eyebrow. "You sound like you're chasing a love story from another lifetime."

"Fairy-tales seem more real than anything else."

I lean back, staring up at the ceiling beams. Maybe I am. Maybe I've ruined my chances chasing someone I never even spoke to.

Maybe Martone was the one. Maybe Blythe was. They were real.

◎

They were here. And I let them go—for what? A bench, a shadow, a memory in perfect light?

Maybe I'm broken. Or maybe… I just know something the rest of the world doesn't. That some things don't need a beginning to feel like a forever.

Brandon shakes his head, grinning. "Dude, you're a shit show."

I laugh, raising my glass. "Yep. Hot mess."

He takes a sip, then smirks. "She could be married, you know. Or raising goats with a cult in Oregon. Or running an underground Fight Club for suburban moms. You don't know her life."

The thought cuts deeper than it should.

Goats smell. *Bad.*

"A chance I'll have to take."

I look back into the fire, searching for something that still feels just out of reach. It'd be easier if she were running that suburban mom Fight Club. At least then I could stop wondering.

The sun poured down across the football field in warm, dappled waves, turning every cap and gown into a patch of blue velvet and gold light. The bleachers creaked beneath the weight of proud parents, grandparents, siblings—all of them leaning forward, scanning the sea of students for someone they loved.

I sat near the front, my dress soft against my legs, hands clasped

tightly in my lap. The program fluttered between my fingers, a heartbeat of movement I couldn't seem to still. A breeze lifted the edge
of the cardstock, and I pressed it flat without looking down. My eyes
were fixed on the sea of blue caps and gowns—scanning, searching.

There she was—Gray. She had my wild curls, the kind no brush
could tame, catching the sun beneath her cap like a crown. Her posture
was strong, shoulders back, chin high, standing with the others—but
apart, somehow. She was always a little apart. I couldn't see her face
from here, but I didn't need to. I knew every tilt of her head, every
way she held her weight. I could feel her energy from across the field.
Steady. Brave. Ready.

Movement beside me made my breath hitch. I didn't turn. Ethan
slid into the seat at the end of the row, a little winded, like he'd rushed
to be on time. His collar was uneven, his tie slightly askew. He leaned
forward on his knees, gaze fixed on the stage. That familiar stillness
clung to him. He didn't say anything, but I felt the glance he sent me.
Brief. Careful. A quiet check-in. I didn't meet it. I kept my face forward, grateful for the midnight armor of my sunglasses. ♪

They hid everything I didn't want him to see. The shimmer in my
eyes. The ache in my chest. The pride. The fear. The way seeing him
here—after everything—still pulled at something I thought had gone
quiet long ago. Behind the dark lenses, I was safe. Unreadable.

I wear them not for the fashion, but for the things I no longer trust.

The moment feels too sharp now—every light too bright, every
look too searching. The truth burns too hot, and everyone's hunting for a weakness. But I sit still, glass-eyed and guarded, watching
the graduation blur and shimmer in the reflection—like it's happening
somewhere far away, behind glass.

♪ *"Sunglasses at Night"* by Corey Hart

He thinks I'm hiding. Maybe I am. Or maybe—just maybe—I see clearer in the dark than I ever did in daylight.

The crowd murmured, the names began, and still I waited. My fingers kept tracing the edge of the program.

For a moment, as the names echoed across the field and tassels swayed in the breeze, I was back in my own graduation seat—my dress sticking to the back of my knees, fingers clutching a paper program just like this one.

I remembered how heavy that day had felt. Not because of fear, but because my future was already being written for me. Berkeley. The scholarship. The plan my parents had gently—and not so gently—laid out. But I'd felt the pull of something else, even then. Something quieter. I hadn't known what to call it, but I'd known I couldn't follow a map that wasn't mine.

Now, watching Gray—strong, sure, full of her own wild light—I knew what I wanted more than anything: for her to choose her own road. Whatever shape it took. Wherever it led.

Then—Her name.

The world tilted slightly. Everything else faded—the chatter, the breeze, even Ethan. I rose slowly, my hands coming together in soft, deliberate applause. My heart felt too big for my chest. My throat ached with the weight of all the things I couldn't say. Gray stepped onto the stage like she belonged there—calm, sure-footed, luminous. She moved with a grace I recognized. But it wasn't mine. It was hers. Entirely hers.

Ethan stood beside me. He didn't look at me, but I could see the pride settle in his face. We stood in quiet solidarity—not as a couple, but as parents. Still bound by this girl. This moment.

When I sat down again, my hands were trembling. I folded them tightly in my lap. Ethan let out a slow breath. I could feel him glance at me again—something soft in it, maybe familiar, maybe even apologetic. But I kept my sunglasses on and didn't turn. I didn't need to. I didn't care—not about him. Not anymore. But he showed up, and I suppose that counts for something.

Gray had crossed the stage. That was everything. Somehow, despite everything, we'd gotten her here. Not as a couple, not even as friends—but as parents. And for once, that was enough.

Golden - Colorado

The light slants through the open garage door—low and angled, the kind that says the day's almost done. Dust hangs in the air, suspended like time, and everything looks a little more golden than it probably is. I'm in Colorado for a quarterly meeting at the corporate office, but right now, I'm far from photo spreads and conference calls—sitting on an overturned paint bucket in Brandon's garage, a cold Sol beer sweating in my hand.

It smells like chain grease and old wood—that specific kind of garage nostalgia. Projects half-finished. Tools exactly where you left them. Time moving slower. Brandon's crouched over a bike that probably hasn't touched dirt in half a year, adjusting the derailleur like it still matters. Bailey, his golden retriever, is curled up on an old blanket near the door, snoring softly—completely unbothered by the clink of tools or the smell of oil in the air.

"I landed in three countries last month," I say, taking a sip. "And I can't remember a single hotel room. Not really. They all blur together—same lamps, same beige curtains, same burnt coffee."

Brandon doesn't look up. Just grunts. "Glamorous."

I smirk, but it fades fast. "I used to love it. The airports, the adrenaline, waking up not knowing what country I was in. It felt like motion meant something. Now I just want to make coffee in my own damn kitchen."

He wipes his hands on a rag and tosses it over the handlebars. "So stay home."

"It's not that simple," I say, even though maybe it is. "The job, the travel—it's been who I am for so long. If I let it go... what's left?"

Brandon leans back against the workbench, arms folded. "You're allowed to change your mind, man. You're not a brand. You're a person."

I huff a laugh. "Try telling that to the magazine."

But even as I say it, I know he's right. I've been running on autopilot—shooting, editing, traveling, repeating. Lately, it's not just the work that's tiring. It's the weight of keeping up with it. Of pretending I still need it the way I used to. The camera feels heavier. The road feels longer. And the silence? It's starting to sound like something I want.

"I want a back door that sticks in the winter. A faucet that drips too loud at night. Meals that don't come in takeout boxes. I want to learn how to fold a fitted sheet without swearing."

"I'm getting tired of traveling," I admit, softer now. "It makes me miss home even more."

⦿

Brandon leans back, wiping his hands on the rag again.

"Home's a funny thing, though. Sometimes you gotta leave it to figure out where you really belong."

I nod slowly, letting that settle. He's not wrong.

What I really want are days that feel like they belong to me.

Brandon eyes me with mock suspicion. "So what—you gonna go full Ann B. Davis? Trade in your camera for an apron and a dustpan?"

I crack a smile. "Hey, Alice looked pretty hot in a blue dress and orthopedic shoes." ♪

He laughs. "I think everybody had a crush on her and didn't admit it."

"She could iron a napkin with the best of them."

I glance toward the open garage, watching the light shift across the concrete. "I look at you and you've got roots. A house. A dog. Friends who know your middle name. That used to terrify me. Now it just looks... good."

Brandon shrugs like it's nothing, but he doesn't look away.

"Settling down doesn't mean settling. Some people just need more time to know the difference."

I let that sit for a moment. He's not wrong.

"I'm just tired," I say finally. "I don't want another passport stamp. I want to fix things that stay fixed."

♪ "Theme from The Brady Bunch" by The Brady Bunch

He doesn't press. He never has.

"Home is where the heart is, Michael," he says.

I glance over. "That's it? That's your big Hallmark moment?"

Brandon smirks. "I didn't say it was original. Just true."

I look down at the bottle in my hand, the label starting to peel. I think about the house waiting for me. The quiet. The possibility that Sophia might be real in all the ways I've imagined—and none of the ways I expect.

"Yeah," I murmur. "For the first time in a long time... I think I actually know where home is."

And this time, I let the truth of it settle. Solid. Unshifting. Like maybe I don't have to be in motion to feel like I'm becoming something.

Brandon goes back to the derailleur like it's the most important thing in the world. I watch him for a moment. I used to race to airports. Now I want to fix something that stays fixed.

Maybe I need a bike too. Not to outrun anything. Just to feel the ground again.

Brandon pushes off the workbench and rummages through a milk crate near the door. He pulls out a plastic grocery bag and a bright blue scooper, holds them out like an offering.

I eye them warily. "What's this?"

He tosses the bag into my lap. "Well, now that you're going all domestic on me, you can go clean up Bailey's shit in the backyard."

I stare at the bag, then at him. "This is how you welcome me into your home?"

Brandon shrugs. "Call it a rite of passage."

I shake my head, but I'm smiling as I push off the paint bucket and head toward the yard—bag in hand, boots on gravel, and for once, not going anywhere at all.

☼

The hose sputtered, then caught, sending a soft arc of water over the kale bed. I moved slowly, letting the soil drink it in. The garden was quieter these days—less laughter echoing across the rows, fewer spontaneous debates about compost ratios and native species. Theo would've had something to say about the spacing on the new squash starts. I could still hear his voice if I tried hard enough.

But he is gone now. The job in Hawaii. A new life. The kind of opportunity you don't say no to. I didn't blame him. I was happy for him, truly. We'd had our season. Our rhythm. And I'd miss him like I miss other things—softly, without regret.

I turned off the hose, winding it back with a practiced flick of the wrist. The afternoon sun filtered through the tall sunflowers along the fence line, casting striped shadows across the worn path. I walked toward the shed, the scent of tomatoes and basil clinging to my sleeves, my boots kicking up warm dust.

Urban Roots isn't mine. Not in the way *Café Sonnet* had been. But that was the point, maybe. I didn't have to carry it all anymore. I didn't have to be the one worrying about payroll and plumbing and whether the espresso machine would survive one more Monday morning. I still missed it some-times—missed the chatter, the smell of cardamom buns in the oven, the way the regulars greeted me like I was part of their ritual.

But I don't miss the fear.

I don't miss holding my breath at the post office box, waiting for another overdue notice. I don't miss wondering if I was chasing a dream or drowning in it.

Now, I show up. I get my hands dirty. I help young volunteers learn how to prune strawberries and plant marigolds. I clock out at the end of the day. I get a paycheck—small, steady, enough. And when I open it, I don't feel shame or anxiety. I feel peace. There's power in being part of something without having to carry the whole thing on your back.

As I shelved a set of hand trowels inside the tool shed, I caught sight of Theo's old clipboard, still leaning in the corner where he used to stash it. I smiled. The friend when I needed one. A reminder that connection doesn't always ask for more than it can give.

I miss him. Not in the way I used to miss people—with longing or ache or that low-grade panic of having made the wrong choice. No, this is something different. Softer. Quieter. The kind of missing that doesn't beg to be fixed. Maybe it just wasn't time. Maybe I wasn't ready. Or maybe I was—and still missed the chance.

A flower can't be forced to bloom.

You can give it water, sunlight, good soil—but it'll open when it's ready. And sometimes, not at all. I think about that a lot now. About how much energy I spent trying to bloom on command. For every-

◯

one. For everything. And maybe Theo knew that. Maybe that's why he never pushed. Why he let it be what it was. Something real, and kind, and temporary.

I stepped back out into the light, stretching my arms overhead. My back ached, my hands were rough, and there was dirt in my hair. But I felt strong. Rooted. And for the first time in a long time, that felt like enough.

There's a kind of freedom in letting go of the version of yourself that was always striving. Always proving. Now, I just grow things. And that's enough.

American 643

The cabin stirs with the usual shuffle—carry-ons thudding into overhead bins, seatbelts clicking, voices low and tired. I slide into my usual seat in the rear, window side. Always the back. Always last to board. From here, I can see everyone—every aisle, every face.

It's a habit I haven't broken. One I don't fully understand. Actually—I'm lying to myself. I understand completely. I know exactly what I'm doing. Not that I expect to see her. But still—I look. I always do. It's not a conscious choice anymore, just something stitched into the routine. Like fastening the seatbelt or or putting the coffee on before my eyes are even open.

A paper boarding pass, of course. I still print mine at the kiosk. Everyone else flashes their phones at the gate, but I like the feel of something in my hand. Maybe it's nostalgia. Maybe it's just me. Maybe I should join the real world and upgrade — no thanks.

So I watch. I watch the faces as they move down the aisle—sleepy, hurried, lost in earbuds and neck pillows. She's never there. Of course she's not. But I still check.

The last few passengers settle in. The flight attendants do their final walk-through. I rest my head against the window. Denver already feels far behind. Too bright. Too busy. Too full of things I thought I wanted and didn't.

I reach into my bag and pull out my sunglasses. Not because it's bright—it's barely dawn out there, the sky still holding onto that early-morning gray—but because my eyes give too much away when I'm tired. Or when I'm thinking about her. Which is always.

They've always been the giveaway—my eyes. I've never been good at hiding what I feel. Not really. I look too long. Blink too fast. Flinch when I shouldn't. But not today. Not on this flight. Today, they don't get the chance.

The sunglasses go on. Habit now. Like the back row or the folded boarding pass. A shield. People think they're about attitude. But for me, they're about protection. Distance. They let me watch without being seen.

Maybe they make me more noticeable—some guy in sunglasses before sunrise, trying not to be looked at. But I don't care. Behind the tint, I'm unreadable.

I lean back and scan every face one last time. Not that she'd ever be on this flight. Not that she'd even remember me if she was. But I still look. And the sunglasses let me pretend it's not hope.

Still... sometimes I wonder. What if—just once—I looked up and saw her? Not someone who looked like her, or reminded me of her, but her. Sophia. Same eyes. Same smile. Same way of carrying the world like she's trying not to spill it.

⊙

What would I do? Would I sit frozen, afraid to disturb the miracle? Let the moment pass like all the others—safe in the knowing that I almost saw her?

Or would I stand up? Say her name out loud, like a question and an answer all at once. Like a thread pulled tight after all these years. Like maybe I was meant to find her in this sky-bound aisle between strangers and carry-ons.

I don't know. I'd like to think I'd move. That I'd do something. But maybe that's why I wear the sunglasses—so I don't have to find out.

So I can keep looking, without the risk of being seen.

The air in the cabin has that distinct recycled quality—slightly dry, with hints of coffee and the antiseptic smell of cleaning products. My ears pop as we climb, a familiar pressure that somehow never gets more comfortable.

The drink cart rattles up the aisle once we reached cruising altitude. I already know what I'm going to say. It used to be ginger ale, always ginger ale, like some kind of flying ritual I couldn't explain. But today, I want something else.

"Bloody Mary mix," I tell the attendant when she reaches me. "Just the mix. Ice is fine."

I think, briefly, about adding vodka—Grey Goose, to be exact. About numbing the noise, the questions, the ache I keep shoving into overhead compartments. But I don't. Not today. I want to feel the descent. Every part of it.

She nods, hands it to me, and rolls on. I swirl the cup once, watch the liquid catch the light. Salty. Cold. Slightly ridiculous at altitude. But somehow, it feels better than sweet and predictable.

I take a sip and settle back, the landscape already giving way to cloud cover. Smooth, flat light. Nothing to capture. Which is fine. I'm not reaching for my camera this time.

I press my shoulder into the window and close my eyes, letting the hum of the cabin fold over me. Something inside loosens—quietly. A subtle shift I can't quite name. Maybe it's just the end of a long week. Or maybe I'm tired of documenting everyone else's story while my own sits parked at the gate.

My reflection in the window stares back—older, sharper around the eyes. There's a weariness that wasn't there a few years ago. Or maybe I'm just noticing it now. Brandon's voice drifts through the static of my thoughts:

You don't have to be in motion to become something.

Easy to say when your world is rooted in place. How does he know all this shit? He's like my grandfather. Wise. Settled. Unbothered. Brandon is so lucky. But me? I've been rooted in airports, rental cars, new cities, new angles. Frame the story. Find the light. Move on.

Fucking Brandon.

Always knows what to say and do. So annoying.
But lately, all that movement feels like noise. Like I'm documenting everyone else's life while mine plays in the background, muted.

The couple across the aisle is already asleep, hands knotted together like it's the most natural thing in the world. I envy them. That simplicity. That certainty. She's not here. I already know that. But I dream of it anyway. I wish it were me sitting next to Sophia, our hands entwined.

I finish the drink slowly. The cabin is quiet now, the engines the only steady sound. The ice melts in my cup, diluting what's left of the tomato mix. Like time diluting intention.

I stare out at the endless stretch of clouds and mountains below. Most passengers see obstacles, barriers. I see something different—a landscape of possibility, always changing with the light.

I want a life—not just snapshots of other people's moments. I want my own story, one that doesn't fit in a viewfinder. I just have no idea how to get there. I want a life—*with her*. For now, I just want to get home. Back to the quiet. Back to the sound of silence. ♪

Steam rises from the water in lazy curls, fogging the bathroom mirror and clouding the small window above the tub. I've lit three ginger peach candles—my small indulgence, always the same scent—their flames steady in the quiet. Something about that particular fragrance has always centered me, reminded me of late summer evenings at my grandmother's house. The sweet ripeness of fruit combined with that subtle, warming spice. It's the scent of safety, of moments suspended in time. The light flickers against the tile, casting shadows that dance and sway like memories that won't stay still.

My bones ache. Eight hours at the Westlake Community Garden, showing a group of eager but inexperienced volunteers how to prepare the raised beds for summer planting. Kneeling in soil, demonstrating the right depth for seedlings, patiently explaining why some roots need more space than others. Dirt embedded beneath my fingernails despite the gloves. Soil worked into the creases of my palms.

◎

The hot water is a mercy I've been thinking about since I watched the sun climb to its peak at noon. I sink lower, letting the warmth rise to my collarbone. Close my eyes. Breathe.

From my phone on the toilet lid, a voice fills the small space. I've always loved this song. The gentle guitar. The story it tells without pretense or embellishment. Just a man trying to call someone who's already gone, asking for help from a stranger who can't really give it. ♪

I open my eyes, staring at the ceiling. There's something about songs like this—they don't try to be pretty. They just tell the truth about longing, about that moment when you realize you're still carrying someone's number long after they've stopped being yours to call. About the dignity in finally letting go.

The song speaks of moving on when you're not ready to, of pretending to be fine when you're anything but. Of that peculiar kind of loneliness that comes from missing someone who might not miss you back. I know that feeling. The weight of it. The way it sits in your chest, not always painful, but present. Waiting.

I think about Theo. The way we worked side by side in the gardens. His quiet laugh. He sent a postcard from Hawaii—all blue ocean and white sand, his new life captured in a rectangle that fit in my mailbox. Just a few lines about the native plants he was working with now. Brief. Friendly. Professional. Nothing about what might have been if one of us had spoken up before he left.

There's something about holding a postcard that a text message can never replicate. The weight of it. The texture. Knowing someone touched this exact piece of paper, that their hand rested where mine now rests. Text messages are efficient but ephemeral—thin ghosts of connection that vanish with a swipe. But a postcard carries some-

♪ *"Operator"* by Jim Croce

thing physical across the distance. Evidence. Proof. A tangible piece of somewhere else, someone else.

And the handwriting—it's cursive. Not the rushed scrawl that passes for cursive now, but real cursive. Looped, deliberate, elegant. The kind barely taught anymore, phased out of schools and quietly disappearing from the everyday. There's something startling about it— like finding a pressed flower in a forgotten book. You can almost feel the time it took, the care. How the words were meant to last. There's something sacred in seeing how a person shapes their thoughts—how their hand moves when they're thinking of you.

I wonder if that's what we've lost in all our instant communication world of today—that pause, that space between sending and receiving. The anticipation. The way a letter forces you to commit to your words, to mean them enough to write them down, stamp them, send them out into the world to make their slow journey. No delete button. No editing after the fact. Just the bare truth of what you chose to say, or didn't.

Maybe this song is about people like us. People who share the same space, the same soil, but never quite manage to bridge the gap between working together and something more. People who let possibility slip away with the changing seasons.

I lift one foot from the water, watching droplets trace paths down my ankle, over my arch, pooling between my toes before falling back into the bath. Such a simple thing, the human foot. Designed to carry us forward, away from places we've been, toward places we haven't. Yet we spend so much time standing still, looking back.

My toes curl slightly against the cooling air. Years ago, I painted my nails religiously—bright colors, careful lines. Now they're bare.

Practical. The small vanities I once clung to seem distant, like clothes that no longer fit but I can't quite bring myself to give away.

The song continues its gentle story, reaching its resolution—that bittersweet moment of letting go, of finding a kind of peace in surrender. Not the surrender of defeat, but of acceptance. Of finally saying the thing you've known all along: that some calls won't go through, no matter how many times you try.

I submerge my foot again, the warm water welcoming it back. My eyes drift to the window, where night presses against the glass, held at bay by the glow of candles and the small fortress of this moment I've created for myself.

The song ends. For a moment, I let the silence settle, broken only by the soft lapping of water against porcelain. Then I reach for the soap—something Gray picked out, with bits of lavender embedded in it—and begin to wash away the day, one careful motion at a time.

Some people need operators to help them place their calls. Others need time in a bathtub, thinking about songs that tell stories they recognize. I'm not sure which kind I am tonight. Maybe both.

My toes peek out from the water at the far end of the tub, pale islands in a sea of bubbles. I wiggle them slightly, watching the ripples spread outward in perfect circles, touching everything before fading away. I think there's something to learn from that.

The water has cooled, of course. The eternal flaw in the bathtub experience—that moment when contemplation bumps up against physics. I reach forward with my toe and nudge the drain plug, listening to the gurgle as a few inches of water escape. Then the familiar creak of the hot water handle, the initial burst of too-cold before the heat kicks in. I've done this dance more times than I can count, this refusal

◎

to leave the sanctuary of the bath until absolutely necessary.Add hot water. Sink deeper. Repeat as needed.

Some problems really do have simple solutions.

I sink deeper into the water, letting it rise to my collarbones again. The fan hums above me, and a soft guitar riff drifts in from my phone. A few tracks pass without really registering—until this one starts. Something about the ease of it, the way it rolls forward without asking for attention. Like someone who's stopped running, not because they're lost, but because they finally know where they are.

It's the kind of song that doesn't tug or chase. It just sits beside you until you're ready to feel something again. ♪

Suddenly, I'm back on the couch with Gray as she watched *Sleepless* for what had to be the fifth time that month. Right before the credits rolled, she looked up at me, all wide eyes and absolute certainty.

"See, Mom? There's a perfect person out there for everyone. You just have to believe you'll find each other."

I think I smiled. But I didn't believe it. Not then. Not really. What if she was right? What if someone is out there? Looking. Still trying. And what if—somehow, impossibly—they're getting closer? The thought feels foreign, like trying on someone else's clothes.

What if she was right? What if someone is out there? Looking. Still trying. And what if—somehow, impossibly—they're getting closer?

The thought feels foreign, like trying on someone else's clothes. I've spent so long being practical, realistic. Building a life around what I can touch, what I can cultivate with my own hands.

♪ "Watching the Wheels" by John Lennon

And yet... there's something about certain songs. The way they bypass all your careful defenses. The way they make you feel seen even when you're alone. This melody spinning around the bathroom feels like it knows something I don't—like it's been waiting for me to listen all along.

I close my eyes and let myself imagine it for just a moment. Someone thinking about me. Someone who noticed me once, who remembers. Someone whose path keeps almost crossing mine.

The water has cooled again. Reality seeping back in with the chill. This is what happens when you let yourself drift into fairy tales—the real world always returns, with its physics and its empty spaces. With its silence where the answers should be. I shake my head. Nobody is looking for me. How could they be? I'm just... ordinary. One woman among millions, tending gardens and paying bills and trying to keep the fern in the kitchen window alive. Nothing remarkable. Nothing that would linger in someone's memory across years, across miles.

And even if someone had noticed me once—had seen something worth remembering—life has a way of erasing the details. Of blurring faces and moments until they're just impressions, shadows of what they once were. I'm probably just a hazy silhouette in someone's past by now. If I'm there at all. But nothing is ever quite what it seems.

For a long time, I believed the reason things didn't work out was because of me. Because I was too quiet. Too reserved. Too serious. Too much in my own head. Too unwilling to bend, or maybe too tired to try.

I've spent years editing myself. Softening the sharp edges, downplaying the things that made me hard to love. Or so I thought.

I look at myself in the tub—the things I can't edit. My body. My face. The stretch marks that never quite faded. The soft curve of my stomach that didn't return after childbirth, no matter how many core exercises I did. The lines around my mouth that deepen when I smile. The gray streaks I've stopped coloring, because I finally got tired of pretending I'm still thirty-five. The veins on the backs of my hands. The practical underwear. The not-quite-matching pajamas.

I used to think those things made me invisible. But maybe invisibility isn't the same as being unseen. Maybe I was the one deciding I had to disappear.

What if the things I thought were flaws—my solitude, my caution, my body as it is now—aren't flaws at all? What if they're just… me? What if they're the shape I've earned, the map of where I've been? And what if the right person won't just tolerate those parts of me, but lean into them? Embrace them? What if those are the very things they end up loving most?

Love me because of them, not in spite of them.

Maybe they won't want to fix or polish or smooth me into something easier. Maybe they'll understand that quiet doesn't mean empty, that scars are proof of healing, and that there's nothing wrong with being slow to trust when your heart has been broken before.

Someday, I want to be loved like that.

I want someone to see me—with everything attached—my doubts, my body, my past, my silence—and not just stay… but choose me like I'm exactly where they've been heading all along.

I stare up at the ceiling. The water is cooling again, but I don't mind. There's something beautiful about the waiting, too. Something sacred in not rushing it.

⟢

04

00:04:30:22:07:22

The fire crackles, glowing embers shifting beneath the iron poker in my hand. I stir the flames absently, watching as tiny sparks rise, dance for a moment, then disappear—brief flashes of light, gone before they're felt.

A fitting metaphor.

The flames curl and shift, casting shadows along the stone hearth, moving in rhythms older than language. I wonder if that's what love is—slow, steady combustion. The kind that warms everything close to it… or consumes what can't withstand the heat. Maybe I've spent too long chasing sparks, when what I really wanted was something that could burn and still hold. Not a flash. A fire.

The floor creaks under my steps—a familiar sound, softened by years. I push open the door to my office, and the quiet wraps around me like a second skin. The room smells faintly of old paper and camera oil, of deadlines and long nights. On the bookshelf, nestled between a row of dog-eared travel journals and a cracked Leica box, the award catches the light.

The old award sits on the shelf where it's always been—centered, dusted, framed by the late afternoon light spilling through the curtains. The NPPA Award for Excellence in Journalism. My name is etched below in clean, precise lettering. A moment frozen in brass and glass.

People always said it was the kind of thing you work your whole life for. And maybe I did. The stories, the images, the time zones and tarmac. All of it chasing something. Truth, maybe. Or purpose. Success looks good in a press release. It photographs well. It fits neatly on shelves and resumes and holiday updates. But the silence around it is deafening.

I should feel proud. Sometimes I do. But right now, all I feel is the space beside it—empty, quiet, unanswered. All the countries, all the flights, all the near-misses and journalism dinners... and I still haven't found her. Still haven't heard her voice. Not really. Not the way I wanted to. And suddenly I wonder—if you capture the world, but never the person who mattered most... was any of it enough?

I press my fingers to the edge of the plaque, tracing the engraving like it might give me a different answer. It doesn't. Outside, the sun shifts. The light fades. And the award just sits there. Shining. Beautiful. And utterly still.

I glance up. Two posters hang crooked on the opposite wall—leftover décor from another version of myself. One is the old Jonny Moseley poster from my Boulder office, all confidence, chaos, and youth. The other is Bob Dylan—the all-knowing enigma—leaning against a brick wall, cigarette in hand, sunglasses on, watching the world like he already knows how the story ends.

⦿

I stare at Dylan.

What would he say right now? Probably something cryptic and maddening. Probably something like how the answer's blowin' in the wind—which is beautiful and infuriating.

But maybe he's right. Maybe it's been there the whole time, just waiting for me to stop chasing and start listening. Or, start searching.

I exhale and lean back, the leather of my chair creaking beneath me. The laptop sits open beside me on the desk its dim light flickering against the whiskey glass at my elbow. I should close it. I should pour another drink and let the night settle over me like every other night. But instead, I type into the Instagram search bar:

Sophia Farraday.

My fingers hesitate over the keys, my breath shallow. I hit enter. Nothing. The familiar ache tugs at my ribs. I should be used to this— chasing a ghost, retracing steps that always lead nowhere.

I delete her last name. Just Sophia. Profiles scroll past, too fast to process. Too many faces, too many lives that aren't hers.

And then—The world stops. My stomach drops as I freeze, my pulse hammering in my throat.

It's *her.*

A photo. A face I know better than my own memory. My breath leaves me in a harsh exhale, as if my body forgot how to hold air.

⊙

I click. And suddenly, she exists. Not just in faded memories or restless dreams. Not as a figment of my past, but as something real, tangible, present. I lean forward, elbows braced on my knees, my eyes devouring the screen.

She's sitting at an outdoor café, a glass of wine in her hand. The soft glow of evening light catches in her curls, still as wild and untamed as they were all those years ago. Midnight black curl spill over her shoulders, framing the same olive-green eyes that have haunted me. She's older. But somehow, she isn't. Time has softened the edges, but it hasn't touched her. She is—

Evergreen. ♪

Her smile—it's effortless, that same quiet, knowing thing that once stopped me dead in my tracks. Like she still holds some great secret the rest of us will never understand.

I reach out, my fingertips brushing the edge of the screen, as if touching the glass could bridge the impossible distance between us.

My hands are shaking. I don't even realize it until I wipe my palm against my jeans, my whole body vibrating with something too big to contain.

The caption is tagged: *Ballard, Washington.*

My breath catches. She's here. Not across the world. Not buried in the past. She's been here. Close. Living. Moving through a life I never knew, in a place I have driven by a hundred times over.

A choked sound escapes me—half-laugh, half-sob. I scrub a hand over my face, but the tears still come, hot and relentless. All these years. All the searching. The restless nights. The wrong turns. She was never lost.

♪ *"Evergreen"* by Barbra Streisand

She was waiting to be found.

I lunge for my phone, my fingers barely working as I dial. The call rings once—twice—before Brandon picks up.

"I found Sophia."

Silence. Then, "Wait—what? Where?"

I swallow hard, staring at the screen through tear-blurred eyes.

"Instagram."

Brandon exhales sharply. "Are you sure it's her?"

I don't even blink.

"No doubt. Time hasn't touched her."

Brandon hesitates, his voice softer now.

"What are you gonna do?"

I shake my head, barely able to form words.

"I don't know... but I think she lives nearby."

A stunned pause.

"No way. That's... that's crazy."

I drag my hand through my hair, my body still trembling, adrenaline still surging.

◎

"Yeah," I whisper, my gaze locked on her photo, the one thing in my world that suddenly makes sense.

"Feels like fate."

Brandon's voice fades, the call disconnecting with a quiet click. The silence rushes in, thick and suffocating. I lower the phone onto the coffee table, but my fingers linger on it, gripping the edge like it might anchor me. My pulse still pounds in my ears, my breath coming in uneven gulps.

She's still the most beautiful site in the world. Not that I ever doubted it. I lean back into the chair, but I can't relax. My whole body hums with restless energy, like the moment before a storm breaks. I stare at the screen, at her, at the impossible truth staring back at me.

For years, I've told myself it wasn't meant to be. That she was just a ghost, a perfect illusion I had clung to for too long. That no one searches for someone this long and actually finds them.

And yet—I did. But now, what the hell am I supposed to do? My hands run through my hair, gripping tight. Every logical part of me screams to slow down, to think. What if she's married? What if she's happy without me? What if I ruin something by showing up?

The cursor blinks in the search bar, waiting. I open her profile again, scrolling. Photo after photo, fragments of a life I was never part of. She looks happy. But not like before. Not like the girl who walked past me that first time in Telluride, barefoot, her sundress catching in the breeze, blowing a bubble like she had all the time in the world. Not like the girl frozen in time in that old volleyball newspaper clipping, eyes sharp and alive.

⚭

There's something else in her now. A weight. A quietness behind her smile. I rub my jaw, my fingers pressing against the tension that won't fade.

Reaching out feels like a risk. But not reaching out? That feels worse.

I stand abruptly, pacing the living room. The fire crackles behind me, throwing shadows against the walls. My whole life has been built on capturing the perfect moment. Waiting for the right light, the right frame, the right second to click the shutter and make it all mean something.

But some moments aren't captured. They're *seized.*

Golden Gardens Park - Ballard

The world slows at Golden Gardens Park. I let my pencil glide over the page, the lines taking shape beneath my fingertips. A curve for the sloping shoreline. A soft stroke for the reflection of sky in the tide pools. The trees framing the park, their bare winter branches reaching toward the pale blue.

The waves hush against the shore, steady and rhythmic, as if whispering something only they understand. Seagulls call out over the Sound, their cries blending with the distant laughter of children playing near the driftwood.

I exhale, pressing the tip of the pencil deeper into the paper, shading in the curve of a path.

Footsteps crunch over gravel. A presence. I don't look up right away, but I feel it—the weight of someone nearby. A quiet pause, a moment of hesitation. Then a breathless voice, worn with exertion.

☾☽

"May I?"

I glance sideways. A man, maybe mid-fifties, wiping sweat from his brow, catching his breath after his run. His gaze flickers toward the empty space beside me, then to my sketchpad.

I hesitate. Not because I mind, but because this has become habit—keeping people at arm's length. Then, something softens. I nod, the smallest invitation.

The jogger lowers himself onto the bench with a quiet grunt, rolling his shoulders back, still breathing deep from his run. He gestures toward my drawing with a nod.

"Mind if I have a look?"

A pause. Then, without a word, I tilt the sketchpad slightly toward him. He studies it, eyes warm with appreciation, then grins and gives me a thumbs-up.

I feel my lips curve, just a little. For a moment, we simply sit—two strangers sharing the same quiet world. The waves roll in, the wind shifts through the trees, the pencil moves again. And for the first time since Theo, I don't feel so alone.

☾

The cursor blinks. A silent metronome, tapping out the seconds, the hesitation, the weight of everything this moment could change. I exhale, rolling my shoulders, rubbing the tension from the back of my neck. Then, slowly, my fingers move.

Dear Sophia,

I pause, staring at her name. Just her name alone feels impossible. Unreal. Like I shouldn't be allowed to type it. But I keep going.

There was a window in Telluride where I used to watch you pass by. Each time felt like witnessing a shooting star—rare, fleeting, unforgettable.

I swallow, memories unfurling in sharp clarity.

You moved through the world as if you belonged to a story I wasn't brave enough to enter. I remember the way sunlight caught your curls, how you'd pause sometimes to blow bubbles, lost in thoughts I could only imagine.

My fingers hesitate again. I press my palm against my chest, trying to quiet the hammering pulse beneath.

You never knew, but those glimpses of you became the measure of beauty against which I've compared everything since.

God, it sounds ridiculous. Overwrought. I should delete it, start over. But I don't. I push forward.

Time has passed, yet the memory of you remains clear as morning light on mountain snow.

I blink, pushing back against the emotion creeping in.

I've traveled the world seeing incredible beauty, but nothing has ever quite matched the simple grace of passing you on the sidewalk.

I lean back, exhaling hard. I hover over the last sentence, rereading it, turning it over in my mind. Too much? Not enough? I want to say more. I want to ask where life has taken her, if she's happy, if she still wears her curls wild and unbound, if she still blows bubbles when she thinks no one is looking. But instead, I type:

I hope life has brought you joy equal to the wonder you once gave to a stranger who never found the courage to say hello.

My hand hovers over the mouse. Send. The word stares back at me, daring me.

Outside the window, a flash of movement—a hummingbird, suspended mid-air, wings beating furiously, yet somehow, perfectly still. I watch it, breath caught. It lingers for a moment, as if contemplating its own decision, then—just like that—it's gone.

I glance back at the screen. My finger trembles over the mouse. The weight of what if presses down. What if she never sees it? What if she does? What if I send it, and nothing changes? What if I don't, and nothing ever will? I close my eyes, inhale deep. The message is still there. Still waiting.

A knock at the door. The handle is cool beneath my fingers. I hesitate, just for a breath, before pulling the door open. And there he is.

The Jogger.

The man from the bench. He stands on my front step, casual, easy, holding a bottle of wine like it's the most natural thing in the world. Like this isn't something big. Maybe for him, it isn't. But for me—

For me, it's the first time in years that I've let someone cross this threshold. The first time I've considered the possibility that maybe I don't have to carry everything alone. That maybe life doesn't have to be an endless list of responsibilities, of pouring myself out for others while never refilling what's left.

Something changed in me. A thought I'd pushed away for years slipped through the cracks—a memory, a song, a girl's voice telling me to believe. I'd dismissed it at first. I always do. But it stayed with me. The warmth of it. The dare in it.

Maybe no one is out there searching. But maybe someone is here. Right in front of me. And maybe the point was never to wait, but to open the door.

He smiles, patient, waiting—not just for me to let him in, but for whatever this is to take shape in its own time. The wine glints under the porch light as he lifts it slightly, an unspoken question in his expression.

I don't answer with words—I never do. Instead, I step back, motioning him in. The door closes behind us with a quiet click—a sound so final, yet somehow, like a beginning.

☾

The rake crunches through the dry leaves, their brittle edges catching the evening light as they scatter into piles. I pause, leaning against the handle, wiping the sweat from my brow.

That's when I see it. A Maine Coon cat, perched on the roof, watching me like some ancient guardian of lost causes. Its tail flicks, unimpressed. I raise a hand in a half-hearted wave. "Hey, buddy," I mutter. The cat does not respond. Just stares, like it knows something.

I shake my head, exhaling, and drop into my rocking chair on the porch. The phone is warm in my hand, waiting, as if it has been waiting for years. I text Brandon.

What if she's happy? What if I'm just disrupting her life?

The reply comes almost instantly.

Sometimes disruption is exactly what we need.
Just try not to end up on Dateline.

Brandon makes it sound easy. Like it's just a text. Like I haven't spent decades measuring my life against the impossible memory of a stranger. I stand, pacing, the weight of my phone pressing into my palm. Every reason not to send the message plays on a loop—she could be married, she could have kids, she could have forgotten Telluride entirely. But what if she hasn't?

Later that night, I sat in the dark of my living room. The message was written. It had been for days. I sat on the couch, staring at it. One tap. That's all it would take. I close my eyes. Exhale. And press—*Send.*

The phone lands beside me on the cushion, the decision final, irreversible. The only movement is the slow rise and fall of my chest as relief and fear tangled inside me, indistinguishable. The room stays still—and then feels darker somehow, as if even the air was holding its breath—

—I reached for the lighter on the side table, thumbed the wheel, and brought the small candle to life. The flame flickered, casting shifting shadows against the walls, a fragile kind of defiance against the dark.

The room stayed quiet, except for the soft crackle of melting wax. I exhaled slowly, pressing my fingertips against the smooth surface of the heart-shaped crystal beside it. A simple ritual. Something grounding. Something constant.. Then—*Chime.*

My phone. I hesitate, blinking against the warm glow of the candlelight as I reach for it. A message. From Michael. A stranger. I frown slightly, adjusting the phone in my hand. The name means nothing. No recognition sparks. Just the simple, unexpected words of a stranger. I read them once. Then again. The weight of them settles over me like a distant echo, like something from a life I forgot to remember.

There was a window in Telluride where I used to watch you pass by...

Telluride.

My fingers tighten slightly around the phone. Who is this man? I read further. The words are careful, deliberate. There's no desperation, no expectation—just a memory, offered like a quiet confession.

Each time felt like witnessing a shooting star—rare, fleeting, unforgettable...

I swallow, my pulse slowing. It's strange, the thought of being seen when I never knew I was being watched. Of being remembered when I never realized I had left anything to remember.

A lifetime ago, in a town far away, someone carried a piece of me with them. And now, he's here. Reaching out. I set the phone down, my thumb hovering over the screen for a moment before I let go.

The candle flickers again, the flame steady, waiting. I don't know what to do. I just sit, listening to the silence, feeling the weight of a past I don't remember—and the presence of someone who never forgot.

The soil is cool beneath my fingers, damp from the morning watering. I press a cluster of bright begonias into place, patting the earth down with careful, deliberate movements. The scent of fresh dirt lingers in the air, mixing with the faint salt of the sea drifting up from the water.

I lean back on my heels, wiping sweat from my forehead with the back of my wrist. A breeze moves through the trees, rustling the leaves, bending the wildflowers. I glance toward the mountains, their jagged peaks steady against the endless sky. Still. Unchanging. Unlike me.

I've always hated yardwork. Give me a backpack and a camera, and I'll hike ten miles before breakfast. But put a spade in my hand and a list of perennials, and I start to lose faith in my own motor skills. I'm still not sure if scarlet begonias want full sun or partial shade, or whether the mulch I bought is even the right kind. Jerry Garcia might've known—but I don't have him on speed dial. But I keep going anyway. ♪

Because despite everything, I want it to look nice. Not perfect. Just... like someone cares. Like someone lives here. Like this place is becoming something.

The rake leans uselessly against the fence behind me—more decorative than practical at this point. I've Googled "how to prune lavender" three times and still don't feel any smarter about it. But the beds are cleaner than they were. The grass is shorter. The chaos is slowly becoming order.

I sit back for a moment, letting the wind find my skin. I used to think beauty was something you went out and found. Climbed mountains for. Flew across oceans to chase.

But maybe it's also something you build. One awkwardly planted flower at a time. Maybe this is how you grow a life—by tending to it, even when you're not sure what you're doing.

♪ *"Scarlet Begonias"* by The Grateful Dead

I sigh, brushing the dirt from my hands before instinctively reaching into my pocket. Nothing. My thumb lingers over the screen, as if staring at it hard enough might force it to light up. But no new messages appear. Of course not. I let out a slow breath, slipping the phone back into my pocket. Maybe I was stupid to think she'd respond quickly—if at all. Maybe it was too much. Too unexpected. Maybe I was too late.

Across the yard, the cat watches me from a sun-warmed rock, his tail flicking idly. He doesn't care. Not about waiting. Not about uncertainty. I push myself up, dusting my hands off. The air feels heavier now, thick with something I can't name. All I can do is wait.

Water spills gently from the can, soaking the soil of the hanging baskets, darkening it, sending the light scent of damp earth into the air. The flowers drink it in, their petals opening slightly under the afternoon sun. Droplets cling to the edges of leaves before slowly surrendering to gravity. The geraniums I planted last month have flourished, their red blooms bold against the weathered gray of the porch railing.

My Grandmother said I had a gift with plants—the ability to coax beauty from soil and seed, patience in watching things grow. I move from basket to basket, giving each its share of water and attention. She taught me everything, how to check the soil with my fingertips, how to listen to what each plant needs. Some thrive with abundance, others wither from too much care. Knowing the difference is everything.

I set the can down, brushing my damp hands against my jeans before sinking into the chair on the porch. The wood creaks in recognition beneath me. And then—I do what I've been avoiding.

I pick up my phone. His message still waits for me, glowing on the screen. My eyes trace over the words again. The way he remembers.

⦿

The way he saw me when I wasn't looking. There's something about it—something careful, something fragile. A window into a past I never even knew existed. I hover over the keyboard. Start typing. Then stop. What do I even say? My fingers backspace until the message disappears, leaving only the blinking cursor.

A flicker of movement catches my eye. A butterfly drifts toward the flowers, its wings delicate and weightless as it moves between the petals. Swallowtail. Black and yellow. Precise in its purpose yet seemingly unconcerned with destination. For a moment, I forget everything else.

The butterfly doesn't deliberate. Doesn't question. It simply follows what calls to it, moving from bloom to bloom with an instinct more honest than any human logic. I watch it navigate the garden I've created, finding nourishment in the colors I've cultivated, a visitor I never planned for but somehow expected.

The beauty of small things. The simplicity of movement without hesitation. My hand moves toward my phone again. But I don't type. I don't send anything. Not yet.

Instead, I set the phone down on the small table beside me and close my eyes. The sun warms my face. A slight breeze carries the scent of lavender from the border of the garden. Time stretches, elastic and generous. The butterfly will decide where to go next. The flowers will continue to bloom. And whatever words finally find their way from my fingers to his screen—they'll come when they're ready, not before.

Some decisions can't be forced. Some moments ask only to be lived before they're shaped into something else.

The weight of my grandfather's Martin guitar settles against my lap, the worn wood warm under my fingers. I strum absently, my touch light on the strings.

"Moonshadow."

The chords are rusty, hesitant, but there. The muscle memory is slow, trying to find its way back. A distant ferry horn hums through the air, vibrating against the stillness. I pause, exhaling, letting the sound fade before trying the notes again.

I don't even know why I picked this song, except... maybe I do. Aunt Donna used to play it on her old guitar, her voice warm and sure, never flashy but always right where it needed to be. She could make it sound like a secret you were lucky enough to overhear. "Moonshadow" was one of those melodies that felt deceptively light. Gentle. But underneath it—something else. Resilience, maybe. Or surrender. The kind of hope that doesn't ignore pain, just carries it differently. I think I've been trying to do the same. Not fix everything. Just let the shadows fall where they may, and keep moving anyway. Maybe that's what the song knows. Maybe that's what I need to learn.

Then, something shifts in my periphery. I glance down at the flower beds—And immediately stop playing. Two deer stand among the begonias, their heads dipping lazily as they tear through my freshly planted flowers. The destruction is slow, methodical, like they're savoring every bite.

On the steps, the cat watches them with an air of complete disinterest. I arch an eyebrow.

"I thought it was your job to keep out uninvited guests?"

◎

The cat blinks, unimpressed. The deer keep eating.

I don't move. I just watch. There's something quiet about the way they stand there, bold as anything, legs delicate, jaws working. No hurry. No shame. They don't even look at me. And really, why should they?

They were here first. Long before the fences, the roads, the flower beds. This isn't trespassing. It's returning. If anyone's the uninvited guest, it's probably me. I sigh, setting the guitar aside. Still no message. Still nothing. Just the waiting.

The wine catches the light as I pour, deep red swirling in the glass. I watch it settle, my fingers resting lightly on the stem. The record player sits waiting. Sliding the vinyl from its sleeve, I feel the resistance of well-worn grooves. There's something romantic about it—this ritual. The soft crackle, the pause before the first note. You have to be present for records. You can't just click and forget. You flip them over. You wait. You listen.

It asks something of you.

The faint crackle sounds as I lower the needle, and then an instrumental begins to drift into the room—soft and ethereal. A breath of sound against the silence. ♪

I close my eyes for a moment, exhaling. Then I move. Settling onto the couch, I reach for my glasses, perching them on the bridge of my nose. The cross-stitch project waits where I left it, the fabric cool beneath my fingers as I thread the needle.

The pattern is nearly complete—a night sky stretched across the cloth, constellations stitched in soft hues. But the center remains unfinished. My hands move instinctively, each stitch precise, controlled.

♪ *"We Move Lightly"* by Dustin O'Halloran

Thread. Pull. Knot.

The rhythm calms me. A tangible thing in a life that's felt anything but. Like the record—slow, deliberate, imperfect in all the ways that matter.

There's something in the repetition that steadies me. Or maybe it's the quiet. Or just the simple fact that something so small can become something whole if you keep showing up. Stitch by stitch, it's a kind of repair work. Not just the cloth—me, too.

I sew to feel the world slow down. To feel myself slow down. Like I'm tethering chaos into something that makes sense, even if no one else sees it but me.

I pause, lifting my gaze to the window. The sky is dark, scattered with stars that pulse faintly in the stillness. A vastness beyond reach. A reminder that the world keeps moving, even when I feel stuck. I take a sip of wine, letting it settle, letting the weight of everything soften— just for tonight.

The wrench slips from my grasp, clattering beneath the Jeep. I sigh, leaning back, rubbing a grease-streaked hand across my forehead. The garage smells of oil and dust, thick with the scent of old metal and time.

This project was supposed to be an escape. Something to keep my hands busy, to keep my mind from wandering places it shouldn't. But here I am, distracted again. Staring at the workbench. At the floor. At my damn phone.

I wipe my hands on a rag and check it anyway. Out of habit. Out of hope. No messages. Still.

◯

It's been weeks. I told myself I wouldn't keep track, but I know exactly how long it's been. I remember what day I hit *Send*. What time. I remember the weight of the air afterward—hopeful, electric, like maybe this time the past might open a door instead of closing one.

But now it's just... silence. The kind that settles in your chest and starts building walls.

I toss the rag harder than I mean to. It hits the bench and slides off, landing in a heap on the floor. My hands are shaking—not with anger exactly. Not yet. Just with the fatigue of waiting. The kind of tired that comes from telling yourself over and over that maybe she's just busy. Maybe it got buried. Maybe she's not sure how to respond.

Maybe she saw it and felt nothing.

I push the thought away like a loose part I don't want to inspect too closely. I step outside.

The night meets me with quiet. A cool breeze drifts across the yard, rustling the trees, brushing the sweat from the back of my neck. I sink into the old chair by the garage door, muscles aching, thoughts heavier than I want to admit.

Above me, the moon hangs low, casting silver light across the landscape. The stars stretch wide, endless. There's something about the way they just exist. Unconcerned. Unchanging. I lean my head back, letting the stillness settle over me.

She didn't owe me anything. I know that. But still—I wish she'd said something. Anything. Even a no. Even a thank you. Even silence with a name.

Instead, there's just... silence.

And for the first time in a long while, I don't know what to do next.

The first stitch is always the hardest. When I started this, I told myself I'd finish it in a week. Maybe two. Now, months have passed, and the center remains empty.

The constellations were easy. The stars, the crescent moon, the delicate swirls of thread forming a night sky across the fabric. The stitches came naturally, one after another, tiny and precise. But the words? I've unraveled them more times than I can count. It's not the stitching itself that keeps stopping me. It's the weight of what they mean.

I run my fingers over the half-finished design, the smooth thread cool beneath my touch. The words should be easy to stitch, just a few loops and lines. But every time I start, something inside me hesitates. A sign of doubt? Or hope?

Across the room, the record player hums, stuck in a soft, looping *skrrt... skrrt... skrrt...* The needle caught, replaying the same second over and over. I don't move to fix it. Instead, I stare at the empty space in my design. The place where the words are supposed to go. Some things are easier to leave unfinished. I set it aside, reaching for my wine.

Outside, the night stretches deep and dark, the stars indifferent to all the questions I don't have answers for. I close my eyes, listening to the record skip. Maybe tomorrow.

I used to measure time by flights—departure gates and return tickets, by the places I went and the ones I left behind. Now, I measure it by

⦿

smaller things. The rust creeping along the Jeep's fender. The way the days stretch longer, minute by minute. The scent of the air—warmer now, threaded with salt spray and something green and new.

The garage smells of oil and old metal. Memory. Grandfather teaching me to change spark plugs. Summers spent elbow-deep in engines. That quiet satisfaction of knowing how things fit together. A different kind of knowledge than framing the perfect shot or bargaining with fixers in countries where I barely spoke the language. Simpler. More rooted. The kind that stays in one place.

I exhale and wipe my hands on a rag, grease clinging to my skin. The Jeep still isn't running right. Or maybe it is. Maybe it's fine, and I just keep tinkering with it because it feels like a problem I can actually solve.

I tell myself that's why I keep coming back to the garage. But the truth is, it gives me something to do while I wait for something I can't name.

Three months. No deadlines. No flights. No bags to pack. At first, the stillness felt foreign, like wearing someone else's life. I kept reaching for my camera. For my passport. For motion disguised as meaning.

But slowly, something shifted. I've started noticing the way the kitchen light changes throughout the day. The pattern of dogs being walked. The way certain neighbors wave and some never do. I'm learning the rhythm of staying put—of watching a place transform slowly, from the inside out.

For years, I've chased the perfect shot, freezing moments just before they change. But what about the slow change that only reveals itself when you stay? What about the kind of life that builds not from highlights, but from repetition?

◎

Travel used to feed something—my hunger for the new, the far-flung, the not-here. But lately, it feels thin. I come back with thousands of images, but they all blur. Places I've seen but never known. People I've listened to but never belonged with.

Sophia was different. She wasn't a subject or a story. She was present. Solid. Uncurated. I can't stop thinking about her. Not because she was perfect. But because she felt perfect in that moment. Because she was real. Because she was there.

I pull my phone out of my pocket. No message from her. Not that I expected one. I slide it away and step outside.

The evening sun burns low, turning the water to hammered gold. Grandfather's property—my property now, though I still can't bring myself to call it that—unfolds in familiar pieces. The garage behind me. The madronas clinging to the hill like old friends, their bark peeling back in slow curls. Wild crocuses push through the soil by the rocky path.

This is where I learned to swim. Where I learned to stay. These are the things that remain. And I'm still here.

For the first time in years, I have no ticket in my back pocket. No departure countdown. No lens between me and what I'm seeing.

I lean against the Jeep's hood, feeling the day's warmth still radiating off the metal. Tomorrow, I'll try replacing the fuel pump. The day after, maybe I'll take the kayak out to Jones Island, if the weather holds. The first orcas of the season were spotted last week—early.

The day after that? I don't know. That's the thing about staying. You don't always need a plan. The days come anyway.

◯◯

I stare out over the water, toward the Olympic Peninsula. Shadows drift across the surface. This is the kind of moment I usually miss—the ones that don't make dramatic photographs but shape a life.

What comes after chasing the world? I don't know. What I do know is this: I'm tired of being the one behind the lens. Tired of being everywhere but never fully in it. Tired of perfect compositions with no one beside me in the frame.

I don't need another solo trip. I don't need more silence disguised as freedom. I need something different now. Something rooted. Something reciprocal. Someone who stays anchored. And maybe, if I'm lucky—someone to stay for. The stars will be out soon—steady, untouchable. They don't wait for anyone.

The stars don't apologize for shining.

I wish I knew how to live like that.

I pick it back up. Not because I want to. But because something about leaving it unfinished feels... wrong. I settle onto the couch, the fabric cool in my hands. The stars are there, the moon, the swirling lines of constellations. The center still gapes empty.

I thread the needle. The first stitch is shaky. The second is better. My fingers remember the rhythm, and soon the words form beneath my hands. Looping, curving, connecting. But as the final letter takes shape, I pause. For months, I thought I knew what it would say.

Love is Written in the Stars.

But now—I don't believe that anymore. Not love. Not fate. Not some cosmic force beyond my control. I pick up my scissors and carefully snip the last few stitches, unraveling the words thread by thread. The fabric sits blank again, waiting. This time, I take my time. I choose the words carefully. Stitch them deliberately. Not about fate. Not about destiny. About choice.

The last stitch pulls tight. I hold up the finished piece, the words stitched in soft silver thread. I stand, stretching the ache from my shoulders. With slow steps, I move down the hallway, passing framed photos—snapshots of a life lived in pieces.

I pause by the empty space on the wall. A deep breath. A decision. I hang the cross-stitch. Stepping back, I study it in the low light.

We Make Our Own Light.

Not borrowed light. Not someone else's warmth. Not a promise written in stars I can't reach. For so long, I waited for something— someone—to illuminate my life from the outside. To spark it. To fix it. But this... this is something else.

This is me choosing to glow anyway. Even when it's dark. Even when it hurts. Light isn't handed to us. We build it—stitch by stitch, moment by moment. In the showing up. In the staying. In the brave, quiet decision to keep going.

I stand there a little longer, letting the truth of that settle into my bones. For the first time in a long time—I believe it. And maybe that's where it begins.

☾

The bench hasn't changed. The wood is more weathered now, silvered by sun and snow, its grain raised in places like old scars. But it's still here, right where I left it—across from the courthouse with its slow, dependable clock. I ease down onto it, feeling the chill of the wood seep through my coat.

I told myself I was staying home. Told myself I wasn't coming back to this bench. Told myself it was about closure. And then—like always—I got on a plane. But part of me knows—I'm still looking for something I should've let go of a long time ago.

Old habits die hard.

The mountains stretch behind the town like they always have— eternal, indifferent. A few kids dart across the street, their laughter sharp in the thin air. A dog pulls at its leash. Somewhere, a car door slams. But mostly, it's quiet.

I think I finally understand why she came to this exact spot. Why she returned to it, day after day. There's something grounding about it—this bench, this view, this little crease in the world where time feels like it slows just enough to let you breathe. Maybe it was never about waiting. Maybe it was about holding still long enough to feel something. To let the quiet catch up to you. And maybe that's what I'd been running from all along.

I run my hand along the backrest, fingertips tracing the grooves I used to memorize like braille. I wonder how many hours I sat here, waiting for a girl I never had the courage to speak to. I wonder how many more I've spent since, trying to rewrite the moment in my head.

Time doesn't rush here. It settles. It settles in your knees, in your spine, in the corners of your memory. I was twenty-three when I first sat here—full of ache and possibility. Now I'm fifty-five.

The ache hasn't left. It's just changed shape.

◍

The world moved on. Sophia moved on. The bench stayed. And I—I chased fleeting moments, collected awards and airline miles... but not love. Not the kind that takes root and stays. Or maybe I did, and I was just too blind—or too afraid—to recognize it. Martone. Blythe. They offered something steady. Something whole. And still, I held back. I never stepped fully into it. Never really let them in.

Lately, I've noticed the small things with my mother—how she moves a little slower in the mornings, how she forgets names she used to recall in an instant. Nothing alarming. Just enough to remind me that time is moving for her, too. I catch her watching me sometimes when I come back from this bench, a question in her eyes she never quite asks. And I never offer it. She senses there's something that keeps pulling me here, something unresolved. But she's never been one to push. Maybe she knows I wouldn't have an answer worth saying aloud. Maybe she understands that some silences are too old, too tender, to name.

For decades, Sophia had become a kind of ghost in my mind—half-memory, half-myth. A girl on a bench in perfect light, frozen in time. But she's not a ghost. I know that now. I found her—or at least the outline of her life—tucked into a quiet corner of Instagram: sunlight on a garden bed, a snapshot of a child's muddy boots, words written in her voice but never meant for me. I sent a message. Just the one. She never responded. And maybe that was answer enough.

She wasn't mine to chase.

She was real. Still is. Living a life beyond the lens I'd tried to hold her in. I lean back, listening to the wind stir through the street. She's not coming. She doesn't live here anymore. But here I am—still waiting on this bench. All I have is the memory of what almost was. And I wonder—was it the moment that never came, or the man who never acted?

03

00:00:44:18:50:48

It's one of those still, silver-lit nights when the world seems to pause in its turning. Moonlight spills through the kitchen window, pooling on the floor, casting soft-edged shadows that stretch and shift. The screen glows ghost-blue against my fingertips, an echo of the light outside. I sit at the table, legs folded beneath me, tea cooling by my elbow, untouched. My phone rests in my palm, the Instagram app open. The message is still there. It keeps calling me back.

I used to watch you pass by. Each time felt like witnessing a shooting star— rare, fleeting, unforgettable...

I let the words linger, blinking slowly. I can't decide if it feels sur-real or inevitable. A stranger. A message. A memory that isn't mine— but somehow still belongs to me.

You never knew, but those glimpses of you became the measure of beauty against which I've compared everything since.

I set the phone down, carefully, like it might break the moment.

Telluride. I was eighteen then. Walking through the world like it was still unfolding just for me. No fear yet. No walls. I wore my hair wild and my hope even wilder. I remember blowing bubbles just because I had them in my bag and it felt like the kind of thing someone unafraid might do. I didn't think anyone was watching.

But someone was.

And now, thirty-five years later, that moment has come back to find me—in a message, of all things. Digital. Unexpected. Disarmingly sincere.

What floors me is not that he remembered. *It's that he saw me.*

Not the woman I built myself into over the years. Not the volunteer in distant places. Not the mother, steady and tired and fierce. Not the café owner with early mornings and practiced smiles. And not the wife. *Especially* not the wife.

That version of me—the one who learned how to shrink herself in small ways, day after day, to keep the peace, to hold the shape of something that no longer held her—I don't think anyone saw her, not really. I don't even know if I did.

There is a particular kind of grief in that. Not just the grief of a marriage ending, but the quieter devastation of losing yourself so gradually you don't notice until you're gone.

But this message… it didn't ask for anything. It didn't flatter. It didn't pry. It just remembered a girl I used to be. The one with ink on her fingers and too many dreams to hold at once. The one who walked through Telluride with no idea anyone might be watching—and seeing. Not the woman who's learned how to stay calm in grocery store lines and cry only in the car.

He saw her. The unjaded version. The pure version. The one who didn't know yet that grace could be chipped away so quietly.

I get up, walk to the window, and stare out into the yard. The garden hums with late sun. A breeze stirs the chimes, soft and metallic. It all feels strange and too still—like the air before something changes.

He doesn't know me. And yet… there's a tenderness in his message that feels like an open hand. He didn't ask for anything. He just gave me back a piece of myself I didn't know I'd lost.

And I still don't know what to do with that. Not yet.

So I sit with it. The message. The memory. The ache. And the smallest beginning of wonder. I carry it. Quietly. Like something delicate and unspoken—tucked into the lining of a coat I keep wearing.

Back home, the night air is cool, carrying the distant hush of the tide rolling in. I sit on the porch, elbows on my knees, fingers pressing against my temples. The weight of waiting—of hoping—has settled too deep in my bones. Months, months with nothing but silence.

The phone feels heavier than it should in my hand, the screen glowing dimly as I scroll through old messages. Messages where Brandon told me to go for it, to take the leap. Messages where I let myself believe that maybe, just maybe, fate wasn't a cruel joke.

I exhale sharply and hit dial. Brandon picks up after one ring.

"Can't sleep?" His voice is groggy but steady.

"I can't keep doing this," I mutter, running a hand over my face. "I've been fooling myself, thinking there was something real to hold onto."

There's a pause, then the sound of him shifting in bed.

"Sometimes things just aren't meant to be."

I close my eyes, the words hitting like a slow, dull ache.

"Letting go feels impossible."

"Letting go doesn't mean you failed," Brandon says. "It just means you're making room for what's next."

I shake my head, staring out into the night. The moon hangs low over the trees, the stars indifferent. "Yeah, but how do you move on when it still feels unfinished?"

Brandon sighs. "It's tough, man. But not every story has the ending we expect. You keep looking back. Maybe it's time to look ahead?"

I press my thumb against the phone, swallowing down the sharp sting of those words. Looking ahead. How do you do that when the past still clings to you like a ghost?

"I've got a trip coming up," I say finally.

"Maybe it'll clear my head. Or maybe it'll just remind me of everything I'm trying to forget."

To my surprise, the cat appears at my side, leaping onto the porch railing, his eyes glowing in the low light. He watches me for a beat before curling up next to me, his warm body pressing against my leg. I reach down, scratching gently behind his ears.

For a while, I wasn't sure if he actually belonged to the house. He came and went on his own terms—aloof, silent, vanishing for days like a ghost that hadn't quite decided to stay.

But now… Now I think he does. Or maybe it's the other way around. I will name him Moseley. He never really leaves for good. At least something is still here.

I glance down at my shoes. One of my shoelaces has come undone again, curling toward the floor like it's tired of pretending it ever wanted to stay in place. K-Swiss—the same shoe I wore in high school. I've been buying the same pair every few years ever since. They still make them, which means I can't be the only one keeping the dream alive. Same white leather, same chunky tongue, same laces that never stay tied no matter how tight I double-knot them.

Martone used to roll her eyes every time she saw them. Said I refused to evolve. The camera's the only upgrade I ever really committed to. Everything else—my shoes, my coffee order, my car—it's all the same. A kind of continuity I never questioned. I told her they were reliable. Comfortable. She told me so was stubbornness. I couldn't argue with that. The lace dangles, unbothered. I don't retie it. Some things never stay tied. But they still carry you home.

⊙⊙

Cafe Hagen - Lake Union

Today I find myself in a café I've never been to before. It's beautiful in that curated kind of way—brick walls, matte black fixtures, Edison bulbs casting just the right amber glow. Behind the counter, a sleek espresso machine hums like a well-behaved engine. Everything matches. Everything knows where it belongs. But it's quiet, and *not* the kind of quiet I like.

I sit near the window, almond milk latte in hand, steam curling faintly in the afternoon light. Around me, every table is full—but no one is speaking. Heads are bowed, not in reverence but in absorption. A sea of glowing laptops and phones casts soft light on blank expressions. Some scroll with mechanical thumbs. Others tap at keyboards, earbuds tucked in, worlds away from the one unfolding right in front of them.

A couple sits nearby. They don't speak, don't even glance at each other—each lost in their own screen. His thumb swipes. Her face glows blue. Some scroll with mechanical thumbs. Others tap at keyboards, earbuds tucked in, worlds away from the one unfolding right in front of them. A few read from Kindles, their faces still, eyes flicking across invisible pages.

I get it—for traveling, for convenience. It makes sense. But it's not the same. The sound of a real page turning. The weight of a story in your hands. The quiet companionship of a book with a worn spine and dog-eared corners. There's something sacred in paper—how it ages with you, how it smells, how it asks you to slow down.

There's a kind of loneliness in this place that doesn't come from being alone. I stir my drink slowly, watching the foam collapse inward. I used to love places like this—corners of the world where strangers overlapped for a moment, where stories bumped into each other accidentally. A smile. A shared glance. A comment on the weather. A beginning.

Now I wonder how anyone meets anymore. How do connections even start in a room where no one looks up?

My phone rests on the table, screen dark. I haven't touched it since I sat down. But I feel it. That invisible tether. That quiet, persistent pull. The message from him, still sitting there, waiting.

I just haven't answered.

My fingers brush the edge of the phone, then pull back. I could. Right now. Be like everyone else. Pick it up. Type something. Anything. But I don't. Not yet. I'm not sure if it's hesitation. Or protection. Or the fact that I'm seeing someone else.

Maybe it's all of them.

Across from me, a young woman holds her phone just above her cappuccino, adjusting the angle, taking photo after photo. She scrolls through filters. I want to ask her what she sees when she looks at it. What she's trying to capture. Or remember.

But I don't. I just sit in the stillness, letting the taste of espresso and almond milk linger.

Outside, two children race past the front window, one shouting about Barbie, the other about spaceships. Their laughter is wild, unfiltered, the kind that doesn't check notifications first. Their mother follows behind, half-laughing, half-calling their names.

I watch them go until they disappear down the block. Then I look back at the table. My reflection ripples in the surface of the cup. The world moves on—fast, connected, untouchable. But sometimes, I wish it would slow down. Or soften.

Just enough for people to look up.

Sleep had abandoned me hours ago, leaving me restless and hungry for something I couldn't name. Or maybe just hungry for Shelby's cinnamon rolls. It's not *Cinnabon* but it's close enough.

I check the time—*5:17 a.m.* Perfect. Early enough to beat the tourists but late enough that Shelby would be pulling in her first batch from the oven.

The headlights of the Jeep cut through the pre-dawn darkness, illuminating the winding road into town. The island feels different at this hour—quieter, more honest somehow. Mist hangs low over the fields, and the silhouettes of deer appear and vanish like ghosts along the roadside. No tourists spilling off the ferry yet, trying to capture everything without experiencing anything.

Just darkness gradually giving way to possibility.

I park outside *Shelby's*, the only storefront with lights blazing in the otherwise sleeping town. Through the foggy windows, I can make out familiar shapes—hunched figures at the counter, steam rising from thick mugs, the steady rhythm of island life that continues regardless of who's watching.

The bell above the door announces my arrival. The scent hits me immediately—bacon, warm cinnamon, butter, fresh coffee. The small space is a cocoon of warmth and light against the blue-black morning.

⟨⟩

"Morning, Michael," calls Shelby without looking up, her hands busy rolling dough. Flour dusts her forearms like snow. "Usual?"

"Yes, please. Thank you."

The usual crowd is already settled in—four or five men, weathered and worn like driftwood. Commercial fishermen mostly, gathering before heading out for the day. They acknowledge me with nearly imperceptible nods. I've lived here long enough to earn that much, but not so long that they include me in their conversations.

Their talk moves like tide—rising and falling around the day's weather, which boats need repair, whose son got into what trouble. None of them look at phones. None of them seem to care what's happening beyond these waters.

I take a seat at the counter, a few stools down from their cluster. Shelby slides a cinnamon roll the size of my fist onto a plate, followed by a latte in a chipped mug that reads "Friday" despite it being Tuesday.

"Thanks," I tell her. She's already moving on, refilling Captain Reed's mug.

I pull out my phone, instinctively checking for messages. Nothing from Sophia. Just a few emails from Jane about an assignment in Croatia starting next month. I should be excited. Instead, there's this quiet reluctance I can't quite name. The truth is, I don't want to go.

The door chimes. A younger couple steps inside, both immediately pulling out their phones—probably checking Facebook, or whatever replaced it. Heads bent. Fingers scrolling. The fishermen glance up, then back down. No one says a word.

I look down at my own phone, suddenly aware of the irony. Technology—blessing or anchor? Sometimes I wonder if my camera, my phone, all these tools for "connection" have just been elaborate ways to keep the world at a safe distance.

Captain Reed's laugh cuts through my thoughts—a sound like gravel shifting underfoot. The fishermen are sharing some inside joke, their faces creased with genuine amusement. No documentation needed. No audience required. Just the moment, fully lived.

I set my phone face-down on the counter and turn my attention to the cinnamon roll, still warm enough to melt the icing. Outside, the sky is lightening to pearl gray. A new day is coming whether I'm ready for it or not. Sometimes being awake when you should be asleep offers its own kind of clarity.

Sleep feels like a distant memory, something I once knew but have somehow forgotten how to do. I've been staring at the ceiling for hours, watching shadows shift across the room as cars occasionally pass on the street outside. I glance at the clock: *4:43 a.m.* Too early to be awake, too late to try melotonin.

The wooden floor is cool against my bare feet as I pad to the kitchen. My old craftsman home creaks in familiar places—the third floorboard from the bedroom door, the spot near the staircase. Ballard is quiet at this hour, the neighborhood settled into a collective exhale before the morning rush.

I stand in the kitchen, caught between choices. The latte machine sits ready, beans from my favorite roaster already measured out the night before, part of my usual ritual. Coffee would be practical—I'm clearly not going back to sleep, and the day ahead is long. The familiar aroma, the comforting routine, the predictable jolt of energy.

But something in me hesitates, hand hovering between the latte machine and the cabinet where my teas wait. Coffee feels too... decisive. Too committed to being awake, to productivity, to moving forward. Tea feels more contemplative, more patient. An acknowledgment that this early hour deserves its own kind of attention.

Tea, then.

I open the tea cabinet, where dozens of tins and boxes stand in neat rows—my own private apothecary. My fingers hover indecisively: chamomile for calm, Assam for comfort, rooibos for warmth. None feels quite right. I push aside the everyday choices, reaching toward the back where special blends wait for particular moments.

My hand finds the small blue tin of jasmine pearl tea—the expensive one I save for celebrations or consolations. Why this one? I hesitate, considering what my subconscious might be telling me. It's the tea I drank the morning after I decided to leave Ethan. The tea for moments of change.

I fill the kettle and set it on the stove, the familiar ritual offering some comfort. This tea won't help me sleep, but it feels important somehow, like acknowledging something I haven't fully admitted to myself yet.

While waiting for the water to boil, I find myself at the kitchen window. The sky holds that particular shade of blue that comes just before dawn—not quite night anymore, not yet day. Liminal. Transitional. Like so many things in my life right now.

From here, I can see my small backyard garden, the silhouettes of

☾☽

raised beds and the apple tree I planted three years ago, finally beginning to establish itself. Somewhere beyond my fence, beyond this neighborhood, beyond Seattle itself, decisions wait to be made.

Messages wait to be answered.

The kettle whistles, and I silence it quickly, not wanting to disturb the quiet. I pour water over the tightly rolled pearls of tea, watching as they slowly unfurl, releasing their fragrance. Like thoughts unspooling, like possibilities opening.

Cup in hand, I settle into the window seat in the front room, drawing my knees to my chest. Through the leaded glass windows—original to the house—I watch as the first hints of dawn touch the rooftops of neighboring homes, each as unique and weathered as my own.

Maybe clarity will come with daylight. Or maybe what I need isn't clarity at all, but the courage to step forward without it.

☽

The dim light from the desk lamp barely touches the edges of my office. Shadows stretch across the walls, thick and unmoving. I stand still, staring down at the worn newspaper clipping on my desk.

Sophia's face looks up at me, frozen in time—the same face I had memorized long before I ever knew her name. The same face that had shaped years of my life in ways I hadn't even realized until now.

The edges of the paper are curled, soft from being handled too many times. How many times have I traced this image, wondering where she was? If she was happy? If she even remembered that I existed?

My fingers move instinctively, brushing over the faded ink. Then—

without thinking—I crumple the paper in my palm. I hold it there for a long moment, feeling its weight, the familiar texture of something I've refused to let go of.

A long breath. I hesitate—then release it. The ball of paper lands softly in the wastebasket.

I stare at it, my chest tight. It should feel like something monumental, like closure. But it doesn't. It just feels… quiet.

My shoulders sink. I rub my face, exhaustion pulling at every part of me. I reach over and flip the switch on the lamp. Darkness.

Pike Place Market

Pike Place swirls with energy—the scent of fresh seafood mingling with roasted coffee, the calls of vendors rising above the din of tourists and locals alike. Crowds weave through the narrow aisles, drawn to the vibrant stalls of flowers, handmade jewelry, fresh produce.

Beside me, The Jogger walks with a bounce in his step, holding up a jar of honey like a prize.

"Local honey, straight from the hives!" He grins, enthusiasm radiating from him.

I glance at the jar, nodding politely, but my attention is already drifting. A few steps away, a street musician strums a familiar melody, his voice low and smooth over the hum of the market.

"Moonshadow."

The sound catches something deep in my chest, a thread pulling taut. I slow instinctively, drawn toward the music.

Near the musician, a couple sways in their own private rhythm, her head tucked beneath his chin, his arms wrapped around her waist. They move easily together, lost in the song, in the moment. Their fingers graze, small touches that speak volumes. Something in my stomach clenches.

"Let's check out the famous seafood place," The Jogger says, oblivious, already leading the way.

I nod, but the smile I offer feels hollow. We move past the crowd, past the musician, past the couple wrapped in a warmth I don't share. The notes of the song drift after me, light and wistful, like a hand reaching out and slipping through my fingers.

The market carries us forward. The Jogger chatters on, pointing at vendors tossing fish, at displays of smoked salmon, at an old neon sign blinking overhead. I walk beside him, but my steps feel disconnected from my body, like I'm watching myself move from a distance.

Then, an art stall catches his eye. Canvases line the walls—Seattle skylines, seascapes, abstract splashes of color. The Jogger slows, drawn to one in particular: a dark, chaotic painting titled *Deer in the Headlights* by Penny O'Reilly.

"Please, take it," the vendor says with a wry smile. "It gives me nightmares."

The Jogger laughs, clearly entertained, but I barely register the words. My fingers brush over the edge of another canvas, the paint raised slightly under my touch. It's a landscape—small, almost hidden among the louder pieces. A quiet meadow beneath an open sky. The kind of place you could breathe. I let my hand fall away.

"Everything okay?"

The Jogger's voice pulls me back. I force another smile, but my throat feels tight. I should reach for his hand. Should tuck my arm into his. Should let him kiss my temple like he did last week when we walked through the park.

But I don't. Because I don't want to. And if I'm being honest with myself, I never will.

☾

I rub a hand down my face, exhaling hard. My gaze drifts, searching for something—anything—to pull me out of this fog. And then I see it. The cross-stitch. It hangs slightly crooked on the wall, the same place it's been since I moved in. The same words staring back at me for years.

Kwitchyerbellyakin.

"I know, Gramps," I murmur. "I wish it was that easy."

I step closer, running my thumb over the frame, brushing away the thin layer of dust that has settled. The fabric inside is still bright, the stitches tight, unyielding.

His voice echoes in my head—gruff, amused, always straightforward. *No use whining about it, kid. Life keeps moving whether you like it or not.* I close my eyes. I want to believe that. But the weight in my chest makes it hard to breathe, let alone move.

I need something. Something to shake me loose. I grab my keys

◯◯

off the hook by the door without thinking. *Shelby's* was closed but I had another idea.

Kings Market

The cereal aisle stretched out before me like a chaotic map of childhood—boxes stacked high in bright colors, mascots grinning, promises of prizes tucked inside. Sugar Corn Pops, Raisin Bran, Lucky Charms, Cinnamon Toast Crunch, Froot Loops—all lined up like old friends I hadn't seen in years.

I stood there longer than I meant to, letting the hum of the fluorescent lights settle around me. People drifted past with carts full of real groceries—produce, eggs, oatmeal, Ensure, responsible things. But I stayed put, scanning the endless rows of nostalgia.

So much had changed. Maybe too much. But somehow, this aisle hadn't. The same promises. The same feeling that somewhere, hidden behind all the noise of growing up, there were still bright, ridiculous things worth reaching for.

My hand hovered. I could've gone safe. Raisin Bran. Grown-up.

To hell with growing up.

Instead, I grabbed the Cap'n Crunch—the one that tore up the roof of your mouth when it was crunchy and went gloriously soggy when you waited too long. No way to lose. Either way, it was still the greatest cereal ever created.

I toss it into the basket, already half-decided: if the checkout girl says anything, I'll just shrug and say it's for my nephew. Easy enough. Safer than admitting the truth—that a fifty-something still loves this shit.

⦾

Starting over isn't always about being wiser. Sometimes it's about remembering who you were before everything got so heavy—before you needed permission to reach for the small, silly things that make you smile.

Maybe it begins with just one small, stubborn act of joy. Maybe it starts here—with a secret prize, a glow-in-the-dark compass ring to guide me home. A reminder that hope can be small and bright and waiting—if you're just brave enough to open the box

The Literary Loft

The air inside hums with warmth—the scent of old pages and fresh ink curling around me like an old friend. The low murmur of conversation fades as the poetry reading begins, the small space settling into stillness.

I sit toward the back, my fingers curled around a steaming cup of tea. The warmth barely reaches past my fingertips. Onstage, a woman named Leila leans into the mic, her voice smooth but weighted with something unspoken.

"In the quiet of the night, your eyes met mine, A spark, a flame, a fire that could never die."

The words drift through the air, settling over me.

A spark. A flame.

That feeling of something igniting—undeniable, impossible to ignore. My gaze lowers to my tea, watching the surface ripple with the shift of my breath. Have I ever had that? Truly?

〇〇

Leila's voice carries on, weaving longing and passion into something tangible, something that presses deep into my ribs.

"We danced in the moonlight, two souls entwined, Passion's embrace, love's sweet, endless sigh."

A couple near the front sits close—his arm draped over the back of her chair, her fingers absently tracing circles on his knee. No hesitation. No uncertainty. Just the ease of two people existing together, the space between them already claimed.

I exhale, the sound barely audible. I don't want a love that is practical, convenient. A love that checks all the right boxes but leaves something missing.

I want the kind that stops time. The kind that feels like fate cracking the sky open. The kind that, with one look, rewrites the whole course of my life. That's the love worth waiting for. The kind I've never found. The kind I still, after everything, can't seem to let go of.

I close my eyes, letting the words of the poem wash over me, settling somewhere deep—somewhere I don't have the courage to name.

The rain taps against the window, soft and rhythmic, a quiet metronome to my thoughts. The house is still. The candle on the coffee table flickers, stretching shadows against the walls.

I shift under the blanket, my phone warm in my palm. Gray's message glows on the screen.

So, how's it going with the jogger?

I exhale, rolling my shoulders, trying to settle the unease I've been carrying for weeks. Months, really.

He's nice, but... no flame. It feels like I'm forcing something that isn't there.

I send it before I can overthink, setting my phone aside. The rain blurs the city lights beyond the window, smudging them into watercolor streaks. I sip my tea, waiting, but I already know what Gray's response will be before my phone even buzzes.

Maybe it's a slow burn?

I let out a breathy laugh—short, humorless. A slow burn. If that were true, wouldn't I feel something by now? Wouldn't there be anticipation when I saw him, a flicker of warmth when he reached for my hand? Instead, there's nothing. Just polite conversation and moments that feel more like habit than connection.

My fingers move quickly.

It's been months. I'm just not into it. I am going to end it.

I send it before doubt creeps in. I don't need to analyze this. I know.

Gray doesn't hesitate.

You'll know when it feels right.

I stare at her words longer than I should. My phone is still in my hand when I scroll absently through my messages, not really thinking—until I stop. Michael. The message I never answered. My thumb hovers. The rain slows outside, softening against the glass. Gray's name flashes again.

◎

What about the mystery Instagram guy?

I blink. My stomach tightens at the coincidence. Slowly, I type.

I never responded.

Three dots appear immediately.

What?! Why not?

I pull the blanket tighter around me. What am I supposed to say? That it felt irrational? That I'd just met The Jogger, and convincing myself to try something safe had seemed logical? That deep down, I was afraid of what answering might mean?

I type, backspace. Type again.

Well, I just met the jogger. Maybe I was afraid. I don't know.

Gray doesn't hesitate as usual.

Yeah, well, the universe doesn't send messages every day.
You don't have to be fearless. Just honest.

The words land in my chest like a stone—and stay there.

Highway 101 - Port Townsend

The road curls west toward the edge of the map—pine-lined and slick from an earlier rain, the clouds pulling back just enough to let the light through. We've got the top down, even though it's not exactly warm. Gray insisted. Said the cold felt good on her face. The heater's blasting at our feet, a compromise.

⟡

Fleetwood Mac plays through the speakers—the layered harmonies and Stevie's voice threading through the open air like fog. Gray picked it. Imagine that. She always goes for the older stuff, claims new music doesn't feel as real. She says it like someone three times her age. ♪

She's not singing, but I catch her lips moving with the words, her eyes on the trees blurring past. One hand rides the wind, fingers catching invisible currents. Her hair's everywhere—tangled and wild and beautiful. I know I'm not supposed to stare, but I do. She's growing up fast. Faster than I was ready for.

And then—out of nowhere—she throws both arms in the air, chin lifted to the sky, hair whipping in the wind.

"I have no fear!" she shouts, loud enough to startle the birds. "I have only love!"

I laugh—startled, then moved. The kind of laugh that sneaks up on you and stays. Her voice still echoes in the air even after she drops her arms and leans back again, calm like nothing happened.

The music carries us forward. The road narrows. Pines lean closer. Somewhere out there, the ocean waits, pulling the horizon tighter. I glance over. She's leaning back, face tipped to the sky, a soft smile playing at the edge of her mouth.

I don't know if she'll remember this drive. This song. This weather. But I will. I'll remember the way she looked just then—free, young, somewhere between girl and woman, unburdened by everything that will come later.

She looks at me and grins. "I see your gypsy, Mom."

♪ "Gypsy" by Fleetwood Mac

⟲

But inside, her words catch. I didn't know it still showed—that restless part of me I thought I'd buried beneath grocery lists and mortgage payments. The part that once chased summer across coastlines. That wore boots through foreign lands and made decisions by feeling instead of fear.

She still sees her. The gypsy. Maybe I haven't lost her completely after all. The mountain road bends again, leading us closer to the sea. But for now, I let the moment stretch.

American 8445

My headphones soften the world around me, harmonies threading through something quiet, aching. A song about waiting. About reaching for someone who might never reach back. It doesn't demand anything—just lingers. I lean my forehead against the window, watching the Washington coastline far below. The cliffs, the waves, the small winding trails that lead to places I've never been. ♪

My finger trails along the glass, tracing the curve of the shoreline. Somewhere down there, Sophia is walking a path of her own. She doesn't know I'm up here, passing overhead.

She doesn't know I've been thinking about her—how a single message can feel like holding something fragile in your hands, unsure whether to grip it tight or let it go.

A contrail cuts across the sky outside my window, high above us—a thin white scar stretching west, etched by someone else's flight. Not mine. But close. I watch it slowly dissolve, unraveling into nothing. Just vapor. Just a trace.

A record of where someone's been Not where they're going.

♪ *"Helplessly Hoping"* by Crosby, Stills, Nash & Young

I exhale, the breath fogging faintly against the glass. The song fades. The sky softens. Something in me unclenches. Maybe this isn't about holding on anymore. Maybe it never was.

Cape Flattery - Washington

The Cape Flattery trail winds before us, damp earth softened by the salty mist rolling in from the Pacific. The waves crash below, endless and restless, gnawing at the base of the cliffs. Gray hikes a few steps ahead, her ponytail swaying, her movements sure-footed despite the wind tugging at her jacket.

I breathe in the briny air, letting it fill my lungs. The horizon stretches out, infinite. The ocean, the sky—vast and open, untouched by the weight of the past. We reach an overlook, where the world feels like it belongs to the elements alone. Wind, water, sky. Nothing else.

I pause, my gaze drifting upward. A jet contrail slices the blue, a perfect white thread unraveling across the heavens. A path drawn in the sky. A path toward something. Or someone. My fingers tighten slightly on the railing.

There was a time when I watched planes and felt a pang in my chest—a longing for motion, for the kind of life that felt untethered. Now, I don't know what I feel. Gray steps beside me, following my line of sight.

"Mom?" she asks, tilting her head. "What is it?"

I blink, coming back to the present. I squeeze her shoulder, offering a small shrug. "Nothing," I almost say, but the word doesn't come.

I watch the contrail begin to dissolve, fading as the wind pulls

☉

it apart. All paths, even those written in the sky, eventually fade. But maybe that's not the same as disappearing.

Tokaido Shinkansen - Japan

The bullet train moves like a whisper, smooth and relentless, slicing through the Japanese countryside. Through the window, the world unravels in a blur—rice paddies, distant mountains, rooftops of ancient temples peeking through the treetops. Fleeting. Ephemeral. Gone before I can blink. ♪

I keep my camera in my lap, fingers tracing its familiar edges. I could capture the motion, the way the landscape dissolves into streaks of color, but what would that say? That time moves too fast? That beauty is impossible to hold? That the moment you try to freeze something, it's already slipping away?

The businessman across from me sleeps with practiced precision—back straight, chin tucked, briefcase positioned exactly parallel to his knees. To my right, an elderly woman carefully unwraps a bento box, each movement deliberate, as if the presentation matters even when dining alone on a train.

Japan is full of these small, perfect moments. Scenes composed with unconscious care. Lives unfolding in quiet dignity. The kind of beauty that doesn't announce itself but reveals itself to those who pay attention.

I've been here three days, and already my memory cards are filling with images that feel both visually striking and emotionally hollow. Temples. Gardens. Crowded intersections where humanity flows like water. The magazine will be pleased. Jane will call them "evocative," "transportive." But something is missing.

♪ *"God Moving Over the Face of the Water"* by Moby

⦾

I turn away from the window, exhaling. The train presses forward, unbothered by questions like these.

As we approach Kyoto Station, I gather my equipment, checking my itinerary. The Philosopher's Path. Kinkaku-ji. Fushimi Inari. All the expected pilgrimages of a foreign photographer seeking the "real Japan." The irony isn't lost on me.

The station itself is a monument to contradiction—ancient city, ultramodern architecture. Glass and steel soaring over a thousand years of history. I frame a shot of traditional wooden sandals displayed in a shop window, the gleaming metal of the station ceiling reflected in the glass. The juxtaposition is almost too perfect, too easy.

Outside, the April air carries the scent of cherry blossoms and exhaust, another contrast that shouldn't work but somehow does. I hail a taxi, showing the driver the address of my ryokan written in careful Japanese characters.

"Sakura," he says, pointing up at the blooming trees, giving me a questioning look in the rearview mirror.

"Yes," I reply, managing one of the few Japanese words I know.

"Kirei. Beautiful."

He smiles, nodding. The first real connection I've made since arriving.

Philosopher's Path - Kyoto

I walk the Philosopher's Path, where cherry blossoms drift down like the slowest kind of snowfall. The air is thick with spring—floral and

◯◯

fresh, the scent mingling with the soft rustle of water running in the canal beside me.

A local guide—Keiko, a university student earning extra money during peak tourist season—walks beside me, explaining the path's history.

"Named for philosopher Nishida Kitaro," she says in careful English. "He walked here every day, meditating on his way to Kyoto University."

"What did he think about?" I ask, watching a petal land on the surface of the canal, creating ripples that distort the reflection of the trees above.

Keiko tilts her head, considering. "Life. Existence. The nature of reality." She smiles. "And probably lunch, sometimes."

Her small joke catches me off guard, and I laugh—a genuine sound that surprises me. It's been a while.

The path isn't empty, despite the early hour. Elderly locals power-walk past us with purposeful strides. A group of school children in matching hats file by, their teacher counting heads. Other tourists pause every few steps for photos, holding up peace signs against the backdrop of falling blossoms.

"Too many people now," Keiko observes. "If you want to experience the path like Nishida, come at dawn. Or in winter, when no one visits."

I make a note to return early tomorrow, before my train ride back to Tokyo. To see the path in solitude, as it was meant to be walked.

The camera finds its way into my hands. I frame the blossoms, weightless and pure, caught in the golden hour light. *Click*.

⬭

A moment, held forever. But beauty like this is easy. It's what I came here to find.

"Not just the flowers," Keiko suggests quietly, noticing my focus.

"Look there."

She points to an elderly man carefully sweeping fallen petals from the path, his movements rhythmic and unhurried. He's fighting a battle he knows he can't win—tomorrow will bring more blossoms, more beautiful decay—but he continues anyway.

I raise my camera again. *Click.*

This is different. Not just beauty, but meaning. The inevitable cycle of falling and cleaning. Persistence in the face of impermanence.

"Mono no aware," Keiko says, watching me review the shot. "It means—"

"The pathos of things," I finish. "The awareness of impermanence."

She looks surprised. "You know this concept?"

I shrug. "I read about it. It's why I wanted to come during cherry blossom season. To capture something beautiful because it doesn't last."

What I don't say is how much this idea has haunted me. How often I've wondered if photography is an act of preservation or just a way of marking what's already gone.

⊚

Serina - Kirkland

The gelato case stretched before us like a painter's palette—raspberry so vivid it looked electric, pistachio the color of soft moss, lemon bright enough to cut through any lingering sadness.

Gray pressed her hands to the glass, her breath fogging it slightly, eyes wide at all the choices. We didn't speak at first. It felt sacred somehow—this moment of simple abundance, of color and sweetness offered up without asking for anything in return. I watched her lean in, studying each flavor like it held a secret. Stracciatella, blood orange, honey lavender. Tiny, perfect worlds spun from sugar and patience.

I felt it then—that ache and wonder that sometimes arrive together. Life keeps unfolding, one bright discovery at a time. There are always new flavors you haven't tried yet. New colors you didn't know you needed. And sometimes, joy finds you exactly where you are—no boxes, no endings. Just beginnings disguised as small, ordinary moments.

She turned to me, grinning. "We should get the weirdest one," she said. I laughed, the sound lifting something inside my chest, and nodded. Maybe that's how you start again—not with a grand plan, but with two spoons, sticky fingers, and the bravest scoop you can find.

Golden Pavilion - Kyoto

At the Golden Pavilion, the temple shimmers like something pulled from a dream, its gilded reflection rippling across the still water. I wait for the wind to still, for the surface to smooth. The symmetry is perfect. *Click.*

It's beautiful. Breathtaking, even. But the kind of beauty that doesn't fight back. It just exists. Untouched. I don't know why that bothers me.

◎

A Japanese couple nearby pose for a selfie, the wife carefully adjusting her husband's collar before they smile for their own camera. The tenderness of the gesture strikes me. I raise my lens, then lower it. Some moments aren't mine to capture.

"Did you know," says a voice beside me, "this is actually a reconstruction?"

I turn to find a Western man about my age, his camera even more professional than mine. The unspoken brotherhood of photographers abroad.

"The original burned down in 1950," he continues. "Some monk set it on fire, then tried to kill himself. Failed at that too."

"I didn't know," I admit, looking back at the gleaming temple with new eyes.

"Makes it more interesting, right? Not just pretty, but rebuilding after destruction." He extends his hand. "Ari. National Geographic."

"Michael. Wander magazine."

We shake, each sizing up the other's equipment with practiced nonchalance.

"Doing the standard circuit?" he asks.

I nod. "You?"

"Six months in rural Hokkaido. Documenting traditional fishing communities before they disappear." He gestures at the pavilion, at the crowds surrounding it. "Just stopped here on my way home. Couldn't resist the cliché."

I feel a flicker of envy at his assignment—something with depth, with time to develop real understanding. My week-long temple tour suddenly feels shallow in comparison.

"What's the most interesting thing you've found?" I ask, genuinely curious.

Ari considers this. "Probably that the most photogenic moments are rarely the most meaningful." He looks at me with unexpected intensity. "You know what I mean?"

I think of Sophia. Of the bench. Of all the perfect shots I've taken that have never captured what I'm really looking for.

"Yeah," I say. "I know exactly what you mean."

We exchange cards before parting ways. His has a stunning black and white image of an elderly Japanese fisherman hauling in nets. Mine just has my name and contact information. Another contrast that stays with me as I continue my tour.

Fushimi Inari Shrine - Kyoto

I arrive at Fushimi Inari as the day begins to fade. Most tourists have left, heading back to dinner in the city. The endless vermilion gates take on a deeper hue in the late afternoon light, shadows lengthening between them.

I move through the corridor of torii gates, their brilliant color stretching in every direction. It's a place meant for capturing—movement, light, shadow shifting with each step.

❪❂❫

A fox statue guards the path, its stone features worn by centuries of reverence. Inari's messenger. I photograph it against the gates, the composition almost arranging itself.

The climb is steeper than I expected. My breathing becomes labored as I ascend the mountain, passing through tunnel after tunnel of gates. Some sections are crowded with names—businesses who donated for their inscription—while others stand anonymous, their benefactors long forgotten.

I pause at a small shrine halfway up, where an old woman lights incense, her lips moving in silent prayer. I wait respectfully, keeping my distance, camera lowered.

When she finishes, she notices me waiting and gestures toward the incense. "You try," she says in limited English.

I hesitate, then step forward. She shows me how to bow, how to light the incense, how to wave the smoke toward myself. I'm not religious, but there's something powerful in participating rather than just observing.

"What do you pray for?" she asks.

The question catches me off guard. What do I want? The question hangs there, exposing a void I've been carrying for longer than I care to admit. I travel the world capturing beauty for others, yet return to empty hotel rooms night after night. I document connection without experiencing it. I frame perfect moments that never feel like they include me.

"Somebody to love," I say finally. "The real kind. Not just conversation. Not just proximity. Something that holds." The words leave my mouth before I have time to rehearse them—raw and louder than I meant, like a chord struck in an empty room. ♪

♪ "Somebody to Love" by Jefferson Airplane

Where did that come from? It didn't feel like something I thought up on the spot. It felt older than that. Like something I've always known but never dared to say out loud. Maybe it's been building for years—through airports and hotel rooms, the faces I've photographed and left behind. Through the silence I've called freedom.

I glance at the woman across from me—expecting a reaction, maybe. But she just nods. As if she understands. And maybe she does.

I take a breath. There's a weight to the truth, but also a strange lightness. Like naming something is the first step to changing it. Or at least, letting it matter.

I continue climbing, the physical exertion clearing my mind. Near the summit, the gates become more spaced out, offering glimpses of the city below, lights beginning to flicker on as evening approaches.

Then—A flash of black, curly hair. My breath catches. I turn sharply, camera lowering.

Sophia?

No. Just a local woman, adjusting her scarf before disappearing around a bend. I exhale, pressing my lips together, heart still pounding against my ribs. How many times has this happened? How many times have I thought I saw her—on a passing train, in a crowded café, across some distant street—only for reality to snap me back?

I grip my camera, raising it once more, but something inside me has shifted. These places—they are beautiful. They have stories. But they are not my story. That story is half a world away. And I'm still trying to find it.

At the very top of the mountain, the path opens to a clearing with

⊙

a view of Kyoto spread out below. The city glows in the gathering dusk, temples and skyscrapers sharing the same skyline. Ancient and modern. Sacred and mundane. All coexisting.

As I begin my descent, I pass a small wooden board hanging among the gates. Visitors have written wishes on small wooden plaques—ema—and hung them here for the gods to consider. Most are in Japanese, but some are in English, French, German. Universal hopes.

Good health for my mother.
For the courage to begin again.
Success in my exams.
Forgive what I cannot fix.
To be seen. To be loved anyway.

I run my fingers over the weathered wood. Someone took these silent longings and gave them physical form, hanging them where the wind could touch them.

The last light is fading as I reach the bottom of the mountain. I pause to look back up at the pathway I've just traveled—thousands of gates, thousands of thresholds, leading up into darkness now.

Tomorrow I'll return to Tokyo, then back to the island. I'll edit these photos, send them to my editor, move on to the next assignment. But something tells me Japan isn't finished with me yet, or I with it.

In my hotel that night, I review the day's images. The old man sweeping petals on the Philosopher's Path. The rebuilt Golden Pavilion gleaming despite its violent history. The fox statue standing guard at Fushimi Inari. The old woman praying. All beautiful, all telling stories deeper than their surfaces.

But it's the last photo I took—the wooden wishes hanging among the gates—that holds my attention longest. These weren't on my shot list. They weren't what I came for. But they're what I found.

I send most of the images to Jane, but I keep this one for myself. Some photographs aren't meant to be published. Some are just reminders of questions still unanswered, wishes still hanging, waiting for the wind to carry them somewhere they might be heard.

The house is quiet. That kind of deep, domestic quiet that settles only after the dishwasher has stopped humming, the lights have dimmed, and everyone's tucked into their own corners of the night.

I lean against the counter, warm mug in hand, watching steam curl into the low kitchen light. Outside the window, the trees shift gently in the wind. A low creak echoes from the hallway as the floorboards settle. My body is still, but my mind won't stop moving.

Not the lonely kind of quiet I used to dread when Gray was little and asleep upstairs. This is a different quiet. The kind that settles after the house has gotten used to someone being gone.

She's just fifteen minutes away—but somehow that small distance has stretched wider than I thought it would. I should be used to it by now. The Sunday night FaceTimes. The shared playlists. The occasional photo of her dorm room when it's clean enough to brag about.

And I am. Mostly. But some nights—like this one—I still find myself listening for her footsteps on the stairs.

I miss her shoes by the door. It used to drive me crazy, the way she'd kick them off in a different direction every time—muddy sneakers, thrifted boots, that pair of checkered Vans she wore until the soles gave out. Now the entryway stays neat, and I hate it. There's something so final about an undisturbed welcome mat.

Funny how shoes tell you everything. The smaller ones that once lined up like little ducklings. The scuffed ballet flats from that stubborn recital year. The hiking boots from her no-makeup, mountain-girl phase. They used to mark time as clearly as a calendar.

Now there's nothing there but space.

She's coming home this weekend, and I've already started setting things aside: the good towels, her favorite granola, the silly little candle that smells like her favorite bakery. It's ridiculous how much I miss her. How much I'm looking forward to hearing her keys rattle in the door. And seeing her shoes in the hallway again. No matter where she leaves them.

I glance at my phone. No new texts. I scroll through our last exchange. A photo of her with her cousins, all fake smiles and goofy poses. A thumbs-up emoji. "LOL." "Miss you." "Be safe."

But not "I love you."

I can't remember the last time I told her I loved her. Really told her. Not just a drive-by "Love you" at the end of a call, not a scribbled note in a lunchbox back in middle school. I mean the kind of I love you that makes someone pause. That roots itself somewhere deeper than the surface.

I take a sip of tea, suddenly uncertain. When did those words become so rare? Is it because I've been holding them in too long? Saving them for someone who never came back?

❂

The words feel fragile and enormous at the same time. Not because they're unfamiliar—but because they're true. They hold weight. Memory. Hope. Risk.

They're the words I didn't say enough to Ethan when it still mattered. The words I didn't say to myself when I needed them most. The words I've never stopped wanting to hear from someone who knew how to mean them.

And now—Gray. My girl, growing up too fast, already slipping into a world I won't always be able to protect her from. I don't want her to ever wonder. Not for a second.

I pick up my phone. Thumb hovers. Then moves.

Just wanted to say—I love you. So much. Always.

I stare at it for a moment. Then press *Send.*

The message vanishes, delivered in a quiet burst of pixels and breath I didn't realize I was holding. No confetti. No fanfare. Just truth. Sent into the space between us. I set the phone down and let myself breathe.

What does *I love you* mean, really?

It's not about romance. Not always. It's not even about certainty. It's a tether. A light left on. A way of saying:

I see you. I choose you. I'm still here.

And sometimes, that's enough. Even if you don't hear it back right away. Even if the space between hearts feels impossibly wide.

⟨⟨O⟩⟩

Love, when it's real, holds its shape in the quiet. Just like this.

American 8446

We're somewhere over the Pacific now—hours into the flight, with nothing but clouds below, stars above, and the lullaby of cabin air. Most of the passengers have drifted into that odd half-sleep of long-haul travel—headphones in, blankets curled, dreaming somewhere between time zones. But, I'm wide awake.

Outside my window, the world is ink-black, the wingtip light blinking like a heartbeat. I shift in my seat, trying to get comfortable, but restlessness creeps beneath my skin.

Across the aisle, a couple sits shoulder to shoulder beneath the glow of a shared reading light. They're about my age—maybe late fifties. The man has a paperback open in one hand, the other resting on his wife's knee. Her eyes are closed, head tilted against his shoulder, mouth parted slightly in sleep. He's not reading anymore. Just looking at her. Quietly. Like she's the most beautiful thing he's ever seen. *

I know that feeling.

He brushes a strand of hair from her cheek, so gently I almost don't notice. He doesn't say a word—just keeps his hand there a moment longer than necessary, like maybe that one gesture says everything he's ever needed to say. The woman stirs, leans in, and whispers something in his ear. Three words.

I don't hear them, but I know what she said. *I love you.* He doesn't answer right away. Just turns his hand over in his lap and takes hers. No fanfare. No performance. Just quiet contact. The kind that doesn't need repeating.

* *"The Slow Regard of Silent Things"* by Patrick Rothfuss

Something in me settles and sharpens at the same time—not envy, not sadness, just recognition. I've said those words before. But never like that. Never with that kind of ease. With Martone, they came out because they were supposed to. Expected. Part of the rhythm of a relationship that looked right on paper. But there's a difference between words you mean, and words you feel all the way through.

I look away, not because the moment is too intimate, but because it strikes something I wasn't prepared to feel. The ache—not the missing-someone kind, but the knowing-exactly-who-you-miss kind.

The truth is, when it's real—when it's right—those words don't feel heavy. They don't catch in your throat or sit awkward on your tongue. They just... fit. Saying I love you is only hard when you're trying to convince yourself of something. When the words are a bridge, not a home. But when they're true, they land like breath.

With Sophia, the words aren't forced. They aren't even a choice. They're simply there—quiet, certain, waiting. What scares me isn't the saying. It's how easy it feels to mean them. Because once they're spoken, there's no taking them back. No pretending they don't matter.

Saying I love you to her wouldn't be a risk. It would be a return. Loving Sophia doesn't feel sudden. It feels remembered, like something I've carried for so long I didn't realize how much space it was taking up inside me. The camera has always made it easier. I could frame the world without being in it, see everything without risking anything. But this—this doesn't fit in a frame. It asks me to step out from behind the lens and simply be seen.

And yeah—if anyone else heard this, they'd probably highlight it and write "seek help" in the margin and tell me to get evaluated for romantic hallucinations. Fall for someone you've never even spoken to? Sounds like a case study in delusion, possibly with footnotes. But it doesn't feel crazy. It feels like finally telling the truth.

I don't know her—not truly. Just a few passing glimpses frozen in memory, and a message I nearly didn't send. But the feeling? It's always been there. Quiet. Unshaken. Familiar in a way that defies logic. That's the revelation. Not that I love her—but that the hardest words I've ever held could also be the most inevitable.

Golden Gardens Park - Ballard

The gravel crunches beneath my tires as I pull into the parking lot. I cut the engine, but I don't move right away. Instead, I rest my forehead against the steering wheel, exhaling slowly, watching through the windshield.

At the water's edge, a young couple moves together in a quiet, playful dance. He twirls her, their bare feet pressing into the wet sand, her laughter lifting into the wind. She stumbles, and he catches her, holding her close—their joy effortless. Natural. Like something that was always meant to be.

They remind me of that couple at *Pike Place*, spinning to "Moonshadow" like no one else existed. That kind of ease. That kind of presence.

I watch them longer than I mean to. There's something about how they reach for each other—unthinking, unguarded. No hesitation. Just connection. And it hits me—not as envy, but as something quieter. Recognition. Longing. It's not that I miss something I had.

It's that I've never had it at all.

Not like that. Not the kind of intimacy that feels weightless. Certain. Not the kind of touch that says you're safe here without a single word. And still, some part of me believes I could. That it's not too late. Or maybe just wants to believe. Or maybe... that hope is the most dangerous part of all.

Above them, just over the water, the day moon lingers—pale and ghostly in the vast blue sky. Faint, but still there. Always watching. ♪

It shouldn't be there. Not really. Not during the day. And yet there it is, like it forgot to leave or didn't want to. A quiet contradiction.

I step out of the car, my sandals dangling from my fingers as I walk toward the shore. The sand is cool beneath my feet, grounding me, though my thoughts still drift.

A weathered bench sits at the edge of the path, its wood smoothed by time and salt air. I pause, running my fingers over the two merging circles carved into the surface—two shapes becoming one, their edges blurred, inseparable.

I sit for a moment. Let the air wrap around me. My gaze lifts again to the horizon. The ocean stretches out endlessly, steady and sure. The wind moves around me, brushing against my skin, tangling through my hair. I close my eyes, letting it carry something away. Maybe the weight of what I've been holding. Maybe the hope of something new.

The day moon hangs above it all—unfazed, unbothered, present. A contradiction. A quiet reminder that not everything needs to make sense to be real. And I wonder—just idly, quietly—if he sees it too.

Michael.

The name still feels unfamiliar in my mouth, but something about

♪ *"Noom"* by Mountain Boy

his message settled in deeper than it should have. The way he wrote makes me wonder. About who he might be. About how someone I've never met could write something that felt less like a stranger reaching out... and more like someone remembering me. Not the woman I've become out of necessity. The younger version. The braver one. The messier one. The real one.

It makes no logical sense. And yet—here I am. Sitting by the sea, eyes lifted to a faint moon that doesn't belong in daylight, asking questions I can't answer. I pull my knees in closer, wrapping my arms around them as the wind shifts.

Maybe it doesn't mean anything. Or maybe it does. Maybe he's out there, somewhere, not thinking of me at all. Or maybe... he is.

What I do know—I'm not thinking about the Jogger. And that says something. I need to stop pretending it doesn't. I close my eyes for a moment and let the wind move through me. I don't know where this goes. Or if it goes anywhere at all. But for now, I'm still looking up.

South Beach - San Juan Island

The sand shifts beneath my boots as I walk the shoreline with my hands buried deep in my pockets. The air smells of salt and driftwood, familiar in a way that makes my chest ache.

Ahead of me, two sets of footprints weave side by side in the damp sand. Someone walked this path before me.

Together.

I follow them without thinking, my gaze tracing the fading impressions, until my feet stop on their own.

◐

I crouch, searching for the right kind of rock—flat, smooth, the perfect weight. My fingers find one, and I straighten, rolling it over in my palm. I take a slow breath, then send it skimming across the surface.

One. Two. Three skips before it vanishes, sinking beneath the waves. The ripples spread outward, then fade, like it was never there at all.

I sink onto a driftwood log, elbows resting on my knees, watching the water pull back and forth in its endless rhythm.

Above the horizon, barely visible in the late afternoon sky, hangs the day moon. I stare at it for a long time. A ghost of something that should only exist at night. A presence that lingers when it should have disappeared.

It makes me think of her. Her face—I could draw it without thinking. It's stayed with me, unchanged, like a photograph the mind won't let fade. Her voice, though—I've never heard it. And yet somehow, she's lived under my skin all these years. Quiet. Persistent. Unshakable.

The moon shouldn't be there. But it is. *So is she.* I lean back, tilting my face toward the wind, breathing in the sea air, letting it press against my skin.

The Jogger. I can't say his real name. I'm not sure why. It's not a secret, not something I'm trying to erase. It just sticks somewhere between my ribs and my throat, like speaking it aloud would make the weight of it too real. His hurt, not mine.

He didn't do anything wrong. That's what makes it harder. He was kind. Thoughtful. Always brought me my almond milk latte without asking—just the way I liked it. He'd press it into my hands like it meant something, like he was offering a piece of himself. And maybe he was.

⚭

But even as I thanked him, even as I sat across from him at the same café table week after week, I felt like I was somewhere else. Not out of distraction or boredom. It was something quieter than that. A distance I couldn't cross, no matter how much I wanted to. There was no spark. No ache. No pull. Just the soft hum of expectation, and the growing sense that I wasn't where I was supposed to be.

He looked at me like he was waiting for the next chapter to begin. And I—I kept turning back to the previous page, looking for something I couldn't name.

When I ended it, I tried to be gentle. I chose my words carefully. I wanted to spare him, even as I knew I couldn't. I watched the way his shoulders dropped, how his voice got quiet. He didn't argue. Didn't beg. But the sadness in his eyes told me everything.

I don't like hurting people. But I've also learned I can't keep living in almosts. And with him, that's all it ever was. Comfort. Not connection. And I think—I've known that all along.

He deserved someone who looked at him like a beginning. And I… I was still learning to stop living in endings.

☾

The world is on the edge of waking, but I am not part of it yet. Somewhere beyond these walls, a ferry horn echoes across the water. A single bird answers, its call sharp in the early quiet. Ordinary sounds. The rhythm of morning beginning again.

I flick on the desk lamp, spilling warm light over the cluttered desk—loose papers, a half-finished cup of coffee gone cold, my camera sitting idle. Moseley is curled in my office chair, paws tucked beneath him like a cat in permanent contemplation. He stirs at the sound, one ear twitching, but doesn't wake.

I don't move at first. My gaze settles on the wastebasket. A deep breath. Then another. I step forward, kneeling slowly, my fingers hovering just above the crumpled newspaper clipping. The edges are bent, the creases deep. For a second, I wonder if I should leave it there—let this be the moment I finally move forward.

But I can't.

People say old love fades. That time softens the edges, replaces the ache with new mornings, new hands, new names. Most of the time, that's true. We trade one story for another, not out of cruelty, but survival. Even the deepest feelings eventually dissolve under the weight of memory—made gentle, made distant, made quiet.

But this one never did. And it never will.

It didn't blur. It didn't vanish. It just settled deeper. Became part of the framework. A fixed point in a life that's kept moving.

Carefully, I pull it from the discarded papers, smoothing it out with deliberate precision. Sophia's face reappears. Even through the creases, through the passage of time, she is still there. I study the image—her standing on the court, frozen mid-motion, the raw, unguarded joy on her face. A girl I've been trying to let go of. I wasn't ready then. Maybe I'm still not. But this... this stays. Never to be forgotten.

The first hints of daylight filter through the blinds, stretching across my desk in golden slats. The clipping rests there now—not discarded, not forgotten. I exhale, rubbing my fingers across my jaw.

Moseley stretches, blinking at the light, then lifts his head with a slow, lazy yawn. I pick him up, pressing my face briefly into his fur before sinking into the chair. The house is still. The world keeps waking. And I'm still here.

Gray is home for the weekend, sitting cross-legged on the couch, balancing a plate of lunch on her lap, completely at ease. She is humming softly between bites, savoring every mouthful like she has all the time in the world—until she doesn't. She moves fast when the mood strikes, when her next idea hits. There is always something stirring just beneath her surface. Always fire.

I sit beside her, but I'm not really present. My phone rests in my hand, thumb hovering over the Instagram icon. The screen glows, waiting. Just a tap. That's all it would take. One tap, and I'd step into something unknown. But I don't. Yet again.

Instead, I watch her from the corner of my eye. Her curls are pulled up into a messy bun, a few loose strands catching the light. Her sweatshirt is oversized, the sleeves slipping past her wrists like they always did when she was little. She looks so much like me at her age it makes my chest ache. But there's more steel in her. More spark. Her personality reminds me of Allison. Unafraid to speak the truth.

She's home—but not mine in the same way anymore. And I miss it. I miss her footsteps on the stairs in the morning, the mess of her backpack in the hallway, the muted thud of her bedroom door closing at night. I miss knowing she's just down the hall, even if we don't speak. Now, I count the weekends. I measure time in arrivals and departures, in grocery lists that no longer include her favorite snacks, in laundry baskets that stay mostly empty. But this is what's supposed to happen. She's growing forward, just like I did. And I'm proud of her—so proud. I just didn't expect it to feel so quiet sometimes.

She laughs at something on her phone, and the sound tugs at something deep in my chest. I smile, even though she doesn't see it. She's here. That should be enough. Still, I already feel time slipping through my hands like something warm that doesn't want to be held.

Gray sets her empty plate on the coffee table and gives me a light nudge with her shoulder. I nudge her back, palm against her thigh. She grins. I grin too. Then, like we're kids again, the gentle shoves turn playful. She smacks my arm. I smack hers. She laughs. I laugh—one of those deep, real laughs that rises up before I even realize it's coming. And just like that, the weight in my chest lifts for a moment.

She stands, stretching as she walks toward the kitchen. My eyes drop to the plate she's left behind. I snap my fingers, pointing at it. Without missing a beat, she turns, mirrors my gesture, and snaps right back. But instead of picking up the plate, she points to the cross-stitch hanging on the wall:

Everything Happens for a Reason.

I used to believe it without question. That life unfolded the way it was meant to. That pain had purpose. That detours were just direction in disguise. But the years wore down that certainty. Loss has a way of rearranging what you think you know. It makes you ask harder questions. And sometimes, the answers don't come.

I've seen good people break. I've watched love falter. I've waited on things that never came back. If there's a reason for all of it, it's not always one I understand. Still—somewhere, deep beneath the ache and doubt,

◎

I want to believe it. That there's a thread tying all of this together. That maybe I haven't missed my chance. And maybe he hasn't either.

The air shifts. The moment holds. I look at the words on the wall— the ones I stitched by hand so long ago, full of certainty I barely recognize now. Gray looks at me, her head tilted, her voice quieter than before.

"Mom... what do you have to lose?"

Maybe everything. Maybe nothing. Gray isn't a child anymore. Not someone to shield from every shadow. She sees things. She always has.

"You already stitched the truth on the wall," she says. "Maybe it's time to believe it again."

Her voice settles into the quiet like it belongs there. No push. No pressure. Just truth, wrapped in something steady and strangely fearless. I look at her—really look at her—and I wonder, not for the first time.

Where does she get this shit?

This clarity. This grit. This knowing. It's like she was born with a compass I've spent my whole life trying to build from broken parts. I reach up, brush a strand of hair behind her ear, my fingers lingering longer than they need to. She doesn't flinch. Just meets my gaze and holds it. I shake my head slowly—not at her, but at the awe of it.

The unshakable wonder of being taught by your own child.

I don't have the answer. But tonight, I might not need it. In my lap, my fingers tighten around the phone. I'm not ready. But maybe being ready isn't the point. Maybe belief doesn't have to come first. Maybe just showing up is enough.

02

00:00:30:21:36:16

The brush glides over the weathered siding in slow, methodical strokes. Fresh white paint covers the years, softening cracks and sun-faded wood with every pass. The old adage floats to mind, clear and familiar:

Paint hides a multitude of sins.

I pause on the next stroke, watching how the bristles smooth over the imperfections—covering, but not erasing. The damage is still there underneath. The rot. The wear. But now it's quieter. Tucked behind something clean. I used to think that phrase was about deception— about covering up, pretending. But maybe it's also about mercy. About offering a second skin to something that's been weathered. Not to fool anyone. Just to begin again.

I focus on the rhythm—dip, sweep, cover. The scent of paint hangs in the warm afternoon air, sharp and clean. Everything is quiet except for the occasional rustle of wind through the trees, like the world is holding its breath while I work.

Above me, Moseley perches on the roof, watching with the lazy judgment only a cat can muster. A good day. A simple one. No noise, no expectations. Then—

Ding.

The sound cuts through the silence like a crack of lightning. My hand jerks. The ladder shifts dangerously beneath me. The bucket tilts—White paint crashes to the ground in an explosion of splatter.

I grip the ladder, heart hammering, breath coming fast. For a moment, I just stay there, hands clenching the rungs, waiting for the world to steady.

Then, slowly, carefully, I climb down, wiping my hands on my jeans, barely aware of the mess at my feet.

I already know before I check. The phone glows in my palm.

Sophia.

The name tightens my chest. I stare. It's real. She's real. And she has written back. I swipe to open it, pulse pounding in my ears.

Michael, your message was an unexpected and pleasant surprise. Thank you for your thoughtful words. They resonated with me in ways I didn't expect. I find myself at a loss for words.

My breath catches. I read it again. And again. Thirty-five years. But who's counting? A lifetime of wondering, searching, imagining. And now, she is here, on my screen, speaking to me. My fingers hover over the keyboard. What do you even say to something like this?

You're very welcome, Sophia. No words are necessary.

I stop. No. Too formal. Too small. I erase it, my thoughts tangled in the weight of the moment. I try again.

Reaching out felt impossible. Hearing from you feels unreal.

I hesitate, my thumb hovering over the send button. The seconds stretch long and thin. What if this is it? What if I ruin it?

Moseley flicks his tail above me, unimpressed. I exhale, pressing *Send* before I can overthink. The message disappears. The wait begins. I don't know how long I stare at the screen. Seconds feel like minutes. The air is thick, unsteady. Then—

Ding.

My heart leaps. My hands almost tremble. I open the message.

Some words find us exactly when we need them.

A slow, incredulous smile spreads across my face. The weight of years shifts, just a little. Moseley blinks down at me, unreadable. But I swear—just for a moment—he looks almost satisfied.

The evening air carried the scent of the Sound—salt and seaweed, cool and endless. A breeze tugged at the edge of my sweater as I sat on the porch, the last blush of daylight painting the horizon in streaks of tangerine and indigo. The hush of twilight had always calmed me, the way it softened everything sharp.

In my lap, the pages of *The Little Prince* shifted with the wind, the familiar weight of the old book grounding me. I'd kept it all these years—ever since the day it was left behind on the café table, folded napkin tucked inside like a secret. I never did find out who left it. Never saw anyone come back for it. But I hadn't been able to let it go either.

My fingers moved to the underlined passage, smoothing the paper like it might offer an answer I'd missed before.

One sees clearly only with the heart. Anything essential is invisible to the eye.

I traced the words slowly, like they might mean something new now. They had stayed with me, haunted me gently. What had they seen in me that day? What part of me had reminded someone of this little book full of stars and solitude and quiet truth?

I didn't know. I'd read this passage a hundred times, but tonight, it lingered differently. The words no longer felt like a riddle I had to solve—they felt like an offering. A small truth waiting for me to grow into it. Maybe we carry certain words with us until we're ready to feel them. And maybe I was closer now.

The breeze lifted the corner of the page again. I let it go, just for a moment, and watched the paper dance. Then I turned my gaze to the sky, breathing in the stillness, letting the words settle into the space between my ribs—where wonder lives, and understanding begins.

My thoughts drifted, scattered like leaves, just as a soft chime broke through the quiet. I glanced at my phone on the table beside me.

A new message. From him.

I hesitate before picking it up, my pulse quickening just slightly. I swipe the screen and—A photo fills my vision.

An ice cream cone, toppled onto the pavement, its once-perfect swirl now melting into the cracks of the sidewalk.

In my world, this is considered a serious tragedy.

A small, unexpected laugh escaped me. I shook my head, smiling. I hadn't realized how long it had been since something as simple as a message had made me feel that—lifted, seen. Like someone knew how to press gently against the silence without demanding anything in return.

I sink back into the chair, the book slipping slightly from my lap, forgotten. My gaze drifts past the railing, toward the distant horizon. The sky has deepened into twilight, the first stars timidly making their appearance. A dropped ice cream cone. A moment that shouldn't matter, but somehow does.

The kitchen hums with the quiet sounds of morning—the low whir of the espresso machine, the gentle clink of porcelain against the counter. Steam curls into the air as I press the button, watching the dark espresso drip steadily into the shot glass, its surface blooming with golden crema.

I reach for my favorite mug. The *Café Sonnet* logo is worn but familiar beneath my fingertips, the edges slightly faded from years of washing. I trace the lines absentmindedly, remembering the day I sketched the design in a battered notebook, never imagining it would

◍

become something real—something people would hold in their hands, just like this.

I pour the espresso into my mug, the rich aroma curling around me, grounding me. The steam wand hisses as I froth the milk, tilting the pitcher just so, coaxing the foam into soft peaks. The pour is instinctive, my hand steady as the milk swirls into the espresso.

A heart blooms in the foam—simple, whole. My signature. I smile, just a little. Then—

Chime.

The sound pulls me from the moment. I reach for my phone on the counter, my pulse quickening before I even see the screen.

A new message. From him.

I swipe it open, and a photo fills my vision. A massive train wreck. Derailment, destruction, total carnage.

What I see in the morning mirror without coffee.

A soft laugh escapes me before I can stop it. I shake my head, bringing the mug to my lips. The first sip is smooth, familiar, warming me from the inside out. I close my eyes for a moment, savoring it— not just the coffee, but the quiet thread of connection weaving its way through my morning.

Funny thing is—I never even liked coffee. Not really. Not until I moved to Washington, where it's not just a drink—it's a ritual, a rhythm, a state of being. People here don't just drink coffee. They orbit around

it. They talk about beans and roasts the way other people talk about wine. They brew like it's a spiritual practice.

At first, I resisted. I was a tea drinker. Quiet, reserved, mildly smug. But Washington wore me down in the best way. The rain, the early gray mornings, the scent of roasted beans curling out of every corner café—until one day I just gave in.

And now, here I am. A convert. A believer. I look forward to it every morning—the measured scoop of grounds, the hum of the latte machine heating up, the sharp hiss of steam. It's become more than caffeine. It's the opening note of my day. The part that tells me: you're here, you're awake, you're still moving forward.

I take another sip and glance back at the screen. Michael's text still glows softly, absurd and perfect in its timing. And just like the coffee, it warms me—unexpectedly. Completely.

The air is thick with the scent of earth and green things growing. Around me, the soft hum of voices blends with the rhythmic scrape of trowels cutting into soil. Someone laughs, a warm, unguarded sound, and the breeze carries it across the garden like sunlight filtering through leaves.

I press my fingers into the dirt, patting the soil around the base of a young lavender plant. Its silvery-green leaves tremble slightly in the wind, already part of something larger—something rooted, steady. I wipe the back of my glove against my cheek, not realizing I've only smeared more dirt across my skin.

Chime.

◎

I glance at my phone, lying on the gardening tray beside me. The screen glows in the afternoon light.

A new message. From him.

I strip off one glove, wiping my palm against my jeans before picking up the phone.

A *Cinnabon* storefront stares back at me, its iconic blue-and-white sign glowing like a beacon of comfort and indulgence.

When I envision Heaven, this is what I see.

A slow smile tugs at my lips before I can stop it. I shake my head, thumb hovering over the screen. The scent of lavender lingers on my fingertips, mixing with the warm earth, the sweat on my skin, the crisp breeze curling through the garden.

I still don't know him. Just a stranger. And yet… this is the third time he's made me smile without trying. Or maybe he is trying, but not in the usual way. Not performative. Just… easy. Earnest. The kind of person who sees a *Cinnabon* and thinks of heaven. That tells me something, doesn't it? Maybe he's someone who still finds joy in small, ridiculous things. Maybe he's someone who shares it when he does.

I exhale, looking back at the tiny plant nestled in the dirt. Rooted. Growing. Something about that feels right.

The scent of vanilla and butter lingers in the warm kitchen as I press my hands into the cool countertop, rolling the last bit of cookie dough between my palms. The dough is soft, pliable—easier to shape than my thoughts. I scoop another spoonful onto the baking sheet, spacing them perfectly apart. Everything in order. Everything controlled.

Chime.

I glance at my phone, dusted lightly with flour. Gray.

So, how's it going with Mr. Instagram?

A familiar, nervous energy ripples through me. I lean against the counter, stealing a quick peek at the cookies in the oven before typing.

It's been good. He makes me laugh.

The words feel too simple, too small to hold the way Michael's messages linger in my mind long after I read them.

I set the phone down, watching the oven timer tick down.

Chime.

I wipe my hands on a dish towel and pick up the phone.

So... are you gonna meet him or what? You need more than a pen pal.

I exhale slowly, my fingers hovering over the keyboard.

I don't know. What if he's not the same in person?
He could be Hannibal Lecter.

I smirk to myself as I hit *Send*, but the humor barely soothes the gnawing uncertainty.

◌

Worst case, you excuse yourself to the bathroom and bolt!
Or he could be... Edward Lewis!! ♪

I shake my head, laughing softly as I check the cookies, golden and rising. But the moment fades. My hands rest on the oven mitts, unmoving.

I don't know if I have the energy for another relationship.

The words sit heavy on the screen. It's the closest I've come to admitting the truth, even to myself. The phone chimes again—Gray, quick, unrelenting.

Mom, it's coffee, not an engagement!
You need someone to take care of YOU for once!

I swallow. The warmth of the kitchen suddenly feels too thick.

But meeting him would make it real.

I set the phone down, running a hand through my curls.

Exactly! Life's too short to play it safe.

Safe. That's what I've been, isn't it? Safe. Careful. Always choosing the path with the least risk. The one where I don't get hurt. I pick up the phone, slowly typing.

How do you know all this?!

Gray's response comes with almost comedic timing.

Speed Racer says if you're not living on the edge,
you're taking up too much space.

♪ *"It Must Have Been Love"* by Roxette

I tilt my head back with a groan. Is she for real?

I am not sure how I feel about my daughter getting advice from a cartoon.

The oven timer dings. The cookies are ready.

You know what I'm gonna say next...

I already do: *What do I have to lose.*

I grab a potholder, hesitating only a second before typing my reply.

Don't forget pepper spray?!

The cookies smell like comfort. Like home. Not just this home, but the kind built through repetition—warm ovens, fogged windows, the soft clink of a mug set on the counter. It's the smell of late mornings and early memories, of Christmas Eves and birthday mornings, of Gray sneaking extra dough when she thought I wasn't looking.

It's the quiet promise of a place where things feel safe. Like the first hiss of the coffeepot at sunrise. The scent of bacon curling through the air. Cinnamon, vanilla, fresh laundry on a Sunday afternoon. The kind of comfort that doesn't shout, but settles in slowly. The kind that tells you:

This is where you're known. But being known… that's the part that scares me. What if he sees past all of this? The kitchen. The carefulness. The version of me I've curated in messages and half-jokes. What if he sees the cracks I've spent so long patching up with cookies and kindness?

And what if—somehow—he still stays?

☾

The thought lingers, strange and unfamiliar. It brushes against something I've kept quiet for years. The idea that being known doesn't always mean being hurt. Maybe it could mean being found.

☾

The afternoon light drapes the room in gold, filtering through the blinds in soft, shifting patterns. I sit on the couch, the familiar weight of Grandfather's guitar resting against me, fingers instinctively picking through the delicate chords of "Moonshadow." The melody is slow, deliberate—hesitant, like the space between breaths. Then—*Ding.*

The sound slices through the quiet. My fingers falter, the last note lingering unfinished in the air. I let out a slow breath, shifting the guitar slightly as I reach for my phone. A single name on the screen.

Sophia.

My chest tightens. I swipe open the message.

Your messages over the last few weeks have been a bright spot for me. But... the idea of meeting up makes me a little nervous.

I stare at the words, my heartbeat loud in my ears. She's nervous. I understand that. I do. But she didn't say no. My thumbs hover over the keyboard. I exhale, pressing the words into existence.

Choosing hope over fear is never easy. I'm nervous too. Very much so.

I hit *Send.* The moment stretches, breath held, waiting.

Ding.

My stomach flips.

☉

Then maybe we should face our fears together?

I blink at the words.

Together.

That word lodges somewhere deep, startling in its gentleness. All this time I thought I had to walk into the unknown alone. And now— she's offering to stand beside me.

I smile and begin to type.

I'd love to face them with you. Especially if there's coffee involved.

Ding.

Want to trade Instagram for coffee then?

I freeze. She's saying… She's saying yes.

I stare at the screen, unblinking. The words blur slightly. My fingers tighten around the phone as the weight of this moment crashes over me. This isn't just a message. It's the answer to something I've been searching for—for thirty-five years. ♪

Laughter bubbles out of me, abrupt, disbelieving. It escapes before I can stop it, rolling through the room, shaking loose something inside my ribs. My hands shake as I type, my pulse a staccato rhythm against my skin.

A thousand times, yes.

♪ "You're the One" by Greta Van Fleet

◐

Send. I press a hand to my chest, trying to steady the pounding inside. The phone vibrates again.

I know a place. Café Hagen in Lake Union. How about Saturday at 2?

My breath hitches. Saturday. Two days from now. She's real. Not just a name on a screen. Not just a memory of a girl on a bench. In two days, I'll be sitting across from her.

The phone nearly slips from my fingers as I reread the message— once, twice. As if the letters might rearrange into something else. Something impossible. But they don't. They stay exactly as they are.

Another burst of laughter—louder, lighter, unrestrained. I rake a hand through my hair, grinning so hard my face aches.

Perfect. Saturday can't come soon enough.

I stare at the screen, barely breathing. I stare at the screen, barely breathing. The three dots appear... then vanish... *Ding.*

Ditto.

I exhale sharply, gripping my guitar without thinking. My fingers fly across the strings, the melody of "Moonshadow" tumbling out, no longer hesitant. The notes are brighter now. Full of something electric, something untamed. Something that feels like light, like laughter, like hope.

This is real. It's happening. And for once, instead of doubt, instead of fear—it just feels right.

I set the phone down and just stand there, the living room suddenly feeling too still—like the moment is waiting for me to catch up.

It's real now. Not a message. Not a maybe. Not a gentle flirtation I can keep at a safe distance. I said yes. He said yes. And in two days, I'll walk into a café and see him—Michael—for the first time. A stranger.

There's no logic to it. I've never heard his voice. I don't know what he looks like, how he drinks his coffee, what he does when he's nervous. I have only fragments—the careful way he chooses words in his messages, the hint of something patient and unhurried in how he writes. Not enough to build a real person from, yet somehow I feel I've known him before.

My fingers tremble slightly as I reach for my tea, the mug still warm against my palm. Something inside me vibrates like a tuning fork struck just right—not anxiety, but recognition. And yet, it doesn't feel reckless. It doesn't feel dangerous. It feels like something I've already said yes to, long before I ever typed the words. Maybe it's foolish. Maybe it's hope disguising itself as instinct. But something in me is certain, even as the rest of me hesitates..

I thought I'd feel panic. Or at least nerves sharp enough to make me rethink it all. But mostly, what I feel is... quiet. Like something inside me has finally stopped pacing. I glance at the phone again, still lit with his last message.

A thousand times, yes.

The words had made me catch my breath when they appeared on my screen. I read them three times, letting each word sink in. Not just

☾☽

enthusiasm, but certainty. As if he'd been waiting to say yes to this very question for longer than made sense.

A small smile pulls at the edge of my mouth. I let it come. In one impulsive motion, I walk to the window and push it open, letting the evening air rush in. The garden scent of damp soil and lavender drifts up from below. Fresh air. A new current.

I don't know what will happen. Maybe it will be nothing. Maybe it will be something I never saw coming. But I said yes. And for the first time in a long time, that feels like enough. Whatever this is, I'm not hiding from it. Not this time.

☽

I set the guitar down carefully on its stand, my fingers still humming with energy. The house feels different somehow—brighter, more alive. As if the old plaster walls have been holding their breath and can finally exhale.

I walk to the window, pressing my palms against the cool glass. The waters of the strait stretch before me, waves catching the last of the light. Beyond, the mainland sits hazy in the distance—Somewhere out there, she's reading my words. Sophia. Not just a memory anymore. Not just the girl on the bench or a name attached to newspaper clipping. A real person, with a voice I'll hear, expressions I'll witness, movements I'll finally see.

I'll need to catch the morning ferry. Plan for delays. Allow time to find parking in the city. The logistics suddenly feel overwhelming and completely insignificant all at once.

I've photographed countless strangers. Captured fleeting moments of lives I'd never be part of. Documented beauty that existed separate from me, untouchable through my lens. But this is different. This is stepping into the frame instead of staying safely behind the camera.

My reflection stares back at me, older than the last time I stood at this window making promises to myself. I run a hand over my face, feeling the slight roughness of stubble. What will she see when she looks at me? Not the young man who watched her from a distance all those years ago. Not the boy too afraid to say hello.

I expected to feel terror—that familiar tightness that comes when something matters too much. But what floods through me instead is a strange, quiet certainty. As if some part of me has been waiting for Saturday at 2 pm all along. As if the universe has finally aligned.

"A thousand times, yes," I whisper to the empty room, tasting the words again. They're true. I would have waited another thousand ferry crossings, another thousand years if necessary. But she said yes. And now time seems both endless and impossibly short before I see her.

I reach for my phone again, scrolling back through our messages. Reading them with new eyes. The subtle humor. The thoughtfulness. I've studied light my entire career—how it bends and shifts across these island waters, how it reveals and conceals—but I've never seen it quite like this. Illuminating a path forward after so long in the shadows.

I've spent a lifetime chasing perfect moments through my viewfinder. But for once, I won't be the observer. I'll be part of the moment itself. And whatever happens—whether it's everything or nothing at all—I'll be there. Present. Finally saying the hello I've waited thirty-five years to say.

I walk the room without purpose, touching objects like they might answer something I haven't yet asked—the worn spine of my travel journal, a chipped mug from Oaxaca, the F5 camera I carried across countless countries. Proof of a life lived wide, but not deep. Not really. I used to think movement made me brave. But maybe stillness does. Maybe staying—choosing one place, one person—is the boldest thing of all.

◎

01

00:00:00:05:15:49

The morning air is scented with damp earth and the distant salt of Puget Sound. I wrap my hands around my coffee mug, letting the warmth seep into my fingers as I settle into the porch chair.

The world moves slowly around me—leaves shifting with the breeze, a car passing by, the muted hum of a ferry horn in the distance. But inside me? A storm.

I exhale, pressing the rim of the mug against my lips, though I don't take a sip. I am meeting him today.

The thought flickers through my mind, still surreal, still something that doesn't quite fit into reality yet. After a three weeks of messages—words carefully typed, moments shared through a screen—it's about to become real.

My phone buzzes. I glance down at the screen.

Michael.

A picture fills the screen—two pairs of blue jeans, two identical white shirts, neatly laid out.

I cannot decide what to wear. These are my options.

A soft laugh escapes me before I even realize it. I shake my head, my fingers instinctively hovering over the keyboard.

I'm loving the variety here.
You'll definitely leave an impression of... consistency.

The second I hit send, my heart flutters—just for a moment. He texts back immediately.

If I'm a no-show that means I passed out from indecision.

Another laugh. My shoulders relax, the anxiety uncoiling just a little. I lean back against the porch railing, my eyes drifting to the sky— the same sky I've watched for years, waiting for something I never thought would come.

☾

The sunlight outside is golden, stretching long across the yard, but the stillness in the house makes it feel like time has stopped. I stand at the window, hands braced against the frame, watching the wind ripple through the trees. It should be an ordinary day. Just another drive, just another meeting.

But it's not. It's her.

I stand in front of the bathroom mirror, hands braced against the sink. The reflection looking back is familiar, but tonight it feels... different. Not unrecognizable, just worn in. A little older, a little sharper around the edges. My hair's behaving for once—well, not really. It never does. But it's doing its best, and maybe that's enough. The shirt is pressed. The jacket's laid out on the bed behind me, sleeves smoothed, waiting. Everything is in place. Almost.

I exhale sharply, stepping away before the weight of the moment presses too hard. I should be excited. I should feel hopeful. But instead, my stomach knots, my pulse ticking just a little too fast. What if she doesn't like me? What if I don't live up to what she's imagined—if she's imagined anything at all?

She's the most beautiful girl in the world. And I'm not Fabio. Hell, I'm not even sure Fabio's still on the roster. But here I am anyway— Average Joe, showing up late to his own life.

All she knows is a message. A name. A few carefully chosen words from someone she doesn't know. Not the mess of the man behind them. Not the years. Not the spaces in between.

She doesn't know the restless energy that keeps me up at night. The way I've second-guessed myself over and over. The way I've convinced myself I was chasing a ghost, only to find out she's real.

Three bottles sit on the counter: Jimmy Choo, Polo, YSL. I pick up Jimmy. Too sharp. Too forward. Back down it goes. YSL—elegant, clean, the kind of scent that impresses in passing. But it's not me. Not really. I reach for the Polo Black. Uncap it. Inhale. Yeah. This one.

It's not flashy. It doesn't announce itself. But it settles into my skin the way it always has—quiet confidence with just enough edge. It's the

◎

scent that's followed me through long nights in Photoshop, through interviews and gallery shows, through half-forgotten hotel rooms. It's lived on my coat collar and lingered in the air long after I've left.

It's familiar. Honest. It suits me.

I spritz once at the base of my throat, then again at my wrist, pressing them together lightly. The scent rises—sandalwood, mango, patchouli—and something in my chest steadies just slightly. Not gone. But steadier.

I meet my eyes in the mirror again. This is the version of me I've chosen to bring forward—not the one shaped by regret or distance or fear. Just me. As I am now. I run a hand down the front of my shirt. Breathe in. Breathe out.

What if I've built her up too much in my mind? What if she's done the same with me? What if we sit across from each other, coffee in hand, and it's just... nothing?

I rub a hand down my face, shaking off the thoughts as I move through the living room. The poster of Donna Weinbrecht catches my eye—Brandon's old joke of a gift, now a permanent fixture on my wall.

He showed up with it the day Monica made him take it down. "There's no room for two women in this house," she'd said, dry as snowpack. So now she lives here—Donna, not Monica—gold medalist, ski legend, eternal flame of mogul glory. Proof that chasing a dream sometimes pays off.

I pause at the top of the porch stairs, scanning the horizon, grounding myself in the vastness of it all. The world hasn't changed.

⦵

But I have. The phone is already in my hand before I realize I've dialed. A few rings, then Brandon answers.

"I'm meeting Sophia today."

A long pause. A meaningful pause. Then—

"Wow… maybe some things are worth waiting for."

I glance down at the wooden planks beneath my feet, tracing the worn edges with my boot.

"Are you telling me to chase the fairy tale now?"

Brandon chuckles, the sound low and knowing.

"Yes. Real love stories don't always follow the rules."

I lean back, letting his words settle. My fingers tighten around the phone. I glance down. Moseley. Silent. Steady. Watching me with that all-knowing feline stare. I reach out, ruffling his fur. He leans into my touch, his purring barely audible over the wind.

I take another breath. Then I stand. Maybe I won't measure up. Maybe I'll disappoint her. Or maybe—just maybe—this is where the story really begins.

The garage doors groan as I pry them open, the rusted hinges protesting against the damp salt air that had crept in over the years. The light inside was dim, filtered through high cobwebbed windows, but it caught just enough to reveal the outline of what I'd come for.

There she was—my grandfather's old Jeep tucked against the far wall, dust layering her like a soft coat, paint dulled from time but still holding that desert tan color. And next to her, the shape I knew better than almost anything in this world:

My Porsche 914.

My loyal companion of decades, the growling little beast of a car. The white paint was still vibrant beneath the dust, like it had been waiting for me to come back and wake her up.

I step in slowly, letting the air settle around me—old oil, leather, the faint scent of cedar soaked into the beams. Time has collected here, thick and patient. I run my hand along the curve of the Porsche's hood, brushing the dust away in lazy circles. The metal is cool under my fingers. Familiar. Comforting.

I open the door and slide into the low seat, the creak of the worn leather a sound I've always loved. My hands find the steering wheel instinctively. The leather is cracked in places, smooth in others—worn exactly where my fingers have always held it. I sit there for a long moment, hands resting on the wheel, eyes closed.

"Well, old girl," I murmur, the words soft in the stillness, "you ready for this?"

The silence answered back like it always had. The light shifted through the window panes, landing across the dash like an omen. I took a breath. Then another. I didn't know what would happen next, only that I needed to be behind this wheel to find out.

The world outside the garage waited. And we were finally ready to meet it as I turned the key.

The engine coughed once, then roared to life—rough at first, like it had to remember what it meant to run, then smoother, settling into that low, familiar growl that lived in my chest as much as under the hood.

I give the gas a gentle push. The tachometer flicked up, needle twitching, dancing like it was shaking the dust off too. 1,500… 2,000… a little higher. The sound filled the garage, echoing off the rafters, alive and expectant.

I smiled, one hand on the wheel, the other still resting on the shifter. We weren't just going for a drive. We were going to change everything. I shift into reverse.

Time to go.

I stand before the mirror, my reflection shifting between familiarity and uncertainty. The soft fabric of my dress flows just past my knees—a light, floral print that feels almost too delicate, too hopeful for something as simple as coffee. I smooth the fabric, then let my hands drop to my sides.

Too casual? Too much? Maybe I should wear jeans.

My hair won't fall the way I want it to. One curl is too stubborn, another too flat. I twist and pin and unpin. Then I stop, letting it be what it is.

Honest. Unruly. Mine.

I reach for my perfume, hesitating for a breath before spritzing the air. Stepping through the mist, I let the scent settle over me, warm and familiar. A small part of me wonders if he'll notice—if scent, like memory, lingers in the spaces between words.

The house is quiet. Shadow watches from the windowsill, tail flicking lazily, as if sensing the shift in the air. Something is changing. I can feel it in the way my breath catches, in the way my hands linger on small decisions—bracelet or no bracelet, hair up or down, shoes that click or don't.

Thirty-five years ago. That number feels too large and too small all at once. How do you step into something that began without you? What if the version of him I've started to imagine disappears the moment we meet? What if he looks like Shrek? Then what? Run?

I press my palm flat against the dresser, grounding myself. The mirror reflects not the girl I was, but the woman I've become. Older, yes. But not faded. Not lost. I've built a life. Raised a daughter. Learned how to begin again. And still... this feels like another kind of beginning. I draw in a breath. Hold it. Let it go.

Then I step into the light.

Mile Marker 221 - Conway

A song I've heard a thousand times drifts from the speakers—soft and unassuming, just a few acoustic chords and the low hum of static. It doesn't demand attention. It waits. The kind of song that sneaks in sideways, pulling something loose in your chest before you realize it's happening. ♪

Floyd.

The freeway stretches ahead, pale and endless under the weight of

♪ *"Wish You Were Here"* by Pink Floyd

late light. The Porsche hums steady beneath me, but I can't shake the feeling I've been on this highway for years. Not this exact one—just every road that looked like escape but felt like repetition.

Same turns. Same questions. Same ache in my chest I've carried across airports and camera straps. Always moving. Always chasing. But chasing what?

The song keeps playing. Not just about loss, but about recognition. The kind that lives between two people who brushed lives at the wrong moment. Like two souls swimming the same circles, searching for something we couldn't name—until one of us finally looked up. Year after year. Same fish bowl, same glass, same ache.

Blue sky and pain.

That's what it's felt like. My life. Beautiful. And empty. A loop of longing that I edited into something nobler. I called it freedom. Adventure. But maybe it was just fear. The same old fears I keep dressing up as ambition.

My fingers tighten slightly on the wheel.

Then, like film flickering across a reel, I remember.

Hiva Oa. The waterfall. The white horse.

The first photo that ever really meant something. Not because it was perfect, but because it wasn't. That wild, still creature standing at the edge of all the thunder. The mist rising like breath. The shutter clicking just before it turned away.

It wasn't about the horse.

It was about that impossible quiet in the middle of chaos. The moment when something holds still, and you know if you blink too long, it'll be gone.

That's what I've been trying to photograph ever since. That stillness. That truth. But maybe it wasn't the camera that captured it. Maybe it was the moment that caught me.

The song hums through the cabin. My chest tightens—not in pain, not quite. Something older. The ache of wanting to be seen. To be known. To stop moving just long enough to be missed.

Sophia. She didn't save me. She couldn't—not from a life she wasn't even part of yet. She just stood still and waited until I remembered how to stop running. How to look up. How to feel the weight of someone staying.

Seattle rises ahead, the skyline sharpening through the haze. It's not just a city—it's a door I never thought I'd get to walk through. And I'm done watching it from a window seat.

I press harder on the accelerator, the car responding like it knows. Every mile peeling something back—fear, silence, the fiction I built to protect myself. And this time, I'm not circling. I'm not documenting someone else's story. This time, I'm choosing mine.

The song fades out. But the ache it leaves behind? That stays.

Not emptiness. Just that quiet space between two people who drifted apart. And might—just might—find their way back. And this time, I'll meet her there. For the first time in my life, I feel it:

A hard rain is gonna fall.

A quiet meow pulls me from my thoughts. I turn to see Shadow, stretched lazily across the couch, her tail flicking with slow amusement—or silent disapproval. Shadow lets out another slow, unimpressed meow—the kind that doesn't answer anything but somehow confirms everything.

I sigh, reaching for my phone. My fingers hover before I type a message to Gray:

Going to meet Mr. Instagram. I can't believe I'm doing this.

Seconds later, my screen lights up.

Some of the best stories start with a little courage and a lot of hope.

I shake my head as I type.

More life lessons from Speed Racer?

The typing bubble appears instantly.

;-)

A pause. Then—

Someone else once taught me that everything happens for a reason.

My breath catches. My gaze flickers toward the cross-stitch on the wall, the words stitched in delicate silver thread.

Everything happens for a reason.

⓪

Another message comes through.

And Mom?

Yes?

Show him your gypsy.

I stare at the words.

Simple. Soft. But they land like truth.

I exhale softly and tuck the phone into my bag. The door clicks shut behind me as I step outside. Spring air wraps around me, laced with the scent of fresh rain and blooming jasmine—the kind of crispness that lingers just before the season fully changes.

The soft fabric of my dress catches in the breeze, brushing against my legs as I descend the porch steps. My heels tap lightly on the walk, steady and sure.

She thinks the gypsy is still in me. Maybe she's right. Maybe today... I'll let her lead.

I should keep moving, head straight for my car, but my feet hesitate. The sunlight filters through the trees, scattering shifting patterns of light across the wooden stairs. I sink down for a moment, my hands resting lightly on my lap. Closing my eyes, I tilt my face to the sky, letting the warmth press against my skin. And just then, the words come back to me:

What is essential is invisible to the eye.

I used to think it was about mystery. About not being able to see the truth in others. But maybe it's simpler than that. Maybe it's this. The weightless way my heart lifts at the sound of his name. The quiet hope that brought me here. The feeling of choosing something real, even if I don't fully understand it yet.

This could be a mistake. Or it could be the beginning of something I don't have a name for yet. Either way—I'm about to find out.

Time to go.

I ease out of the driveway, the tires rolling smooth beneath a sky washed in soft June blue. Ballard unfolds in steady frames—craftsman homes with bright doors, cafés with sidewalk tables half-filled, trees arching over the road in full summer leaf. The light here is filtered, diffused—like the sun never fully commits, but shows up anyway.

The window's cracked just enough to let the breeze in. It smells like cut grass, and diesel for some reason. I pass the co-op, the bookstore I wander in on Saturdays, a man tuning a guitar on his porch with his bare feet resting on the rail. Everything feels familiar but slightly tilted.

As if the edges of the world have gone soft around the fact that I'm about to do something I never thought I would.

A woman walks her dog past the old bakery, the leash slack between them. She waves at a man sweeping his stoop. It's just another day for them. But for me, everything feels like it's about to change.

I don't turn the radio on. I don't need to fill the silence. It's not the heavy kind, not anymore. It's the kind that lets you think clearly.

I glance at the clock on the dash. I left a few minutes early. My hands tighten slightly on the wheel. Not from nerves—at least not the bad kind. It's something else. That quiet awareness before something shifts.

Each street brings me closer. Each stop sign, each patch of filtered sunlight sliding across the windshield. I don't know what I'll say. I don't know if he'll be someone I remember—or someone entirely new. And for the first time in a long time—I just want to be seen.

But I'm not driving away this time. I'm driving towards something—

North 85th - Green Lake

—the afternoon sun casts sharp shadows across the hood of my car. I grip the steering wheel, my palms damp. This is just coffee. Then why does it feel like the ground beneath me is shifting?

I stare straight ahead as the stoplight glows red. Everything feels suspended—this moment, this breath, this quiet stretch of time before the inevitable.

What if I'm making a mistake? What if he sees me and I'm nothing like the woman in his head? I glance at my reflection in the rearview mirror, but I don't recognize the expression staring back at me—a mixture of longing, fear, and something dangerously close to hope.

The light flicks to green. A decision made for me. I press the gas, the hum of the engine vibrating through my hands. The Interstate looms ahead. Whatever waits for me on the other side of this choice—I want it to be real. I want it to be mine.

No turning back.

⦿

Mile Marker 175 - Northgate

The sun beats down hard, glinting off the curves of the road as the Interstate hums beneath me. Heat shimmers above the pavement, blurring the edges of everything but the lane ahead. I keep my hands steady on the wheel, eyes fixed forward, the blur of asphalt pulling me closer to something I can't quite name—but finally, finally, I'm headed toward it. ♪

The freeway rushes beneath the wheels like a film reel unspooling. The sound of it—steady, low, endless—matches the rhythm in my chest. The road doesn't ask questions. It just moves. And right now, that's all I want. Movement. Momentum. A direction that finally makes sense.

I'm steady on the outside, but inside—I'm anything but. What if she regrets saying yes? What if I've spent my whole life chasing something that was never real? I exhale sharply and shake the thoughts away.

A breeze slips through the cracked window—

Mile Marker 173 - Green Lake

—A scent of something warm—honey, maybe. Or coconut. Faint but sharp enough to pull me out of my spiral. I glance to the left, instinctively, but the cars blur past—faces unreadable, gone before I can register anything more.

Still... the feeling doesn't pass.

There's a shift in the air. A hum beneath the noise. Not déjà vu. Not memory. Just... presence. The strange sensation that someone is close. That something is close.

♪ "Jupiter 4" by Sharon Van Etten

Then—A flash of green on my right. I barely register it at first. Just another car. But it catches in my chest, sharp and sudden. I grip the wheel tighter. Check the mirrors. Nothing unusual. Just traffic. Just sunlight. Just the blur of the freeway rising to meet me.

And yet—I feel it. That flicker of something just out of reach. I shake it off. Adjust the mirror. Refocus.

It's probably nothing.

But some part of me stays alert, like I've brushed the edge of a thread I didn't know I was following.

After a few miles I flick on my blinker and ease off the gas. A vintage green Karmann Ghia slips into view in the right lane. I fall in behind it. The license plate catches my eye:

SONNET.

I tap my fingers on the wheel, considering it. A poet at heart? A person who loves words? Or maybe just someone who thought it looked good on paper.

A Ghia isn't practical. It's light, a little stubborn, a little magic. Romantic, even. You drive one because you want the ride to matter more than the destination. Because you're not in a rush to arrive—you're in love with the getting there.

The plate, the car—none of it felt accidental. Whoever was behind the wheel had chosen carefully. Someone who didn't mind being a little different. Someone who still believed small things mattered.

Probably nothing, again.

Still—it sticks. Like a spider's web you walk through without seeing, thin and invisible until it clings to you, and suddenly, you're caught.

The Ghia signals right, taking the Lake Union exit.

So do I.

I trail behind it, following the curve of the off-ramp. Not because of the car. Just because that's where I'm going. And yet—the hairs on the back of my neck lift. Like I've stepped into something that's been waiting for me all along.

Exit 166 - Lake Union

I ease to a stop at the light at the bottom of the offramp, the rhythm of traffic pressing in around me The world narrows to the rearview mirror. A Washington license plate comes into focus. My breath catches.

POWLIFE.

That plate. That car.

My fingertips pressing into the leather. I lift my gaze back to the mirror—I can't see the driver. The sunlight glints off the windshield, blinding me to the face inside. Just a shadow, just an outline.

The city swells around me—horns blaring in short bursts, the rumble of a delivery truck bouncing off glass storefronts, a skateboard rattling over a sidewalk crack. A cyclist whistles as he weaves between cars. Someone laughs from an open café window. Tires buzz against sun-warmed asphalt, steady and sure.

But I barely hear it.

The sounds slip to the background, blurred by something heavier. Something unspoken. Something remembered.

The light turns green.

I don't move. A flicker of uncertainty holds me in place, as if the very air around me has shifted. A pull—so faint yet undeniable—urges me to look beyond the mirror, beyond the moment.

But to what?

A gentle *HONK* jolts me back. I blink, inhaling sharply, fingers flexing on the wheel.

Move, Sophia.

With a press of the gas, the car rolls forward, turning right—away from fate, or toward it?

I glance between the rearview and side mirrors, catching glimpses of the Porsche still following me. A test. A hesitation. A decision. I make a turn onto Yale. The Porsche follows. A left on Thomas. Still there. My heartbeat thrums in my ears.

I ease into a parking spot near the cafe and kill the engine, my breath unsteady. A moment later, the Porsche glides past. And then— it's gone. I stare after it, frozen.

Then—something stirs in the back of my mind. A feeling, not a memory at first. Just a familiar pulse, like a song I almost remember but can't quite place.

Telluride. A glimpse of a white Porsche turning onto Pine Street, disappearing around the corner before I could wonder why it felt important.

Later. Idling in front of my house. Not long enough to be suspicious. Just long enough to make me pause.

Seattle. A flicker of white in the blur of traffic on I-5. That same familiar shape. A passing thought—a skier's plate. Colorado. Mountains. Memory.

I told myself it was nothing. A coincidence. But still, it stayed with me—not fear, exactly, but something circling. Near, but never named. I never gave it weight. Never gave it meaning.

Until now.

A shiver runs through me. The kind that makes you wonder if the universe has been whispering to you all along. My lips part, a slow, stunned smile forming.

I step out of my car, scanning the street. The Porsche is gone. I should feel foolish. Maybe I am. But the sensation lingers—that strange, knowing feeling settling into my bones like something just out of reach.

The sound of voices nearby draws my attention. A small crowd has gathered, their faces tilted skyward. I hesitate. Then, curiosity pulling at me, I join them. I follow their gaze—but there's nothing there. I frown, glancing back at the street. Searching. For what? For who?

Nothing.

I smooth my hand over my skirt, trying to quiet the flutter inside me. But my fingers are trembling now. I notice it suddenly—barely visible, but there. Like my body knows something before I do. Like it's bracing for impact.

My heart is racing—too fast, too loud—as if it knows something my mind can't admit yet. Not fear. Not exactly. Not hope, either. Something in between. Something waiting.

I press a hand to my chest. It doesn't slow down.

Something's coming. I don't know what it is, but it's close. Closer than I've let myself believe. The air feels different now—thicker somehow, like the sky is holding its breath. And maybe I am too.

The city hums around me as I step out of the Porsche, stretching my fingers once before slipping my phone into my pocket.

I have my sunglasses on. Habit. The sun is sharp, but as I start toward the sidewalk, I pause. A shop window catches my reflection— dark lenses, expression hidden—and for a second, I barely recognize myself. A man shaped by distance. By waiting.

I consider leaving them on. Letting them do what they've always done. Protect. Conceal. Give me just enough distance to keep from unraveling. But not this time.

When I meet her, I want nothing between us. No filter. No shield. Just my eyes—because if she sees anything in me, anything worth trusting, it'll be there. I take them off, fold the arms slowly, and slip them into my jacket pocket.

The smell of roasted peanuts drifts from a food cart nearby. A woman laughs behind me, high and unfiltered. Someone's perfume catches in my throat—something floral and too sweet. It's all too much, and yet not enough. My heart pounds against the quiet in my chest, and I can feel it: something is shifting. I round the corner onto the sidewalk—and pause.

I'm not ready. But I'm here. That has to count for something. Every version of this moment I've imagined—every time I rewrote it in my head—it never looked like this. It was always cinematic. Perfect. But maybe that's the point. Real things never arrive the way you plan for them.

I think about turning around. Just for a second. Not to leave—but to delay. To breathe. To buy myself a few more heartbeats before whatever this is becomes real. But I don't. I can't. I've waited too long for this moment, even if I don't know how it ends.

People are gathered, their heads tilted skyward. Their expressions are a mix of wonder and quiet awe. Some have their phones raised, capturing whatever it is that has stolen their attention. I follow their gaze—but the sun is too bright, the light too sharp. I squint, shielding my eyes.

Nothing.

I glance at my watch:

2:58.

Still set to *Telluride* time.

A breath. A step...

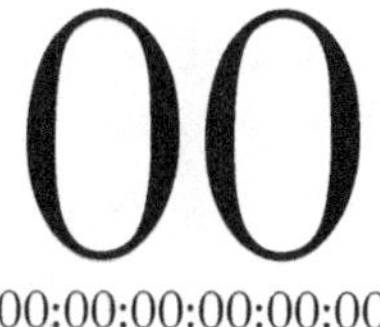

00:00:00:00:00:00

The world changes. The light shifts—not like the slow fade of dusk, but something stranger. More unnatural. Shadows stretch long and distorted, bending at odd angles. A collective hush settles over the street. ♪

I weave through the gathered crowd, my pulse a steady drumbeat in my ears. There's an energy in the air, an almost sacred silence as heads tilt skyward, all eyes drawn to something unfolding above.

The brightness softens—at first like the world slipping into golden hour. Then darker. Stranger. The temperature drops. Goosebumps rise along my arms.

The sun disappears behind the moon, leaving only a burning ring of light in the darkened sky.

Totality.

♪ *"On the Nature of Daylight"* by Max Richter

◎

A gasp ripples through the crowd, followed by a silence so thick it feels sacred. The world stops spinning. The constant urban hum of traffic fades to nothing. The air cools against my skin, carrying a strange electricity. For just these precious minutes, even Seattle is holding its breath - no car horns, no distant conversations, just collective awe as day becomes something else entirely.

I glance up, briefly. It's beautiful. Otherworldly. But this spectacle isn't why I've come.

As cheers erupt, scattered applause and awed voices around me, I continue through the crowd, careful, deliberate. My pulse quickens. Every few steps I scan again—faces, silhouettes, posture. A flash of dark hair. A shoulder turned just so.

I know exactly who I'm looking for. My eyes lock on the spaces in between. The ones that could hold her. I'm not guessing. I'm not wondering. I know who I'm here for.

The girl with the quiet gravity. The one person I want to see in this fractured light—the one person I want to find while the world resets itself. And just as I start to think I've missed her, I see her.

Sophia.

She stands just ahead of me, bathed in the eerie eclipse glow. The light touches her like it remembers her. Her outline shimmers with that same impossible softness I've carried in my memory.

I stop moving.

And for a moment—just a moment—time collapses, and I'm on

that fateful sidewalk in Telluride again, when a simple passing became the moment my life split into before and after her.

The crowd blurs. The city fades. The hush around us evaporates. My vision narrows until it's only her. Still as stone. Her hair caught in the breeze the same way it always has—untamed, alive. A long dress brushes her calves, the hem lifting slightly like a page turning.

She's still looking up. She hasn't seen me yet.

She shifts slightly. Tilts her head like the wind has whispered her name. Her shoulders turn.

Then—her face.

The light bends for her. She looks like a dream I had too early in the morning to hold on to. Like a lyric I never fully understood until now.

Something pulls at me. That invisible connection—tight, unbroken. Stretching across decades and decisions and all the hollow spaces in between. Still holding.

She turns fully.

Not a version of her. Not a memory. Not some imagined conclusion to a story I've spent my life trying to rewrite. Just her.

She blinks once. Then again. Her gaze sweeps past me. Then catches. Locks. Holds. The world narrows to just us two.

Everything I have been—everything I have become—collapses into the man standing here now. I don't breathe. I don't move. I just look at her, and for the first time in years, I stop waiting.

She is real. Not a phantom haunting airports and crowded streets. Not an empty space on a park bench where I waited day after day. Not a possibility always slipping through my fingers. Her. Here. Now. And I am still the boy who never stopped believing in this moment.

I step forward, afraid that if I break the rhythm, she'll vanish again. But she doesn't. She stays.

I see the soft curve of her lips, the rise and fall of her breath, the faint tremble in her hands.

One final step.

And then, I'm in front of her. Closer than memory. Closer than grief. Closer than I ever let myself imagine. I don't trust my voice. But somehow, the words find me.

"I almost gave up hope I would ever see you again."

My voice catches as I say it. Her eyes search mine. There's something in her expression—something like knowing. Like recognition. She takes a small step closer.

"Maybe we just needed time to find our way here."

Her voice is quiet, but it crashes through me like a tidal wave, washing away years of silence. It's the first time I've heard it. After all the decades, all the imagined conversations, the silent stories I told myself—this is the sound I never knew. And it's everything. Soft, steady, like she's not used to saying things out loud.

Then, she moves. Or maybe I do. All I know is that suddenly we're here, in each other's arms, and the moment is too vast to hold. Years of searching collapse into this single point of contact—her solid warmth against me, real and undeniable.

At first, we hesitate—uncertain hands finding their place. Then, we anchor. Her scent hits me—warm, sunlit, like coconut and honey. Something tropical and wild and entirely out of place in this Seattle air. My hand trembles as it finds the small of her back.

She lets out a breath—quiet, unsteady—and her fingers tighten slightly, holding on like she's afraid the moment might slip away. I feel it too. That same grip in my chest. That same fear that if I move, even slightly, this will vanish like everything else I couldn't hold on to.

I squeeze my eyes shut, feeling the weight of it all. The years spent searching. The moments almost lost. She is real. She is here. And for once, so am I.

"I didn't realize how much I could miss someone I'd never even met," I whisper.

Slowly, she pulls back, just enough to meet my eyes. She studies me, as if I am something both familiar and impossible. As if she, too, is trying to make sense of how it all led here. Then, in a whisper, she says the words that undo me completely.

"Why do you feel like a warm memory?"

Something breaks open inside me. I don't try to stop the tear that slips down my cheek. It's not sadness. It's something heavier. Older. Like a thread pulling loose after being knotted for too long. She sees it, and her expression doesn't change—just deepens. Like she's known all along.

◎

Cafe Hagen - Lake Union

The cafe hums around us—espresso machines whirring, low murmurs of conversation, the occasional clink of a spoon against porcelain. But I don't hear any of it. All I hear is the silence stretching between us.

Michael sits across from me, hands trembling slightly on the table. I watch them, fascinated, before my gaze moves to his face—his eyes locked on mine, as if he's afraid to blink and miss something.

His breath is uneven. I tilt my head, softening.

"You're not going to pass out, are you?"

His lips show the smallest ghost of a smile.

"I haven't decided yet."

I laugh, the sound surprising even me. Light. Real. It fills the space between us, melts the tension, makes this feel less impossible. His shoulders relax—just a little. Then, his expression shifts, something deeper settling into his gaze as he studies me. As he leans forward, something faint stirs in the air— sandalwood and something citrus fills the space between us. Just enough to make me pause.

"I've never seen so much beauty in one place," he says softly.

My hand moves instinctively, tucking a loose curl behind my ear. A familiar habit. His eyes follow the movement, like he's memorizing it. I take a slow breath. The past is crashing into the present, shifting everything. This isn't just a meeting.

It's a reckoning.

"I want to know every tiny detail about you," he says, voice steady but laced with something raw, something unsaid. "But… there's really only one question on my mind."

My heart stumbles. The world outside—the street, the strangers, the slow-moving clouds—narrows to this small table. I lean in slightly, searching his face.

Without thinking, my hand inches forward—just enough for our fingers to brush. The contact is feather-light, but it grounds us. More real than anything I've felt in years. Maybe more real than anything I've ever known.

"And what would that be, Michael?"

His gaze drops for a moment, gathering courage. When he looks back up, the intensity in his eyes nearly steals my breath. His fingers still tremble next to mine. A pause. Then—

"Would you rather have a spring or summer wedding?"

I stop breathing. His voice is steady, but the weight of it sends a shockwave through me. A wedding.

Not *if*. *When*.

No one's ever looked at me like that. Like I'm the answer, not the question. Like the story was always going to end this way. I wonder what it's like to live with that kind of knowing.

My fingers tighten involuntarily around his. I try to speak, but my throat locks. Tears sting my eyes before I can stop them. I feel his trembling begin to ease as our fingers intertwine.

I drop my gaze for just a second, blinking rapidly, trying to regain control—but it's useless. A single tear slips down my cheek. I wipe it away quickly, my lips pressing together in a trembling smile.

He's waiting. Holding his breath. Finally, I look up, and everything spills out in one quiet, undeniable truth.

"Spring."

My voice wavers, but I don't care.

"Definitely spring. It feels like the world is waking up."

Michael's grip tightens, like he's holding on to something fragile but fiercely important. His own eyes are glassy, his breath unsteady.

The weight of decades presses into this moment. We both struggle to contain it, to stay here, in the now, without letting the past overwhelm us. I squeeze his hand, grounding myself. Grounding him.

"There was one thing I always knew about you," he whispers, voice thick with emotion. I swallow, trying to steady my heartbeat.

"And what was that?"

His thumb brushes the back of my hand—a quiet, steadying motion.

"I knew every second spent with you would be a gift."

The tear I'd been holding back finally falls. But this time, I don't wipe it away. Because for the first time in a long time, I believe what he said. I let out a watery laugh, shaking my head.

"It won't always be Christmas with me, Michael."

His lips turn into a smile.

"I would hope not," he says, "it would make for a boring flight if there was never any turbulence."

I laugh—really laugh. A sound I hadn't even realized I missed. My heart feels too full. Too fragile.

"We may have our first argument on who the lucky one is," I whisper.

Michael bites his lip, like he's holding back another question.

"I do have one more question…"

I inhale sharply, bracing.

"Oh, dear," I murmur. "I'm ready. I think…"

A pause.

"What do you have in your beautiful hair that smells like tropical sunshine? Or is that just you?"

I blink. He noticed.

Then—laughter bursts out of me, real and genuine and effortless. The tension, the waiting, the decades—it all dissolves into something light, something beautiful.

Through the window, the afternoon sunlight washes over us,

painting everything in warmth. And for the first time in a long time, I stop thinking.

I just exist. With him.

For a moment, I just sit still, taking it all in. But something inside me has started to move again. Not in a rush. Not in a flood. Just a quiet thaw—like spring waking up inside my chest. Not a question. Not a maybe. Just...*Yes.* Small. Quiet. Certain. But there.

Michael is looking at me, something quiet and serious in his eyes. Like he's remembering every version of this moment that didn't get to happen. Like he's deciding—finally—to believe it's real.

"What are you thinking?" I ask.

"That I've crossed enough oceans in my life."

I tilt my head, a little curious. "Oceans? What do you mean?"

"That you're sitting across from me... and that distance feels like the size of an ocean. I just—" He hesitates, then exhales. "I just want to be beside you from now on."

For a second, I forget how to breathe. Not from nerves. From recognition. From hearing the words I didn't realize I've been waiting for.

A smile tugs at the corners of my mouth—gentle, inevitable.

My fingers are still wrapped around his, with the quiet determination of someone who's learned not to let go. Not when it matters.

"Then let's make it the last ocean either of us has to cross," I whisper.

◐

He squeezes my hand once—steady, certain. I've spent too many years watching horizons, waiting for something to appear. I look down at our hands entwined. This time, I'm holding on.

Because I want that too. I want the version of us where we don't stay on opposite sides of the table. I want the story where no one has to cross anything alone anymore.

Outside, a child passes holding a balloon—yellow, bobbing lightly in the breeze. A bird hops along the sidewalk, searching for crumbs. A bike leans crooked against a tree. The world moves. Small, ordinary, alive.

Gas Works Park - Lake Union

The sun is warm on my face as we walk hand in hand, the Seattle skyline rising like a memory behind us. Lake Union glints under the late afternoon light—a restless shimmer of gold and blue. The gentle lapping of water against moored boats carries across the park, mingling with distant laughter and the soft rustle of leaves.

We pause at the crest of the hill, the grass soft beneath our feet, the breeze tugging gently at her hair. I catch the faint scent of coconut and something distinctly her—a warmth I've come to recognize even with my eyes closed. I turn toward her, tightening my fingers around hers, as if to memorize the way they fit—how right it feels. Like we've been reaching for this without knowing it.

And for a moment, it hits me—I'm holding her hand. Not in a dream. Not in a memory I made up to comfort myself. But here. Now.

I thought this moment would never come. That it couldn't. She was a ghost, a flicker at the edge of memory, someone I'd glimpsed and imagined more than I should've. But now—this is real. Her skin, warm against mine. The way her thumb brushes lightly across the back of my hand, like a confirmation that yes, she feels it too.

It's surreal. Beautiful. A little terrifying.

I don't say anything at first. I just hold her hand a little tighter. As if that might anchor me to the moment. As if letting go would undo it all.

"Sophia?" I say, my voice quiet, steady, despite the drumming in my chest.

She looks at me. "Yes, Michael?"

"Now that I've held your hand, I'm never letting go."

Her eyes meet mine—steady, unblinking. For a long moment, she doesn't speak. Then—just one word, soft enough to feel like a secret.

"Promise?"

Something tightens in my chest—a sweet ache that makes it hard to breathe. I lift her hand to my lips, fingers trembling slightly, and kiss her slowly, deliberately. Like a vow written in touch, not words.

"In this lifetime," I whisper, "and whatever comes after."

She doesn't smile at first. Just watches me, letting it sink in. Then—something shifts. That quiet smile rises, the kind that says she believes me.

The breeze moves again, warm against our skin. Behind us, the lake sparkles like it's listening. We keep walking, the gravel path crunching beneath our shoes, the golden light stretching long across the grass.

Lake Union shimmers to our left, boats bobbing like they're in on some secret.

Sophia slows beside me, her gaze lifting toward the soft afternoon sky. The eclipse we witnessed together is long gone, but something about the light still feels altered—tilted, changed. Like we're walking in the afterglow of something significant. Like something aligned, not just in the sky, but in us.

She shields her eyes with one hand, her voice soft, sure.

"Apparently the universe had plans for us."

I glance at her, caught off guard by the simplicity of it. The weight behind the words.

There's a pause—long enough for something to stir. And then, without meaning to, the lyrics come to me. Gentle. Familiar. Like a thought I'd been carrying for years without realizing it.

"Maybe we were always being followed by a moonshadow... and we just didn't know it."

She turns to me slowly, the words sinking in. Not just hearing them—feeling them. I see something shift behind her eyes. A recognition. Like a thread pulled tight between past and present just now clicked into place.

"Followed," she repeats, her voice quieter now. "Or chased?"

I meet her gaze, something turning over in my chest.

"Is there a difference?"

She thinks for a second. Then:

"I spent a lot of years running from things that were never chasing me."

Her voice is barely above a whisper. She squeezes my hand.

"I'd rather be followed."

The quiet smile that follows is the kind that stays with you. The kind that says, Yes. I've always known.

She doesn't speak. She doesn't need to. And neither do I.

The light stretches long across the grass, soft gold catching in her hair, and we keep walking—together, just ahead of our shadows. We're almost back to where we started when I clear my throat, suddenly nervous again.

"So... how do you feel about Bob Dylan?" I ask, trying for casual, even though my pulse betrays me.

Sophia stops walking. Turns to face me fully. Her expression is serious—almost concerned—as if she's deciding whether this might be a deal-breaker.

"Bob Dylan?" she repeats slowly.

I shrug. "I thought you should know what you're getting yourself into."

She stares at me for a beat longer than necessary—then cracks.

Her laugh is real, unguarded, the kind that lights up her whole face. She squeezes my hand.

"His voice sounds like a cat caught in a blender." She leans in, eyes dancing with mischief.

We keep walking. She slips back into step beside me, brushing shoulders.

"So," she says, "how do you feel about ketchup on a hot dog?"

Ketchup on a hot dog. A felony. A jailable offense according to Dirty Harry. I think the Hot Dog Man might have something to say about it, too.

Nobody—and I mean nobody—puts ketchup on a hot dog.

And just like that, we're off—into new conversations. The weight of the moment balanced by the lightness of discovery. There's a rhythm forming between us already, quiet and effortless.

Each question feels like a small treasure, each answer a kind of promise—not grand or sweeping, just real. I find myself leaning in, not to impress her, but because I want to know. Everything. Every detail. Every thread that makes her who she is.

I think of all the waiting on the bench. The silence. The long walks. The moments I spent talking myself out of hope. All the questions I never got to ask—until now.

And the truth is, she's everything. Beautiful, yes—but it's more than that. She's thoughtful, sharp, kind in ways that don't feel rehearsed. Everything I hoped for in those late-night imaginings.

Everything I told myself I was probably getting wrong. But I wasn't. She's real. And somehow, impossibly, she's even better than the fiction I built to survive the waiting.

She tells me my idol sounds like a cat in a blender. She puts ketchup on a hot dog like it's not a crime. I'm flying into turbulence already— but this time, I'm not bracing for impact.

I'm laughing. And for the first time in a long while, I catch myself smiling, and I don't try to stop it.

I'm not flying alone

I knew it the moment I passed her on the sidewalk. There was a shift. Not lightning-bolt dramatic. Just quiet and absolute. The kind of knowing that settles into your bones.

Like a piece of the story had finally found its place.

"Sophia?"

She glances over, already preparing herself for another random question. "Yes, Michael?" she says, her voice edged with a smile.

I pause just long enough to feel it. The moment. The truth of it.

"I actually never gave up hope. I just didn't know where it would lead."

She doesn't answer right away. Just watches me, eyes steady, like she's measuring the shape of that truth. Then, softly:

"Maybe hope doesn't need a map. Just a reason."

Maybe this—this right here—is the reason.

We keep walking. I don't want the moment to end. I don't want to let go of her hand.

The sound of our footsteps mixes with distant laughter, the soft bark of a dog chasing something just out of reach. The lake shimmers under the weight of afternoon light, and the city rises behind it— familiar, but not.

Everything feels quieter now. Calmer. Like the volume of the world has been turned down just enough to hear what matters.

I think about the coffee I never drank back at *Café Hagen*, still sitting on the table, cooling in the glass like it was never meant to be touched. Just a prop in the story.

My whole life… narrowed to that single cup. Not because of what was in it. But because of what it meant to sit across from her—finally. To watch her eyes lift to meet mine. To realize hope didn't leave me behind after all. It just… took its time.

Hope doesn't always arrive loudly. Sometimes, it's just two people walking side by side—saying nothing, saying everything. I glance at her. She's looking out over the water, wind catching her curls, expression unreadable. But she's here. Real. Breathing.

I would never say she's mine. But I will always say I'm hers.

I take a breath that feels like the first one in years.

One untouched cup of coffee. And everything after.

◍

EPILOGUE
+02:00:22:22:36:15

I used to hate yardwork. Hated the dirt under my nails, the way the mower rattled my arms numb, the endless battle against grass that didn't care if you showed up or not. It felt like wasted energy, something to get through on the way to somewhere better.

But that was before Sophia.

Now, here I am, mowing the lawn in the late afternoon heat, sweat rolling down my back, headphones clamped over my ears, listening to a song that sounds like her—soft, certain, unhurried. The words drift through me, and I find myself smiling. The porch door's open. The air smells like grass and garlic. And for the first time in a long time, I'm not moving toward something. I'm already there. ♪

The song shifts—synth rising, voice clear and aching—and suddenly I'm not just mowing the lawn. I'm remembering what it felt like to be

♪ "Come Away With Me" by Norah Jones

twenty, chasing light through a viewfinder, thinking I had to keep moving or disappear. I didn't know then what I was really searching for. ♪

But I do now. Forever young. It used to sound like a wish you made at midnight. Now, it sounds like a promise—one I want to keep, not for myself, but for her. For us.

If I get to spend my days like this—shoulder to shoulder, building something that doesn't need to be captured or published or proved— then maybe that's what forever really is.

Somehow, without even trying, she made all the things I once dreaded feel like privileges. I don't mind the ache in my back after haul- ing bags of soil for her garden, or the clatter of dishes stacked beside the sink after we cook. I love it—all of it—because it's for her. Because there's a quiet kind of joy in doing anything that makes her smile.

Even my cars—the Porsche and the Jeep that once held most of my attention—feel a little neglected these days. I find myself wan- dering toward the Ghia instead, wiping down her sun-warmed hood, adjusting things that don't need adjusting, just for the excuse to run my hands over the machine that brings Sophia home to me. Funny how easily my priorities shifted. How easily the world narrowed to the things that actually mattered.

After everything, I offered to move. Ballard, Seattle proper, any- where she wanted. I would have packed it all up in a heartbeat if she'd asked. But Sophia fell for the island life almost faster than I did. She sold her house without hesitation, planted herself here with me, and never once made me feel like she had sacrificed anything. I told her then—and I tell her still—that whatever dream she wants to chase, I'll be the first one in line cheering her on. Her own gardening business. Her writing. Whatever she wants to build, I'll build the scaffolding.

♪ *"Forever Young"* by Alphaville

I never really understood what it meant to love without condi-tions. Without the unspoken ledger of who gave more or who owed what. Not until her. Loving her isn't heavy. It doesn't demand. It frees. It makes every part of my life lighter, easier, better than anything I could have imagined when I was younger and too restless to stand still. She gives without asking anything back, and somehow that makes me want to give her the whole world in return. And she never demands. Always offers. Always leaves room for choice. But the truth is, there's no choice anymore. If she's there, I stay.

Sometimes I catch myself wondering how I ever lived without this—without her—and the thought feels so distant it's almost like remembering someone else's life. All the searching, the waiting, the half-formed prayers I didn't know I was sending up—they were worth it. Every second of it was worth it, just to find her. Just to know what love could actually be when you stop bracing for it to vanish. Some things you don't even know you're missing until they finally reach you.

And somehow, in finding her, I got Gray too. Smart, funny, stub-born Gray, who carries the best parts of her mother and still manages to surprise us both with how wise she is. I used to think I was here to guide her in some small way. Turns out, more often than not, we end up taking our cues from her.

When life tangles itself into knots, Gray's the one who hands us the scissors and says, "Here. Cut yourself loose." Half the time, Sophia and I just look at each other in awe and say, "What the fuck?"

Gray. The daughter I never had. And more than I ever deserved. I love her to the moon and back, even though she's chosen to follow the dark side: snowboarding. ♪

I forgive her.

♪ "Imperial March" by John Williams

Next month, we're driving out to the Gorge to see Fleetwood Mac—and Dylan, too, because he's the greatest, of course. I got the usual rolled eyes when I floated the idea, but they laughed and agreed anyway. That's the thing about them. They make room for my stubbornness the same way I make room for theirs. We belong to each other now, all of us, in a way that feels earned.

I think about all the places I used to run to—countries that blurred together, landscapes framed in my lens and left behind like souvenirs—and I realize none of them ever felt like coming home. They were beautiful, sure. But they were never mine. Not the way this life is. Not the way she is.

I pause at the end of the last row, wiping my hands down the front of my jeans, and glance toward the road out of habit. And there she is—the low hum of the Ghia threading through the quiet, the gleam of sun caught on the windshield as she rounds the bend toward home. I kill the mower, pull one side of my headphones away, and stand there for a moment, just watching. Something catches in my chest—a quickening pulse, a warmth that spreads from my center outward, familiar but never diminished by time. After all these years, just the sight of her still does this to me.

She pulls into the garage, the car shuddering softly as she turns off the engine. Through the glass, I can see her resting her hands on the steering wheel, her face tilted slightly down, smiling to herself in that way she does when she thinks no one is watching. My chest tightens—not with pain, not with sadness, but with a kind of awe so quiet it barely has a name.

This is it. This is *everything*.

Not the places I once chased across maps, not the photographs stacked in my archives. Not the future I thought I had to carve out by force. Just this. The way she looks up and finds me standing there like she expected me to be. The way the air softens around her when she smiles.

Coming home doesn't mean what it used to. It's not the island, or the house, or even the life we've built here. It's her. It's always her. I lift a hand in a slow wave, feeling the heat of the afternoon settle around us. And just like that, I remember what all the waiting was for. Sophia—the still point in a world that never stops spinning.

A pink bubble stretches in front of my face, trembling on the verge of bursting. I pop it with a soft *snap* and pull the gum back between my teeth, smiling to myself.

My beloved Karmann Ghia hums up the gravel driveway, her engine low and content, a sound that settles into the rhythm of home. There's something about driving an old car—the way you feel every shift, every purr, every protest. It asks more of you, but it gives more back. You don't just arrive somewhere; you *experience* getting there. ♪

Like dropping a needle on a record instead of tapping a song on your phone—it's slower, imperfect, alive. The kind of thing Michael and I both understand, and maybe even love.

As I round the bend, I spot him—Michael, pushing the lawn mower across the yard with determined focus, headphones clamped over his ears. His movements are methodical, almost mechanical, like someone performing a duty rather than a labor of love.

I pull into the garage and let my hands rest on the wheel, watching him through the windshield. He hasn't noticed me yet, too absorbed in his battle against the grass. A smile tugs at my lips. He hates yard work—has always hated it—finding it mundane and repetitive compared to framing the perfect shot. Yet here he is, week after week, maintaining these straight, even lines across the lawn.

♪ *"To Build a Home"* by Cinematic Orchestra

◉

For me.

Because I once mentioned how much I love the smell of freshly cut grass. Because I said the sound of a lawn mower reminds me of childhood summers. Because I find beauty in ordinary things maintained with care. And because he loves me.

He looks up finally, seeing my car in the garage. Even from this distance, I can see his face shift—the concentrated grimace melting into something softer. He stops for a moment, pulls one side of his headphones away from his ear, and smiles. A simple wave of his hand—acknowledging my presence before returning to his task, determined to finish what he started.

For a moment, I stop, watching him resume his neat lines across the lawn, listening to the quiet hum of the Ghia's cooling engine. This is what love looks like after the grand gestures fade—mowing a lawn you hate, wearing headphones to make it tolerable, offering a small wave because you know she understands you need to finish.

And suddenly, inexplicably, I find myself holding back tears. Not from sadness, but from the overwhelming weight of being known, being loved in such a specific, mundane way. The kind that doesn't make it into movies or photographs.

The kind that simply endures.

My gaze flickers to the rearview mirror—to the house beyond, to what waits inside. I step out of the car, the cement cool beneath my sandals, and move toward the back of the garage. My eyes catch on the license plates—

SONNET and *POWLIFE,* side by side.

⊚

A smile tugs at my lips.

On the far side of the garage, against a stack of forgotten boxes and old ski gear, a poster leans sideways—Donna Weinbrecht, frozen in time. Discarded. Unnoticed.

Michael's past self, like mine, slowly being left behind. I smile. He told me there was only room for one woman in the house.

Me.

Inside the house, the afternoon sun slants through the windows. I unpack groceries onto the counter—coffee, fresh fruit, vegetables—small, simple things that make a home feel lived in. I slide a pint of raspberry gelato into the freezer, tucking it behind a bag of frozen blueberries, and smile to myself. The Cap'n Crunch goes into the cupboard, a cheerful rebellion against all the responsible choices piled neatly around it.

Little things. Ordinary and ridiculous and perfect. Pieces of a life finally starting to feel like mine.

A worn sign hangs above my espresso machine.

Every cup served with Love.

And beside it, just as it always has:

Kwitchyerbellyakin.

My eyes flick to the mantle as I pass through the house.

Our house.

◯◯

In the living room, a row of framed photos lines the mantle—wedding pictures, standing neat and proud.

Our wedding.

I reach out, tracing my fingers along the edge of the frame. Our hands clasped. His smile—soft and stunned, like he couldn't quite believe I was real. My dress flowing like ink into the background, catching the late-afternoon light just enough to glow. The wind had lifted the veil at the perfect moment, like even the weather had paused to say yes.

I remember the way he looked at me at the altar—not with nerves, not with surprise, but with certainty. Like he was seeing something he'd always known was waiting for him. Like I was the answer he'd carried long before he ever knew the question. The same look he gave me at *Café Hagen* the day we met.

This was always where our story was headed. We just didn't know the ending. Until that day.

And then there was Allison—my maid of honor, of course—who announced loud enough for the first three rows to hear, "If he doesn't bend you over a chair after that look, I swear to God, I'll do it for him."

I didn't laugh then—too many eyes on me—but I remember biting my cheek to keep it in. Now, I let the smile come freely. That was Allison's gift, really. She never let things get too serious—even the sacred stuff. She has a way of pulling me back to earth, reminding me that joy wasn't something you had to earn. Typical Allison. Irreverent. Loud. Always pulling me back to earth and exactly right when it counted.

I smile, the memory warming something behind my ribs. The feeling it stirs isn't lightning or fireworks. It's quieter than that. Steadier. The kind of feeling that stays.

Beside it, a smaller frame. Gray, on her college graduation day. Her curls wild under the cap, her grin wide and unfiltered. The light had caught her just right, haloing her shoulders like the universe was nodding in approval. I shift the frame slightly, aligning it with the others.

Michael took that photo. He didn't say much afterward—he never does when something matters—but I saw it in the way he looked at her. Gentle. Solid. Proud in a way that asked for nothing in return.

She's not sure what comes next. And I haven't pushed. The world will tell her to decide, to leap, to define herself in bullet points and elevator pitches—but I won't. I know better. Sometimes clarity doesn't arrive on a schedule. Sometimes it shows up quietly, years later, wearing a different name than you expected.

So I let her wander. Let her wonder.

She talks about a dozen different futures—grad school, nonprofits, a bookstore by the coast, Fleetwood Mac groupie. Maybe all of it. Maybe none. But she carries something solid, even in her wondering. A quiet thread, woven deep, that won't come undone.

I remember the quiet moment after the ceremony, when Ethan and Michael crossed paths on the lawn. No posturing. No awkward silences. Just a nod—an unspoken agreement passed between them. They didn't need to compete. Gray wasn't a prize. She was a person they both loved in their own way.

They understood that they each held a piece of her story. It wasn't friendship. But she wasn't a divide between them—she was the bridge.

And maybe that was enough. Maybe it was something else too. Acceptance, perhaps. The kind that matters more as you get older.

He loves her like the daughter he never had. Not with declarations or big gestures, but in the way he listens. The way he remembers small details. The way he gives her space, and still makes her feel seen.

I'm not sure when that happened—when our stories began to braid together like that—but it did. Quietly. Without ceremony. Like everything else that's ever mattered.

Gray saw it too. I caught her watching him one afternoon, when she thought no one was paying attention. He handed her a mug of tea, said something small—something only she would understand—and she smiled in that rare, private way of hers. That was when I knew. She trusts him. In the way that matters.

That same weekend, the two of them went down to Mt. Hood for a ski day. When she pulled her board out of the car, Michael raised an eyebrow and gave her this look like she'd just confessed to a felony.

"Snowboarder, huh?" he said, with the kind of mock dismay usually reserved for betrayal.

She just shrugged. "Try to keep up, old man."

And to his credit, he did. He took her anyway. And they had a blast. They came home sunburned and sore, talking over each other as they rehashed runs and wiped out on the kitchen floor demonstrating something called a butter. I stood there watching them, thinking—this is what it looks like when the pieces finally fit.

I reach out and straighten the frame. His hand in mine. Her laughter frozen mid-motion in the photo beside it. A family, not by blood—but by choice. The most enduring kind there is.

Two years married nearly, and I still find myself studying him when he sleeps. When we first met, I worried about what he would have to give up. His life had been defined by movement, by capturing the world in all its remote corners. Mine had been defined by staying, by finding depth in familiar places. The gap seemed impossible to bridge without one of us losing something essential.

"I don't want to clip your wings," I told him one night, tracing the lines of his palm as we lay in bed. "Your photography, your travels—they're who you are."

He'd looked at me then with such certainty. "They're what I do, Sophia. Not who I am."

I didn't believe him. Not fully. How could I? I'd read his articles, seen his photographs—the way he captured light breaking through temple windows in Kyoto, children playing in the streets of Montserrat, the cold brilliance of starlight over K2, scattered across the Himalayan sky like something holy. His work breathed with a passion that seemed inseparable from his being.

Yet here we are. He's turned down assignments that would have taken him away for weeks, even months. Renegotiated his contract with *Wander* to include more domestic projects. When the magazine called with the Antarctica expedition—the one he'd talked about as his dream assignment—he declined without hesitation. "I can't be away from you for six weeks," he told me simply, as if the choice required no thought at all. As if all those years of chasing the perfect shot across continents had been preparing him for something else entirely—his life, with me.

I never asked him to choose. But he did, time and again, choosing us over everything else. For Michael, the world had narrowed to what mattered most—Me.

The sacrifice seemed entirely his. One evening last spring, I found him on the porch, reviewing photos from our weekend trip to the Olympic Peninsula.

"Do you miss it?" I asked. "The big assignments, the far-away places?"

He was quiet for a moment, scrolling through images of tide pools and ancient forests—none of them exotic, all of them within a few hours' drive of our home.

"I used to think photography was about capturing what other people couldn't see," he said finally. "Bringing back images from places they'd never go."

He paused, selecting a photo of me, crouched beside a tide pool, examining a starfish. My profile in silhouette against the setting sun.

"But I think I was wrong. It's about seeing, really seeing, what's right in front of you."

He looked up at me then. "And I was missing so much."

He has found beauty in the familiar.

When the Italy assignment came up last month, I expected him to turn it down like the others. Instead, he asked if I would come with him. Not as an afterthought, not as a concession, but as an essential part of the experience.

☾

"I want to see Tuscany through your eyes," he said. "I want to know what you notice that I miss."

We spent two weeks there—winding through olive groves, lingering in hilltop towns, sitting beneath vine-draped pergolas as the world unspooled around us. His photographs from that trip are different from his earlier work. Still beautiful, still capturing perfect light and composition. But there's something new in them.

A stillness. A presence.

Many include me—not posed, but caught in moments of genuine discovery. My hand brushing over sun-warmed stone walls. My face turned toward the dappled light filtering through olive branches. My reflection wavering in a weathered terracotta basin filled with rainwater and fallen petals.

He didn't sacrifice his art. He transformed it.

We found a rhythm then—he captured images, I captured words.

Different ways of witnessing the same moments.

The other day Michael stirred beside me, his eyes slowly opening, finding mine immediately as if he sensed me watching.

"Morning," he murmured, his voice still rough with sleep. "What time is it?"

"Early," I said, shifting closer to him. "Go back to sleep."

He smiled, eyes already drifting closed again. "What were you thinking about?"

⌾

"Just that I'm glad you kept your promise."

"Which one?" he asked, already half asleep again.

"All of them," I said softly.

His arm tightened around me as I closed my eyes, listening to the steady rhythm of his breathing.

"Have I ever told you I love you?" he murmured softly. ♪

"Every day and twice on Sunday," I replied.

"I will double my efforts Monday through Saturday then."

I smiled. I never had this kind of love before—one that felt like both an anchor and wings. Before Michael, love had been comfortable but predictable—like a well-worn path I followed without questioning. This was different. This was choosing each other every day, seeing and being seen completely. This was love that transformed rather than confined.

"Sophia?"

"Yes?" I said.

"Am I really waking up next to you, or is this still a dream?"

I didn't answer right away. My eyes were still closed, but I could feel the weight of his gaze on me—soft and steady, like he was trying to memorize the moment.

I'd asked myself the same thing more than once. Whether this

♪ *"Today"* by Jefferson Airplane

- 660 -

life—this love—was real. Whether it could be this easy and this true at the same time.

I shifted just enough to press my forehead against his.

"If it is," I whispered, "let's not wake up."

Outside, the world was waking up—the ferry horn, birds calling, life moving forward in all its ordinary wonder.

The kind that's worth staying for.

My fingers trail against the wooden railing up the staircase, pausing where the wall is lined with cross-stitch frames, each one holding a truth I once struggled to believe.

We Make Our Own Light.
Everything Happens for a Reason.

The last one is the newest. The words carefully chosen:

Love is Written in the Stars.

I stand there for a moment, letting them settle. Letting their meaning finally reach me. Maybe it's not all fate. But maybe—just maybe—some things are meant. Maybe cosmic forces really are a thing. Or maybe… it was all just coincidence. A beautiful, impossible coincidence.

.The sound of keystrokes fills the small office, steady and rhythmic. Sunlight spills through the window, warming my back as I type. Words flow from my fingers, giving shape to thoughts I've carried for years—our story, finally finding its way to the page. My novel—almost complete now, after so many false starts and abandoned drafts.

⊙

In the corner, the Selectric waits. Boxy, unapologetically stubborn. I still use it—just not today. These pages need the efficiency of a blinking cursor, not the chime of a carriage return or the clatter of keys that leave no room for doubt.

I glance at it. The ribbon is nearly dry. Again. And I ran out of white-out two poems ago. Still, there's something about it I can't let go of. I use it when I need to feel the weight of a word, when I need to hear the truth hit the page like a declaration. For poems. For letters I never send. For the kind of writing that feels like breathing through paper.

But today... today is for getting it done. I turn back to the screen, the cursor blinking patiently. Waiting. I stretch my fingers and keep typing. The Selectric doesn't mind. It knows it'll be needed again soon. It's strange how life circles back on itself. That scholarship I gave up all those years ago—the one that had my parents questioning everything they thought they knew about me—wasn't lost after all. Just dormant. Waiting for the right story to tell.

And what better story than ours? The ski bum who saw me before I saw him. The bench at three o'clock. The way time and distance and circumstance kept pulling us apart until something stronger finally drew us together.

For years, I couldn't write. Not the way I once did, when words came as naturally as breath. I traveled, I helped, I built things with my hands instead of my mind. I convinced myself it was enough. But something was always missing—that quiet space where thought becomes language, where experience transforms into something that might outlast it.

Now the words come again, flowing like water returning to a dry riverbed. Each day at this desk feels like reclaiming a part of myself I'd set aside. Not wasted time—just a long, necessary detour that brought me exactly where I needed to be.

I pause, rereading the paragraph I've just written. It's about the moment we finally met—really met—after all those near misses. The bench, the eclipse, the way the air felt right before it shifted. I smile, remembering.

Some things are worth waiting for.

I lean back in the chair, eyes drifting from the screen to the far wall of the office. My gaze settles on the poster still hanging there—Bob Dylan, eternally unimpressed, eternally unreadable. His hair is a mess, cigarette tucked loosely between two fingers, sunglasses guarding whatever secret truth he's not telling.

The man whose voice, I maintain, still sounds like a cat caught in a blender. Michael's idol. His patron saint of wandering souls and restless questions. I used to roll my eyes every time he quoted Dylan.

Don't think twice, it's all right.
You don't need a weatherman to know which way the wind blows.

Half the time it sounded like nonsense. But he'd say them with this little smile, like the words held more weight than I could hear.

"Dylan is an acquired taste," he always tells me.

"And you've clearly acquired too much of it," I always reply.

But the truth is, I've learned to listen—really listen. And I think that's what love does. It nudges you toward things you wouldn't have chosen on your own. You pick up pieces of each other like sea glass—weathered and strange and beautiful in ways you didn't expect.

◍

There's a stack of records by the turntable, alphabetized by no one's system but mine. I nudge Dylan toward the back—just a little. He notices, of course. But he lets me. Another quiet gesture in a long list of them. Like how he buys almond milk without asking. How he sets my book down facedown so the spine won't crack. How he leaves his camera behind when he knows the moment belongs to us—not the lens.

Love is compromise, yes—but not the kind that shrinks you. The kind that softens the sharp edges. That says, I see you, even when we don't always agree on the soundtrack.

Maybe it's not even compromise, really. Not in the way we're taught to think of it. It's not giving up parts of yourself to make something work. It's more like... adapting. Growing alongside someone, not around them. It's making space for their quirks and rhythms the way you make room for furniture that doesn't quite match—but somehow belongs.

It's the quiet understanding that you don't need to become each other—you just need to stop resisting who the other already is.

I glance back at Dylan's face—half-defiant, half amused. I don't understand him. Probably never will. But I understand Michael. And that's more than enough. Well—mostly. I never understood those old shoes he always wore.

I got tired of watching him trip over those damn laces. Every few days it was the same thing—he'd stop in the middle of the sidewalk, mutter something under his breath, and crouch down to fix them like it was a surprise they'd come undone. So one morning, while he was in the shower, I tossed them. Left them by the trash can like a breakup note he'd never get to read. And in their place, I left a new box by the door—nothing fancy, just something that stays tied.

Victory.

He stared at the new shoes like they'd materialized out of thin air, holding them like they might explode. I just shrugged and told him to try not to trip over the concept of change.

I turn back to the keyboard. Fingers hovering. Then moving. The words pick up again. And this time, I know exactly what I want to say.

After a while, a quiet presence fills the doorway. I know it's him before I turn. Michael leans against the doorframe, watching me with that steady gaze that still makes something flutter in my chest. Not saying anything, just observing—the way he always does, finding the story in the moment.

"You planning to stand there all day?" I ask without looking up, my fingers continuing their dance across the keyboard.

He crosses the room, his movements fluid and certain. His hands rest on my shoulders, thumbs working small circles at the base of my neck where tension always gathers. I lean back into his touch, into the scent of cut grass and cedar that clings to him.

"How is the novel coming along?" His voice is low near my ear.

I glance at the screen, at the words spilling across the page. The final chapter of the story I thought I was writing—before life handed me something better.

"It's almost finished."

Michael moves to perch on the edge of the desk, his eyes finding mine. In the afternoon light, the flecks of gold in his eyes seem to catch fire.

◐

"What happens next?"

I don't hesitate. The answer is easy.

"Well, that's the best part." I reach for his hand, my fingers sliding between his.

"We get to write it together."

His breath hitches, just slightly. And then he bends down, kissing me— slow, unhurried, deep—like he's been waiting all day for this moment.

As he pulls back, I catch sight of the framed newspaper clipping on the wall. Me playing volleyball in high school, once crumpled in doubt—now carefully placed in glass and light.

He follows my gaze, squeezing my hand gently. I wrap my arms around Michael again, holding him like I'll never have to let go. Over his shoulder, my eyes drift back to the poster of Dylan hanging crookedly on the wall—and for a second, I swear he's winking at me behind those sunglasses. Like he knows something I'm only just beginning to understand.

Somewhere inside, I smile. Maybe Bob wasn't meant to be understood. Maybe he just knew something it takes the rest of us a little longer to figure out. Maybe all love really does begin with a "Simple Twist of Fate."

A breeze stirs through the open window. Shadow and Moseley curl into each other on the couch, tucked in like they belong together.

Like us.

The curtains flutter gently like pages turning, like time moving forward—toward whatever comes next. ♪

♪ "Moon Over the Sun" by Nina June

www.ingramcontent.com/pod-product-compliance
Lightning Source LLC
Chambersburg PA
CBHW050057120726
47904CB00004B/1121